WOLFBITTEN

WOLFBANE SERIES: BOOK 4
CELIA HART

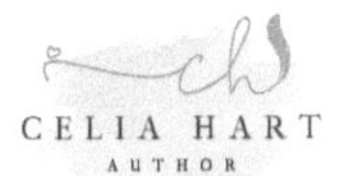

Celia Hart LLC

WOLFBITTEN
WOLFBANE SERIES: BOOK 4
by Celia Hart

Copyright © 2026 by Celia Hart

All rights reserved.

Edited by Corbeaux Editorial Services
Cover design by Emily's World of Design
Chapter heading artwork by Barbara

Print ISBN: 979-8-9864024-8-2
E-book ISBN: 979-8-9864024-9-9

CONTENT WARNING

These content notes are made available here so readers can inform themselves, if they want to. Some readers might consider these "spoilers." If you don't like spoilers, look away. You've been warned.

- **Bad language**: strong and frequent

- **Sex**: several fully described and explicit sex scenes, including cunnilingus and fellatio

- **Violence**: several graphic and explicitly violent scenes, including torture

- **Other**: domestic abuse, fatphobia, homophobia, mentions of war, murder, pregnancy (not main characters), purity culture, sexual assault

If you'd like more information on any of the above content notes prior to reading, please reach out (celia.hart.author@gmail.com) and I will be happy to elaborate so that you may make a fully informed decision before choosing to turn the page!

For my exes.

You don't deserve it, but surviving you made me stronger, wiser, and freer. Like a phoenix, I've risen from the ashes. While you're all still losers, I'm out here publishing my fourth novel. Thanks for the material!

NOTE

Chapter 1

Theresa

Half-full. Between the two options, that was the one I preferred. It wasn't that bad things never happened—I was only mortal after all. But attitude was everything. And a good attitude was particularly important at that very moment as the crushing weight of a sandbag dug into my shoulders, snow crunched under my winter hiking boots, and wind cut at the exposed sliver of skin between my gaiter and hat.

"*Faster!*" my father telepathically barked through mindlink, snapping me out of my thoughts. His tone was as uncompromising as the Alaskan cold we were battling. "*College made you weak.*" Retirement hadn't softened him one bit. Although my brother Tyce had succeeded him, the notorious former Alpha Lance wasn't one to let his legacy fade quietly.

I gritted my teeth and redistributed some of the weight on my shoulders. The *heavy as duck* sandbag I was carrying had to be at least a hundred pounds. I continued my climb, each step more precarious than the last. None of this was safe. If I slipped, I'd tumble down the mountain like an avalanche. I could already imagine my father's dismissive reaction. "You'll heal," was all he'd say.

He wasn't wrong. But it wasn't like it wouldn't hurt like all heck.

I am tough. I am strong. I am alpha female! The silent mantra carried me forward, while outwardly I panted like a dog.

Above me, my father's wolf form moved effortlessly over the rocks, his huge, lethal claws cutting through the snow to get a good grasp on the frozen earth. He stared me down with his severe, unforgiving amber eyes. While some people remarked I had the same ones, they'd often follow the comment by stating that mine were somehow gentler, friendlier. His gaze was anything but. If there'd been a time when my father was warmer, I'd never known it.

My shoulders and upper arms burned.

"*Pick it up!*" he snapped again, and I let out a low growl, forcing my legs to move.

By the time we reached the summit of the small mountain, I could barely feel my limbs from both the intense climb and the merciless winter biting at them. While most of Alaska was known for its hard winters, up north, where we were, was particularly unrelenting.

My father motioned for me to drop the sandbag. I heaved it off my shoulders and let it fall with a thud before collapsing into the snow. I readjusted my gaiter, thankful he wouldn't question why I was so covered up at this time of year. I didn't know how long I'd be able to hold my family off from finding out what I'd done.

I glanced down. Unfortunately, even with my night vision, I couldn't see much. I hadn't seen the sun since I'd gotten home for winter break, and it would be almost another month before it rose again. My gaze wandered to the sky. In the perpetual night of winter, the stars shone brilliantly, a stark contrast to the cold, dark earth below.

My peaceful moment was cut short as I was back on my feet, hoisting the sandbag onto my shoulders, with Dad mushing me back down the slope. The trek down was no less grueling. The icy ground threatened to betray my footing at every step.

When we finally made it back to the snowmobile, I promptly turned away before my dad could shift into his human form without warning. He was so used to being among pack warriors who thought nothing of constant shifting, he often forgot how uncomfortable it was for me to see him naked. I'd, very regrettably, caught him unclothed far too many times.

The *bzzt* of his snowsuit zipper informed me that it was safe to look again. I turned around and strapped the sandbag to the back of the snowmobile. My muscles throbbed. Each movement sent an aching protest through my limbs, begging for relief after the hours of relentless strain.

"Not bad today, Terri." His grudging approval was rare and yet, nevertheless, came with a barb. "But you're not as strong as you were before you left. I'm disappointed. You promised to keep up with your training."

"I have been." I tried not to sound defensive. "It's just hard sometimes. I have classes, homework, exams—"

"And friends and drinking," he cut in, throwing me a sharp look. "I'm not stupid. I know what goes on at college campuses. Figure it out next semester. I don't want to have this discussion again in the spring."

I nodded and readjusted my gaiter to hide the flush of irritation rising in my cheeks. He climbed onto the snowmobile, and I followed. The engine's growl drowned out any lingering argument as we sped away. The cold wind cut across my face as I looked up at the dark, starry sky while we drove back toward the pack.

Just as the large gates came into view, my phone vibrated in my coat pocket, signaling that we were back in range of the cell tower on our pack land.

My dad hopped off the snowmobile as soon as we parked, grabbing the sandbag to bring inside on his way in. At least he wasn't going to make me do that too.

Just before disappearing into the packhouse, in a rare act of fatherly affection, he called over his shoulder, "Hurry inside. It's freezing."

I stayed behind for a moment and pulled out my phone.

The screen lit up with three new messages from an unknown number.

My chest tightened, my lungs contracted, and a chill crept up my spine. My fingers trembled as I stared at the screen. My breath quickened, fogging the air. I impulsively glanced around, the eerie feeling of being watched taking hold of me. My thumb hovered over the Block button, but I hesitated. Blocking the number wouldn't stop him. He always found a way.

He doesn't have power over me. I won't let him. He's already taken enough.

After a steady breath in and out, I hit block and shoved the phone back into my pocket.

The warmth that greeted me in the packhouse was a welcome relief. I peeled off most of my heavy layers but left my gaiter on. The smell of food guided me to the dining room, where my mother sat at the long table, picking at her plate.

"Dinner's almost ready, Terri," Tasha, our cook, called from the kitchen. I slid into a seat across from my mom, and Tasha appeared moments later.

The water with lemon was brought out first, shortly followed by a salad with some pan-grilled chicken strips on top. I sniffed the dressing. Honestly, I didn't have to do that. I already knew it would be low-fat. Altogether, the meal she placed in front of me couldn't be more than eight hundred calories. Mostly devoid of carbs and flavor. I'd definitely be raiding the pantry later for a couple of my brother's protein bars. When no one was watching.

"I let Tasha know what you'd like," my mom stated, as if it were me who had chosen this meal.

"Thanks," I said, forcing a smile.

"Alpha Nikolai's due back soon from his land search," my mom remarked with as little emotion as the food had flavor. "Just in time for the big hunt." Considering what had happened to my mom's former pack months earlier, which had forced them to move here from halfway across the world, I'd expected more grieving.

I nodded in response.

"He's staying with us," she added with an odd glint in her eye.

My fork hovered over my plate. "You mentioned."

"He's an alpha," she continued. "It's only right to show him proper respect. We found families to host everyone else, but I made sure the alpha stayed in the packhouse where he belongs."

"Of course," I said cautiously, "I'd never consider being disrespectful to an alpha."

Her eyes lingered on me. "He's single, you know."

I set my fork down, biting back an annoyed groan. Normally, this was the part where she warned me to keep my distance from unmated men. "Okay, I'll—"

"I know your father insists you wait for your fated mate," she interrupted, her voice dropping into a conspiratorial murmur, "but if someone of higher rank takes an interest . . ." She trailed off, and her lips curved into a small smile. "Well, how would he know the difference?"

I blinked.

Before I could respond, she rose abruptly, leaving her empty plate behind as she disappeared down the hall.

I sat there, stunned, her words ringing in my ears.

Had my mother just suggested what I thought she'd suggested?

Chapter 2

Nikolai

Forty. That was how many pack members were left in Severnaya Zvezda Pack, including me. A nice, even forty. Our pack had never been particularly large. As opposed to some packs in Russia and other post-Soviet states, where numbers could climb to ten thousand, ours had always maintained a balance of around a thousand. Now only scraps remained of what we had been.

After months of coordinating with my late beta's aunt, Yulia Tikaani (née Vovchenko), we finally arrived at her pack. When we first fled our war-torn home, we traveled in our wolf forms, bringing only what we could carry as we crossed into Moldova. From there, it took nearly three days by air to reach Alaska.

We had left just about everything behind, and only a sliver of hope remained.

As generous as Luna Yulia's invitation was, we couldn't depend on her hospitality forever. Our pack needed stability—a place to truly call home. With my newly elected beta, Sasha—a man as ruthless in battle as I was—at my side, I set out to survey the terrain, searching for the perfect location to rebuild. It had to be remote yet sustainable, a stretch of untamed wilderness where we could endure for years, if necessary, even without electricity or running water, until we had the means to establish proper infrastructure.

From what I'd gathered, Alaska was largely lawless, which worked to our advantage. Not being citizens would make purchasing land difficult, so we'd likely have to squat.

Sasha and I had traveled in our wolf forms for weeks, enduring the relentless darkness and brutal cold, with temperatures plunging to between negative thirty and negative forty degrees Celsius. The wind howled through the barren landscape, slicing through our fur like icy blades, but we kept moving.

At night, we sought out whatever shelter we could find. We huddled together as we slept, pressed against each other to keep warm. It was a strange shift. We had always been friends, but never *this close*. Before the war, our interactions had been limited to a firm handshake, a nod of respect, a high five. We had never touched beyond that.

But war and survival didn't care for social norms.

When we returned to civilization, I wasted no time stepping into a hot shower, savoring the way the steaming water soothed my exhausted muscles. After weeks of surviving on raw game, the thought of a hot meal was more than alluring.

How I also longed for a *banya*, the social center for warriors back home. There was nothing I'd have liked more at that moment than the lash of a birch *venik* on my back. But the days of simple pleasures were now over.

"Ah! Alpha! You're home!" Luna Yulia greeted me at the bottom of the stairs. "I must introduce you to my daughter, Theresa. She's finally home from school for winter break. I told you what a good cook she is, of course?"

"Yes, you mentioned," I responded, annoyed by this bombardment. It was common for mothers to boast about their daughters to me. Fruitless, as I'd never entertain anyone as my mate except my fated one. Though perhaps I'd entertain them in other ways—ways their mothers certainly didn't have in mind. In the past, I'd found amusement in the game, but now, it was just a grating irritation. I no longer had time for female company. I was too busy leading what was left of my pack.

"I'll have her cook you a meal after the full moon passes."

"Thank you, but there is no need. Tasha does a sufficient job. I am thankful for the hospitality your pack has offered me and mine. No reason to go out of your way for me." I tried to say it as politely as possible. The last thing I needed was the alpha's sister fawning all over me. It would put me in an uncomfortable spot with the family that was hosting us, and I was not in a position to be making more enemies.

"She will make you our family's borscht recipe," Luna Yulia responded and turned away, heading out of the room. I let out a breath and made my way into the kitchen.

"Alpha," Tasha greeted me. She was a courteous middle-aged woman with chestnut hair that was always pulled back into a tight bun. Her manner of speaking was straightforward, and she never offered any sort of polite conversation, which I appreciated. While in the past there were things to laugh and joke about, these days I preferred solitude, or at least minimal social interaction. "Yulia asked me to make chicken with buckwheat for you today."

Tasha had been the daughter of my pack's cook when Luna Yulia lived there and had made her way over here soon after Yulia did. I understood that they were lifelong friends.

"Thank you," I grunted.

"It's been a long time since she's asked me to make buckwheat, or any of her other favorite Ukrainian foods. She must be trying to impress you."

I nodded. *More like to seduce me on behalf of her daughter.* I had known her family well growing up. And if she was anything like the rest

of them, she was an opportunist. A good quality, but also one to be aware
of.

That evening, the entire Jade Moon Pack gathered in front of the pack-house. The excitement penetrated the air and almost forced itself into my frozen heart. Almost. Many wolf packs that lived in highly isolated areas took part in the great hunt, including mine. And there was a point in time when I'd looked forward to the night before the full moon every month. It was something we dreamed about as young pups. Our fathers would show off their kill to us, and tell us stories of how they tackled wild beasts with their buddies.

But now I couldn't bring myself to feel pleasure even in what was previously my favorite activity.

"How's it going, Volkov?" Sasha's heavy palm landed on my shoulder.

I shrugged, offering no real response. He gave me a knowing look.

"Let's take it out on the animals tonight," he said, attempting to hype me up.

"You act like that's not what we've been doing for the past two weeks," I replied flatly.

"Tah, but that was for survival. Tonight is the great hunt. Plus, I have some vodka to look forward to after."

"*Mudak!*" I scoffed. "Wasting money on booze."

"Relax. It was a gift from my host family. We deserve a drink after what we've been through. Now, go out there and bloody some bears. Show them what a real alpha is made of."

Before I could reply, Alpha Lance approached, his presence as over-bearing as ever.

"Alpha Nikolai!" he greeted, offering his hand.

I took it, returning a firm shake.

"Ready for tonight?" he continued. "If you're anything like me, I'm sure you can't wait to sink your teeth into some meat. There's nothing like the taste of warm blood when you first bite into Bambi's neck."

I offered him a curt nod.

From behind him, Luna Yulia's voice rang out over the crowd. "Where's Terri?"

Lance barely spared her a glance. "Who knows? That girl's been strange ever since she got home." Then his gaze landed back on me. "Have you met Terri yet?"

"Not yet."

"She's supposed to be here tonight. But if not, there's always tomorrow at the full moon ceremony." His tone was casual, but as soon as Yulia was out of earshot, his demeanor shifted. His grip tightened around my forearm, and his eyes narrowed, glinting with unspoken warning.

"You're going to be living in close quarters with her for the next month," he said in a low, firm voice. "And you better stay the fuck away from my daughter if you know what's good for you. My hospitality only extends so far."

I met his gaze, unwavering. "Understood. I have no time for women now."

His expression relaxed into something that almost resembled approval. "Good. Then we'll get along just fine." He clapped me on the back with what would seem like camaraderie to an outsider. "Now, go fuck some animals up."

With that, he walked away.

"Want some company tonight?" Sasha asked as we lingered at the edge of the crowd.

"I need to be alone," I replied.

He nodded in understanding. "*Ni pukha!*"

"*K chortu,*" I muttered, accepting his good wish.

Alpha Lance called for silence and led the pack in a series of religious chants, the words reverberating in the cold night air. When he dismissed everyone, they dispersed, bodies twisting and bones snapping as they shifted into their beast forms.

Sasha gave me one last pat on the back before following the others.

I waited until most of the group had disappeared before I headed out, finding a safe spot to dump my clothes before I shifted. While it had been good to be human again, there was something so satisfying about succumbing to my animal brain. Everything was so much simpler. I ran on instinct, with all my human thoughts and trauma fading into the background.

I swiped my bladelike claws through the snow, cutting through ice easily. The frosty wind ruffled my fur, I inhaled the crisp Alaskan air, and then I was off.

My instincts took over as I brought my snout to the ground, chasing the scent of fresh game. While tracking didn't give me the same thrill it used to anymore, I was still fully invested, especially in this form. I couldn't return to my host pack without bringing something back for their full moon ceremony. It would just be wrong. And I intended to make it good. Not just a couple of rabbits. It was all or nothing.

I headed farther out, farther than I imagined anyone from the pack going. I must have traveled for an hour when I finally saw it. A huge caribou in the distance. My claws were already tingling with bloodlust, my incisors watering. While I may have not vocalized my agreement with Alpha Lance, I certainly felt exactly as he did. There was nothing more satisfying than tearing into the throat of unsuspecting prey.

I got into attack position, readying myself for the tackle. I took a deep breath, and inhaled something unexpected. It was something I'd never scented before, and my first thought was it must be some sort of plant that was capable of blossoming in the dead of winter, the nectar of its flower carried on the wind. But while the scent was slightly sweet, it was also carnal, like the damp, glistening skin of an aroused woman. But no, this wasn't any woman. This was the type of woman I could have lusted after for months, to finally indulge in the satisfaction of kissing her soft skin, inhaling the scent between her thighs. This was the kind of scent that, if it made a sound, it would be a siren pulling me to my death. I'd risk everything for that scent.

During those seconds that I lost my concentration and found myself distracted, I saw her. The most stunning wolf I'd ever seen. While I couldn't quite make out the color of her fur, I knew it was dark and thick, glowing under the moonlight. I was captivated, watching every inch of fur flowing back with the wind as she leaped into the air in the most elegant and deadly way. It was almost catlike, how she made it seem so effortless, as if she were simply dancing. Her claws sank into the body of the hapless caribou, and in nanoseconds, she was tearing its throat out. Just as quickly as the prey had become aware of its demise, it was gone.

I was about to step forward and offer to carry her kill back for her. But she was too quick. She flipped the humongous beast onto her back and sprinted into the darkness of the night as if she were merely carrying a hare. Whoever she was, I had to know.

I crept closer, circling the red stain left behind in the snow. Beyond the pungent smell of blood, that slightly sweet, lascivious smell lingered. Had that been hers? Was it possible for someone to smell so fucking good?

Knowing I couldn't return empty-handed, I turned to continue on my trail. But I just couldn't get her off my mind. All I knew was that, whoever she was, I had to stay away. That was exactly the sort of distraction I didn't need in my life right now. Not while I had thirty-nine pack members depending on me to help them through their grief and resettlement.

Chapter 3

Nikolai

"Za zdarovye," Sasha and I toasted each other, and I took a gulp of the vodka. After piling our kill in a shed the pack had for exactly that, he invited me over to the beta wing of the packhouse to throw back a few.

"Not bad, eh?" he asked.

"Not bad."

He gave my shoulder a shake. "Hey, Volkov, loosen up. Life's getting better. We're free now."

I grunted.

Sasha was my good friend going back to when we were pups. People had always remarked we could pass for brothers. They clearly lacked keen eyes. Sure, we both sported thick blond hair and tall frames—although I had at least a good ten centimeters on him—our facial shapes were much different. His was more rotund, and his cheeks constantly reddened with emotion.

My features were far sharper, hardened, and had become even more so in the past year. At times, I looked in the mirror, and I saw my late father staring back at me. His ghost haunted me from the beyond, shaping my features to mimic the forehead furrows, lifeless eyes, and permanent scowl I'd always associated with him.

I took another sip of the vodka.

"Have you checked out any of the girls around the pack yet?" Sasha asked.

How could he be so relaxed, talk about such meaningless things, especially after he'd lost almost his entire family except his sister and niece? He'd had to carry the poor fatherless girl on his back for kilometers since she couldn't shift yet. I, myself, had carried an orphaned boy.

"There are more important things than girls," I replied.

"Like what? The pack was nearly wiped clean. If you ask me, reproduction should be at the top of our priority list. We should be paying our pack members to have sex."

I let out another grunt.

"Hey, come on, you have to have a sense of humor. Otherwise, life's just damn depressing."

"Life's damn depressing either way," I replied.

We silently sipped on our drinks and munched on chips Sasha had dug up from the packhouse cabinets. There'd been a time when this would have been fun. When drinking had meant joking and laughing and giving our friends shit. But now, I only had one friend who hadn't left for the other realm.

The alcohol numbed me a little. It wasn't enough to take it all away, but it was something. The two of us drank until there was only half a bottle left, and I was feeling the effects—something that took a lot for an alpha. But I was pleased that, when I got up, my head was a bit light, and my shoulders slumped into a relaxed position.

"You need some pussy, big time." Sasha shook his head at me. "I'm telling you. It'll be like ten therapy sessions in one. Your balls must be so heavy. When was the last time you emptied them?"

"Stop being so vulgar," I responded, swatting him over the head. With that, I headed toward the alpha wing and proceeded upstairs to my bedroom.

The Tikaani family had been more than generous. The bedroom they provided was better than the one I'd had back in Ukraine at my own packhouse. And the fact that they were willing to host my entire pack without asking anything in return was flabbergasting. I vowed to repay them, and then some. One day. Once I was able to get my own pack settled and functioning independently.

It was well past midnight, and the halls were silent. I was about to turn right to head toward my room when my nose caught that scent.

Fuck, it was amazing. I breathed it all into my lungs, as if I were inhaling the best drug in the world. It instantly melded with my buzz, and soon my feet were carrying me in the direction it was coming from. *Boginya*, what I wouldn't do to bottle it up and snort it every day.

A door creaked open in the hallway and out stepped an angel. My eyes traced from her bare toes, which were painted a tropical orange, up her baggy black sweatpants that hung low on her hips, to her stomach that peeked out from a cropped, long-sleeve shirt and was more toned and sculpted than possibly even some of my warriors'.

She wore a scarf—no, a blanket, really, with how much it covered her chest in thick, concealing folds. While I was not usually one for excessively lewd thoughts, I suddenly could think of nothing but tearing it from her neck, revealing everything she was hiding underneath. I could already imagine how her bare breasts would feel in my hands after I pushed her against the wall and shoved aside the superfluous fabric between us—

Boginya!

What the fuck was wrong with me? I didn't even know her name.

She stepped forward with her head down and long, dark waves shielding her face like a curtain. Then, slowly, she looked up. My eyes locked with the most remarkable amber gaze I'd ever seen in my life. The whole earth seemed to tilt beneath me, the world faded into nothing, and suddenly we were the only two people, everything else long forgotten.

"*Paru.*" The word forced itself onto my lips, and I almost choked when I said it. Could she really be—?

"What?" she said in a deep, honeyed, throaty voice, furrowing her brows.

Did she not feel it too?

"Sorry, what did you just say?" When I didn't respond immediately, she continued speaking. "Why are you looking at me like that? Do I have something on my face?" She brought both manicured hands to her cheeks.

I shook my head, trying to clear my mind.

Unexpectedly, she smiled widely, revealing all of her perfectly straight, white teeth. The most perfect teeth I'd ever seen. They'd put any movie star to shame. "Oh! You must be Alpha Nikolai Volkov! Hi! I'm Terri, Terri Tikaani. I'm Alpha Tyce's sister and Julia's my mom. She's already told me so much about you." She put her hand out.

"Do not you—?" I started, not sure exactly what to ask.

"Don't I what?" She tilted her head, observing me. I stared back into her inquisitive amber eyes, unable to tear myself away from them.

Was she fucking with me? I mean if we were . . . Shouldn't she feel it too?

And then a bleaker thought came to me. What if someone had bewitched me to believe she was my mate when she wasn't? Could someone do that? Would they? And why? It was the only explanation I could think of immediately, unless she really was just fucking with me. But I also wondered why she'd do that. We'd never met each other, and most women were desperate to be with an alpha. So what would be her reason to pretend not to be mated to one?

"You seem sad. Are you okay?" Her expression suddenly changed. She looked up at me through her long, dark lashes, her eyebrows downturned in almost a look of pity.

"What?" I barked.

"It's almost like I can feel it." She glanced down at her hands as if they held some answer to a question she had and muttered, "And you seem perplexed. I don't understand."

"Good night," I grunted and turned on my heel to head to my bedroom. I had to get away. The alcohol was clearly affecting me more than I thought it was.

"Good night!" she called out. "It was nice to meet you, Alpha Nikolai. See you around!"

Boginya, she was peppy. And that was when I knew there was no way she could be my mate. She was exactly the type of girl that grated on my nerves. The kind with no worries, no responsibilities, who walked around like life was just some big fucking party. A *princessa*. And she had to be a princess, having been raised in this oversize mansion with so much money she was probably used to always getting what she wanted.

I shut the door behind me and let out a breath, relieved to be in the privacy of my bedroom. As I threw off my clothes and got ready for bed, thoughts swirled around my head. Distractions. I couldn't seem to get her out of my mind. *Boginya*, she was so beautiful. Stunning. I couldn't recall ever seeing a more gorgeous woman in my life.

The resemblance to her alpha brother was undeniable. The same tan skin, dark hair, and striking amber eyes. Their facial features shared a similar structure, but where his had a rugged edge, hers were soft and cherubic. Her cheeks were full, dimpling when she smiled with those plush, pillowy lips.

And her scent.

Was that how she smelled naturally? Or had she been wearing an elusive perfume? I'd heard mates were supposed to smell particularly nice, but I still couldn't make sense of what just transpired.

I tried to push it from my thoughts but found I simply couldn't. I tossed and turned, and soon found myself painfully stiff. *Blyad*, this was exactly what I didn't need right now! Especially living in the same home with two alphas who would have my neck if I even thought about touching her. Fuck my life.

Chapter 4

Ginger

My twin sister, Paige, finished twisting the last bit of my hair around her curling wand and sprayed it down with hairspray. "I miss this." She let out a deep sigh, sitting back on her heels, her body collapsing a bit. We had gathered on the floor of her bedroom while getting ready for the evening. The bedroom that wouldn't be hers much longer. She would be the last to fly the coop, leaving our parents to an empty nest—something our mother couldn't stop being melodramatic about. Her wedding was in a matter of days, which was the reason I had flown back to Vermont with my mate, Tyce.

"It's not that much different from when I was in school," I replied, my stomach squeezing a little, but I needed to put a positive spin on our situation.

"Yeah, but you were at least home for the entire summer then. Now, I'll probably only see you a week a year or something like that."

Nonchalantly, I blurted, "Maybe the family can move to Alaska." At first, I meant it as an offhand remark, but then I thought, why not? I straightened up with the confidence of a great idea.

"Funny," Paige responded, clearly not amused.

"No, but seriously. Why not?" I said more enthusiastically. "I'm stuck in Alaska because Tyce is alpha of his pack. But what's *really* keeping all of you here?"

"Are you serious?" Paige squinted at me.

"Yeah, I'm serious. I hate not having you guys out there."

"They don't even allow female warriors in your new pack," Paige responded. "And Dad would probably have to start all over. You know how warriors are with newbs. Even if Tyce put him in as a senior warrior, they'd never really respect him coming in as an outsider. And what about Heidi? Are Hunter and Evan going to move to Alaska with Kelli?" Paige brought up the big, fat family secret. While Paige and I were both informed of the fact that our older sister, Heidi, and her best friend, Kelli, were mates, everyone else in the pack, including our parents, thought they were actually mated to their husbands and beards, Hunter and Evan.

I blew out a breath and slumped my shoulders.

"Have things at least improved with the in-laws?" Paige asked.

"I don't know. Not really. They still think I'm a fat cow with a fucked-up wolf."

"Oh, Gigi." Paige threw her arms around me.

"Please don't." I shrugged her off. "I'm fine. Everything's fine. Things between Tyce and me have never been better, and that's what really matters." I forced a big smile on my face. "And tonight's going to be fucking awesome!"

"Yeah," Paige responded, biting her lip, clearly not as excited about the impending event as I was.

"What's wrong?"

"Lucy caught wind of the bachelorette party and basically took over planning the entire thing. Jasmine said it was just easier that way, especially since she's so busy with being luna and her twins. She was really apologetic about it. And said if it sucks, she'll take us out for dinner or something."

I burst into laughter. "Oh my Goddess. I was there when Lucy found out too! That girl is nuts. But that just means tonight's gonna be better than I was expecting."

"What, you think Jasmine can't plan a fun party?" Paige defended her best friend, putting her hands on her hips and giving me a pointed look.

"Paige, I love Jasmine as much as you do. For a lot of things, she'd be perfect. Like tackling big bad wolves, perfect. Squat competition, also perfect. Help with calculus homework, there's no one I'd trust more. But bachelorette party? I think we need to acknowledge that is not one of her strengths."

"But Lucy is such a train wreck!"

"Yeah, she is. That's why tonight's going to be epic." I laughed, already imagining all her probable antics. Because I'd be getting married a few months after Paige, Jasmine took on the task of hosting a joint bachelorette party for us. Of course, I understood why this may have been a huge undertaking. Being the luna of her pack, the female leader married to the alpha, along with having a couple of babies that were only months old, would certainly be sucking up a fair amount of her time.

I pulled out a portable mirror to apply my tinted moisturizer, and Paige took a seat in front of her full-length mirror to apply her own makeup.

After some time, I broke the silence. "So how's the marking situation going? Are you going to make it to your big day?"

Paige snorted. "Goddess, I hope so. The wedding is literally five days away. But now I totally get what Jasmine meant. I'm going to die if I don't mark him soon. What about you?"

"Tyce has been biting my ass sometimes. Honestly, it feels kind of good." I giggled. "I think it's the venom in his fangs. You should try it!"

"What is wrong with you two?" Paige pushed my shoulder. "And we don't have venom in our fangs. We're not weresnakes!"

"Then why does it feel so good?"

"Probably his drool." Paige giggled.

"He does drool all over my ass."

"Okay, I think I've heard enough about your ass and Tyce for the night."

"I'm only getting started." I smiled slyly.

We met at the pack entrance gate as instructed by Lucy. Heidi, her belly straining against a coat that looked bulky everywhere else, was already waiting with her mate Kelli when Paige and I arrived. I threw my arms around her, so happy to be reunited with my other sister. "Where'd you get the coat?" I asked.

"It's an old one of Dad's. It's the only thing that fits anymore."

"I thought it looked familiar." I gave one of the sleeves a tug.

"Paige! Gigi! You're here!" Lucy popped out from seemingly nowhere with Jasmine trailing behind her. "Don't worry, our ride's on the way. They just got a little lost. But I've got it handled." She pulled out her cell phone and walked away.

"Any idea what she has planned?" Paige asked Jasmine, who stayed behind with us.

"You think she told me?" Jasmine laughed. "Like I said, if things get too crazy, we can always leave early."

"I'm sure it'll be fine." Paige bit her lip.

"Lucy's been better behaved lately. I will give her that."

"I don't need well-behaved!" I butted into the conversation. "I need the train-wreck crazy version of Lucy to host my bachelorette. I need a night that I'll remember and smile about when I'm kept up all night by

Tyce's little screaming brats. I need male strippers, lines of coke, and so much penis paraphernalia that I become dicknotized!"

"Gigi!" Paige exclaimed. "Have you ever even *done* coke?"

"Well, no. But my bachelorette party is the perfect night to lose my c-card!"

"I'm not going to be your sober babysitter tonight," Heidi said. "I'm too far along for that. If you pass out in the bathroom while coked out of your mind, you're on your own."

"So much for having a sister's back!" I replied.

We all stood in a group laughing and catching up. Jasmine and Heidi pulled out matching veils and sashes for Paige and me. As we were in the middle of taking cute pictures, a bus with tinted windows pulled up to the pack gates. Lucy lugged a huge cooler and waved us onto the bus.

"Wow! This is nice!" I exclaimed as I entered, taking in the black and colorful fluorescent lights and plush leather seats. I plopped down on one, bouncing a bit. "What's in the cooler?"

Lucy gave me a mischievous look and a wink. "Once everyone's seated and we're on our way, you'll find out."

"It's probably just her special punch," Paige loudly whispered to Jasmine.

"Okay, that is in there," Lucy admitted, rolling her eyes. "But that's not all."

"Does coke need refrigeration?" I snickered.

"No drugs," Jasmine chimed in. "It's on the list of ground rules I gave Lucy."

"Goddess, you're so boring!" Lucy whined. "But I followed them, okay?"

"What else was on the list?" Paige asked.

Lucy pulled a paper out of her small purse and cleared her throat. "No drugs, no strippers . . . Please, Jasmine, you think Blake cares?" She rolled her eyes again and continued, "Nothing illegal, no crossing international borders, no Jell-O or mud wrestling, no wet T-shirt contests, no topless mechanical bull riding, no nudity in general, no tattoos, no happy-ending massages, no orgies, no driving any vehicles of any kind after drinking, no asking police officers if they'll use their handcuffs on you or going in the backseat of their cruiser, no asking firemen to use their poles or hoses, no pantsing, no mooning, no pornography."

"So sex clubs are okay?" I asked, giggling.

"Add that to the list of noes!" Jasmine exclaimed.

"Too late!" Lucy smirked. "I've already paid, and it wasn't on the list."

Jasmine narrowed her eyes and appeared as if she was readying herself for a fight.

"I'm just kidding! Jeez, no reason to get your granny panties in a twist."

"Okay, so what *can* we do?" I asked.

"Well, I'm so glad you asked!" Lucy bounced up and gave her long blonde hair a shake. She flipped open the large cooler. "I think we can all agree that no good bachelorette party starts without some drinking!"

She fished out a large pitcher and began pulling glasses down from a cabinet in the bus.

"I guess we should help." Kelli glanced at Jasmine. Jasmine nodded in return. The two of them stood up, clearly putting aside whatever disdain they held for Lucy.

"Hold the glasses while I pour. And, Jasmine, put these straws in them." Lucy shook a bag in front of Jasmine's face. Jasmine took the bag and opened it to peek inside, her face reddening in response to whatever she discovered.

"Not only did you have to get penis straws, but you had to get the biggest, veiniest ones possible, huh?" Jasmine rolled her eyes, holding up a purple plastic phallic object that looked more dildo than straw.

"I figured we'd all want to succeed tonight. Suck. Seed. Get it?" Lucy burst into laughter, then grabbed the straw from Jasmine and shoved it into the glass she just poured. "Here, you start, PJ. You and Blake don't have any problems in that department, right? Why don't you show us how it's done?"

Part of me felt a little bad for wanting to laugh at Lucy's quips, considering Jasmine was my friend and Lucy most definitely wasn't. But it was entertaining to watch the two of them bicker. They both clearly had some deep-seated resentment that had never gotten properly resolved.

Once all the drinks were passed around, we settled into our seats, and Kelli hooked up her phone to play music.

"So, are you going to reveal where we're going?" I asked.

"I figured we'd do something different and go into a human town. This one is super cute, very New England, and gets all decorated for Christmas. I found it online. And it's not too far from us." It wasn't typical for werewolves to venture outside their pack much. Most felt more comfortable among their own. I was the exception and had spent most of my teenage and adult years in boarding schools and away at college because I'd lost my wolf when I was only twelve. I thought I was facing a future of being wolfless until my mate Tyce helped me get mine back over the summer.

I had grown up in Vermont but moved to Alaska not long after I turned back into a werewolf, since my mate was an alpha and had an obligation to lead his pack.

I sucked a big load of my drink into my mouth, wanting to savor the evening. I knew I wouldn't have many more nights like this with my sisters in the future. It took almost an entire day to travel to Vermont from Alaska, so it wasn't worth the trek except for special occasions. I glanced over at Heidi, who was rubbing her round belly while sipping on a mocktail. My stomach tightened with the realization that soon we'd likely all start having families, meaning we'd be pulled further apart from each other.

"You're going to suck that cock dry!" Lucy teased, waking me from my melancholy thoughts and bringing my attention to the fact that I had already sucked almost my entire drink down. As usual, Lucy was quick to refill my cup. She was a good hostess like that. In reality, she probably just did it for the plot, but who could blame her?

I willingly put my cup out for more booze, taking full advantage of the fact that I was no longer a lightweight in comparison to my fellow werewolves. Paige and Jasmine, as expected, nursed their drinks. Heidi had, obviously, opted for a mocktail, and Kelli followed suit in solidarity. I was suddenly thankful I had Lucy here, even if she was an unwelcome guest, because at least she was reliable for a good time.

After my third drink, I was feeling it, my head a bit light and my vision getting a little unstable. Whatever Lucy's secret recipe was for her cocktail, it was no joke.

About a half hour or so after we left, we arrived in a cute little downtown area that was all done up for Christmas, with the colonial-style houses, buildings, and trees decked out in evergreen garland, large red ribbons, and string lights. As if on cue, small snowflakes drifted down from the sky as we pulled into a parking space. While this town was super cute, it didn't exactly scream bachelorette party, and now I was suddenly questioning what had happened to Lucy since I left Vermont. What happened to the crazy girl that flashed an entire nightclub just months earlier?

"Okay, this was not what I was expecting," Paige said to Jasmine. "Maybe you're right. Lucy *has* calmed down."

"This sucks," I blurted out to the two of them.

"You do realize you're about to become a luna," Paige responded.

"So? My pack isn't here. This is the perfect opportunity to act crazy for one night."

We filed off the party bus onto the sidewalk, trying to avoid the particularly slushy parts so we wouldn't get our white sneakers wet.

"Please tell me we're at least going to a bar!" I shouted. "Not just doing some touristy Christmas stuff."

"Who do you think I am?" Lucy glanced back at me as she led the way down the festive street, bringing us past cozy shops and restaurants, the lights of their interiors spilling out onto the wet sidewalk. Before long, we found ourselves in front of a towny-looking pub, where the vast majority of the populace inside was middle-aged men downing tap beer.

I looked over at Lucy.

"Okay, I really thought the people out tonight wouldn't be so . . . old," she said.

I sighed but figured I should just make the best of it. Maybe once I got back to Alaska, I could meet some friends who knew how to party for real. Not that there were many places to go out in the middle of nowhere where I lived. And it was so strictly conservative too. More so than the pack I'd grown up in, which was saying something.

"Here, take these!" Lucy handed Paige and me fake IDs that, as usual, looked nothing like us. She then draped about a pound of penis necklaces on everyone.

We all marched in, and everyone's eyes instantly went to us. Lucy made a beeline for the bar and started ordering us drinks before anyone could protest. I followed her, excited to get my drink on. The bar was playing my favorite Mariah Carey Christmas song, and I was ready to start dancing.

After we all had our drinks in hand, an older man with a gray beard asked, "What is this all about? A birthday?"

I blinked a few times, thinking how obvious the veil and phallic jewelry were. But I was feeling the alcohol and decided to engage in his dumb questions. "A bachelorette party!"

"Woo!" Lucy cheered before taking a big gulp of her drink.

"A bachelorette party? What's that?"

"Never heard of such a thing, Bob," his seat companion said. I studied his face, to check if he was joking, but he said it without even a slight smirk.

"You've never heard of a bachelorette party?" I responded, taking a sip of my drink, about to roll my eyes.

"Nah, have you heard of a bachelorette party, Al?" he shouted to a man sitting on the other side of the bar.

"A bacha-what?" Al asked.

"Bachelorette."

"What the hell is that?"

"No clue. Hey, Jim!" He waved down the bartender. "These girls are having a bachelorette party. Any idea what that is?"

"I think I saw that on TV. That's a show, right? *The Bachelorette*?" Jim stroked his beard.

"Ah! Are you all famous?" Bob asked, glancing at each of us.

"Is this a joke?" I asked.

"A joke?" Bob replied. "Do I look like a joker to you? Lou." He looked over at the man next to him. "Am I a joker?"

"Not at all, Bob," Lou replied. "I didn't hear you say anything funny."

"Why don't you explain what a bachelorette party is to us?" Bob said.

"Can't you tell?" I tugged at the veil on my head.

"Are you getting married?" Bob asked.

"Ah! I know! These girls are having a party to celebrate her upcoming nuptials!" Lou said.

"Oh! I see!" Bob responded. "Well, in that case, you've come to the right place. Our town's brides also celebrate before their marriage. But we call it a Bride Fight."

I blinked a few times. "Bride Fight?"

"Well, you see, before any broad gets married here, she's gotta engage in a duel with a giant chicken."

Jasmine and Paige stifled laughter behind their hands. "Seriously?" Paige asked.

"Absolutely!" Lou nodded. "Poultry farming is our town's biggest trade. So any lady that's to be wed must prove herself in matters of wrangling chicken."

Was it just me or were the men sitting at the bar struggling to hold straight faces?

"Oh, Gigi will definitely triumph. What do you lovingly call your fiancé?" Paige elbowed me. "Tyson Chicken?"

"Oh hell yeah! Chicken fight!" Lucy sang while pushing a shot into my hand.

"Hey, wait! Paige, you're getting married sooner than me. So you should really be the one challenging the chicken."

"You're the one that wanted a crazy bachelorette party. So this crazy is all you," Paige responded.

"I wanted to do coke, not *duel cock*!" I replied.

"Hey, hey." Bob chuckled. "There's an easy way to settle this. You can just pull on a wishbone. And the person who gets the short end has to fight."

"And you just have wishbones randomly lying around?" Lucy asked.

"Always. For times like this." The bartender, Jim, pulled one out of what seemed like thin air.

I grabbed for it and held it out to Paige. "Let's go!" I shouted.

Paige rolled her eyes and pulled, taking part of my half of the bone with her as it broke. *Damnit!*

"Gigi, is it? Looks like it's all you." Bob got up and his companions at the bar began helping him move some tables and chairs around.

"Lucy, where the hell did you find this place?" I asked as we all watched, and a crowd began gathering in the area being cleared.

"Isn't this fun, though?" She clinked her shot glass against mine.

What the hell? I downed it, the burn of tequila familiar in my throat.

After I thumped the shot glass on the bar, I exhaled with a satisfied sigh and exclaimed, "Okay, I'm ready! Let's go!" I may have slurred that a bit. The alcohol was really hitting me now.

"Okay, warrior." Paige snickered.

"You can do it, Gigi!" Lucy cheered.

Jasmine patted me on the back as we moved closer to the now-cleared area.

"I'm looking forward to seeing this giant chi—" Heidi stopped before finishing her sentence as a man with a huge beer belly wearing a chicken suit strutted out onto the floor. The whole bar cheered, clinking their beer mugs.

The room went quiet, and all I could hear were murmurs and some snickering as the patrons of the restaurant all gave each other looks, lifting their eyebrows, glancing to their friends and then toward the chicken man. "The Chicken Dance" blasted from the restaurant speakers, and the men who had been chatting with us at the bar cheered.

The man in the chicken suit put up his hands in a chicken-beak gesture, opening and closing them. "Come on, Gigi." He waved me to come to him. "It's time for a chicken—"

Before he could finish his sentence, I was already sprinting toward him, not listening.

Alcohol blurring all thought and common sense, I went into fighter mode, the practiced moves pulling at my muscle memory. Tyce had made me practice every beginner warrior move with him for hours every day until my legs were like jelly, my fingers numb from the Alaskan frost, tears frozen solid to my skin, core muscles screaming to stop.

The last thing I saw was fear in the chicken man's eyes as they made contact with mine. And it was at that moment it came to me: perhaps he wasn't actually looking to fight. But it was too late. I was already in the zone. I gripped his shoulders and swung my leg behind his. In a matter of microseconds, his back hit the ground with a loud thump.

I turned to face my audience to celebrate my victory. A loud, collective gasp sounded through the crowd, and the music stopped abruptly.

Oh, damn.

"Holy shit! That broad took you right down!" Bob from the bar rushed over to the man currently sprawled out on the floor, moaning.

The chicken-suit man blinked a few times.

"How many fingers am I holding up?" Bob brought three fingers to the man's face.

"He was just going to challenge you to a chicken dance-off!" Lou from earlier pulled on my elbow and gave me a look of severe disappointment. "Why'd you have to get so violent for?"

"I . . . I . . . I didn't know."

"Hey! You told her she would have to battle him! Next time be more specific!" Lucy butted in. "Gigi is training to be a warrior. You picked the wrong bitch to fight!"

"A what?" Lou asked.

"Sorry, we've all clearly had a bit too much to drink," Jasmine cut in before Lucy could say more she wasn't supposed to.

It reminded me of the time at the nightclub when she threatened humans with her "beta," which had a far different connotation to humans than werewolves. I almost snickered out loud thinking about it, but I knew that wouldn't look good at this particular moment and stopped myself.

"Is he going to be okay? Can I call anyone for help?" I asked, trying to fix the situation.

"I'm a'right!" The man wheezed a bit as he slowly got up onto his forearms. Lou and Bob helped him stand.

"I'm so sorry!" I exclaimed. "I didn't realize."

"You were on your way to murder before I'd even finished my sentence!" the chicken-suit man replied.

"Is there anything I can do to make it up to you? Buy you a drink?"

He smirked a bit and pulled on his white, unkempt beard. "You and your friends could join me in the chicken dance-off, and we'll have a vote to see who wins fair and square."

"Uh, okay," I replied, looking around at the ladies who had come here with me. They nodded, clearly also feeling bad about the situation, which had gone from odd to bad to very odd.

"Okay, get in position!" he said, dusting himself off.

"Goddess, this place is weird," Lucy whispered as she took her place next to me, handing me yet another shot and clinking the one she had in her other hand to mine. We both downed them, and then the song started.

We all began quacking our hands, flapping our wings, and shaking our butts. As the song went on, we got more and more dramatic. At one point, Paige and I hooked elbows and danced around each other. The man in the chicken suit spun and dipped Lucy. And Jasmine, Heidi, and Kelli grabbed hands, dancing in a circle.

As the song ended, the crowd cheered, and the bartender came around to hand us all free drinks.

"You girls aren't s'bad. Stick around!" the man in the chicken suit said, giving us all high fives. He then grabbed a microphone and announced, "I concede to the ladies. They have out-chickened me!"

We cheered, and everyone who'd seemed hesitant about getting too crazy was now heartily downing their drinks. I noted that Lucy was especially quick to make sure that Jasmine was never empty-handed.

Before long, everyone, except Heidi and Kelli, was clearly feeling it. I was now to the point where the whole place was spinning and blurring. Yep, definitely couldn't see straight. And, wait, what? Was Jasmine agreeing to get on a table to dance with Lucy? *Holy shit*!

I rushed over to witness the momentous event. By the time I reached the table, Paige was joining the two of them as well. I cheered them on and snuck my phone out for some photographic evidence-slash-black-mail.

We drank and danced for so long that we shut the bar down and barely made it back to the party bus. I almost fell into a dirty puddle at one point, but Paige and Kelli grabbed me before I could.

Once the bus started moving, it wasn't long before most everyone drifted off to sleep. I was just nodding off when I caught the sound of hushed voices.

"Thanks for planning this, Lucy," Jasmine whispered. "I've barely managed to keep up with my luna duties lately. It's been . . . a lot. And I really appreciate that you stuck to all the rules. I know I gave you a crazy list. It wasn't fair of me not to trust you, or to ignore how much effort you've been making to better yourself. For what it's worth, I had a lot of fun."

"I'm glad you let me plan this," Lucy said with a heavy sigh. "Honestly, it means a lot. And . . . Jaz?"

"Yeah?"

"I'm sorry. For everything. For all the problems I caused you. I should've been more understanding about you being mated to Luke."

Silence stretched between them. For a moment, I wondered if Jasmine would respond.

Finally, she said quietly, "Apology accepted."

"Thanks," Lucy murmured.

"And I'm sorry too," Jasmine added after a pause. "For how you found out. We should never have kept it a secret from you."

"Thank you for saying that," Lucy replied softly. After a beat, she added, "I hope . . . maybe one day, we can be friends again."

A long moment passed before Jasmine answered, "One day."

Chapter 5

Tyson

'Twas several nights after the winter solstice (and one night after Christmas) when all through the packhouse, not a creature was stirring, not even a mouse. And thank the Goddess for that, because we weren't really big fans of mice around here. At least I wasn't. Although, I had come to warm up to rats . . . Well, some very specific pet rats. Other than that, still wasn't a big fan.

But you know what I was a fan of? T and A, especially when that T and A was attached to my perfect, voluptuous, thick AF fiancée and mate. My mate who was very conspicuously missing from my bed. I had gotten used to having her warm body next to mine at night, and every inch of my skin was practically tingling with the loss of her. Because her family was devout, it had been decided that she would stay at her parents' home, and I at the packhouse of my ally, the Midnight Maple Pack.

I knew she planned to go back to school during the spring semester, but damn, this was torture. For years I was totally fine being on my own, in fact preferred it. But somehow, now, it felt totally foreign and unnatural.

I rolled over and flipped my pillow, trying to get comfortable in the bed with far too much space. Goddess, what I wouldn't do for—

The door creaked open slowly, and the most luxurious, perfumed scent drifted in. Her feet padded across the floorboards, and I could instantly tell she was drunk because she was doing the shittiest job sneaking ever, clumsily tripping and giggling as she made her way to the bed.

I shifted and made room for her as she crawled in under the covers.

"You're awake!" Gigi exclaimed quietly as soon as I opened my eyes.

"I'm always awake for you, baby," I replied, pulling her closer.

She brushed her fingertips along my biceps. "My, Grandma." She snickered. "What big arms you have!"

"The better to snuggle you with," I responded, squeezing her to me. "Mine," I added with satisfaction.

"My, Grandma, what big, glowy eyes you have!"

"The better to stare at that fat, delicious ass while you're making gains during your deadlifts." I gave one cheek a big squeeze. Her pelvis instantly shot right to my crotch, rubbing against the massive boner I'd been sporting since her arrival.

"My, Grandma, what big pecs you have!" She pushed her hands under my T-shirt and inched them up my chest, conveniently ignoring what was really big and in need of her attention at that moment.

"The better to . . ." I paused. "The better to lift you up and onto my cock." I smiled, baiting her in that direction.

She gasped. "Grandma! That's not appropriate to do to your granddaughter!" She swatted at my chest and smirked. "Now where was I?" After a pause, she continued, "My, Grandma, what big quads you have."

"The better to fuck you from behind with," I quipped.

"No, Grandma! You can't do that to your granddaughter!"

"I officially hate being a grandma."

"My, Grandma, what big fingers you have." She brought my hand to her face and slipped a digit into her mouth, gently sucking on it.

"I like the direction this is heading." I groaned a little, now very aware of how much my cock was throbbing, begging to be in her mouth instead. "The better to undress you with." At that, she bit down. *Hard!*

"Hey!" I pulled my hand from her mouth. I got up and pinned her down, straddling her body and pushing her arms down onto the bed so she couldn't move. "Didn't anyone ever teach you not to bite the hand that fingers you? What terrible manners!"

She struggled a little, trying to get free from my grasp, meanwhile giggling.

"Someone needs to teach you a lesson, you naughty little redheaded girl."

"My, Grandma, what big teeth you have!" she exclaimed.

"The better to eat you with," I replied, flipping her onto her stomach and immediately pushing her hips up until I had perfect access. Holding her wrists behind her back so she couldn't move, I used the other hand to push the skirt of her dress out of the way and rip her panties clean off.

"Hey! I liked those!"

"Not anymore," I replied, finally letting go of her wrists and bringing my mouth right to my favorite meal. My tongue slipped between her ass cheeks, and if she'd been planning to protest initially, she definitely wasn't anymore. Every muscle in her body rapidly relaxed, and the only sounds coming from her were soft moans as I licked the perimeter of the opening of her behind.

I pulled away and sat back on my heels, taking an appreciative look at the sight in front of me.

"Hey, don't stop!" She turned her head to glance up at me.

"Oh, who's okay with Grandma all of a sudden?" I teased, pulling my T-shirt off with one swift movement. I moved closer to her. "I think it's time for Grandma to put her injured hand to work doing what it's meant for. Is that okay with you, Grandchild?"

She got up on her knees, pouted, and crossed her arms across her chest. "Fine."

"Anyway, I'm not your grandma. I'm the big bad wolf." I pushed her back onto the bed, flipping her onto her back. "Now where was I? I think it's time for me to use my big mouth to finish my meal." I pushed her knees apart and brought my lips to her pussy, which was glistening with wetness. I kissed it up and down until I found her sweet little bean and sucked it right into my mouth where it belonged. She let out a passionate cry in response.

Goddess, I love that sound!

I eagerly lapped at her clit, stroking back and forth, allowing her enthusiastic moans and the mate bond to guide me. I was officially pussy-whipped, a prisoner to my mate's perfect pink cunt. I would spend the rest of my life happily rubbing, licking, massaging, tasting, inhaling, and doing anything else it needed to be fully satisfied.

"Oh, Goddess, Tyce," she cried out, and I could tell she was close. Her legs were trembling, and her hands were entwined in my hair, grasping firmly at the strands. I gave one final effort, putting everything into the focused flicks of my tongue, dancing it across her clit, until she let out a vehement concluding scream that I quickly muffled by sticking my fingers into her mouth to prevent her from waking the pups in the room next door. Blake wouldn't be such a gracious host if he found his twins woken and introduced to sex ed about thirteen years too early.

She was left panting and had never looked so beautiful, with her face flushed, her hair astray, the skirt of her dress crumpled across her stomach to reveal her legs that, because of her dedication to warrior training over the past few months, had transformed to be firmer and more muscular.

"Tyce," she whispered, brushing her fingertips along my thighs.

"Yes?"

"I'm still horny."

I smirked down at her. *How did I get so lucky?* "You don't have to ask twice." My boxers were off in under a second. Her legs fell open, and I was unable to hold back the groan that escaped my lips. I fisted my cock and guided the tip right to her opening, teasing her a little by swiping it up and down the edge. She sucked in a breath, her nails dug into my thighs as she pulled me closer, and I could sense her desperation. I couldn't hold back anymore as I inched my way inside her.

She gasped with satisfaction, lifting her chin and inviting me to trail kisses along her neck as I thrust into her slowly, gently building the pace, trying to savor every moment. It was short-lived, because before long she was moaning out, "More, Tyce."

I pushed forward harder and faster, covering her mouth with mine, swallowing her impassioned whimpers. A shudder ran down my spine, and before I knew it, I was fucking her like I was trying to win an Olympic race. I gave in fully to the pleasure of my cock being encompassed by her tight little wet pussy. Gigi writhed underneath me, her limbs shaking, and I could tell she was close. I stroked her clit until her nails were clawing so hard at my skin I wasn't sure she hadn't broken it. I gulped down her screams while she unraveled underneath me. My orgasm crashed inside me like a wave, and I pulled out just in time, spilling my come all over Gigi's stomach. *Fuck! That was so good!*

"Mmmm . . ." Gigi inched closer to me, her breath heavy, and her skin damp and glistening. I inhaled her intoxicating scent, not able to get enough. After our canines receded, the sign of our unmarked mateship, I grabbed my T-shirt from the floor, quickly cleaned her, and threw it toward the hamper.

As I drifted into sleep with my arms wrapped around her, I whispered, "Happy nutting to all, and to all a good night."

Chapter 6

Theresa

The excitement in the air was palpable. The whole pack had gathered on the airplane runway. This was the one part of the pack land that was consistently plowed so we'd continue to receive food and supplies throughout the harsh winters, even after we gave up on plowing the roads that led to the main highway. It was how I was able to get back and forth from school during the holidays.

Full moon runs were a longtime tradition of our pack's and one of my favorite celebrations during the long, sunless winters. Even when seasonal depression tried to sink its way into my bones and pull my spirit away, these runs tended to give me the adrenaline I needed to keep going. There was something magical about an entire community coming together to expel all our energy in the wilderness and subsequently feast on the kill we'd contributed to the celebration. My heart was full of gratitude knowing that, no matter how tough things got, this pack would always have each other's backs.

I spotted my friends in the crowd and pushed through to make my way over, simultaneously staying aware of my surroundings. I knew he was here, and the last thing I wanted was to have to interact with him. During the past few months in school, I'd done so much work to find acceptance in the situation and learn to move forward. But I knew I was still on thin ice. Seeing and interacting with him could easily form cracks in the delicate, newly formed ground I was standing on. No, it was best I stayed away. What was done was done, and I couldn't change anything now.

"Hey, girl!" Sophia, one of my closest friends from forever waved me over. A balaclava covered her naturally voluminous, curly blonde hair, and she'd donned a snowsuit that would be easy to zip off for the run, similar to what many others were wearing. It was definitely a balancing act to find something that would keep us warm in our human forms but be easy to slip off when shifting.

I was about a yard from my destination when I felt a firm grip on my shoulder. I instantly turned to come face-to-face . . . well, face-to-ski mask with my mom.

"Are you trying to rob a bank or something?" I tried to joke with her.

"Come," she responded, not even acknowledging it, grasping my wrist and pulling me along. My mom may have been a petite lady, but she definitely wasn't weak. She fought every lump, wrinkle, and sag like she was at war with her mortal enemy, and she was no stranger to the gym.

Within seconds, she planted me right in front of Alpha Nikolai. Okay, let's be honest. He was hot! Like really, really hot. It was rare that I felt any attraction to anyone. I mean, sure, I'd had crushes in the past. But that crazy, lustful, need-to-get-my-pants-off-right-now feeling? I thought it had to be made up in books and movies. Because I'd never felt that with anyone, at least not when first meeting them. I googled it once out of curiosity. I knew I wasn't demisexual, because I did feel solely physical attraction sometimes, and I was certain I'd never be able to date someone based on personality alone. There were tons of people I enjoyed being around who had amazing personalities, but I didn't feel attracted to them. After my long search, I finally settled on graysexual. It was kind of asexual, but not really. It was the best I could come up with to try to label myself. And I wasn't even sure that label was quite right.

But this man? Holy wow.

His scent hit me first—musky, raw, undeniably masculine, and far too many pheromones. Like a good version of a men's locker room. Goddess, that sounded so wrong, but it made sense in my head. It shouldn't have stood out among the mishmash of scents around me, but it did.

My heart thudded, and heat crept up my neck. He was massive, casting a shadow over my mom and me in the moonlight. Under all his winter layers, I knew he was built like he could uproot an entire massive tree.

I looked up into his silver eyes—yes, definitely silver, not gray—and a deep sadness emanated from him. Granted, I was a pretty empathetic person and great at reading facial expressions, but this was different. It was almost as if I were feeling my own emotions, but they were definitely his. How strange!

"Nikolai! You've met my daughter, Theresa, right?" My mom pushed me forward. "I'd like you to take her on the run tonight. You just never know what's out there in the dark wilderness. It would be good for her to have an alpha watching out for her while her brother is out of town and her father is preoccupied leading the run."

He looked me up and down, and didn't say anything.

"You'll do this favor for me, won't you, Alpha?" My mom crossed her arms and stared him down. Although she was shorter than me, my mom knew how to intimidate.

"She looks capable," he finally replied.

Gathering that he was not a fan of the idea, I started to say, "I can just run with my frie—"

"Hush, Theresa," my mom cut me off. "As a mother, I worry about my pups, especially my daughter. You'll understand when you have your own one day. Now, come, Alpha, take her with you. After all, we've done so much for your pack. What is this small favor in comparison?"

It was clearly difficult to argue with that. I could sense him weighing the options in his mind. But Julia knew what she was doing.

"Yes, Luna Yulia. I will do this favor," he finally responded, and I could tell it was hard to grit out each word. He pressed his lips together in resignation, and then forced the corners of his mouth into a half smile.

"Wonderful," she replied. Without another word, confident she'd made the correct chess move, she turned on her heel and left the two of us to socialize, I suppose.

His eyes bore into me, his face expressionless. He did have a pretty good poker face, but I could still sense everything he was feeling, and it was definitely something along the lines of irritation. But he didn't speak.

Making an effort to avoid awkwardness, I began rambling like I always do in these situations. "Are you excited? It should be a lot of fun tonight! It's slightly warmer than it has been."

"Hm." He gave a small nod. Well, okay then.

"How has it been joining our pack? Are you getting everything you need?"

"Fine."

"Let me know if you have any problems with my brother Tyce. He comes off rough sometimes, but he's a good guy."

No response.

"What do you like to do for fun?" Why was this like pulling teeth with him? Why was I trying so hard?

I tilted my head, studying him, making it clear I was waiting for a response. He stared back. Once again, I was reminded what a nice face he had. He clearly hadn't shaved in a few days, which left him with stubble covering his angular and well-sculpted face, giving him a sexy, scruffy look. He was like a supermodel, so gorgeous it was simply unfair.

For a moment, something flickered in his silver eyes—pain, hesitation?—but it was gone before I could place it. His face hardened once more. "We don't need make conversation," he muttered. "Let's just finish this."

Ouch! I was just trying to be nice. And, to think, I could have been running with my friends, having a great time. But his sadness still made its presence known, and I squared my shoulders. His bad attitude probably had nothing to do with me, so I shouldn't take it personally.

"Jade Moon Pack!" My father's voice rang out, hushing the large crowd. He continued on to give his monthly speech to the pack. Well, not so much his anymore. Ever since he'd found his mate, Tyce changed. While I always knew he had it in him, it wasn't easy being raised to be alpha by two alphas who very much were not going to give up their power without a fight. He'd really stepped up lately. Which I'd noticed even though I wasn't home from school much.

As my dad's speech ended, the crowd dispersed. I followed in Alpha Nikolai's footsteps. I guess I probably could have split at this point, and promised not to tell my mother if he didn't run with me. He'd be relieved as it clearly wasn't in his plans to babysit a full-grown woman tonight.

But, I can't lie, I kind of liked the idea of spending some time with him. Maybe he'd open up more and—okay—he was hot! Who wouldn't be ecstatic if their mom dumped the werewolf equivalent of Austin Butler in her lap?

When we'd barely made it past the edge of the gathering, Nikolai began shrugging off his coat.

"Oh, uh, sorry, I'm just going to go a little farther in. But meet you back here?" Not that I would mind getting a glance at what he looked like underneath the heavy coat. I just didn't exactly feel comfortable stripping here, in front of him, and basically anyone in the pack that might walk by.

He grunted with a small nod. That was probably the best I was going to get.

I crunched through the snow to find a rock to hide behind. Once I found a good spot, I looked around just to make sure I was safe. Only then did I unravel my scarf along with everything else. Once I'd gotten the last sock off, I shifted. My bones stretched my skin to rearrange themselves, nails turned to claws that tore through the tips of my fingers and toes, and fur sprouted to be immediately blown back by the chilling Alaska wind.

I sank my paws into the snow and headed back to where I'd come from. I'd been told my wolf looked like the smaller version of Tyce's. I think they only said that because we had similar, black-tipped brown fur. I'd seen pictures of our wolves together, and I didn't see much of a resemblance outside that. We had totally different face shapes, and that lucky son of a gun had gotten the long, lush fur. I'd taken more after my mother in that respect. Her whole family had much shorter fur, albeit thick to survive the cold eastern European winters.

Silver lightbulbs tipped me off to his location. Not that I needed them to identify the person I was looking for. I could smell him from yards away. Goodness, that scent!

Maybe if I teased him a bit, it would get him to lighten up.

As soon as I reached him, he launched forward, barely even acknowledging my presence. I followed right after him. He picked up speed, and I wondered if he was trying to outrun me. Tough luck with that! With my dad's training plan of torture, I had no problem keeping up with anyone. When his run turned into a sprint, I followed, racing him deep into the frozen tundra. I easily dodged the rocky outcroppings he did and hopped across frozen rivers, following right in his paw prints. As we approached a rugged, snow-covered ridge I was very familiar with by now, I hatched a plan to shake him up a bit. He continued running down an opening that was a path during the summer, and I sprinted up a small ledge, doubling my speed. I got there with perfect timing, leaping up and landing right in front of him, sinking into the snow.

He tried to stop but still ended up slamming right into me. I'd had just enough time to get low to the ground, so he tripped over the top of me and went flying into a pile of snow. He growled and flailed frantically as he got himself up.

If I could have, I would've laughed. Any one of my friends would've thought it was the funniest thing ever. We were constantly playing around in our wolf forms, play wrestling, racing, and playing silly tricks like the one I just did. But when he glanced at me, there was no humor in his eyes. Yikes, he really was a grump.

Just as quickly as he'd tumbled, he got right back to it, flying across the snow-covered expanse. I followed right behind. At this point, I was determined to get him to see that I was a fun time and not just a little puppy who had to be babysat. I gained some speed on him. When I was well in front of him and right at a fork in the trail, I fell to the ground and howled as if I were injured. He immediately stopped and approached me. He brought his snout close, sniffing me everywhere while I continued to moan and cry out. As soon as he lifted his head, I got a good swipe of the snow with my paw and sprayed it into his face, sticking my tongue out as soon as I did.

He froze. His eyes pierced right into my bones. *Eek!* I thought that would have at least gotten *some* humor out of him. It wasn't like it hurt. Zero for two.

He turned his back to me, practically swatting me with his huge alpha tail, and got right back to it. Once again, I followed. This time, he was definitely trying to get rid of me. I felt like I was one of those dogs in an agility competition. But he clearly didn't know me and my history. My grandpa and dad trained my brothers and me as if we would constantly be at war. Fortunately, being so isolated in middle-of-nowhere Alaska, that wasn't really the case. But as my grandpa would say when he was still alive, war is unpredictable and unfair, and it only takes one misstep to fall to your death.

Eventually, Nikolai began to slow down, and I could sense he was finally getting tired after running at full speed. Thank goodness, because

I didn't really know how much longer I'd be able to keep up with him, although I was determined to. I slowed down much more, falling behind. This could go one of two ways. Either he would stop to rest with relief once he determined he lost me. Or he'd come looking for me because he felt responsible after my mom's talk with him. I supposed it would be too much to hope he genuinely cared about my well-being. Although, he had seemed concerned when I'd faked my injury. So there was hope!

With faith in my heart, I ripped a bit of my fur out with my teeth and then used my crazy-sharp claws to scratch the top of my head. I cringed at the pain, although I had grown pretty used to it throughout the years. It was important to get my scent really concentrated in this area, and the head bled far more than any other part of the body. It left a nice red splattering in the snow and then closed right up. I carefully climbed the jagged rock face, using every muscle in my body to hoist myself up by my claws, and then found a nice sturdy ledge to rest on.

Moments later, my heart fluttered as a cream-colored wolf with a silver undercoat backtracked with his snout close to the ground. *Wahoo!* I prepared myself, my insides vibrating and adrenaline rushing. Steady, steady. He crept closer until he was standing above the crime scene I'd left for him. And was that a whine? Milliseconds before I put my plan into action, I hesitated as I sensed the kind of anguish I'd never in my life felt—the kind of despair that chokes you and leaves you with no more will. My chest tightened, and I almost forgot how to breathe. But I had already sprung into action, and the feeling was gone just as quickly as it had appeared. I leaped onto the thick ledge, shaking all the snow that had accumulated on it to dump onto Alpha Nikolai.

I wish I could laugh in this form. Because that had to have been one of my best pranks yet. I climbed my way back down the rocky surface to find Nikolai clawing his way out from the snow pile. I quickly dashed behind a snowbank before he got above ground. As soon as he was out, he frantically looked around and I jumped out, letting out a bark that sounded as much like "boo" as I could manage.

He shuddered, jumping back by instinct. And then his eyes met mine. I stuck my tongue out in a playful gesture.

He was not happy.

Not at all.

If looks could kill. I took a few steps toward him, thinking I'd try to comfort him. Bad idea. He bared his teeth and crinkled his nose—a face that said, *You're about to die*. I lifted one paw, and he growled the most menacing growl I'd ever heard in my life. That was pretty impressive considering I'd grown up with three alphas. When I didn't immediately move, he leaped closer, getting right in my face, and snapped at me. I backed up and he inched closer still, continuing to threaten me with his teeth and growls, making it very clear that I was no longer welcome.

I swallowed, my face, neck, and ears feeling impossibly hot, and, with my tail between my legs, turned to go. My mission to get Alpha Nikolai to lighten up had failed spectacularly. And I'm pretty sure I may have made things worse.

Chapter 7

Nikolai

For the first time in a very long time, I didn't wake with the sensation of my lungs caving in, a lack of will to live, a darkness choking me to the point I wasn't certain whether or not I was drowning. I woke to a stillness. And something else. A pull, a heat curling in my gut, a raw, aching hunger that had nothing to do with survival.

For the first time in months, my focus shifted to how stiff my morning wood was—swollen with what had to be every drop of blood in my body. I groaned. I didn't masturbate much these days, but *boginya moya*, my dick was hard and desperate for some attention.

I shifted onto my back, only to realize my arm was pinned down by something warm. Something solid. I forced my lids open, only to be met with a mess of dark hair spilling over my arm, her warmth seeping into my skin. And then there was that addictive, haunting aroma that had taken up permanent residence in my brain no matter how hard I tried to scrub it out.

My pulse kicked up. How the fuck had she gotten here? Was this some kind of trick?

Right when the last thing I needed was a distraction, I was being bombarded with the most gorgeous, impressively athletic but maddening woman I'd ever met. Granted, she was a spoiled princess, and definitely not someone I'd normally pursue. I swear to Artemis someone was trying to seduce me for nefarious reasons.

She let out a slight whimper, interrupting my thoughts, and *fuck!* Just when I thought my dick couldn't get any harder, that did it. It twitched painfully with an excruciating need, an all-consuming hunger I'd never felt before.

Why is she in my fucking bed?

Why does she smell so fucking good?

Could she actually be—?

I eased her off my bicep, where she had apparently made herself comfortable. While I really should have been confronting and interrogating her about why she thought it was appropriate to just crawl into my bed while I was sleeping—*had she ever heard of consent?*—I couldn't bring myself to do it.

And then I relaxed. Again, I noted, I could suddenly breathe. I was not weighed down by everything that had happened in Ukraine, the death of my whole family, and the responsibility I had to my pack. The ache in my soul was somehow more bearable. I was just here, in this bed, maybe not happy, and perhaps still unhappy, but able to appreciate the moment in a way I hadn't been sure I'd ever be able to again.

A flicker of movement. Her lips parted, letting out the sexiest moan I'd ever heard. *Blyad!* That sound. It should've been innocent. It wasn't. Her scent coiled around me dangerously. It was everywhere. In my lungs, in my bloodstream. I gritted my teeth and sat up against the headboard, trying to regain some control over my body that was betraying me. But I couldn't tear my thoughts from her.

Through the barrier of blankets, her silhouette was unmistakable. The fabric dipped between the contours of her legs. It was difficult not to imagine bringing my head between those same legs to feel her thighs trembling against my ears, her back arching as my mouth coaxed breathless, desperate sounds from her lips. That blissful expression she wore in sleep wouldn't be from some fleeting dream, but from my tongue stroking her, savoring her, unraveling her. And suddenly, there was nothing in the world I wanted more than to taste her cunt.

What the fuck was wrong with me? I had Severnaya Zvezda Pack to lead and rebuild, morale to foster! And here I was, focusing on pussy. No, this wasn't right. I had to wake her. Had to shove her away. I was just about to move—

Then her eyelashes fluttered open, revealing those same mesmerizing amber eyes that haunted me in my dreams. And, once again, that sense . . . that sense that she was my mate came to the forefront. But she wasn't, was she?

As soon as she made eye contact with me, her eyes widened, her whole body shuddered, and she shot up to a sitting position, jerking away from me and pulling the blanket to her chest. "Wh-wha—" she started, not finishing the word. She glanced around, her hands tight on the fabric of the blanket she was holding. She panted, clearly gasping to gain control of her breath. "How did I get here?" she finally asked.

"Why you ask me that? I should ask you!"

"I don't sleepwalk." Then her eyes narrowed, and her brows furrowed. She pointed at me accusingly. "Did you bring me in here? Are you a pervert?"

"What!" I practically choked. "I am not a pervert!"

"You snuck into my room while I was sleeping and brought me in here to—" She scrunched her nose in concentration. "To . . ." her voice trailed off. "Why did you bring me in here? Are you some weirdo that just likes to watch people sleep? Because let me tell you, I thought that part of *Twilight* was creepy, okay?" Then she looked down toward my lap, and *ebat*! "Oh my gosh!" Her face, ears, and neck all reddened. She immediately stumbled out of bed at the sight of my hard-on, which was still very much tenting the blanket and very much not inconspicuous.

Her leg got caught up in the sheets, and she tumbled to the floor with an *oomph*.

"You okay?" I asked, the sight of her getting hurt yielding the instinct to do everything in my power to help her. I was out of bed in milliseconds to help her up. She got up onto her knees, and, *nifiga sebe*! This girl did not dress modestly for bed. She was in a loose, light pink tank top with a plunging neckline. The soft brown nipple of one breast was openly exposed, and the other may as well have been with how thin the material covering it was.

My entire body locked up, and heat punched through me. She was so beautiful I could barely breathe.

I didn't mean to look, but for fuck's sake!

I'm sure I did a terrible job hiding my gawking because she followed my gaze downward and reddened even more, her entire chest flushing scarlet. As soon as she brought her hands up to adjust her top and cover herself, I compelled my eyes upward. I was clearly not being a gentleman. I forced myself not to think about how remarkably pert and flawless her breasts were—the perfect handful that would fit so nicely in my palm—while painfully aware that my cock was still throbbing, and my inner wolf was clawing at my insides with a carnal need to mount her. I'd never felt so out of control in my life.

Don't look, don't look, don't look.

I clenched my jaw so tight my teeth ached, forcing my gaze anywhere but where my instincts wanted it to go. She was looking downward, so I couldn't make contact with her eyes. I just had to find a neutral place to focus, and ultimately chose the most immediate spot my eyes could find. Her neck.

And then I saw it.

She must have seen the shift in my expression, must have felt the exact moment I noticed, because she immediately abandoned adjusting her top to instead cover the offending part of her neck. Her palm pressed against the spot like she could erase it, hide it from my sight.

Too late.

Her face turned ashen, her eyes squeezed shut.

Every muscle in my body tensed. Heat burned through me like a wildfire. My pulse raced a million kilometers an hour.

A strange pressure seized me, tightening around me like a noose. The mark. A mate bond already sealed. Mine— *No. Not mine. Never mine.* The realization shredded through me.

The boner I didn't think I'd be able to get rid of was instantly killed. The human part of me no longer had any control. I reached out instinctively toward her mark before yanking my hand back as if I'd been burned. Misery—no, *betrayal!*—flashed through me. A pained howl echoed inside my chest.

My wolf was in charge as I bared my teeth and glared at her. Anger pulsed through my veins. I knew I'd given her *that look* by her reaction.

Tears pooled in her eyes, and the hand that wasn't on her neck abandoned covering her sheer top, instead kneading the part of her chest right above her heart, as if she was trying to stop the pain. She hung her head.

"You are marked," I gritted out. "You are fucking marked!" Why this angered me so much, I didn't even know. No—it was because she had bewitched me to believe she was my mate. Maybe her mom had bewitched me. Someone had bewitched me! And all this time, she already had a mate! *That bitch!*

Her lips trembled slightly before she spoke. "Please don't tell anyone," she squeaked in an emotion-choked voice. Her chin lowered to her chest in defeat.

Running on pure rage, I shoved out of my bedroom. The walls were closing in, her scent was still thick in my lungs, my muscles were coiled too tight.

I needed out.

I needed to fucking breathe.

If I didn't shift immediately, I couldn't guarantee I wouldn't hit or destroy something. I sprinted down the stairs and out the closest door to the outside world. I didn't even bother going somewhere more isolated. It would be far from the packhouse anyway, which they had bafflingly placed right in the center of the pack. I threw off my T-shirt and stripped myself of my sweatpants and boxers in one swift movement. I was so hot that the Alaskan winter felt balmy to me.

My wolf thrashed against me and forced me to shift before I'd barely stripped off my last piece of clothing. The snap of my bones barely registered through the haze in my head. I dug my claws into the ground, trying to anchor myself before I lost control completely. But it was futile. The moment I hit all fours, my wolf ripped any control I had away from me and took off. Snow exploded beneath my paws as I bolted out of town, past the last house, past the lights, past the edges of the pack's land.

I needed to run. I needed distance. I planned to find a mountain to climb and howl until I went hoarse.

My thoughts went all over the place, scattering and surrounding me, until it began to feel like an argument between my human and my wolf side.

She was a spoiled alpha princess. A brat.

She was mine.

She didn't read the fucking room.

She played with me. She wanted me to chase her.

She was marked. Already claimed.

Stolen!

She already had a fucking mate, and that really should have been the end of it. But it nagged at me, especially in this form. Someone had sunk their teeth into what was *mine*. I should be making some bastard pay for stealing an alpha's mate.

And then, I wondered, what happened when someone else took your mate as their own? Would I still be able to tell? Would I still feel it? Was I now mateless? My stomach sank and my head throbbed.

My wolf let out a low, mournful howl. It was an aching sound, raw and unfiltered. The kind of sound a wolf makes when something inside him has been ripped away.

The wind howled back, as if mocking me. As if the Goddess herself were playing the cruelest joke on me yet.

Fuck my life.

Chapter 8

Ginger

Exactly one year after the big alpha wedding, I witnessed my baby twin sister tie the knot. She looked so beautiful in her simple white A-line gown. Heidi and my mom had FaceTimed me while she went dress shopping so I could be a part of it. Oh, Goddess, and here I went, getting all emotional.

Tyce gave my hand a squeeze. He looked so handsome in his suit. It wasn't often I saw him all dressed up since he preferred T-shirts and sweatpants, and honestly, his job mostly required clothes that could be stripped off at a moment's notice, which I didn't mind at all. But *this*? *This* was nice. It fit so well on his broad shoulders, thick chest, and muscular thighs. He'd had the same seamstress in his pack that had done his suit tailor my bridesmaid dress. With how awful the dress looked when it first came in the mail compared to how it looked when she was done, she was a miracle worker! What had originally made me look frumpy and lumpy, now perfectly accentuated my womanly curves.

In werewolf weddings, it was uncommon to have bridesmaids and groomsmen, but for anyone that did, the custom was for their bridal party to stand with their mates, as the mate union was considered holy in our religion. So I stood with Tyce, and Heidi stood with her friend and pretend-mate, Hunter. Heidi was due to give birth in two weeks, and she'd been worried she wouldn't be able to fit into her dress. It was a fair concern as her belly was straining against the material. Any bigger and she wouldn't have. Heidi was the reason I'd ended up with this shapeless monstrosity, since there weren't many options that would work for both of us. But, as usual, Tyce came through with a solution.

"Your ass looks spectacular in that dress," he mindlinked me. I subtly elbowed him in response. Because I wasn't luna yet, I couldn't mindlink him back in my human form. Otherwise, I'd tell him to stop staring at it in front of the entire congregation. Which I wouldn't put past him. As alpha, he did a lot of inappropriate things, because he knew he could get away with them, but I liked to put him in his place.

While Dylan said his vows, tears tumbled down Paige's cheeks. For someone who had fought tooth and nail to not get married, she was completely over the moon in love tonight. Dylan, the gentleman he was, pulled out his pocket square and wiped the tears from her eyes. She could barely get through her own vows, as what had been some sweet tears turned into a full-on sob.

Everyone cheered as they kissed and subsequently marched back down the aisle to head to the reception. Tyce and I followed in their footsteps, and I felt so much pride hooking my arm with his. *That's right, bitches! Alpha Tyce is my man!*

The reception was small and simple. Paige neither wanted anything fancy, nor did our family have the means to provide it for her. Tyce had offered to chip in, but my parents refused his help. "Just take good care of our Gigi," my dad had said to him. "We can handle our other daughter's wedding. We'd planned to pay for three, so we're already saving money."

A heated tent had been set up in the back garden of the temple, which wasn't much of a garden at present, and simple catering was brought in from the pack sub and pizza shop, who did this often. They'd set up a buffet with meat, pasta, and salad. Some pack members were hired to bartend and DJ. Heidi, Paige, my mom, Dylan's mom, and I had worked hard the week leading up to the big day to decorate the event, including all the flower arrangements. Honestly, after all our work, it looked fantastic and didn't feel like a budget wedding at all.

The warm glow of the candles we'd scattered around the tent cast a soft golden hue over the tables. The scent of fresh flowers and warm Italian food lingered in the air. As we made our rounds greeting the guests, the tent was bursting with music and chatter punctuated by laughter and clinking glasses as guests shared funny stories with each other.

It was, of course, a much smaller affair than the big alpha wedding had been the previous year. But it was cozy, and it was nice to know everyone in attendance.

"This'll be us soon," Tyce wistfully said as we slow-danced. "I can't lie, I'm dying to fuck the shit out of you on our wedding night and sink my teeth into that creamy little neck." He nuzzled into me, planting kisses around the area where he planned to do the deed.

My heart stuttered at his words. *Our wedding night.* It wasn't the first time we'd talked about it. Tyce was never shy about claiming me, about making me his in every way. But something about hearing it here, in this moment, made it feel real in a way that sent shivers down my spine.

"Then you'll be stuck with me forever." I gave a self-deprecating laugh.

"Stuck with that fine ass? Those sweet tits? And that spicy personality of yours? There are worse things I can think of." He winked and gave me a sweet smirk. Goddess, I loved him.

After the cake cutting, some of Dylan's friends pulled us outside to help decorate Dylan's car. For fun, I decided to paint a couple of chickens in bride and groom attire using the window paint markers. I knew it would give Paige a laugh.

"You have an obsession with cock," Tyce whispered, his hot breath close to my ear.

"That's why I'm marrying one," I teased him back. "Tyson Chicken!"

"We really need to talk about that nickname."

"No, we don't. It fits perfectly."

"Goddess, you're infuriating." He nibbled on my nose.

"Is that why you're practically eating my face out right now?"

"When you're moaning, you're not talking." He trailed kisses along my cheeks.

"Sounds like you're going to be busy keeping me moaning all the time then," I replied, leaning into his kisses that were now moving to my neck. My insides flooded with warmth, and my nerves tingled with pleasure from his every touch as he danced sparks along my skin.

"Bow chicka bow wow!" Blake loudly sang, putting a stop to where things were headed as we immediately separated.

"Cockblocker!" Tyce teased. "I'll remember that next time you're well on your way to making another heir."

"You think singing a song is enough to stop my moves from work-ing?" Blake joked back, wrapping his arms around Jasmine. "I know her fail-safe weak spot." He brought his mouth to her ear.

"Blake, stop!" Jasmine cried out, but it didn't sound very convincing. She was simultaneously trying to get away from him while her body didn't seem to want to move. She finally broke free of his grip.

"Fail-safe, huh?" Tyce playfully punched Blake in the shoulder.

"Guys, stop! This is a family event," Jasmine exclaimed.

"Okay, but this isn't over. As soon as we're behind closed doors . . ." Blake gave her a big, loving wink.

"Closed doors? Pshh. I think it's time we try out the whole exhibi-tionist thing, Gi." Tyce elbowed me.

"Bold of you to think people would be impressed by your moves," I teased.

"Funny, that's not what you said last night," Tyce rebutted.

"I don't know what you're talking about. We're perfectly unsullied mates that have separate sleeping arrangements until marriage." I giggled.

Tyce shook his head. "You got me."

As the night wound down, Paige and Dylan escaped amid a line of sparklers and all their friends and family cheering. A tear trailed down Paige's cheek once she saw the car.

She raised her arm to quiet the crowd before she got in. "Everyone, thank you so much for making this the best night of my life. Dylan and I appreciate everyone who helped with this wedding so much, and we will never forget."

Dylan pulled out his pocket square to wipe her eyes once again and gave her a kiss before they finally got into the car.

After they left, a few of us lingered behind to help clean up. Blake pulled out his phone, stretching as he dialed. "Hey, Miriam! How are the pups?" His face softened as he listened. "Yeah? Good, good. We're just about wrapped up here . . . That Ryker! Already an alpha." A broad grin spread across his face.

Jasmine perked up. "What did my mom say?"

Blake smirked, tucking his phone away. "She said she got the pups down for bed and that Ryker is already doing push-ups."

Jasmine snorted. "She did not say that."

Blake raised a brow. "What else do you call it when he pushes himself up from his stomach?"

She huffed, crossing her arms. "Okay, I'll give you that one."

Blake chuckled, dropping a kiss onto her head. "C'mon. With two warrior parents, of course he's doing push-ups at three months. It's in his blood."

Blake then approached us and clapped Tyce on the shoulder. "Ready to head back to the packhouse? Want to walk with us?"

Tyce turned to me with a warm gaze. "You coming?"

I swallowed, glancing toward my parents, who were loading the last of the wedding supplies into their car.

"Tyce, you know I can't . . ." My voice trailed off.

His lips curled into a smirk. "Then I'll see you later?"

I hesitated for just a second longer, drawing out the moment before flashing him a teasing smile. "Maybe."

Okay, so I had been sneaking around a lot since being back in my old pack. Which I'm pretty sure my parents noticed. And it wasn't like there was much they could say about it, which made me wonder why I even bothered. But my mom could be so melodramatic, and my dad would only ignore it as long as I kept up the image of being chaste.

So I played along. For now.

It didn't really matter anyway. Paige's wedding was over, and in just a couple of days, we'd be heading back to Alaska.

Tyce smirked, brushing his lips against mine one last time. "Don't worry, I'm going to turn that maybe into a yes." His voice was full of confidence, his touch lingering. "See you later, baby."

I sighed as I watched him walk away, my heart tugging in his direction. Dragging my feet, I made my way to my parents' car, the reality of our impending separation settling heavily on my shoulders.

I had planned to go back to school at the end of January. It was my dream to study medicine, to learn the biology of the body, and, most importantly, heal people. It was something that had always felt like mine, something separate from my forthcoming title, from my mate, from the life I was destined to step into. But every time I thought about leaving Tyce, a deep ache settled in my chest. The idea of being so far from him felt unbearable.

And if I gave up on school . . . what then? Would I slowly become just Alpha Tyce's mate? Would my life revolve around pack duties, politics, and raising pups before I even had the chance to figure out who I was?

Would I regret it? Would resentment creep in over the years, making me bitter, making me wonder *what if*?

I thought about Dr. Luna—the woman who had inspired me, the one who proved that you could be both a luna and a doctor. I held on to that.

It would only be a few years anyway. And what were a few years in a lifetime together?

Chapter 9

Miriam

29 years ago

Long before I moved to the East Coast, met my mate, and became Luna Jasmine's mom, I belonged to the Jade Moon Pack. My parents, Luna Catherine and Alpha Bruce, were strict, overbearing, and ruled with iron fists.

At fifteen, I had only two regrets. The first was that I didn't fully understand how sex worked. I had a vague idea—a male and a female got naked, kissed—but beyond that, things were a little . . . fuzzy. What exactly happened between kissing and making a baby?

I liked thinking about it sometimes—okay, maybe a lot—and always with someone specific in mind.

Jeremy.

With his long rockstar hair, lean build, and complete disregard for school, he was the kind of boy my parents would disapprove of instantly. Add in his reputation for doing drugs, and he was practically forbidden. But none of that mattered to me. I was 100 percent in love.

I spent hours daydreaming that we were mates. Because if we were, no one, not even my parents, could keep us apart. The mate bond was sacred, an unbreakable connection. Rejecting it was the greatest sin a werewolf could commit.

But I was too young to meet my mate.

So instead, I fantasized about the moment I turned eighteen, about locking eyes with Jeremy and just knowing. And then, of course, I imagined kissing him while naked.

I knew what he looked like naked too. My friend Trish had found a perfect hiding spot where we could spy on the boys in our grade training in their wolf forms.

I always pretended I wasn't interested, that looking at naked boys was gross. But secretly, I loved that Trish made me give in. It gave me an excuse to watch Jeremy, to memorize the way his body moved, to imagine running my fingers through the forest of curly brown hair under his belly, to wonder how his skin would feel beneath my touch.

But I would never admit to thinking about any of those things.

Because I was a good girl. And good girls didn't.

The second thing I regretted—more than anything—was bringing Carrie into the packhouse.

She was a senior, and since I was a sophomore in a senior-level science class, we ended up paired together for a big AP Chemistry project early in the school year. When she suggested working on it at my place, I knew exactly why.

First, she wanted to see inside the packhouse, everyone did. And second, just like every other girl at school, she had a crush on my oldest brother, Lance, the future alpha.

Carrie was beautiful. Not just regular pretty, but the kind of pretty that made people stare. Her hair was perfect—Cindy Crawford-level perfect. And I knew from the moment she asked that letting her into the packhouse was a terrible idea. She was exactly the type of girl who would go after my brother, and my brother wasn't exactly known for turning down pretty girls. Neither of them was, really, but thankfully, Gabe was away at college, so at least I didn't have to worry about him.

Still, I gave in. I think she may have bribed me with an invite to a senior party. Not that I'd ever be allowed to go anyway.

And if my brother had been the one to sleep with her, that wouldn't have been so bad.

In fact, it would have been a million times better than what actually happened.

Because what happened was this:

That day, Carrie showed up in a sweater, but underneath, she had on a crop top and a push-up bra that made her boobs look twice their normal size. The second she stepped into the packhouse, she yanked off her sweater, fanning herself like she was overheating. I didn't think much of it at the time.

We settled in the living room, huddled over the coffee table, deep in our project. And then my dad walked in.

To this day, I still feel sick when I think about it.

He came over, asked us what we were working on, but his eyes went straight to Carrie's low-cut top and never left.

When she was getting ready to leave, he caught her at the doorway and offered to show her something in his office. I told myself that was all it was—he showed her something in the office.

I wasn't wrong.

He did show her something.

But it turned out that what he had shown her was his *thing*.

And after that day, he showed her several more times.

The whole school found out because Carrie actually *bragged* about it. She told her friends she had slept with *Alpha Bruce*.

I threw up the day the rumor got back to me. Then I threw up several more times.

Every time I thought about Carrie touching my dad's *thing*, I wanted to hurl all over again.

My dad was old! And he was *my dad*!

Then Trish told me that she heard Carrie had sucked on my dad's dick and *swallowed his jizz*. I didn't even know what jizz was, and neither did Trish. But it sounded disgusting. I ran into the bathroom, threw up again, and cried.

The only way I got through the project was by telling Carrie I'd just do it myself and give her credit. She was more than happy to let me. At least that way, I wouldn't have to sit across from her, pretending not to think about her mouth on *my dad's dick*.

Three weeks later, on the day of our big presentation, I handed Carrie a stack of index cards. After I finished my part, I elbowed her to start reading hers. She opened her mouth . . . and projectile vomited all over the classroom.

Turned out, morning sickness was a symptom of pregnancy.

Yep—my dad had knocked up my high school chemistry partner.

Less than a month later, Carrie was banished from the pack.

That was the day I learned an ugly truth: alphas were rarely faithful to their mates.

One of the first of many hard lessons about the world.

"What happened was pretty messed up," Lance said one afternoon, grabbing a snack while I sat at the kitchen table, doing my homework.

"Just promise me when you're alpha, you won't ever sleep with any of your kids' chemistry partners!" I blurted out.

"I'd never be unfaithful to my mate," he replied, taking a seat across from me. "Look, I don't agree with everything Dad does."

"You sure had me fooled. You're like his little puppy the way you follow him around."

He wrinkled his nose in annoyance. "Do not."

I snorted. "Please. When's the last time you didn't do exactly what he told you to?"

He sighed. "It's just easier that way. You know how Dad is."

Yeah. I knew.

Our dad was brutal, and it was always safer to obey than to push back. Because the alternative was something none of us liked to think about. I'd never had it as bad as Lance, but I knew what it was like to be on the receiving end of our father's wrath.

We sat in silence for a while, him eating, me staring at my homework without really reading a word. Finally, I worked up the courage to ask what had been on my mind for weeks.

"Lance . . . can I ask you something? And you have to promise not to tell Mom or Dad."

He raised a brow. "Yeah, sure."

The nice thing about Lance was that he was usually pretty reasonable. Unlike Gabe, who could be tricky sometimes.

I took a deep breath. This was going to be the most awkward conversation of my life. But I had no one else I could ask. "How does sex work?"

Lance froze midbite. "What?"

I shifted uncomfortably. "Like . . . how do you make a baby?"

"Holy Artemis! You seriously don't know?"

Heat crawled up my neck. "How would I? It's not like Mom ever told me, and they don't exactly teach it in school!"

"Goddess, this is weird." He rubbed his face. "Okay, how about this—I have a magazine. It has pictures. But if you ever tell Mom or Dad I gave it to you, I swear to the moon, I'll kill you."

"I'd never!"

"Good. You can borrow it, but I want it back when you're done. They're not easy to get around here."

Nothing was easy to get where we lived. If it was, I would've just found a book instead of asking my *brother*. That was one of the biggest reasons I planned to leave for college, far away. Gabe had gone, and I would too. Boston, if I had my way. Harvard was my dream, but I had a few backups.

"Can I ask you something else?"

Lance sighed. "You've already made things weird as hell, so go ahead."

"What is jizz?"

His eyebrows shot up. "Jizz?"

Goddess, I was burning. I knew I was as red as a cooked king crab, and he could definitely tell how embarrassed I was. "Trish told me Carrie swallowed Dad's jizz."

"Damn it, Mir! I did *not* need to know that!"

"You think I needed to know that?"

"Fucking Artemis." He pushed his palms into his eyes. "I'm erasing this conversation from my brain."

"But can you at least tell me what it is?"

He groaned. "Fine." His ears were red. They always went red when he was embarrassed. "When a guy orgasms, a white fluid comes out. That's how a girl gets pregnant. That's jizz."

"Orgasms?"

"Goddess, I can't believe you don't know any of this."

"You don't have to make me feel stupid."

Lance exhaled. "Okay, sorry. It's just . . . weird. I assumed everyone knew this stuff."

"Trish doesn't know either."

"All right, fine. So when you—uh—rub a guy's dick, either with your hand or . . . other ways, it feels really good. And if you do it long enough, it feels extra good, and jizz spills out. Just . . . don't let him get any inside you, because that's how you get pregnant. Got it? Do everything but."

"I'm not planning on doing anything unless it's with my mate."

"Good. It's better that way."

"Then why do you do it with people who aren't your mate?"

His ears burned. "That's enough of this conversation. Do you want the magazine or not?"

"Yes!"

I followed him upstairs. He reached under his mattress and pulled out a well-worn magazine. The cover featured a petite woman with huge, perfectly round breasts—breasts that made my tiny bug bites look even more pathetic.

Was that what Jeremy wanted? Or would he be okay with mine?

That night, I devoured the magazine, studying every page with fascination. I couldn't tear my eyes away. For the first time, it all made sense. This was sex.

And now, a whole new world of fantasies opened up. Now that I understood exactly what Jeremy and I would do once we found out we were mates, I couldn't wait.

The next day, I went to return the magazine to its hiding spot under Lance's mattress, where I found two more. Curiosity getting the best of me, I pulled them out. Flipping through the first one, I found it to be similar to the one I had borrowed—more of the same. But the second . .
.

The second made my head spin.

My vision blurred, and for a second, I thought I might pass out. Because this one wasn't like the others. It was all men. Men doing the types of things that were only supposed to be done between a man and woman.

My stomach twisted. *Why would Lance ever have such a disgusting magazine?* A rush of nausea hit me, and I shoved the magazine back under his mattress, my hands shaking. I didn't see that. I imagined it.

By the end of the day, I had almost convinced myself it had never happened. That it had been a dream, a strange, impossible dream. And now that I was awake, everything was back to normal.

But one thing kept me from truly forgetting.

"Thanks for returning my magazine," Lance said that night when we were finally alone.

"Thanks for letting me look at it."

"You didn't have to put it back. I could've done that myself."

"It was no problem. I figured it was easier that way."

There was a brief pause before he added, "You just put it back, right? You didn't . . . look to see what else was there?"

My heart skipped. "No. I just put it back."

He studied me for a second. "Because if you did, not all of it was mine."

I forced my face into neutrality. "I didn't see anything else."

"Good. Just—if you did, know that it wasn't mine."

"I don't know what you're talking about."

"I was holding a magazine for a friend. For safekeeping."

"Lance," I said, looking him straight in the eye, "I have no idea what you mean."

His shoulders relaxed just a fraction. "Okay. Good."

Chapter 10

Theresa

It had been almost a week since *the incident*. Nikolai was so stealthy I barely caught a glance of him during all that time. I rubbed at my mark, fingertips pressing against the sensitive skin. My pulse spiked. Would Nikolai say something? Would he just casually mention it in conversation? *Oh yeah, Terri's mark—*

A shiver ran down my spine.

He probably wouldn't think twice. Why would he? To him, it wasn't some dirty secret, something that made my skin crawl every time I thought about it. To him, a mark was a mark. A sign of commitment. Something mates did and didn't hide. No one else in the world thought getting marked was a secret.

"*Uggghhhh,*" I moaned out loud. I knew you weren't supposed to worry about things you couldn't control, but I was in anxiety overload. My stomach had been churning nonstop since he saw it. Every time my mom seemed slightly annoyed or frustrated with me, the hairs on my body stood up, waiting for the other shoe to drop. Every passing comment from my father made my skin prickle, waiting for the moment he'd say it, the moment his disappointment in me would show all over his face. The moment they'd both know.

But, as of yet, nothing.

I thought about seeking Nikolai out. Either cornering him outside his bedroom, or maybe tracking him down when he went for a run. But I hesitated. The way his emotions played out burned in my memory and, quite honestly, low-key scared me.

Sure, I expected anyone to be shocked by my mark. But that kind of anger? That depth of fury? It was the kind of reaction I would have expected from my father. *Maybe* my brother. Not from some random guy I'd only spoken to a handful of times, and you could barely even count any of those times as a full conversation.

And then, what was up with my sleepwalking? At first, I honestly believed it had been Nikolai who had brought me into his room. That he was some huge weirdo creep. Maybe he had a bizarre obsession with me? I mean, he didn't exactly seem like the type, but you never knew! That would explain the anger. But no, it turned out I was actually *full-on* sleepwalking, something I'd never done before in my life.

A couple of nights after the incident, I'd woken up sprawled out in front of his door, the cold wood of the floor pressing against my cheek.

I blinked and scanned the dark, empty hallway. Disoriented, my mind scrambled to piece together how I'd ended up there. And then it hit me.

Sleepwalking.

A wave of dread settled in my gut. What if I hadn't woken up in time? What if my parents had found me lying there? Worse, what would Nikolai think if he opened his door to see me curled up outside like some obsessed freak?

And then it happened again the following night.

I looked up causes for sleepwalking online, trying to get to the bottom of this newly developed habit. *Sleep deprivation, irregular sleep patterns, stress and anxiety, fever, and alcohol or drug use.*

Perhaps it was all the stress and anxiety. I certainly had plenty of that these days.

But something about that explanation didn't really sit right. Something told me there had to be more to it than that. Especially because, why had I been specifically ending up outside of Nikolai's door of all places? It just seemed like . . .

I inhaled deeply and then blew out all the air in my lungs. *It will all be okay. It will all be okay.* I kept repeating that to myself. I'd gone through hard things before and always came out on top. This time would be no different.

My cell phone vibrated.

Before I even looked at it, I knew.

Unknown

> You can't avoid me forever. I saw you at the full moon run. Your little circle of alphas won't always be around.

My little circle of alphas. I turned those words in my head.

Memories started flooding back to me.

"Maybe you should do fewer chest exercises. Your tits are so small," he'd said to me one day while we'd been naked, lying in bed. His eyes were scanning my body in an excruciating way. I felt so exposed. I wanted to tell him to stop staring at me, but he was so sensitive. Sometimes the smallest things, things that didn't even seem offensive in the slightest, would make him snap.

It was best to keep the peace and just lay there, letting him drag his eyes across my body and determine every flaw.

"Honestly, Terri, your body is kind of masculine. You have too much muscle. Men like a more feminine figure."

I'd tried not to let it get to me. But he was probably right. It wasn't normal for a woman to train as hard as me. The women in movies were all so slender without much muscle definition. That was what men liked.

Looking back, that had been a red flag. I should have left the second he'd said something negative about my body. But the thing was, both my grandfather and my father had always been highly critical of their mates. Those were the relationships that were modeled to me growing up. As sad as it was to say, that criticism, that feeling of never being good enough, that was normal. That was what love had always felt like to me. No matter how hard I tried, in school, in training, in eating, the goalposts were always moved. I was never smart, strong, or thin enough in my parents' eyes. And so it made sense that it would be the same with my boyfriend, another person who was supposed to love me.

One day, he'd said we should go to the gym together. At first, I thought that was a great idea. I was always at the gym, and I loved the idea of bonding over a shared hobby. Maybe he'd even be impressed by all the work I'd put in and the results I'd obtained after years of hard work. But I soon learned the flaw in my thinking.

After warming up, we started with bench press. He had me go first. I layered on some weights for a warm-up set. Two forty-five-pound weights on a forty-five-pound bar. I swiftly did eight reps and let him take his turn.

He got through that just fine. I layered on more weights. On my third set, I decided to finally load the bar up to what I normally lift on an eight-rep day, which was 270 pounds. This was pretty standard, if not low, for a male warrior in my weight class, but I knew it was a lot for a female. My expectation was he would be impressed, the same way Tyce and Trav always were when I worked out with them.

But I shouldn't have been so naive.

When he went after me, he started out fine with the first four reps, grunting through them. But once he got to the second half, with the way he was wincing and his limbs were trembling, I could tell he was struggling.

"Here, I'll spot you," I offered, slipping my hand under the bar.

"Don't fucking spot me!" he snarled in a voice laced with fury. "You're fucking embarrassing me!"

"Oh, sorry." I stepped back and fidgeted with my hands. He ground his teeth, and scrunched his entire flushed face while he groaned through his fifth rep. On the sixth rep, he squeezed his eyes shut, every vein in his body seemed to twitch, and he just barely got the bar up.

By the seventh rep, there was no doubt he wouldn't be able to do it. He was growling so loud that people were looking. A sickening sense of dread crept over me as his arms visibly shook, and the veins in his neck bulged as he tried to force the bar up. I knew I should help him. There was no way he was going to get that bar up. But I stood glued in place, unsure what to do. I must have looked so stupid and awful to everyone else, not helping someone who was clearly failing. This was terrible gym etiquette.

Finally, after spending far too long staring at him struggle, I couldn't take it anymore. I stepped forward and helped him lift the bar to the J-hooks.

He immediately got up, and once again, I knew I'd made a mistake before he even said anything. His nostrils were flared, and his hands were balled into fists. His cold, hard eyes met mine. "You bitch. I told you not to spot me! I was going to lift it!"

"I'm sorry," I practically whispered.

"Fuck this!" He flung his hands up, face flushing with rage, before he stormed out of the gym without a backward glance.

My stomach twisted. I'd screwed up.

A few people exchanged smirks, whispering behind their hands. A couple of gym-goers snickered under their breath, and then, loud enough for everyone to hear, someone chuckled and commented, "Damn, that dude was pissed!"

Heat rushed to my face. I clenched my fists, wishing I could disappear, sink into the rubber flooring, anything to escape the stares.

From that day forward, whenever I'd go to the gym with him, I made sure to always choose weights that were "normal" for a woman my size to lift—ones I knew he'd easily be able to lift himself. And if I did that, he was happy, and so was I. But there'd been something that had nagged at me. Wasn't it wrong that I'd had to shrink myself down so his ego wouldn't be bruised?

How could I have been so stupid? Why did I think any of the things he did were okay?

Now, I just wished he'd disappear forever. If I never saw him again, it would be too soon.

There had to be a way to get rid of him, and to get him to stop contacting me, short of getting him banished from the pack. Gosh, why was I always so nice? Truly, I should have been dying for him to be banished. Just one word to Tyce, and I knew he'd willingly do it, no questions asked. We had trust like that. But still, there was that part of me that knew he was just a scared little boy inside. He pushed me down because he felt inadequate. Not that it made any of the things he did right. But still, I couldn't help but have empathy for him.

I just didn't have it in me to get him banished—to pull him away from all his friends and family. He hadn't always been bad. There were good parts of him too.

And maybe, maybe it was the mark. Maybe he'd accomplished exactly what he set out to. As long as I wore his mark, I couldn't hate him. And as long as I didn't hate him, there was still a chance for him to slide back into my life. No matter that I had blocked him on everything. No matter that I did my best to avoid him when I was home. No matter that thoughts of him evoked cold, hard dread and fear.

Or maybe it was that I knew that one person couldn't be fully evil. I knew that *he* wasn't 100 percent evil. There had been times when he was sweet and vulnerable and made me feel all soft and cozy inside. There'd been a time when just seeing his face brought butterflies to my stomach. And those bits of goodness made me hesitate.

So maybe I couldn't hate him . . . not completely.

But I didn't have to love, or even tolerate, him either.

Chapter 11

Theresa

A couple days later, my brother Tyce finally returned home with his mate, Gigi. "Tyce!" I screamed as he walked in the door, throwing my arms around him.

"Hey, Terr Bear," he replied, messing up my hair as he pulled away. I pushed his hand off my head and gave him a shove.

"Welcome home, Gigi!" I exclaimed to my soon-to-be sister-in-law and pulled her in for an even bigger embrace.

"Thanks, Terri," she replied, returning the hug. I liked Gigi so far. She was good for Tyce. Every time he glanced her way, a smile would sneak onto his face.

As I let go of Gigi, I said, "I feel like I've barely had a chance to get to know you. We should hang out tonight, if you're up for it of course. I know you just got in from a long flight."

"I'd love that," she replied with a big smile and no hesitation.

"Yay! How about we head down to the local pub for dinner instead of staying in?"

"Yeah, that would be great!"

"You can hold down the fort with the 'rents." I gave Tyce a wink.

"You owe me one." He pinched me playfully on the arm.

I was about to say something else when we were interrupted. "You're home." My mom appeared in the doorway, perfectly poised, her layered, dark hair that ended just past her shoulders impeccably blown out as usual.

"Hey, Mom," Tyce said.

"Hi, Luna Julia. It's nice to see you!" Gigi straightened, mimicking my mom's perfect posture, and planted a smile on her face. "Tyce and I brought back some gifts from Vermont for you. Let me go unpack, and I'll bring them down."

"Are you hungry?" my mom asked, completely ignoring how hard Gigi was clearly trying. "I'll have Tasha make you something." She then turned toward the kitchen and was soon gone.

Gigi let out a breath and said, "Tyce, I'm just going to run upstairs and get settled."

"Here, let me help you with your bags," he said, picking everything up off the entryway floor.

That evening, Gigi and I met downstairs, bundled up for the walk over to the pack pub. One nice thing about going away to college was how much more there was to do in Anchorage. Here, we were so isolated. We didn't even have internet until 2005, and we finally put up a cell phone tower around 2012. I suppose cell phones weren't a necessity seeing as how we could just mindlink in our wolf forms, but at some point, we had to join the modern world.

As soon as we stepped outside, the icy wind slapped our faces. "And I thought Vermont was cold!" Gigi exclaimed.

"I've heard Alaska is hard to get used to," I replied. After a beat, I continued, "But honestly, even after living here my whole life, I still somehow always forget how dark the winters are. The twenty-four hours of sun during the summer are good at wiping it from your memory. But it's easier in Anchorage anyway. Tyce told me you'll be starting at UAA at the end of the month?"

"Yeah." She let out a breath and didn't seem as excited about it as I thought she'd be.

"What's wrong?"

"Nothing's wrong. It'll just suck being away from Tyce, you know?"

"I'm sure he'll visit. And you can always come back here. It's only for a few years, right?"

"Well, I was going to go to medical school, but I don't know. I'm rethinking it now."

"I'm sure you'll figure it out. And I'll be around too if you ever need someone to talk anything through."

Fortunately, with the packhouse right smack-dab in the middle of downtown, we were at the pub in no time. Most people who lived farther out would take their snowmobile in, or just run over in their wolf forms if they weren't expecting to carry anything back.

We climbed the steps to enter the pub, the warm air inside instantly defrosting my cheeks. We both slid off our heavy coats and found an empty booth. Because this time of year was unpredictable, as far as what was available for food, they printed a new menu regularly on eight-and-a-half-by-eleven printer paper. The ones they gave us had clearly gone through quite a few hands already, judging by the stains and the way some of the printed words ran.

"Honestly, I'll just have bread, bread, and more bread," I joked to Gigi.

"I love having friends who like to eat! Especially when it's carbs."

"Just don't tell my mom."

"*You* don't tell your mom!" She snickered, and we shared a thieving look. "So does that mean we should just order a couple of bread baskets with smoked salmon chowder to dip it in? And what is this mystery-meat stew?"

"It's whatever game they were able to hunt down or came in the latest shipment. I think it's usually a mix of caribou and moose. Maybe musk ox. I think every once in a while they get Dall sheep. And sometimes it's plain ol' beef or pork. They always have stuff like mystery-meat pie or mystery-meat lasagna on their menu."

"Looks like they have a lot of chicken options." Gigi examined the menu. "I guess they get it from the pack chicken coop, so that makes sense."

"I'm so sick of chicken," I lamented. "It's so easy to get relative to everything else, plus it's lean, so that's basically the only thing my mom ever lets me eat during the winter. That, salmon, and eggs."

Gigi reached her hand out and brushed my arm with compassion. I almost flinched at the touch, it was so unfamiliar to me. My family wasn't touchy-feely like that. While I did make an effort to hug my siblings and friends, and found so much comfort in the gesture, it still always felt foreign after so many years of not receiving that type of affection from my family.

"Hey, I didn't bring you out here to trauma dump on you! Let's talk about something else," I said. Too much information. Too much oversharing. Why did I always do that?

Gigi leaned closer and opened her mouth as if about to speak, but then something distracted her. Her eyes moved from left to right as she followed something behind me. I turned to find Beta Liam, the beta of our pack, with Beta Sasha from the Severnaya Zvezda Pack, lining up at the fully packed bar. This place was very popular during the winter. There really wasn't much else to do.

She then turned back to me. "Goddess, that Russian accent is so hot! It's so Mafia or Bratva. Whatever they call the Russian mob."

"Mm," I replied, not sure how to respond.

"What do you think of Alpha Nikolai?"

My cheeks burned uncontrollably at the mention of his name. I desperately hoped Gigi didn't notice and tried to play it cool. "He's all right. I haven't talked to him much."

"I mean the beta is also good-looking. But the alpha is hot!"

"Yeah, he's handsome." Oh gosh. Why was I talking like my grandma?

"Not as hot as Tyce of course."

"Sure, Tyce is very handsome." I needed to stop using that word. But it wasn't like I was going to call my own brother hot. *Blech!* And, sure, I was comparing him to my brother, but truthfully, I found Nikolai much hotter. Like, Nikolai was the type of hot that made me feral and necessitated a change of panties. The type of hot I had never been sure actually existed outside of airbrushed and filtered fitness influencer models.

"Alpha Nikolai doesn't talk much though. He's really standoffish." Why was Gigi choosing him of all people to talk about tonight?

"Well, I can understand," I responded. "He lost his entire family and most of his pack recently." Stating it out loud made me tear up a bit. Something about this man. He made it so hard to control my emotions and my hormones. Sometimes I thought I was losing my sanity when he entered my consciousness.

"Yeah." Gigi slumped her shoulders and balanced her head on her hands. "That really sucks. I can't even imagine."

"Hello!" We both jumped as the waitress popped out of seemingly nowhere. "Can I start you off with a drink?"

Gigi bit her lip. "I'll have a Sprite, please."

"Nothing harder?" The waitress winked at her.

"I don't think . . ."

"We're on pack land. If you look like you could be close to old enough, we don't ask. And, besides, you're about to be luna."

"With vodka," Gigi said.

"'Atta girl! And you, Terr?"

"I'll have the same," I replied. It'd been so long since I'd had a sugary drink, and I was looking forward to it.

"I'll be back with your drinks and to take your orders." She shuffled away.

"I guess Tyce never brought you here?" I asked.

"What's the point, right? We have a private chef at the packhouse."

"I don't know. To get out and have fun?"

"He's really busy." Gigi shrugged. "Before the roads got snowed over, we would take day trips and stuff to other places. But we haven't been able to do that lately. He's also taking his alpha role really seriously now, and I know that takes up a lot of his time." She glanced up then back at me, smiled slyly, then continued, "And a lot of the time, we want to snuggle on the couch and just hang out alone." Her cheeks pinkened, tipping me off that the *s* word she meant was not actually *snuggle*. I appreciated her not sharing what they actually did most nights, because I preferred to pretend my brother was celibate, although the whole pack knew otherwise.

We soon ordered our food, and Gigi told me all about her family and the joint bachelorette party she'd had with her twin sister back home. We were two and a half drinks deep at that point, both starting to feel it (they didn't pour light here—after all, we all had werewolf tolerance), and she suggested we move over to the bar where it was much livelier.

I agreed, so we grabbed our coats and crossbodies and headed over. The betas had found seats by then and were both concentrating on the hockey game up on the TV screen. As we approached, my scent must have tipped him off because Beta Liam turned around.

"Hey, Terri!" He stood from his stool in greeting. "You coming to hang out at the bar?"

"Indeed," I replied.

"Here, ladies, take our seats," he said, patting Beta Sasha on the shoulder. He immediately grabbed his drink and vacated his seat.

"Oh, no, it's fine! We don't mind standing," I said, feeling bad.

"We insist," Beta Liam said, gesturing at the stools.

"What kind of gentleman lets two beautiful ladies stand?" Beta Sasha said in his thick Russian accent. "Besides, you do us favor keeping company. We get enough of each other all day." He gave Liam a playful punch in the arm.

I'd grown up with Beta Liam, and he was essentially part of the family, like a cousin. He was over a decade older than me and had already been the beta of the pack for about ten years. He was one of a small group of people who could maintain and pilot our bush plane. In general, everyone loved Beta Liam. While my father had ruled with intimidation and brute force, Liam, and his father before him, always led with respect and kindness. Like good cop and bad cop.

I wondered what the dynamic was like between Nikolai and Sasha. Not that I'd spoken to him much, but Sasha did seem to be far more outgoing and jovial. I sometimes noticed him making jokes to his alpha, while Nikolai just stared at him with barely a reaction. Yeah, kind of like when I tried to play those pranks on him during our run. Which obviously hadn't gone over very well. My cheeks burned and my stomach churned when I recalled the events of that day and the morning after. I pushed them out of my mind, not wanting to ruin the evening with Gigi.

"So, how are you liking Alaska so far?" Gigi asked Beta Sasha.

"I do miss home. But I know there is better future for me. And here—here is where future is," Beta Sasha replied.

I turned his response around in my mind. So did he mean that because he was here there was better in the future, or there was better in the future irrelevant of where he may be?

"I miss home too," Gigi replied.

"You are from other side of country, yes?"

"Yep, from Vermont. But I'm getting used to being here now. And, of course, my mate is here. I suppose that's what really matters at the end of the day."

"Right. Mate bond is sacred."

"Sasha, you see any potential mates in our pack yet?" Liam winked. "What about Terri? Did you look in her eyes?" he teased, giving me a pat on the back.

I laughed uncomfortably. Sure, Sasha was a good-looking guy, but I didn't feel any attraction to him, and joking about it made me uneasy.

"Her mother was beta's daughter," Sasha said. "So, of course, it makes sense she is destined for beta. Or alpha, like her father. But, regretfully, she is not my mate."

Contrary to his statement, he didn't seem to regret it much, which I was relieved by. The last thing I needed was for someone under the same roof as me to have a thing for me. *But what about Nikolai?* My stomach quivered.

"Late Beta Andrey, and ones before him, were good men." Beta Sasha took a big gulp of his drink. "Your mother, she came from good family, Terri. All intelligent, ambitious, resourceful."

My mom never spoke much about her family. I had learned they'd all perished in the war in a manner that was more logistical than emotional. Whatever sadness she felt, she never showed. But I sometimes wondered if she did feel that heaviness but, perhaps, thought it would make her appear weak or vulnerable to display it openly.

Had she mourned them in silence? Did she grieve behind closed doors? Or had she buried her past so deeply that even the memory of her family had been erased?

Although I'd never been close to him, I'd still cried and found moving forward in my day-to-day excruciatingly difficult when my grandfather passed. After all, he was my family. I'd grown up in the same home as him. To know that one day I'd left for college, and then would never return home to see him alive again haunted me. How did my mom feel knowing she'd not only never see her family again, but nor would she ever see her pack as she'd known it?

As soon as Gigi and I finished our drinks, Beta Liam bought us another round, swatting Sasha's hand away when he attempted to take out his wallet. I was well aware they didn't have much, essentially surviving off our pack's goodwill at the moment.

We mostly just made small talk for the rest of the evening. Toward the end of the night, when I was about to ask Gigi if she was ready to go back, Liam leaned into Sasha. "So when do you head out again?"

"In few days," Sasha replied.

"Head out where?" I asked.

"We found land, and now going back and forth, building shelter. We hope to move there permanent in few months, maybe when weather is warmer. Good place to settle. Nothing much around." He smirked and continued, "As you Americans say, no one to hear you scream."

Chapter 12

Nikolai

Exactly twenty of my pack members showed up to warrior training on Friday morning. Half my pack was now makeshift warriors. Before the war, I'd had more than double—fifty of my strongest and bravest men. Now I was left with a random jumble of people that met the only criteria of being between the ages of eighteen and sixty. As they say, for a poor man and a thief, any clothes fit.

I let out a breath as I scanned the group. Perhaps Sasha was right, some breeding among the pack wouldn't hurt. Not that it was a good time for any of us. We were still mourning the loss of our families. We didn't even have a home yet. We would soon, but it wouldn't be equipped with electricity or running water when we first settled. We'd be living off the land for who knows how much time before we figured it out. The last thing I could imagine was bringing more children into our dire situation. The ones we had now suffered enough.

"Okay, warriors!" I shouted, far louder than need be, considering how few people were gathered. "Let's warm up. Give me four laps around the track, twenty push-ups, twenty sit-ups, and the normal stretches."

Alpha Tyce had reserved the warrior gym for us for four hours every other day. The times varied depending on when his pack needed to use it. His men were still allowed to come in for individual workouts outside of their normal training schedule, but he promised there usually weren't many that chose to do extra outside of what was already required.

"Are you training pups or warriors?" Sasha quipped, his eyes following the pack members as they began their jog around the track.

"It's a warm-up. And these people have never trained as warriors before. If they wear themselves out now, they won't be good for the real work later."

"Without effort, you won't even pull a fish from a pond."

I rolled my eyes at him, not bothering to respond. I understood where Sasha was coming from. I should have been working everyone much harder than I was. But the pack, as it was, was in a fragile state. Although I had gotten everyone here, there was no guarantee they'd continue to stick with me and respect me as their alpha. Dissent was a real possibility. These people had followed me across borders, left their homes, their dead, behind. For what? A land where they had nothing? If I pushed too hard, if I lost their trust, they might leave. And then what?

After they completed their warm-up, we moved out of the track room and into the weight room. I had to admit, the training facility in this pack was impressive. What we had back home may as well have been a shack in comparison. Granted, I believed you only needed some basic equipment and land to run on, but it was nice having the luxury of options. They had a whole damn rock-climbing wall.

As soon as I brought my warriors to the barbell area which, of course, had a whole line of weight racks and benches, I was accosted with . . . I couldn't decide if it was hell or heaven on earth. Hell because I couldn't tear my eyes away, and it would be the death of me as a composed and in-control alpha. But heaven because, *blyad*, I'd never seen such a perfectly sculpted, round ass in my life. The *princessa* of the pack was deadlifting, just sticking out her glutes without a care as to who might be hypnotized by their perfection.

And how much weight was she lifting? My thumbs and fingers would probably touch if I wrapped them around her waist, and yet, she was lifting as much as a male warrior. I think I forgot to breathe as she drove up and straightened out of her hip hinge. Where did she learn to lift like that? And what was she doing in the warrior gym? I could have sworn only men were warriors in the Jade Moon Pack.

I did my best to pry my eyes away and hoped no one noticed me staring at her like a lecher. I cleared my throat, completely forgetting what exercises I'd planned for the day. "Okay," I finally said. "We're going to start off by doing some bench press. I want everyone to work up to their one-rep max so we know what we need to double in the next three months."

"Three months?" a woman in her forties, Mariya, gasped.

"Yes, three months," I replied firmly, making it clear I wasn't bullshitting. "Any other questions?"

"What happens if we don't?" Mariya challenged.

"Double the work," I replied. She seemed as if she was about to argue further, so I continued, "You are all that's left of this pack. You are the only thing standing between the life and death of this pack and those too weak to fight. So I suggest you consider that during these training sessions. Now, everyone, pair up and find a bench."

I supervised as they attempted to lift their heaviest, not letting them stop until they clearly failed. I exhaled a heavy breath. This was not promising. I wasn't used to training the general populace, nor to how little the average person could lift.

I knew I had no choice but to play the cards I'd been dealt.

Meanwhile, I was trying my best to keep my concentration focused on my pack and not the unexpectedly athletic she-wolf just meters away, lifting more weight than possibly all my pack members combined could.

I crossed my arms and clenched my jaw. "We have a lot of work ahead of us. Right now, we have no chance to win any fight. If what happened in Ukraine happens here, there will be no more pack. I said I wanted you to double your one-rep max. Change that to triple. Moving forward, the days we don't meet in the gym, we will be running outside. Whether in human or wolf form will change depending on my mood that day."

Mariya gasped.

"Is there something you have to say?" I asked in a sharp tone, glaring at her.

After a beat, she finally replied, "No," and looked down at her feet.

"Good. I'm not going to take challenges lightly. You are all warriors now, and I expect you to act like it. That means no arguing with me, your alpha and leader. I can guarantee that anyone who does will regret it. This is a matter of life or death. Now, everyone, grab a pair of heavy dumbbells, heavier than you think you should. Then I want you to do front and lateral raises until you can't lift your arms anymore. Sasha will supervise while I set up our next program."

Sasha simply shook his head, surely thinking exactly the same thing I was. We were fucked.

I took some steadying breaths. At least this was a start. They wouldn't be shit forever. And what were the chances we'd have to defend ourselves any time soon? We were in another country now, where no one knew of our pack. At the moment, we were protected within the Jade Moon Pack. By the time we set out on our own, everyone would be far more trained.

But definitely not trained enough.

Yep, we were fucked.

I entered the storage room to grab the TRX straps I'd seen Tyce's warriors using on one of the days I'd come in to do my own workout. Before I even took a couple steps in, I was confronted by that scent—that delicious, sweet, erotic scent that wouldn't leave my dreams. Without meaning to, I let the door shut behind me. Terri was on her tippy-toes trying to reach something up high, but the sound of the door slamming shut distracted her, and she promptly turned to face me.

"What are you doing in here?" she asked, and her voice almost seemed accusatory. She placed her hands on her hips and went rigid, glaring at me.

"What are *you* doing in here?" I responded, giving her attitude. How dare she accuse me when she wasn't even supposed to be using this gym? "Strange shirt. Not every day someone wears *vodolazka* in gym."

"A what?" she asked.

"You know, big collar, covers neck."

"A turtleneck?"

"Turtleneck." I copied the word, trying to commit it to memory. While my English was quite good since we studied it in our pack as part of the school program, and had access to innumerable English-language TV shows and movies, there were still words I needed to learn.

"It's what I wanted to wear," she said, keeping her head held high.

"Why you ask me not to tell anyone?" I asked, suddenly feeling like this was the most important question in the world.

"You didn't tell anyone, did you?" she asked instead of responding, bringing her hand to the place where I knew the mark was located. The way it looked was seared into my brain. And I hated every time I thought about it.

"No."

"Thank you."

"Was it premature marking? Is because your parents difficult?"

"Something like that."

"*Nu*, what is it?" I crossed my arms and narrowed my eyes at her. "I think I have right to know why I keep such big secret."

I stared her down. That mark. Every time I even thought about it, something inside me ignited, like my blood was on fire, burning me from the inside out. I clenched my fists, trying to hold it together. Because at that moment, I wanted to lay into her. Call her a whore.

But then I looked into her eyes—really looked. The whites that surrounded the most beautiful golden orbs reddened, becoming glassy with tears. Fucking Artemis! How could I be mad at her when she looked so pitiful and vulnerable?

"I . . . I . . . I can't . . ." she started, practically choking as she spoke. She closed her eyes and just stood there for a moment, taking deep breaths. And I understood. She was trying not to cry. Finally, she said, "It's personal."

"Fine," I conceded. Why was it my fucking business? Why did I even care? And here I was, making this poor girl cry when she didn't owe me any explanation for anything that went on in her life.

"I'll go," she said, trying to sneak past me without touching me. But while she was slim, it was quite a narrow room, and I took up a good amount of space. I probably should have moved back to let her through more easily, but something stopped me from doing it. Something within me wanted to feel the warmth of her body brush against mine, to touch even the slightest bit of her skin. And before I could stop myself, I stepped closer just as she was trying to get by me.

"Wh—" Her head shot up as our torsos touched. Her cheeks reddened. *Boginya moya*, she looked so beautiful flushed like this.

"You getting something?" I asked. It was the first thing that came to mind as an excuse for why I'd stopped her from leaving. "I help you."

"Oh." She parted her lips slightly, and her eyes didn't leave mine. Her tongue darted out, touching her lips before retreating back into her mouth. It was taking everything in me not to claim that tongue.

She arched her back, and I stepped back a bit. Partly because I was hard as a rock now, and I was standing so close to her that she was bound to feel it if I moved just slightly in the wrong direction, but also because this whole situation was wrong. It was everything I didn't want to happen.

But holy Artemis. She looked so gorgeous at that moment. The gym shirt she was wearing was so tight, and her nipples were pebbled into stiff peaks, just begging to be admired and touched. What I wouldn't give to cup those perfect breasts in my hands.

Our breaths were heavy. The tension was so thick you could cut a knife through it.

"What you want?" I finally asked. The words came out strained, almost a moan.

"The ab roller," she replied.

I easily plucked what she needed off the top shelf and handed it to her.

"Thank you." She bowed her head slightly.

"Do you always use warrior gym?" I asked, not wanting her to leave. Suddenly, it was my mission to keep her in this small enclosure as long as possible.

"Yeah. It has better equipment than the other one. And fewer people bother me."

I was about to say something else when the door swung open, and I came face-to-face with the former Alpha Lance.

"What is going on in here?" Lance's nostrils flared and he took on a sharp, assessing expression. *Blyad!* I knew that look. A predator sizing up his prey.

"Nothing," Theresa cut in before I could speak. "Alpha Nikolai was just helping me reach something." She held up the ab roller like it was a shield, then pushed past him to exit.

Lance didn't move. His eyes flicked to mine, then to the door she slipped through, then back.

"Helping?" He stepped forward, too close. "Because from where I was standing, it looked like something else."

I held my ground, forcing my shoulders to stay relaxed. "Like I said, I have no time, no desire for women now. My only priority is my pack." While I was able to sound convincing while I said it, it felt like a lie.

Because what just happened had definitely not been nothing. Whatever that she-wolf was doing to me, my emotions, and my self-control was the complete opposite of nothing.

Lance didn't blink. Then, finally, he stepped back. "Good," he said, voice flat. "Let's keep it that way."

Chapter 13

Theresa

What just happened? I brought my hand to my racing heart, even though I was well aware the gesture was not going to steady it. I had planned to finish my workout with some ab exercises, but now I wasn't sure whether I wanted to stick around. Would it be wrong to just take the roller home with me? It wasn't like I couldn't just bring it back the next day.

That moment between Nikolai and me had been so strange. I couldn't figure out if he hated me or not. And when we'd touched, the oddest feeling came over me. It was like tingles where we connected. I'd never felt anything like it.

My whole body had reacted—an involuntary shiver running down my spine, a rush of warmth spreading from where our skin met. My fingers twitched at my sides as if they wanted to reach for him again, just to see if it would happen a second time. Was I imagining things?

He *was* hot. And he was making me react in all sorts of unexpected ways. I could still picture his imposing stature. The way he took up so much of that small space in the storage room. How I could see the outlines of his hard muscles through the thin T-shirt he wore. That heady scent that wafted off him. He shouldn't have smelled great after working out, but holy wow, I think the sweat actually made it more potent and that much more intoxicating.

I was uncomfortably warm thinking about it, but in maybe the best way possible? Was there a word for when you were so turned on it was excruciating but it also somehow made you feel energetic and alive at the same time?

I glanced back at the storage closet, where my dad still stood in the doorway, and made a final decision to split. That was pretty awkward, and I wasn't sure how I felt about dealing with Nikolai and my father sharing the gym with me at the same time. To get to the exit, I had to walk past Nikolai's pack members, who were stuck doing jumping jacks.

"*Bystreye!*" Beta Sasha barked out. While my mother was a native Russian speaker, she'd never spoken it to anyone other than our cook and most definitely had never taught her family. It was too bad because I'd always thought it would've been nice to know a second language.

All I could tell was that Beta Sasha was not happy, and he was getting in the face of some poor buxom woman. Her full breasts were clearly not well supported and were bouncing wildly with each jump. That couldn't be pleasant. He yelled the same word again. "*Bystreye, Mariya!*" She crossed her arms over her chest, and he slapped her hands as she did it. "*Ruki vverkh!*"

She looked so defeated as she moved her arms back into the jumping jack position that I felt I had to intervene. I knew it wasn't my business, but sometimes I just couldn't help myself. "Stop!" I shouted at Sasha. "She doesn't have the support to jump like that."

"What?" he snapped at me, glaring with cold, hard eyes.

"She's not wearing a good sports bra. Can't you see she's in pain?"

"Why you not wearing good sports bra?" he asked her in English, undoubtedly for my benefit.

She was already red from the workout, but her face took on an even rosier hue. "I don't have."

"Why not have?"

Her eyes bugged out as if to say, *Are you stupid?*

"They're not cheap," I offered. Sure, I wasn't exactly an expert in this area, as my ex had made quite clear. But my friend Sophia was always complaining about how difficult-to-find and expensive her sports bras were, and that she had no choice but to buy them because the pack required us all to be able to run a mile in under nine minutes, even as civilians. Mariya nodded in agreement.

Sasha blew out a heavy, annoyed breath and then pressed his lips into a thin line, his whole face taking on a pinched expression.

"Obviously, it's an issue," I said to Sasha, taking pity. "As the pack sponsoring Severnaya Zvezda Pack, I'll ask Tyce to put aside some funds so we can purchase them for the ladies who need them. They're important so you can become independent."

Sasha didn't say anything, but Mariya's shoulders sagged like a weight had been lifted off them. I gave her a friendly smile and turned to go, figuring my job was done. Especially since Sasha had nothing else to say, and I was still trying to escape being in the same place as both my father and Nikolai.

I found my winter boots and coat in the corner of the gym, since this one didn't have a women's locker room to store them, and pulled everything on. I then slipped out into the cold, dark late morning.

My breath came out in clouds, illuminated by the glow of my night vision. I trudged down the freshly plowed road. We'd gotten a new layer of snow overnight.

It didn't take long to get home. As soon as I kicked off my boots, I made my way into the kitchen. I was starving. Tasha had my lunch ready in no time. Boneless, skinless chicken breast, rice, and broccoli. I choked it down. It wasn't that it was bad (Tasha did at least know how to make even the blandest food palatable), but—gosh—what I wouldn't do for some fried chicken instead. That was one nice thing about being away at school. There was no one to monitor what I ate. While others complained about the cafeteria food, I couldn't help but indulge in being able to eat fats and sugars for once in my life.

There had been times that Tyce, Trav, and I had convinced Tasha to let us cook our own meals, especially when my mom was distracted with other things. Honestly, looking back, I think my brothers had done that for me. They were always the ones acting like they actually *wanted* to learn how to cook, but perhaps they'd just felt bad that my food was so monitored, and they realized that gave me an opportunity to actually eat something good for once.

I suppose our dysfunctional family had the effect of bringing us closer together. The three of us did tend to watch out for one another. And it gave me hope for the future. That perhaps the Tikaani family wouldn't always be so *intense*.

After I finished my meal, I made my way to Tyce's office to check if he was in, to discuss the whole sports bra situation. The door was slightly ajar, but I heard a female voice giggling inside, and I thought twice about pushing it open. The last thing I needed was to be traumatized for life after walking in on my brother with his mate doing things I had no desire to see.

I knocked on the doorframe.

"One minute!" Tyce shouted. Then there was more giggling and rustling. Yep, glad I knocked. After some time, he finally said, "Come in."

"You do realize the door was open and I was about to be doomed to a lifetime of therapy bills," I said as I entered.

"Sometimes things just happen." Tyce shrugged.

Gigi adjusted her shirt and shifted in her chair but didn't say anything.

"I think we'd all appreciate it if fewer things happened where we could accidentally walk in on them."

"I'll note it." Tyce leaned back in his office chair, placing his hands behind his head in a relaxed position. "So what brings you in here, Terr Bear?"

I took a seat and told him what I'd witnessed, pleading my case for quality sports bras for Nikolai's pack. Gigi chimed in and wholeheartedly agreed, saying she needed some more herself for all the training she was doing, and how the ones she had couldn't get washed fast enough. Once Gigi took my side, Tyce was instantly convinced.

"Does that mean you'll be bringing it up at the next budget meeting?" Gigi teased. "Is that going to be your big agenda item? Sports bras?"

"I'm just glad I have a reason to talk about boobs during those boring-ass meetings," Tyce replied. "It's about time we talk about something actually important. Not road repairs and plow trucks. Though I don't mind a conversation about a dump truck now and then." I couldn't avoid noticing how he slyly pinched the side of Gigi's derriere. She pushed his hand away, but also couldn't stop the amused expression that formed on her face, her nose crinkling a bit.

Goodness, they were so nauseating. But so cute. It was hard not to believe in love when I observed the two of them together. It was clear by how Tyce looked at Gigi that he adored her. And she seemed smitten with him as well.

A sharp pang twisted in my gut. Would I ever have something like that?

Had I ruined my chance now?

I swallowed past the lump in my throat and pushed the thought away, finishing up my conversation with Tyce before heading upstairs.

I threw myself into my usual ab exercises, trying to distract myself, trying not to think about Nikolai, about what I'd lost, about the uncertainty of my future. But no number of sit-ups or planks could stop the what-ifs from creeping in.

By the time I finished, my mind was no quieter. I peeled off my workout clothes and stepped into the shower, letting the hot water scald my skin in an attempt to chase away the unease curling in my stomach. But as soon as I wrapped myself in a towel and caught my reflection in the fogged-up mirror, my breath caught.

My mark.

The jagged bite was an angry, inflamed pink, standing out starkly against my skin. I traced my fingers over it, wincing at how tender it felt. Some days it was itchy, a dull irritation that never fully went away. But today . . . today, it felt like a raw and pulsing open wound.

I pressed my palm against it, trying to soothe the discomfort, but it didn't help.

In the beginning, I'd try to research if there was a way to remove a mark. I went by the hospital, where I knew they kept archives of wolfy ailments. I tried flipping through some of the books, making up an excuse about how a friend had some questions about her mark she was too embarrassed to research herself. But, ultimately, I could find no evidence that it was possible, and I had to return to school anyway, cutting my time short.

I confessed everything to Sophia, and she tried to convince me to tell my parents. But I just couldn't do it. I couldn't stand the thought of the disappointment in my parents' eyes. Sure, Tyce had screwed around his whole life, but he was a *male* and the *alpha*. It was different for women. The standards for us had just never been the same.

I got dressed and threw on a thick turtleneck. For now, that would do. It was winter, and there was no reason to question my choice in wardrobe. I'd be going back to college at the end of January, so I'd have several months before I came back to the pack. I could even enroll in summer classes and just stay in Anchorage. Maybe permanently.

Chapter 14

Ginger

"These plowing fees are outrageous!" Tyce's mom complained.

"Mom, I told you, Trav did the math, and it's cheaper to keep the roads to the Spruce Winter Pack plowed than to fly back and forth all the time," Tyce responded with an annoyed inflection to his voice.

"So why aren't they helping pay for it?"

"Because they're in debt to their asses."

"And whose fault is that? They're the ones that embezzled two hundred million dollars."

"*Alpha Vic* embezzled two hundred million dollars, and he's dead now. Now that Trav is *luno* or whatever, we have a blood alliance. So sucks to suck for us."

Luna Julia let out a heavy sigh.

"And I'll be using those roads today."

"For what?"

"Apparently Alpha Sara has news."

"That girl is no good." Luna Julia tutted and shook her head. Then she stopped and blinked a couple times. "News?"

"Yeah," Tyce responded.

"Of course we know what it means when a woman has news." Julia lifted the sides of her mouth into a rare smile. "Finally, I'm going to be a grandmother! It's about time!"

"Hold up!" Tyce sat up straight from the slouched position he was in. "That is definitely not the news!"

Julia grabbed a catalog off Tyce's desk, rolled it up, and tapped it on his head. "Tut tut, Tyce. So much for you to learn." Then she walked out of the room, swaying her hips as if she were dancing to a tune in her head. That was probably the happiest I'd ever seen her.

"Do you actually think Sara's pregnant?" I asked once Julia was out of earshot.

"There's no fucking way."

"If they go at it as much as we do, there's definitely a way." I giggled.

"I can't imagine Sara getting pregnant. Can you?"

"I mean, she has the hardware as far as I know." I shrugged.

"That girl is definitely on triple birth control. There's not a motherly bone in her body. She probably takes BC and makes Trav wrap it *and* pull out. She's trying to figure out if there's a way to get Trav to carry her heir as we speak."

"Not a half-bad idea." I let out a laugh. "Tyce, can you carry your own heir? I'll just show up at the birth and say some encouraging words as you push our spawn out of your ass."

"Stop reading all that omegaverse shit." Tyce pulled me into his lap as I let out a loud squeal. "It's giving you some really fucked-up ideas. And just for that, I'm going to come inside you next time."

I stopped laughing and stiffened.

"What's wrong?" Tyce asked, clearly noticing my change in mood through the bond.

"You wouldn't really do that, would you?"

"I was just joking."

I nodded and bit my lip. "I know. And I do want us to have a family one day. But I also really want to finish my degree first and get a job at the clinic and everything."

Tyce softened his voice. "I know that, Gigi. I promise I was joking. I want you to get your degree too. And I know our pack forbids it, and there would probably be a huge uproar if we lifted the ban on contraceptives now, but maybe we should consider going to a human doctor so you can get on something. Until you're ready, of course."

I nodded. I had been raised very conservatively just like Tyce. So even though I could have gotten on some sort of contraceptive while in my first year of college, it still somehow felt wrong. Even if I wasn't personally religious. I guess it was hard to shake a lifetime of values being force-fed to you.

"All good?" he asked, rubbing my back affectionately.

"All good," I replied, leaning into the movement of his hand and the trail of soothing sparks it left behind. I inadvertently let out a whimper.

"Fuck, I love when you do that." Tyce's other hand grasped my hip. "Do we have time?"

"No," I responded, practically whimpering again. "We promised Trav we'd be there at two."

He groaned, "Okay, fine."

We finally managed to unwind ourselves from each other and made it out to Tyce's douchey car. I did have to reluctantly admit, it worked great in Alaskan conditions. We made the trek to Trav's pack on the expensive plowed roads and made it just about on time.

When we arrived, I couldn't help but glance at Sara's stomach. She certainly didn't look pregnant. She was just as sinewy as ever. She may have bulked up a bit, but mostly in her arms and legs. Definitely not in her torso.

"What's good, little bro?" Tyce slapped Trav's hand and pulled him in for a man-hug, patting his back a few times.

"Welcome back, Gigi." Trav gave me a hug in greeting after Tyce. Sara simply nodded at us. Not the affectionate type, that one.

We then converged in Trav's bougie living room, unchanged from when Alpha Vic ran the place. I imagined that, although it likely was to neither of their tastes, they also weren't the type to take up interior design. I then wondered if I'd be allowed to make some changes to the packhouse I lived in after I officially became luna, or if those decisions would continue to be Luna Catherine's and Luna Julia's. It was odd to think that although I'd officially be luna soon, I really wouldn't have much control at all, furthering my desire to have something I did have control over, such as my career.

"So, news?" Tyce asked after we'd settled in our seats and Trav had brought over some waters and snacks for us.

I nervously fidgeted with my water. Now that Julia had gotten it into my head that Sara was expecting, I couldn't imagine the news being anything else.

"I'll let Sara tell you," Trav said, giving her sturdy thigh a squeeze. *Oh shit. Maybe Julia was right.*

"This." Sara undid the lid of a jar and handed it to Tyce. "Smell."

He sniffed it and looked up at her with confusion on his face. "Alpine Snow Pack? From Anchorage, right?"

"I found someone's fur frozen in ice and brought it back."

"From where?" Tyce handed me the jar to smell and shook his head in a gesture that said he'd known his mom was wrong. He then turned back toward Sara and leaned forward, raising his eyebrows at her.

"Not too far from here," Sara replied. "I've been doing my normal rounds, traveling within a twenty-five-mile radius of our packs, and those motherfuckers are coming up here now. They clearly want something from us."

"Why would you assume that?" Tyce asked.

"Because there are no other packs in this area except ours," Trav replied. "What other reason could they possibly have for coming here, especially in the dead of winter? There's literally nothing except dark, cold, and oil rigs."

"But we have no disputes with them."

"No known disputes," Sara corrected. "Neutral packs become enemy packs all the time. It's all about who gets to them first and has something to offer."

"It's that pack from near Galena. They're probably still pissed we refused to join their lame scrimmage a couple years ago," Tyce said.

"We can't assume anything," Trav replied. "Anyway, we appreciate all the help you've been giving our pack, so we'll have our warriors keep an eye on things for now and keep you posted on any new developments. So far, they haven't come too close to our borders."

"Good," Tyce responded, clapping his hands together. "So now that we have that news out of the way, want to do a little sparring?"

Sara jumped right up. "Let's go!"

Sara and Trav brought us over to their warrior gym, which, hot damn, was impressive. It seemed like something that would fit in far better in LA than out here, in a dilapidated pack, where the sun never came out.

"Trav, you take your brother!" Sara shouted as soon as we stepped into the sparring court. "I've got Gigi."

The way she said it felt a bit threatening. A shiver traveled up my spine. I'd learned more about Sara in the past few months. She was ruthless and had tortured and attempted to murder her brother's mate. But there was no way she'd do that to me, right?

Tyce and Trav got right to work.

I turned to Sara, and she had a pretty malicious smile on her face. *Fuck! Should I be scared?*

"You start," Sara offered, showing her palm and bowing slightly. Okay, that was pretty polite.

I decided to practice one of my kicks, since that was something Tyce and I had spent the last couple weeks working on. Sara stood stock-still, her hands behind her back, as I came closer to her. I noted that she hadn't even put her hair into a ponytail but had left her long blonde bob, which always looked shiny and perfectly blown out, loose. I ran toward her, ready to kick. But as soon as I extended my leg, her palm closed around it. I swear to Artemis, she barely even moved a muscle as she lifted my leg until I lost contact with the ground and then fell crashing down to the wood floor with a loud *oomph*. As my back made impact, I swear both my lungs popped.

"Hey! Go easy on her!" Tyce practically flew to my side. He had murder in his eyes as he limbered up his shoulders and neck as if he was readying himself for a fight.

"She sucks," Sara stated simply.

"She doesn't suck!"

Sara rolled her eyes at him. "Goddess, you have to be blind *and* stupid to think she doesn't suck. It's kill or be killed, and this bitch is getting killed because you've gone way too easy on her. Now get out of the way." She shoved Tyce, then turned to me. "So, Gigi, are you going to train for real or accept your death?"

I groaned as I got myself up onto my palms. It was true. Tyce did go easy on me. He'd never actually put up a real fight. How was I supposed to battle our actual enemies? Especially now, with the threat of some pack from near Anchorage casing our territories—a pack that would have easy access to me once I went back to school.

"Sara's right. You are too easy on me. I need someone who will challenge me."

"*She's psycho!*" Tyce mindlinked me. I waved him off.

"See. Your girlfriend knows what's up." Sara smiled that same devious smile again, like she knew she'd be carving me for dinner tonight and would enjoy every second of it.

I got up, in position to fight. Tyce lingered a bit but eventually turned back to his brother. As soon as his back was turned, Sara approached, and swooped her right leg under my feet, instantly tripping me before I even had a chance to react.

Again, I crumpled to the floor, slamming against the hardwood. Tyce, again, turned his entire attention to me and looked as if he was about to slice Sara open.

"Tyce! I'm fine!" I yelled. "I can't do this with you watching me!"

"Bitch doesn't even know how to block." Sara shook her head.

"Watch who you're calling a bitch!" Tyce shouted with clenched fists, clearly barely holding himself back from driving them into her.

"Pardon," Sara said, not really sounding apologetic, but that was probably the best he was going to get from her.

"It's okay, Tyce!" I said, wishing he'd just let up.

"Maybe she's right, Tyce," Trav intervened. "Gigi is going to have to learn how to defend herself. And you're too worried about her getting hurt to train her properly. She's a werewolf. She'll heal. Maybe let Sara train her for a while."

I could see there was conflict in Tyce's eyes. I knew how he felt about Sara, that she was a psycho and probably not safe to leave me alone with. Though he couldn't say that to his brother about his mate. But, also, Trav and Sara were both right. Tyce wasn't going to train me properly. He *was* too afraid to let me get hurt. And Sara was really fucking good. If I could learn to even be half as good as her, then maybe I'd have a chance at survival, if it ever came down to it.

"She *is* right," I said with confidence. "And Trav is right too. I am a werewolf. I will heal even if Sara fucks me up. I need this, Tyce. No pain, no gain, right?"

"I don't think you understand how fucked-up you can get and still heal," Tyce said.

I got up and rebutted, "Well, maybe it's time for me to understand! I'm not ever going to be a half-decent luna if I don't train like an alpha!"

He crossed his arms across his chest and pinched his lips together. We all stared at him, waiting for him to respond. Finally, he exclaimed, "Fine!" And before anyone else could speak, he approached Sara, and with clenched fists and hard eyes, he said, "But if Gigi ends up in the hospital or you do any permanent damage to her, I will kill you with my bare, cold hands. I don't care if you're my brother's mate."

"Tyce, don't be dramatic!" I tried to pat his arm. But it was solid, flexed, and unmoving. I'd never witnessed him like this before. Trav also seemed to have paled a bit.

"I think that's enough sparring for today." Trav finally broke the silence.

"I'll see you tomorrow at noon." Sara nodded at me and walked away without another word.

Chapter 15

Theresa

"There you are!" My mom grabbed me by my mock-neck collar as soon as I entered the dining area. My pulse quickened at the gesture, but I instantly relaxed upon seeing she was facing the other direction and dragging me toward the kitchen. At least this wasn't about *that*.

I hadn't even had the time to imagine why she was dragging me by the collar as if I were a dog when she planted me in front of our cook. "It's about time you learn how to make borscht. Your future mate will be expecting it," my mom said. "Every good Ukrainian wife knows how to make a good borscht."

"Every good Ukrainian wife?" I asked, lifting an eyebrow. While I knew I was technically half-Ukrainian, I'd certainly never been raised as if I were. We never ate her home country's food, even with a cook who was from her home country. And in all likelihood, I'd find my mate in the very country I was currently standing in. So it defeated all logic for her to suddenly state that I needed to prepare to be a "good Ukrainian wife."

"Yes, yes, Terri. Tasha is going to teach you tonight. I've already invited Alpha Nikolai to eat dinner with us. I'm sure you'll do a good job for him." She tilted the corners of her mouth upward in what, I think, was supposed to be a smile, gave me a nod and a wink, then turned and walked away.

"Ready?" Tasha asked, gesturing toward some large cabbages that were sitting on the counter.

"I guess," I replied. My goodness, this was so weird. But part of me was a bit curious about borscht. I'd never tried it before, and certainly never cooked it.

"We start with the stock. We got a shipment of pork the other day, so we have that." She patted a slab of meat. "Here." She handed me a chef's knife.

I followed her instructions, and she observed and corrected my errors as I went. Soon we had the meat boiling with vegetables to create the broth. She then showed me how to cut the cabbage properly, and we peeled and grated the beets and scrubbed and cut up potatoes together. Once the broth was ready, we added the grated beets and potato cubes. We then sautéed the carrots and onions until they were caramelized and added them to the soup along with the cabbage.

Two hours later, the soup was ready.

"It'll be better tomorrow, but Yulia wants to eat it tonight," Tasha said. "Here, let's prepare the sides."

We chopped up some fresh parsley, which presumably came from the greenhouse. Tasha then put me to work dicing garlic while she surprised me by pulling a loaf out of the oven. "I made the traditional brown bread to go with it," she said. "You can take credit in front of the alpha." She gave me a wink and pinched my cheek. "He's a beautiful man, that alpha. Very quiet though. He needs someone talkative like you to fill the silence."

"There's nothing wrong with quiet," I responded, not sure what else to say.

"No, but it's lonely. A happy home is one filled with lots of love and noise. So you can't think about how wrong everything is, because everything that's right is distracting you too much. Now, let me go see if everyone is seated yet, so you can start serving them the meal you made. Just like a good Ukrainian woman." She elbowed me playfully as she stepped past me to check the dining room.

I leaned against the counter and let out a breath. The door to the kitchen swung open and my eyes darted upward, expecting the return of Tasha.

Instead, I was greeted with his luxurious scent and silver eyes.

"*Privet!*" I greeted him, using one of the very few Russian words I knew.

"*Privet,*" he mumbled in return. He sniffed a few times but didn't say anything. He just stood, staring at me, his eyes piercing into me.

"Are you looking for something?" I asked.

He opened his mouth but was distracted by Tasha reentering the room. "*Alpha, poydem.*" Tasha tugged at his arm and pulled him out of the kitchen. I was both a bit thankful, since he always seemed to make things pretty awkward, but also a bit disappointed. There was something that drew me to him. Something I didn't really understand.

Tasha was soon back, and we filled bowls together. She pushed me to bring the first two out. I entered the dining room to everyone gathered around the table—my grandma, my parents, Tyce and Gigi, and Nikolai.

"First bowl goes to our guest of honor," my mom said, gesturing to Nikolai, as soon as I entered the room. I gently placed it in front of him. "See how talented my daughter is?" she boasted. "Beautiful, educated, and a good cook. A perfect mate."

"A great mate for her *fated mate*," my dad interjected as I placed his soup in front of him.

"Are you so sure she hasn't met him yet?" my mom responded. "Perhaps the fated mates are just shy about announcing their bond."

"Julia, what are you going on about?"

"I'm just saying, I can understand if Terri or anyone else in this house might want to wait a bit before letting us know about their bond. It's nice to get to know each other as mates first and involve parents after."

"Woman, stop involving everyone in your delusions," my dad replied. "You have two mated children now. Terri's time will come when it comes."

I returned to the kitchen to fill and bring out some more soup bowls, and Tasha followed after me. Soon we had everything laid out, and I took a seat in front of mine.

"What is this?" my grandmother, Catherine, asked. "Why is it red?"

"It's borscht," I replied.

"What is borscht?"

"It's a beet soup from Ukraine."

"Why are we eating this for dinner? We never eat this."

"I'd like to know too," my father agreed.

"We are just trying to make Nikolai welcome!" Mom replied. "I'm sure he misses his favorite foods from home. Here, add some sour cream, garlic, and parsley." She handed my dad the bowl of sour cream.

"This is pretty good!" Tyce chimed in. "Is that pork? It's cooked perfectly. Nice and tender. Nice job, sis!"

"It's really good, Terri! I really like it," Gigi agreed.

"It's not part of my diet," Catherine said, pushing her bowl away, getting up, and walking out of the room.

"Sorry about my grandma," I said to Nikolai, thinking he might get offended that she didn't like the food from his home. "She lost her mate a few months ago and hasn't been the same since."

"I'm sorry," Nikolai replied. "I don't know how it is to lose mate . . . but loss, I understand." And a cloud seemed to be cast on the table.

I reached for the sour cream to try adding some of the toppings my mom recommended we add.

"That's not for you, Terri," my mom snapped at me. I pulled my hand back, and she handed me the parsley instead.

My dad moved his spoon around the bowl and didn't say anything.

After Tyce took some sour cream for his own soup and then offered some to Gigi, my mom glared at the couple. Tyce glared right back at her as he added sour cream to Gigi's bowl.

"Well, Alpha, what do you think?" my mom asked as Nikolai took his first sip of the soup.

"It's good," he replied.

"It's nice having a beautiful woman cook you a hot meal, right?"

My cheeks heated. Goodness, why was my mom making this dinner so awkward?

"Mm," Nikolai responded noncommittally.

"Terri can cook all sorts of wonderful dishes. What would you like to try next?"

Nikolai let out a breath and then said, "I am happy with Tasha's cooking, and I am happy also to eat American food. Terri does not need to make extra effort for me."

"But Terri is more than happy to make extra effort for you."

Could my mom make it any more obvious what she was doing? My body was on fire with embarrassment. I was ready to tear my mock-neck off with how uncomfortably hot my neck and chest burned.

"No need, Luna," Nikolai replied politely. He finally set his spoon down, his expression unreadable. But for a moment, I swore I saw something flicker behind those silver eyes. Annoyance? Frustration? Or something else entirely?

"Of course there is! We are hosting you here in our home, and we must treat you as the valued guest you are."

"Fucking Artemis, Julia! Will you lay off the man?" my dad snapped.

My mom began to open her mouth, and he cut her off before she could speak. "And do we have anything else to eat?"

"This is a special mea—" my mom started to explain.

She didn't even finish her sentence before he got up, letting his spoon drop, splashing soup in its wake. The legs of his chair scraped against the floor as he pushed himself back from the table. Without another word, he turned and strode toward the kitchen. My mom rose too, as if to follow, but then she just stood there, watching him disappear behind the closed door.

I supposed that may have answered the mystery as to why we'd never had Ukrainian food previously.

"Big pimpin' out Te-e-ri," Tyce sang out. "We doin' big pimpin' up in Jade Moon P."

Gigi snickered behind her hand. Nikolai just continued to look down at his bowl, acting like nothing out of the ordinary was happening around him.

I was ready to crawl under the table, lie down, and die. I was so dizzy with mortification, I couldn't guarantee I wouldn't do just that. RIP Terri Tikaani.

"Tyson!" my mom barked. He immediately straightened up and stopped. She then sat down in front of her own bowl of soup, and with defeat in her shoulders and a quiet sigh anyone could have easily missed, she picked at her own soup. The whole table was silent.

I glanced down at my bowl and moved my spoon around. My stomach was heavy with nausea. And even though I lived in a constant state of starvation, I couldn't bring myself to eat it. I wanted to ask to be excused from the table, but I knew it wouldn't go over well. So I just stared at the swirling reddish-pink liquid, pretending I wasn't there.

My father eventually returned with some leftovers Tasha must have reheated for him. With contentment on his face, he sat down and happily ate his meal. Everyone ate. Silently. I wanted to throw up.

How was I supposed to continue living in the same house as Nikolai after everything that had happened up until this point? Especially with how my mom acted tonight, offering me up to him like prized livestock so shamelessly.

When everyone finally started to finish up and file out, I couldn't sprint out of the dining room and into my bedroom fast enough. I had to be in my safe space. Maybe forever. I just wouldn't leave my bedroom until it was finally time to go back to school.

I was about to crawl under my covers and listen to loud music to try to block everything out when a knock on my door sounded. I froze. Shoot. What if it was Nikolai? Oh gosh, I definitely couldn't face him. Maybe I could just ignore it. Pretend I already had my headphones on and couldn't hear.

Knock knock.

Knock knock.

"It's Tyce. Open up!"

All the tension released from my body. "Come in."

The door creaked open and he stepped onto the threshold, his huge alpha body taking up most of the doorway. Sometimes I forgot how huge he was, because I'd grown up with him and still remembered how small he'd once been. Not that he was ever that small for a kid, but relative to his size now. "Hey, are you okay?" he asked. I looked up, and he had his eyebrows drawn together in concern, his eyes warm with empathy.

"Yeah, I'm fine," I replied, thinking that would be good enough. Then he could feel good that he checked on me, but he didn't have to worry about me because I said I was fine. It was like an unwritten rule in our family. Just act like everything was okay so no one was ever uncomfortable.

"Are you sure?"

"Yeah, why wouldn't I be?"

"You just . . ." He paused, took a breath, and continued, "You didn't look fine during dinner. And what Mom did was really weird. And not okay. And if you want me to talk to her, I will."

"You don't have to do that."

"But I want to." He paused again, rubbed his neck, and glanced down at the floor. After a moment, he looked back up. "I know I haven't always been the best brother or much of an alpha really. But I'm making an effort now. And I've realized that part of being an alpha means you stand up for people that don't have the power to stand up for themselves. Ever since I brought Gigi here, I've realized how fucked this family is and how shitty they treat everyone. And you don't deserve that, Terr."

He stepped forward, reaching his hand out. I stiffened, not used to affection from him. He paused, as if he was unsure if he should touch me or not, but finally resolved to pat my shoulder. Very awkwardly, I must add.

"I'm okay," I said, not sure what else to say. I wasn't ready to have some sort of heart-to-heart with my brother. Part of me wanted to—to just let everything go, to tell him how I felt, let the tears flow. I knew he'd understand. After all, he'd grown up in the same house. But I just wasn't at a point where I could be vulnerable like that. I wore my happiness like armor. As long as everyone believed I was fine, I was strong and in control.

"Okay," he said, following that unspoken rule. When someone told you they were okay, believe them. He finally removed his hand from my shoulder and stepped back. Before he turned to go, he said, "But if you ever want me to talk to either Mom or Dad, for any reason at all, just let me know. I promise I will, 'k?"

"'K."

He nodded, satisfied with my response, and left. I shut the door behind him and fell into my bed. And then I let go of what I was holding in. The tears flowed. Not from embarrassment or sadness. But from happiness. That someone cared. Someone had taken the time to come to my room to make sure I was okay. Because someone had noticed I wasn't well at dinner. It must have said something that I cried over that moment. Because how many times had that actually happened before in my life?

Chapter 16

Julia

29 years ago

By the time I got to high school, I had one goal. Get out of this shithole.

While perhaps there may have been some advantages to being part of the beta family, no one was untouched by the poverty caused by communism. And while most had accepted this as a card they'd been dealt, there had always been a fire deep within me that knew—yes, just knew—that I was not meant for this middle-of-nowhere country-bumpkin life. In my heart, I could sense that I was too big for the pack I'd been born into.

My older brother would be beta one day, even if it was in some dilapidated pack where the electricity didn't even work half the time. Being a beta's daughter, however, meant that I wasn't destined for anything more than to be some nobody forest-boy's mate. If I stayed here, I'd never have even the slightest chance of meeting someone outside Severnaya Zvezda Pack.

But once the Soviet Union fell a few days after the winter solstice in 1991, I began to have some hope. Perhaps one day my feet would touch the soil of another country.

And so began my campaign. I would go to university in America.

How did I do it? I convinced everyone I wanted to be a pack doctor, something we and the nearby packs desperately needed. My grades were top tier (my mother made sure of that), and I always presented myself as mature and polished. Once I applied and got into a great premed program in the US, all the nearby packs came together to come up with the funds necessary for the exorbitant tuition. I probably should have felt a little bad. Maybe there was a pinch in my chest a couple of times. But I pushed it down. The important thing was that I was out.

A couple weeks into school, I met Gabe.

He was the only other werewolf in my Biology 101 class, and so we naturally became lab partners. And when I found out his father was the alpha of his pack, his fate was sealed. If there was one thing I was good at, it was seduction.

And Gabe was easy. So, so easy.

It started with a lot of touching and complimenting. I could tell that this man, who had always been overshadowed by his brother, needed the validation. "You are so smart," I would say every time he came up with an answer to our work. "Goddess, I wish I were as intelligent as you." He was too stupid to notice that I'd been doing most of the work the whole time.

After a week, he began asking me to hang out with him outside of class. I made sure I always had plans. I knew he'd need to feel like he'd pursued and conquered me. All men needed to feel that way. Especially insecure ones who needed to believe they were hunters that could take down any prey, even the quickest, cleverest, most elusive prey. And I needed to paint myself as exactly that—not something easy, like a rabbit any man could catch. I was a wild tiger.

I learned his schedule and where he frequented. Partway through October, I sat myself down at the campus café with a tea and my school books.

"Fancy meeting you here," a familiar voice chimed from behind me. A moment later, Gabe dropped into the chair across from me, making himself comfortable.

I barely spared him a glance. "That seat is taken."

He grinned, leaning in slightly. "You sound so sexy when you talk in that accent. Say something in Russian."

I exhaled, flipping a page in my book. "You do not have homework to do?"

"Say that in Russian."

"I'm busy."

"I see that." He grabbed one of my books, tilting it toward himself. "Writing and Communications, huh? I'm in the same class. Who's your professor?"

"Albertson."

"Same. Are you also working on that damn speech?"

"That is what I came here to work on," I replied.

"How's that going?"

I gave the most vulnerable look I could muster and thought of the saddest thing I could think of, watching my little sister pass away at only four years old from leukemia. It was my time of month, so the tear slipped out easily.

"That bad?" he asked, leaning forward and putting his hand on mine.

"It is just so hard, when English is not my first language." I looked up at him through damp lashes. "I wish I could speak like you."

His chest puffed up. "I could help, you know."

"You would do this for me?" I whispered, bowing my head slightly in gratitude.

He straightened his shoulders, basking in the moment. "Why don't you come by my dorm this weekend? We can work on your speech together."

I hesitated, letting my fingers skim the rim of my tea. "Oh, I couldn't. What people would think? Me, go into your dorm room alone?"

"No one will care. I have people over all the time to study. It'll just be as friends."

I let the silence stretch just a moment longer before flashing him a grateful smile. "Oh, okay." Then I bit my lip and dropped my gaze again. "I have to admit something."

"What?"

I leaned forward, my lips brushing his ear as I whispered, "I have never been alone with man before."

I sat back in my chair and fluttered my eyelashes. His Adam's apple bobbed as he swallowed.

It wasn't until the first week of November that I finally let him kiss me. He was a horrible, sloppy, very wet kisser. He didn't know what he was doing with his tongue. But I figured I could slowly teach him to be better. Or perhaps, over time, the kissing would become less and less. Either way, the life he could offer me was worth the small inconvenience.

As the month wore on, he became desperate to fuck me. I threw him breadcrumbs. One day, I let him touch my breasts while fully clothed. Then, a few days later, I unbuttoned my blouse and let him touch them bare. Each new boundary he crossed made him bolder, more frantic, more obsessed.

One evening, I wore a skirt and let him slip his fingers past the elastic of my panties. His breath hitched as he pressed against my entrance, teasing, testing.

"Just do not put them inside," I murmured. "I am saving myself for my mate."

"You're so fucking wet though," he groaned, tracing the slickness with the tip of his finger. "I can make you feel so good."

I let my lashes flutter. "Do they have to go inside?"

His nostrils flared. "Have you ever had an orgasm?"

"What's that?" I asked with eyes wide, playing the role of the innocent, untouched girl he so badly wanted to corrupt.

"Oh, fuck," he choked out. "You're driving me crazy, Julia."

"Why?" I tilted my head, feigning confusion.

"I need to make you orgasm. It's the best fucking feeling in the world."

I hesitated just long enough for him to think he had a chance. "Can you do it without putting your fingers inside me?"

"No."

Was he that clueless, or was this just another attempt at manipulation?

"Oh," I sighed, pulling back just enough for his hand to slip away. "I guess I will have to wait."

He let out a frustrated groan. "Goddess, I'm so hard right now. It *hurts*."

I smirked inwardly but kept my expression blank. "You need to see doctor?"

"No," he huffed. "It just needs to be touched. Please, Julia. Just a little. It'll make it feel better."

I bit my lip, hesitating. "I don't know. My mother told me not to do anything before I meet my mate."

"It's just touching," he urged, taking my hand in his and running his thumb over my palm. "Like when we hold hands."

I pretended to consider, then pulled my hand away. "But we are not dating."

"Of course we are," he responded with no hesitation.

"Oh?" I blinked up at him. "Then I should stop seeing Rich and Scott."

His entire body went rigid. "Who the fuck are Rich and Scott?"

"You know them," I said airily. "Rich is in our bio class. Scott is in my chem lab."

His hands shot to my hips, his grip possessive, bruising. A lesser girl would have gasped at the force, but I only smiled inside. *There it is.*

"You're fucking *mine*, Julia," he growled.

And that was when I knew.

I didn't give him the hand job that day, but I did finally give in a few days later. I was pleased at his generous size. His alpha genetics were on full display as I stroked him to satisfaction. And when he came, he cried out as if he'd finally been gifted everything he'd ever wanted.

"Wow," he sighed. "That was so fucking amazing."

As time inched closer to finals, he only became that much more desperate to be inside me. The closest I would let him get was stroking him as he rubbed his body against mine while we were both naked.

"Goddess, when will you finally let me show you how amazing sex is?" he asked.

"I told you, that is only for my mate," I replied as I dressed myself.

I had just bent to pick up my discarded blouse when his hands caught me, pulling me flush against his bare chest. "I could be your mate," he said with conviction.

I blinked up at him. "What?"

He grabbed my waist tighter. "I mean, c'mon, why not? We're in love, right?"

I let the pause stretch, just long enough to make him second-guess himself, before answering. "But . . ." I started, voice small.

"No buts," he interrupted. "I'll bring you home over Christmas break. We'll tell my parents together. That I'm choosing you. Taking you as a chosen mate." He searched my face, desperate for agreement. "It makes sense anyway, right? You're the daughter of a beta. Alpha and beta families mate to form alliances all the time. My dad can't say no to that."

I let my lips part slightly, as if his words had left me breathless. "And then we could be together . . . for real."

"Exactly."

"You are so smart, Gabe. I would be lucky to have mate like you—so strong, so handsome . . ." I let my voice drop lower, eyes wide with faux innocence. "So good at teaching me how to be woman."

His whole body tensed. His pupils darkened. He was already getting hard again.

"I can't wait to make love to you," he groaned, pulling me closer. His hands skimmed up my thighs, fingers slipping beneath my skirt, into my panties—finding me without hesitation.

I let him have that moment, let him think he was getting somewhere, then tore myself away just as quickly. "Not until we mark each other," I said firmly.

His frustration twisted into something darker. "I said we're mates," he snapped. "It's as good as done." He reached for me again, but this time, I stepped out of his grasp.

I let a flicker of doubt cross my face. "How I can trust you?" I whispered. "How I know you will not say this now, then leave me for your fated mate?" My voice trembled, sharp with doubt. "More you push, more I think this is what you will do."

His mouth dropped open, but before he could argue, I grabbed my shirt, threw it on, and slipped out the door.

Then I avoided him for the next few days. Until he finally tracked me down and put a plane ticket in my hand. "I'm your mate. Now tell your family you won't be seeing them for winter solstice."

Chapter 17

Nikolai

There hadn't been much improvement in training. I reminded myself we'd only been here for a short while. These things took time. In our pack, we had never expected anything of our women, not even to pass the bare minimum physical requirements that packs in the US apparently had. While I'd come to understand that Tyce's pack was considered traditional for the standards here, they were still far more progressive than the vast majority of packs in Eastern Europe.

Before the war, it had made sense. Women were to be protected and cherished. They made a house a home, a dead animal a meal, a mating a family. Each gender brought its own strength. But what if a pack was only forty, half of which were women? Then what?

We no longer had families. We ate for survival, not for enjoyment. And mates? What of them? Sasha wasn't wrong. We did need to increase our numbers. But it was also irresponsible. We hadn't set up our permanent residence. We were still reliant on the Jade Moon Pack for everything. It wasn't right to bring them more mouths to feed and heads to bed.

No, I needed to be a leader to my pack. I needed to make us independent. And that was why, in the dead of this Alaskan winter, I was once again going to venture out to set up our pack. Sasha would stay behind and lead and train our people. I was the alpha, and I was ultimately responsible, so I would battle the relentless cold.

I packed what I could fit into my carry pack. It wasn't really enough, but Sasha and I had at least fixed up a small, abandoned cabin we'd found the last time we'd gone. So I would have some form of shelter, granted it had no heat or running water.

I made my way downstairs to have my last home-cooked meal before my journey. Tasha had gone above and beyond this time, well aware of my plans. She placed a stack of a half dozen fluffy pancakes, a three-egg omelet, fried potatoes, and thick sliced, perfectly cooked bacon in front of me.

I savored every bite as I wolfed it all down. It would be a long journey, and prey was sure to not be abundant. I needed all the calories I could get.

"Where's Sasha?" Yulia stopped me and asked just as I was swinging the travel pack over my shoulder on my way out the door.

"It's only me this time," I replied.

"You can't go out alone. Not out here."

"I'll be fine."

"No." She crossed her arms, and her eyes pierced me. "You could be leaving your pack without an alpha. It's not safe out there. I don't care how trained you are. The winter here turns even the toughest men into feeble boys. How would anyone know to help you if something happens?"

"I'll be fine," I reiterated. She acted like I didn't *come from* the cold. As if the climate wasn't the same where I'd been born, raised, and trained. As if my own father hadn't forced me to survive in pitch-black bitter cold for weeks at a time. As if we hadn't won battles simply because opposing packs *couldn't* survive the climate that we could.

"Why isn't Sasha going?" she asked, not letting this go.

"The pack needs training. They need a leader here while I'm not."

She continued to stare me down, her arms stiffly folded across her chest. She was a petite, polished woman, one who didn't have the appearance of someone who had ever even stepped onto a battlefield, but she had mastered the alpha stare. I was sure she'd drawn a whimper from a man or two with that look.

"I'll be off," I said and was about to turn to go when she grabbed my arm to stop me.

"Take Theresa with you."

"What?" I choked on my breath and took a step back.

"She's well trained. She knows what to do in emergencies. And she's not busy. She doesn't go back to school until almost February."

"I assure you, I'll be fine without Theresa," I replied. It took everything in me not to yell. My heart pounded and heat flushed through my body. I'd had enough of her trying to set me up with her daughter. How many times could I rebuff all her antics before she'd get the hint that I wasn't interested. Not in anyone, and most certainly not the sister of the alpha of the pack I was currently indebted to.

"Lance!" Yulia called, and I let out a heavy breath. I should've known she wouldn't take no for an answer. "Come with me." She pulled on the sleeve of my coat. And while I could've easily shaken her off and left, I knew I had to be polite. Because she was still the former luna of the pack my entire pack was inhabiting. And it would not do well to piss her off. Especially since she was the only reason we'd been able to come here.

I let her drag me toward her mate's office like a dog on a leash.

"Lance!" she shouted again as she pushed the door to his office open.

"What?" His eyes shot up to the two of us. "Goddess, what is it?"

"This young man wants to go out into the wilderness alone. He is crazy. No one should ever go out there alone."

I shook my head. "I am fine. My pack must train, and beta must stay to train them. I already went this path. I am used to cold."

"Julia, let him be. He's an alpha. He knows what he's doing, and you're not his mom." Lance turned back to his phone.

"He should take Terri with him," Yulia explained. "She could help him if something happens. We never allow anyone in our pack to travel alone. It's for good reason."

"You know what." Lance looked up, and a smirk appeared on his face. "That girl has been getting weak. She slacked with her training in school. Time out in the Alaskan wild would be good for her. I've been going too easy on her."

Yulia nodded her approval.

"Go get Terri ready to go. I'll have a talk with Nikolai," Lance said and gestured to the chair in front of his desk.

Yulia practically skipped out of his office. I likely lost a centimeter of teeth from grinding them so hard. It took everything in me not to flip Lance's desk. What could he possibly be thinking?

He pulled a knife out of the top drawer of his desk and stroked it between his thumb and pointer finger. A typical threatening alpha tactic. "I'm assuming you'd like to make an heir one day."

"I would," I confirmed, not sure where this conversation was heading.

"So you'd say your balls are important to you?"

I kept my expression neutral, though my grip on the chair tightened. Lance smiled at that.

"I'm trusting you out there with my daughter. That means she better come back alive and in one piece, completely untouched."

"Of course I make sure your daughter is safe," I responded.

"And untouched."

"And untouched," I repeated.

"Completely, 100 percent untouched. Not even a paw accidentally brushing up against her."

"I assure you, I will not touch your daughter. I have no interest."

"Good." He smiled a pretty fucked-up smile. "Because while stabbing assholes is my favorite torture activity, I quite enjoy slicing balls off too." My fingers twitched slightly at that. "And I can't guarantee I won't do both if I have you chained up."

I knew he wasn't fucking with me. I knew he had every intention to do what he'd threatened me with, and it would bring him nothing but pleasure. But I was determined to stay in control, focus on my pack and only my pack. "As I said, I have no desire to touch your daughter."

"Then it sounds like we can expect an heir for your pack eventually." Lance nonchalantly slid the knife back into the top drawer of his desk.

"With all this worry, how dangerous this trek will be . . . why allow your daughter to go at all?" I asked, hoping he might see some sense and allow me to go alone.

"It's not the trek I'm worried about," he replied, leaning back in his chair. "Let me put it this way. My Terri can handle the coldest of winters and the most rabid of bears. It's men I don't trust. So if you have no desire to touch her, as you say, then I see no need to worry."

I glanced down toward my lap, giving in.

Before long, Yulia returned with Terri by her side. "She's ready to go." Yulia pushed her daughter toward me.

I gave a curt nod, careful not to show any emotion. On the inside, I was seething. The last thing I needed was to babysit the pack princess and put up with her annoying pranks again. I walked past both Terri and her mom, and as I strutted toward the front door, I said over my shoulder, "Let's go." Every follicle on my skin was tingling with the need to shift. I was pissed.

I didn't even bother to glance behind me, but I knew she was following because I could scent her. It was another reason she was more of a burden than a resource. That scent was fucking distracting. And now that I would be forced into my wolf form, it would be that much harder to hide the effects it had on me. *Boginya moya*! It was like I was a teenager all over again! My dick getting hard from just a slight breeze on it.

As soon as we stepped outside, I began stripping. If I didn't shift soon, I couldn't guarantee I wouldn't flip out.

"Oh, um," she started. I looked up and she immediately glanced at the ground. Her cheeks were rosy—but it wasn't clear if it was due to the cold or embarrassment. "I'm just going to go find a rock or something to shift behind."

I nodded and she walked away, taking her damn scent with her.

As soon as everything was tightly packed into my travel pack, I shifted into my wolf form, then put the strap into my mouth and swung the pack so it would land on the back of my neck. It wasn't the most comfortable way to travel. In fact, it was the opposite of that, but there wasn't much other choice. I needed equipment, and we couldn't exactly drive where we were going at this time of year.

As soon as Terri reappeared in her wolf form, I sprinted ahead. Her scent followed not far behind me. I just had to stay the course and focus on the destination. Nothing else. Fortunately, there would be no conversation, which was one of the downsides of traveling with Sasha. Since he could mindlink me, I had to listen to his chattering, something I no longer enjoyed. But since Terri and I were in different packs, it would be perfect, sweet silence with only the howling of the frosty wind in the background.

She obediently followed me across the tundra. Not that she had much choice but to do so. We eventually fell into a comfortable pace (for me, at least). If Terri thought it was too fast, she didn't let out even one whine to indicate so. While I tried my hardest not to care, there was a part of me that wondered if she was okay and worried she was maybe just playing tough. Perhaps I should have been more considerate. After all, it wasn't like she'd asked to come with me. She'd been forced into the situation as much as I had been. But I couldn't soften myself. I'd gone through far worse than this. It was time for little miss *princessa* to learn some mental toughness.

We traversed the snow for hours. By evening, Terri's stomach grumbled, cutting through the silence of the frozen wilderness. I turned my head to sneak a peek at her, and she kept her focus facing ahead, marching on.

Again, her stomach grumbled.

I had planned to make it farther before attempting to hunt, as I had learned game was a bit more abundant a good dozen or so kilometers away still, but something inside me stopped my feet in their tracks. I physically couldn't ignore her hunger. It was as if my willpower had been overtaken by the aching need to fix what was wrong with Terri. She stopped next to me and tilted her head in a look of confusion.

I pointed my nose toward the open tundra and nodded. I'm sure she understood. She followed me into the pitch-black landscape and switched off her night vision as soon as I did. It was time to hunt using our other senses.

We stuck side by side as we crept into the icy terrain, scenting along our path, perking our ears for any sounds of scavenging. Terri crept along, just as stealthy as me. Not a single crunch of snow under her paws could be heard. We both moved swiftly, synchronized, weaving around rocky outcroppings and snowdrifts, as if we had coordinated a dance. Well . . . that was unexpected.

Perhaps, I grudgingly admitted to myself, my irritation with her earlier was more out of habit than for a valid reason.

Suddenly, Terri stopped. We both heard it. The snap of a willow twig and a heartbeat. The wind carried the scent of the unsuspecting prey toward us. Moose.

In a matter of seconds, we were both rushing toward it. This would be no easy feat. Moose were huge and known to take out actual wolves. I, myself, had witnessed one being swung into the trunk of a tree, its ribs shattering upon impact. Real wolves only hunted them when their need for food outweighed their fear of death.

However, we were werewolves. Which meant that even if a moose dealt a terrible blow, we'd heal. So we were better off attempting to take this one down than continuing our search for prey, which was hard to come by this time of year. Either way, I was now driven by my innate desire to make sure I fed Terri, and as soon as possible. So even if I thought another animal could be found, I wouldn't have been able to turn away.

We chased the moose until we were able to get it cornered against a steep, snow-covered ridge. I placed myself in front of the moose and turned my night vision on to better see what I was doing. There was no longer any point to keeping it off. I went in for the kill. Snapping at its nose and slashing my claws at its face. Terri immediately joined in, doing the same from the back of the moose.

It attempted to kick and bite at us. Between my dodges, I glanced toward Terri, and I almost found myself forgetting what I was doing as I watched her catlike precision in weakening the animal. She had the most beautiful, feline leap, and she meticulously slashed her claws into the flesh in a way that was almost artistic.

At one point, she dodged an awkward, unexpected kick, and I flinched, anticipating her fall. But she landed perfectly, not a single hair out of place.

The moose slammed its hoof into me, and I stumbled backward into a snowbank. *Blyad*! That was stupid. And embarrassing!

As I was righting myself from my fall, I glanced up. Although Terri had been going hard before, she was now clearly giving it her all. She went from simply fighting to killing. She slashed and bit until the moose was sufficiently weakened. Finally, she plunged her claws into its chest and pulled its pulsing heart free. She slammed her entire bodyweight into it.

The large mammal toppled over and crashed into the snow, splattering its blood and darkening the unsullied white earth.

My jaw fell to the ground.

I'd never seen a she-wolf hunt like that.

She tilted her head and gestured to the animal, as if she were saying, *Ready for your meal?* And then I realized a woman serving me a human meal maybe didn't do that much for me, however, a woman serving me the hunt she just killed in front of me was definitely my kink. A kink I had no idea I had until that moment.

I nodded toward the moose, silently urging her to take the first bite. After all, I was a gentleman. She held my gaze for a moment, then finally gave in, sinking her teeth into the warm flesh. I watched, amused, as she tore into the meal with unrestrained hunger. A strange satisfaction settled in my chest—something primal, something deeper than mere duty. I had provided for her, and that simple fact filled me with an unexpected sense of contentment.

I eventually pried my eyes away and similarly chowed down. We stayed like that for some time. Just standing around a moose carcass in the silent, dark Alaska wilderness, the only sound that of our chewing. And while I had hunted and eaten my kill with many others in the past, somehow this instance felt much more intimate. For a brief moment, I even forgot everything that had been worrying me. I just enjoyed the moment for what it was, inhaling her beautiful scent, sharing a meal we'd worked together to procure, and savoring the fresh, warm meat.

After we'd finished and continued on our journey, I decided to become more considerate of my companion. While it was clear she could keep up with me, I still decided to watch my pace, and observe her to make sure she wasn't overly exerting herself. Fuck. When did I start caring about how she was holding up?

It seemed like perhaps the outer edge of my frozen heart had formed a crack.

Chapter 18

Theresa

There was a shift in Nikolai. I didn't even know how I so definitively understood this. One moment, he was his usual grumpy self, with dark clouds hanging over him. And the next moment, something just seemed lighter about him.

At first, I thought I imagined it. But as we traveled, something was . . . different. His shoulders weren't as tense. His ears weren't flicking back toward every sound like they usually did. And when I stumbled over uneven snow, his head turned—just for a second—before he returned his focus forward.

I didn't think I'd ever felt so in tune with someone before. I'd never been so aware of someone's mood, especially someone that was well practiced at keeping a poker face. But the longer we traveled together, the less I could ignore it.

After following him for over twelve hours, he made an abrupt stop. I can't lie. I was relieved. My legs felt like they would give if we continued much longer, but I knew not to complain to an alpha. I'd learned that lesson over and over again in my life. If I ever showed any type of emotion that was inconvenient to my father, or even one that made me appear weak, it never went over well. When I was a child, it was more in the form of neglect. Negative emotions would cause my father to pull away from me. If I cried, he'd walk out of the room and slam the door behind him, muttering that I needed to buck up on his way out. But as I got older, and he became more involved in my rearing, it meant that he would only push me that much harder or make me complete tasks that were that much more difficult.

I still vividly recall my father making me jog through snow in my human form, in just a T-shirt and shorts, and no shoes, in the dead of winter, at only thirteen years old. It'd felt as if needles were piercing the veins of my feet, and the cold wind burned my arms and cheeks. My muscles stiffened so much, I could barely force my joints to move. My teeth clattered so violently that I couldn't believe they didn't fall out. I grew number and number, tears froze on my cheeks and turned to icicles on my chin.

"Stop crying and run faster," he said. He didn't even yell it. And that somehow made it worse. It was as if he had no emotional capacity, not even enough to react in anger. He was dead inside. A robot training me to be a robot like him. And the next time around, he said, "We're going to do it again. If you don't cry, we can finish in twenty minutes. If you do, we'll drag it out to forty."

So, over time, I learned that negative emotions were to be avoided at all costs. They were a liability. If I wanted love and approval, I had to be pleasant, happy, accommodating, and most of all, complacent.

Nikolai turned right, and I followed behind him. Before long, we arrived at what appeared to be a chunk of icy stone covered in snow. He immediately began digging into the white powder, scraping his claws against the ice. I moved in to try to help, but he gently nudged me out of the way. So I just stood there and watched. I really wished we could mindlink. Just so I could ask what he was doing and how I could help. For a brief moment I considered shifting just so we could finally have a conversation, but that required me being naked. And him being naked to respond.

While it was somewhat normalized in many packs, ours still leaned conservative. Furthermore, I barely knew the guy. Usually a man at least took you on a date before he got to see you naked, right?

After a few minutes, he seemed to finish. He turned, looked up, and made eye contact with me, then gestured toward the hole he'd dug. I followed after him into the hollow, made just large enough for his wolf form to fit through. I easily slipped in behind him through the alpha-size cavity.

I glanced around at the cavernous area we'd entered, my night vision reflecting off the icy walls. He'd found a cave. Presumably for us to sleep in. I supposed that answered that question.

He then flipped the travel pack he'd been carrying off his neck and onto the ground and pulled out his coat. He laid it out and pointed at it with his snout. When I didn't get it right away, he pointed again. Oh, okay. I padded over and lay down on it, curling up into my wolfy sleeping position.

He then curled up right alongside me, his warm body curving perfectly around mine, as if we were two puzzle pieces snapping into place. The gentle beating of his heart thumping against my back. The rise and fall of his chest pushing and pulling against me.

Oh.

Oh!

Well, I supposed it made sense. That was how wolves slept during negative temperatures. But I was not expecting it.

And although our thick fur created some sort of buffer, it still felt supremely intimate. My skin was extra sensitive, tingling from the contact. My stomach fluttered with nervousness. I was far too aware of my breathing. Did he find this totally normal? Because I wasn't sure I'd be able to sleep with this close contact with him. I mean, he was Nikolai! He was so hot, and he was an alpha! And I was alone with him in a cave, spooning! Spooning!

I did my best to not think about it. I let my thoughts wander to anything but the moment I was in right then. In time, I finally did drift into sleep.

And when I woke up, I felt more refreshed than I had in a long time. I guess there was nothing like an ice-cold, pitch-black cave in the middle of winter, snuggled up next to the hottest man-wolf I'd ever seen in my life, to get a good night's rest, right?

As soon as it was clear I was awake, Nikolai separated from me and stood up. I soon followed, rising from the makeshift bed. As soon as I stepped away, he gathered it into the travel pack and swung it back onto his neck. We didn't waste any time exiting our sleeping quarters.

I felt like we should have had some sort of conversation. Hello? Good morning? How did you sleep? But it was useless. We couldn't communicate in our wolf forms. But it felt so wrong. We'd just spent the night together, and we continued as practically strangers, me tagging along on his venture that I'm sure he had no desire for me to be a part of.

We continued through the snow, heading to some destination only Nikolai knew of. I assumed he knew where he was going. Although, there was a possibility he perhaps didn't. After all, Alaska was a huge state, with a whole lot of wilderness and not many signs. But, of course, I was sure Nikolai was well trained in navigation. It was me that had never learned this skill growing up. I supposed my father never thought I'd need it. After all, women rarely, if ever, go on any sort of missions in our pack.

We'd been traveling for a number of hours when a familiar scent entered my nostrils. I sniffed in disbelief. We were so far away. How was it possible? I sniffed again.

Alpine Snow Pack. I was very familiar with the scent as a few of their pack members attended the same school as me. A small familiarity among a lot of newness.

College was the first time I'd felt so different from everyone else. I'd lived with werewolves my entire life, in a very isolated area. And while I blended in easily with humans, it still felt uneasy in some ways. I had to be careful not to make my differences so obvious. Some things could be explained by growing up in an isolated village, but others couldn't.

The sight of tracks took me out of my daze. I put my nose to the ground, following them, my instinct leading the way. As soon as Nikolai noticed I was no longer trailing him, he turned and began following me, then joined me in sniffing the trail.

Something didn't feel right. My chest tightened and my heartbeat throbbed loudly in contrast to the quiet, dark morning. Why were they here? So far from home?

Then I looked up, and before I could even comprehend the scene in front of me, a terrible, burning sensation pierced the skin of my shoulder. I cried out, unable to concentrate on anything except how much pain my left front leg was suddenly in. Stars burst behind my eyelids, and nausea formed at the pit of my stomach. It was wolfsbane. I'd never experienced the pain of werewolf's kryptonite before, but some instinctive part of me knew exactly what it was. Before long, I was losing my ability to stand, collapsing on myself.

Two wolves and one naked man with a dart gun appeared from seemingly nowhere. Nikolai instantly stepped into action and lunged toward the naked man. I watched from my helpless state, paralyzed by the pain I was in. I was surprised the shot hadn't killed me. And as the pain spread from my front leg to the front half of my body, part of me wished I would die, just so the pain would stop.

In a matter of seconds, the naked man had gone from standing to his blood spraying across the white snow. But he was merely a pawn, because both the other wolves instantly ganged up on Nikolai. They slashed their sharp claws through his skin, bit at his legs, used the weight of their bodies to knock him down. He fought back, getting hits in where he could, but he was outnumbered.

I watched as they pulled patches of fur off his body, hot, dark red blood spilling from his wounds. As they bit so hard into his legs, their teeth scraped against his bones. As they got a good shot into his chest and plunged in so deep, he was seconds away from death. At the last moment, he was able to flip himself and pull the wolf's paw from his body.

Nikolai was losing. Blood stained the snow. His body was slowing, muscles trembling under the relentless attacks. My vision flickered, the wolfsbane keeping me pinned in place. But the sight of him—struggling, bleeding—sent something razor-sharp through my chest. It wasn't fear. It wasn't even survival instinct. It was rage. The kind that burned through every ounce of exhaustion and sent me lunging forward before my body even registered what I was doing.

Adrenaline pumped through me. The strength I thought I lost from the wolfsbane returned. Suddenly, the only thing that mattered was keeping him safe. If he died, I died. It was just how it was. If I wanted to continue on, he had to as well.

Every single thing my father had ever taught me rushed into my bones, my limbs, my muscles. And I was fighting. I was slashing, biting, rolling around the snow with a wolf that had to be double my size attacking me right back.

His incisors pierced my skin, and I cried out. He clawed across my face, leaving slash marks that burned even more as salty tears and frigid air mixed inside the wound. But I couldn't collapse. I had to keep going.

I jumped onto him, trying to get a good hold of his back. I latched my claws to his body as if he were a piece of rock I was climbing. Thick blood stained my paws. He bucked, but I kept hold of him, riding him as if he were a wild bronco. Nausea bubbled in my stomach. The wild ride was not mixing well with the wolfsbane that was still in my system. I swallowed back the vomit and tightened my grip on him. I would not give in to the wolfsbane or to him. I had to keep him away from Nikolai. It would be far beyond impossible to fight two wolves at once. Especially such big and well-trained ones as these. Alpine Snow Pack had certainly not sent their runts out here.

The wolf kept bucking, and my grip began to slip. My claws slid down his back. While it did have the effect of lengthening the scratch wound I was leaving in his flesh, it also left me less stable as he kicked up his hind legs, shook himself side to side, and then finally shook me loose. I flew through the air to land in an icy patch, my body banging against the hard ground, bones bruising from the blow.

I stood back up on wobbly legs, and hot, acidic vomit ejected itself from my insides, smoldering my esophagus and throat as it came up. Pain seared inside and outside of me. Black dots danced in front of my eyes. But I had to keep at it. The wolf advanced toward me.

My night vision was fading. I'd have to rely on my other senses because sight was no longer going to be an option.

Before my night vision was gone for good, I got one last glance at the wolf. He shifted into his human form. But why? Before I could think about it more, a needle pierced my neck, and agonizing pain surged through me again. Copper filled my mouth, more nausea bubbled up in my stomach, and the world began to fade.

I tried to move. I tried to stay in the fight, but my limbs were heavy. So so heavy. I could barely lift my legs. I could no longer see. Darkness took over. My claws receded, fur disappeared back into my pores, and soon I was defenseless against the cold. I collapsed into the freezing snow, naked and vulnerable. The only thing I could do was await death.

My consciousness faded . . .

I forced my lids open. The world was blurry around me. I couldn't get my eyes to focus. Every limb, my chest, my back, everything stung. It stung like I had been cut up and battery acid had been poured over the open wounds. I shuddered as I breathed in and out. My lungs burned with every breath I took. I let out a choking cry, unable to withstand the pain that had overtaken my body.

"Shhhh," a male voice hushed me. And that was when I noticed that his skin was touching my skin. He had his arms wrapped around me, we were chest to chest, with his legs enfolded with mine.

And then I realized, the pain I was feeling was not just mine. It was his too. I was simultaneously feeling both at the same time. My pain was far more in the forefront, piercing and stabbing at me from all angles. But then there was also a subtle background noise, staticky pain that was also there, just not as prominent. His pain. His pain that I could somehow feel while I was so close to him. But how?

"Ni . . . Nikolai?" I managed to get out, even though it was so painful to speak. "Where are we?"

"Sleep," he said. "You need to heal."

I wanted to insist he tell me, but I was in so much pain that I gave in. I let my head relax against his shoulder and snuggled into his warm body. No one had ever held me so close to them. My body had never fit so perfectly against anyone else's. I gave in, and let my eyes shut, and drifted back into sleep.

I woke again. My body was still sore, but it was a timeworn soreness. My healing must have progressed from when I'd previously opened my eyes. The fire in my insides had dimmed to embers, still burning, but bearable now. A soft moan escaped me.

It was cold. Bitterly cold. The hard ground beneath me pressed into my skin, and while we were indoors, the chill seemed to seep from everywhere. Nikolai was wrapped around me, his warmth a much-needed barrier against the freezing air. I noticed now that parts of my body were bandaged, and layers of his coat, and perhaps other scraps, were piled over us.

I shivered, my teeth chattering uncontrollably. Though Nikolai's body was warm against mine, the exposed parts of my skin prickled painfully with the cold. I tried to speak, but all that came out was, "Brrr ... brr ..."

"I add more wood," he whispered. "It helps."

He carefully pried himself free of me, and I instantly felt his absence, a deep emptiness that went beyond the cold. It wasn't just the loss of his warmth—there was something about having him close that calmed me. Without him, it simply felt wrong.

I turned over, to see where he'd gone. It was a bad idea. Pain stabbed at me from every limb. I let out a loud groan, clutching at myself. I squeezed my eyes shut in agony and waited until the feeling passed. *Note to self, do not move unless absolutely necessary.*

When I opened my eyes again, Nikolai was crouched nearby, concern etched deeply into his expression.

"I'm okay," I said weakly, trying to reassure him. "Just can't move."

He nodded but didn't speak. His eyes lingered on me. I let my own gaze wander over him. The firelight reflected against his silhouette in golds and shadows, illuminating the contours of his body. His broad shoulders, sculpted chest, and defined abs gleamed faintly. The fine trail of blond hair on his lower stomach caught the light as it trailed down to his pelvis. My eyes drifted lower in greedy longing— Oh goodness, what was I doing? Heat flooded my cheeks.

I squeezed my eyes shut. I was hot, so so hot. My face and body were on fire. But, wow. Wow wow wow. When I opened my eyes again, he had turned away, and I found his back to me as he crouched over a fire he'd presumably built in this dark place that had no light. It appeared to be some sort of cabin.

After the sound of some logs being thrown on the fire and the resulting sparks, he returned and crouched down beside me. "Is okay if I . . . if I lie down with you again?" he asked in a hesitant voice. "We cannot shift, and it's best way to stay warm until we can again."

"Um," I stammered. "Yeah, that would be good."

He crawled back toward me, and I awkwardly opened my arms to him. He eased himself against me, wrapping his limbs around me as if it were the most natural thing in the world, allowing warmth to seep back into me. "Not for too much longer," he said. "You look much better now than at first."

"What happened?" I asked. "Where are we?"

"You were really good," he responded, answering some third question I didn't ask.

"Really good?"

"At fighting. I wish women in my pack could fight like you. You were . . . amazing."

Heat fluttered in my chest at the compliment. "Thanks," I said shyly.

"It was thanks to you I did not die out there. I owe you my life. Alone, I could not fight both wolves."

"But you did," I insisted. "Fight them both. I passed out. I'm surprised the guy I was fighting didn't finish me off. It wouldn't have been hard."

"He didn't want to kill you," Nikolai said grimly. "He wanted bait."

"Bait?"

"He thought you were my mate. Or someone close with me." His words hung heavily in the air. I studied him closely, sensing there was more he wasn't saying.

"But why did he need bait?"

Nikolai's eyes flickered, and he hesitated. "I don't know," he said, but the lie was clear, not in his voice but in the way I could feel it—innately. I decided not to push but filed it away for later.

"Mm," is all I said in response.

"The wolf I fought was good as dead by time you passed out. Seeing you like that gave me strength to finish him. But not soon enough. The one you fought shot me with wolfsbane. I almost passed out, but I promised your father to bring you back safe. That gave me strength to finish the other one. It was not too hard. When he shifted into human, he could not go back to wolf with his injuries. I bit off his head with what strength I had left before I was too weak to stay wolf anymore."

"Oh my," I said, clinging to him harder, so thankful he was able to survive after I passed out. We lay like that in silence for some time as I reflected on what had happened. While my pack had gone to war during my lifetime, it was never on our land. I had always been so far removed from our pack disputes, I'd never experienced anything like I had that day. I'd never come so close to death. It was taking me time to process it. Finally, I asked again, "Where are we now?"

"It's cabin Sasha and I found, fixed up. Our pack will move here."

"Did the other pack know about it?"

"No. I never met that pack before."

"I know that pack," I said.

"They are American?" he asked.

I was a bit taken aback by the question. But then I thought maybe he thought they might be Canadian. Any other country would be crazy to think of in this isolated of an area. "Yes, American. From Anchorage. The largest city in Alaska. It's where I go to school. That's how I know them."

A shiver traveled the length of his body. I could sense fear. Somehow this information scared Nikolai. But why?

"What country did you expect them to be from?" I asked.

His body stiffened, his grip tightening slightly around me. "I don't know," he said. A second too late. I let the silence stretch, waiting. He didn't add anything. But I could feel it. Something was off. Something he wasn't telling me.

"Are you sure you don't know?" I asked.

"We should rest," he responded curtly. "We need to heal." The way he said it so brashly made it clear it was the end of the conversation. I conceded, having no energy to argue.

His muscles were rigid as he clung to me. His vibe was off. Something about the conversation had stressed him out, and it in turn made me uneasy.

After at least an hour of being so acutely aware of his emotional state that I was unable to fall asleep, I took his hand and clenched it in mine. I intertwined our fingers together.

As soon as I did that, I internally panicked. What just came over me? Why was I holding his hand so intimately? Would he take it the wrong way? What other way could he possibly take it besides an extremely intimate gesture? Would he be upset that I was being so affectionate toward him? Would he think I was intending to make this thing between us (did we have a thing between us?) something it's not?

But he didn't say a word. Instead, his breathing evened and his muscles loosened. His entire body sagged against mine. The grip he had on me softened. And it didn't even seem like he noticed what I'd done. He just allowed his hand to stay in mine and simply drifted into sleep. My own slumber followed shortly after.

Chapter 19

Ginger

My legs wobbled like Jell-O, barely holding me up. My arms were heavy like lead. Each labored breath stabbed my lungs. I wasn't sure how much more I could take.

I was sweating like a hog at a barbecue. Which was quite a lot considering I was outdoors in the middle of the coldest winter I'd ever experienced in my life. Long story short, Sara was kicking my fat ass.

For our first day of training, she took me out to an open area where the snow was so deep I could barely walk. Every time I tried to move more than a foot, I was out of breath. I had, of course, worn a full snowsuit, knowing we'd be training outdoors today. And very much regretted my choice.

You'd think she would go easy on me for my first lesson, but no. Not at all. Not even a bit. Didn't pull any of her punches. Well, okay, she hadn't actually punched me, but she had knocked me into the snow so many times that my whole core was burning from how many times I'd had to get myself back up from a horizontal position.

Sure, Tyce had trained me consistently since I'd arrived at his pack. But Sara was right. He was going easy on me. I couldn't recall ever feeling as defeated as I did at that very moment.

"Again!" Sara shouted.

I groaned, forcing myself onto my knees and compelling every muscle in my body to get itself together so I could stand.

"We're not stopping until you either block me or pass out. Whichever comes first. And if that doesn't happen until tomorrow morning, then so be it."

I'm not going to cry. I'm not going to cry. I'm not going to cry.

I wanted to collapse on myself. But I couldn't pass out. I had to do it. I had to prove to myself that I could be a warrior, just like I always wanted.

Sara gave me her usual malicious smirk. Goddess, she made Tyce's alpha face look like a child's imitation. She exuded pure evil, especially with her coal-black eyes, which looked even more ominous lit up by her night vision. It was downright terrifying. I was pretty sure she was enjoying every second of torturing me.

I got into position. I did appreciate that she waited for me to do that at least, well aware that in battle there would be none of that courtesy. As soon as I had my legs staggered and my arms up, she began her sprint toward me. How was she so fast in all this snow?

She'd been surprising me with a different move every time we practiced, so I had no way to predict what she would do next. This was obviously by design. But it made it supremely difficult for a beginner like me. For the little time I'd attended a werewolf school before I lost my wolf, they had always told our opponents exactly how to attack and how we were to block them. And Tyce had done the same.

And Sara was fast.

My reflexes were never good enough to catch up with my eyes.

My pulse was in my throat, and my muscles compressed in anticipation. She ran at me with her arms up as if she were about to tackle me with her upper body. I prepared, certain I figured it out in time finally. As she got closer, I ducked. But instead of stumbling over me like I hoped, she swung her leg out, catching me behind the legs and knocking me to the ground.

I plunged backward into the white powder. *Fuck!* I really thought I'd gotten it that time, but she tricked me!

She looked down at me and shook her head. "Again," she said in a way that made it clear she thought I was pathetic, then walked away, giving me space to get back up. I couldn't hold in my wheezing breaths as I pulled myself together again. Tears gathered behind my eyelids, threatening to fall. My limbs all felt too heavy to move. But I couldn't give up. I had to prove this to her and to myself. I could do it.

But the longer this went on, the less I believed it.

We'd already been training for hours at that point. The first hour had been Sara putting me through different exercise drills, and the remainder of the time was this—Sara handing me my ass.

I wondered if she would really keep me here until morning if I never passed out. At this point, it seemed more likely I would pass out well before then. But if I didn't?

We continued. Just like that. For at least another hour.

And just as a tear had almost loosened itself from its tight hold behind my lashes, I heard a familiar voice in the distance. "Gigi?" Tyce's voice echoed in the crisp, chilly air. "Are you seriously still training?"

I straightened my shoulders and fixed my posture. I couldn't let Tyce see me looking so pathetic. I had to show him I could be a strong, useful luna. All the years I was without a wolf would not hold me back.

"Yeah!" I responded.

His figure came into view as he approached the edge of where my night vision could reach. "Okay, well, you need to wrap it up. Because I need to head back to the pack now."

I glanced toward Sara, wondering if she'd hold me hostage like she'd threatened. She folded her arms across her chest and looked Tyce up and down. "One more time, and then she'll be ready to go," she responded.

Tyce nodded in agreement and similarly folded his arms across his chest. Well, here went nothing. Maybe I'd get lucky and finally block her while he was watching. I shrugged my shoulders a few times, danced back and forth on my feet until I got them into a good position.

Sara, again, lunged at me. I watched her like a hawk, trying to decipher what she would do, checking her body language for even the slightest movement that would give it away. But it was hopeless. I jumped, and she did too, in unison, grasping my shoulder. As I fell backward, from the force of the push of her hand, I glanced up. The light of my night vision caught a glint of metal in her other hand.

My back made impact with the ground, and she moved her body in an impressively flexible and athletic way to land with her feet on either side of me, squatting over me, with the long blade of her knife just centimeters from my eye. I gasped, every hair on my body standing on end.

"If I wanted to, I could have taken out an eye," Sara taunted. "Remember that for next time." She swiftly closed her switchblade and hid it within the confines of her clothes. She then walked away without looking back, disappearing into the distance. I didn't fail to notice Tyce glaring daggers at her, but I was proud of him for not intervening. We had a long talk the night before about how he wouldn't unless Sara *actually* hurt me to the point where I ended up in the hospital. And anything less than that, he would stand back. But I could certainly *feel* his anger and frustration through our bond.

"Are you okay?" Tyce rushed over to me, taking my hands to help me up. I was in too much shock to even try to get up, but he lifted me as if I weighed nothing. I instantly went from horizontal to vertical, with Tyce's arms wrapped around me.

"Yeah," I sighed.

"You were out here for hours."

"I know."

"You don't seem happy about it. You don't have to keep training with her if you don't want to. Whatever she's training you to do, I can do it too. I'm an alpha too, Gigi. And you've met my dad and grandpa. They trained me, and they didn't fuck around."

"But that's why you're so good!" I cried out, tears I could no longer hold in tumbling down my overheated cheeks. "Because they didn't go easy on you. And that's why Sara is so good. Because her parents probably didn't go easy on her either. I need this. I need Sara. I need someone that isn't going to go easy on me. And you always do, Tyce!"

He didn't say anything after that as we walked to his car. What could he say? He knew I was right. And soon I'd be back at school, forced to take a break from my training. I had such limited time to make some real progress. Then an idea came to me.

As soon as we were seated in the car, and on our way back to the pack, I took Tyce's hand in mine, and asked, "Did you ever get any more info about the Alpine Snow Pack?"

"Nah, haven't heard anything yet."

"And it's not likely they're actually a threat to us, right?"

"No clue. They could be out there for any number of reasons. We definitely can't assume they're out to get either of our packs, especially since they haven't even come within the normal range where our warriors do their rounds. Sara's just the crazy one that travels hella far."

I nodded.

"Why?" He glanced toward me.

"I know they're not really our allies per se. But would it be possible to make some sort of arrangement with them, so they could continue my training when I go back to school? Maybe we could pay them or offer something in exchange. I just hate that I'm going to miss out on a semester's worth of training and won't be able to continue until I come back for the summer. And with a pack just outside Anchorage, I mean, why not?"

Tyce squeezed my hand but didn't say anything right away. When the thought popped into my head, I felt so hopeful, but now I was readying myself for disappointment. I didn't fully understand all these werewolf politics, but there was always some convoluted response when I asked about something going on with this pack or that pack.

"I'll think about it," Tyce finally replied. "I'm not sure they'd agree. After all, we wouldn't want strangers from packs we have no alliance or anything with coming into our pack, watching how we train, and learning all our strategies. So it's unlikely they'd want it either. But I guess it never hurts to ask. So I'll think about how we can get them to agree."

"Thank you." I rested my head on Tyce's bicep. "I appreciate you at least trying."

"Of course, baby. Anything for you."

The moment my head hit the pillow, exhaustion swallowed me whole. My body felt bruised and battered, but at least I could finally rest . . .

Until my phone rang, shattering the silence.

I jolted awake with a gasp and fumbled for my phone in the dark while Tyce groaned, trying to pull me closer to him. I swatted him away once I finally got the phone up to my face. Paige. Of course, my family always forgot about the time difference.

"What!" I answered the FaceTime. I didn't even care that my face was totally shielded in darkness. "It's"—I checked the time on my phone—"four in the morning here!"

"Oh, shit! I'm sorry!" Paige replied. "I keep forgetting!"

"Can this wait until a normal hour?" I whined. Then I blinked. "Wait, are you at the clinic? Why does your background look like the clinic?"

"That's why I called!" Paige smiled widely. "I wanted to introduce you to our new nephew!"

"Oh my Goddess! What!" I jumped up and ran to flick the light on, ignoring Tyce's moans as he covered himself with a pillow. He could deal. This was big. Very, very big!

"Hang on! Let me take you into the room!"

I settled cross-legged in the bed, jittering with anticipation.

Paige moved to stand beside Heidi's bed, so both of them could face the phone at the same time.

"Heidi, how are you?" I practically screamed.

"Well, I didn't die." She chuckled, but I could tell she was worn out. Her skin was shining with sweat, and her eyes were dull and glassy.

"She did great!" Kelli popped into the frame. Paige then flipped the camera view so more of Kelli was in frame. She had a tiny, wrapped-up, itty-bitty thing in her arms.

"Say hello to Grayson!" Paige said from off-screen. She zoomed in on his little scrunched-up red face, with his eyes closed tight.

"Grayson! You're adorable!" I shouted. "Tyce! Look at our new nephew!" I shook him awake.

He was a good sport and sat up, taking my phone from me. "Look at that munchkin." He grinned. "Congrats, Heidi, Kelli!"

"Thank you," Heidi responded with a huge smile on her face.

"Isn't he the best?" Paige was back in frame now.

"Yeah, I wish I was there to hold him!" I tried not to let the homesickness I'd been pushing down come up. My whole family was in Vermont celebrating the birth of my nephew, and I was thousands of miles away.

"Don't worry, we'll be seeing you soon!" Paige replied. "Dr. Luna said there shouldn't be any issues with Heidi traveling since she should be fully healed by March. We're all so excited for your big alpha wedding!"

"I'm so hap—" I sniffed and rubbed away the tears I could no longer hold back. "Happy that you're coming here. I miss you."

"We miss you too!" Paige replied. "Don't cry! You have Tyce! Your mate! And your wolf! Things are good. And you'll get to meet Grayson in person soon."

"I know. It's all good." After a pause I added, "Can you FaceTime me with Grayson again tomorrow?"

"Yeah, of course!" Paige replied. "Now get some sleep. Heidi needs some rest, and as you pointed out, it's early out there. We'll talk again tomorrow, okay?"

"Okay, good night," I whispered, and Paige hung up.

"Are you okay?" Tyce asked, pulling me toward him, wrapping his large arms around me.

"Yeah, I'm fine," I said, but I couldn't help but sob into his chest. Everything was great, just as Paige reminded me. I'd gotten everything I wanted. But if that was true, why did I have to work so hard to convince myself that everything was great? Was it really, if I missed my family so much it hurt?

Chapter 20

Theresa

The next time I woke, he was still wrapped around me, holding me as if his life depended on it. His even breathing informed me he was still sleeping. I didn't want to accidentally wake him, so I lay as still as I could. Not that it was exactly a burden.

Something about his touch sent a slow, delicious warmth coursing through me. At first, I barely noticed it as something other than the comfort of shared body heat. But then . . . then it became something else. The faintest friction. A shift in his breathing. The tension between us changed, thickening in the cold air.

A soft vibration traveled from the surface of my skin to my bones, energizing me from the inside out. My nipples were stiff and peaked against him, and not because of the cold. I couldn't help but try to bring myself closer, greedily gliding up against him while it was socially acceptable. A soft, deep moan escaped his mouth and echoed off the walls of the small cabin.

The warmth of his body seeped into mine, his arm tightening around my waist. My breath hitched. Was he still asleep? Or was this something more? The slow, subtle shift of his fingers along my hip sent ripples through me. My body reacted before my mind caught up, leaning into the touch, reveling in the way he pulled me closer.

His hand grasped my hip, pulling me toward his pelvis. I was crushed against something rock-hard. It took me a second to realize it was his male appendage. His—*holy wow*—it was massive. I could have mistaken it for a boulder.

My breathing grew noticeably louder along with his. We went from lying still, wrapped up in each other, to a step below humping. The hand that had been clutching my love handle was now traveling to my bare stomach, making its way toward my belly button, his pinky grazing the bush I hadn't thought I'd needed to shave. My cheeks warmed in slight embarrassment. My ex had always berated me when I missed a spot. And this was a pretty huge spot to miss.

But I was relieved that Nikolai didn't seem to notice or mind. He continued trailing his hand along my lower abs, his fingers brushing lower and lower, venturing deeper into my hairs. I knew this was probably wrong, and we shouldn't be acting like animals who couldn't control themselves simply because we were unclothed and, well, sleeping together. But, gosh darn it, what he was doing felt so good. Each swipe along my skin let off small pleasurable tremors. My thigh muscles contracted against his.

He inhaled noisily, and I reacted by tilting my head back. Soon the tip of his nose was brushing against my neck. I whimpered, desperate with need. Then it was his lip, sampling my neck, barely touching the skin. But every time it did, it practically sent a shockwave through my body. Before long, his mouth was on my neck, planting soft kisses along it. His hand slid farther up my torso, until it found my small breast, encompassing it fully and giving it a testing squeeze. I was panting, begging for more with every breath. His fingertips traveled the small mound until they found my erect nipple. He traced, caressed, and plucked at it, and I let out a small cry. I didn't think I'd ever felt anything so heavenly before. It was as if I'd been traveling in a desert for ages and finally got my first sip of water.

Growing bolder by the second, I lifted myself off the ground and brought my legs on either side of his large body to straddle him. I took all of him in, greedily tracing the contours of his body with my eyes. His modelesque face, his thick neck, his sturdy shoulders. The way his pecs and biceps flexed with each small movement. The way the dim light of the fire danced along his smooth skin, reflecting off the baby-fine blond hairs on his arms and chest. He was all raw, robust man.

He stared up at me, the silver glow of his night vision taking me in. His mouth dropped open, and only his panting, gasping breaths came out. I couldn't recall ever feeling so desirable before. The look he gave me said everything, and I couldn't stop myself. I wanted to take what I needed.

His hands continued to explore my humble breasts. He seemed to appreciate them in a way they'd never been previously. "So perfect," he groaned, praising me. I shuddered with lust, the apex of my inner thighs pulsing with need and soaked with arousal. Had I ever been this turned on before?

It was as if my pelvis had a mind of its own as I rubbed myself along his stiffness. The light of his eyes disappeared when he closed his lids and let out a loud moan. I thrust my hips back and forth, savoring the sweet, sweet friction. It was electrifying. His hands traveled down the length of my upper body, from my breasts, down the sides of my torso, until they found my love handles again and grasped them firmly. At first, he simply rested his fingers and palms against the bones, allowing me to continue the motion, selfishly drawing as much pleasure as I could from each movement along his hard length. Forward, I slid along his firm skin, and back, I savored every bit of friction. At first slowly, but with more haste with each round until I was trembling with raw pleasure.

I was getting close, and I was no longer able to see reason. My moans came out loudly, shamelessly, unwittingly. I had never taken pleasure from someone so freely. I'd never given in to my desires like I was at that moment. It was as if I were possessed by a sex demon. My thighs convulsed against him, each rub back and forth added to the buildup. I was so close. Just anoth—

His hands strengthened their grip, and his fingers dug into the flesh of my bottom. Midstroke, I was halted, unable to finish what I'd started.

His breathing was ragged. His hands were trembling against my skin, torn between pushing me away and pulling me closer. His lips parted, as if he was about to say something, but nothing came out.

I didn't know how to react. I had been so close, just at the cusp of being swept into a hurricane. I tried one last time to move, but he had me in a death grip, walling me off from proceeding. Without meaning to, I let out the saddest whimper that had ever come out of me.

I immediately burned with shame. Shame that I had gotten so carried away, just assuming he wanted the same thing, not checking in and making sure—not even pleasing him before I went ahead and did myself! And shame that I had reacted like a toddler when I didn't get what I wanted.

He stiffened beneath me, jaw clenching. "We can't," he choked out, voice thick with regret. "This is wrong."

I simply nodded and climbed off him with my metaphorical tail between my legs.

"I promised your fath—" he started, but didn't finish his sentence. "I . . . I cannot do this now. I have pack to lead. I—" He closed his eyes and shook his head. "You are so beautiful. But I cannot be with you now."

Thickness settled in my throat. Tears built up behind my eyes. I staved them off. I was just having an emotional reaction. I knew I shouldn't have done that. He was just reacting like he was supposed to. I was just being emotional. *I was just being emotional!*

"Terri," he said in a gentler voice, touching my upper arm. "If circumstances were different . . ." He let out an audible breath. "What I mean . . . it is not that I do not want you. It is that we cannot be together. Your brother is alpha of the pack that hosts mine. And my pack needs me. I must be good leader for them. I cannot be . . . cannot be doing what we just did. Think how it would look."

I didn't know how to respond. What could I possibly say? He was right. It was always like that. People never wanted to be with me because they feared what my brother or father might do to them. Who wanted to be caught sleeping with the alpha's sister? If he intended to kill you, you were as good as dead. It was the reason no one knew what had happened to me, except one of my friends. It was why I kept *his* secret. Because even if I hated him, and some days did want him dead, I couldn't bring myself to send him to his grave. He hadn't been all bad. Or I kept telling myself that, but was it really true? What had really been good about him? Now that I tried to think of something, I couldn't.

"Anyway," he continued, "you have someone? You are marked, yes?"

I rubbed at the mark. For a brief moment, while in the throes of passion, I had forgotten it existed, forgotten the constant physical reminders like the itching, the tingling, the burning. For that brief moment, I'd felt normal, and as if I had a chance at a normal relationship.

All I could do was say, "Yeah." Perhaps I should have elaborated, explained that the person who marked me was not someone I had any intention to be committed to now or any day in the future. But I was already overwhelmed by my regret and shame about what I'd done, then and moments ago. I'd made a fool of myself, and I wasn't sure how I'd be able to even look Nikolai in the eye once we returned to the packhouse and were supposed to act like everything was normal, we'd never seen each other naked, and I hadn't used his body as a sex toy.

"Hey, are you okay?" Nikolai affectionately wrapped his large hand around my forearm.

"Yeah, fine," I responded, figuratively brushing myself off. I straightened my shoulders and put on a bright smile like I always did. "You're right, what we did was totally wrong. I don't know what came over me. It was just a weird mistake. Too much hormones or something, you know? Us being naked and cuddling and . . . Well, it won't happen again. We don't have to say anything to anyone about it." *Stop rambling, stop rambling, stop rambling.* But he wasn't responding, so I kept going. "It'll just be our secret. What happens in the cabin stays in the cabin. All business from here on out!" *Shut up, Terri!*

He let out another breath and said, "Thank you." That was it. That was all he said, and relief flowed off him. Even though logically, I understood his predicament, I couldn't help but feel devastated by his response. Wasn't there a part of him that enjoyed it and didn't want it to just be our dirty secret that was going to be forgotten forever after today?

He got up and added more wood to the fire. He then turned to me, touched my arm, and said, "You seem better now. You can shift to be warm. I'm going to chop wood and repair this cabin. That's why I came here."

I nodded. Yes, of course, I could shield my naked human body now.

The hand he'd placed on my arm tightened for just a second—just long enough for me to wonder if he was about to pull me back. His jaw clenched, his silver eyes flickering with something I couldn't quite name. Regret? Longing? But then, just like that, it was gone. He let go, turning away from me, his voice tight with restraint. "Run. Warm up your legs."

"How long do you plan to stay here for?" The question finally came to me. I realized I hadn't asked when I'd been thrust into this adventure.

"Only few days. To make the most important repairs. I wanted to stay longer, but better we go back soon. Too much happened."

Too much indeed.

Chapter 21

Nikolai

I couldn't get her out of my mind. She was consuming my waking and dreaming thoughts. What she did. How she had climbed on top of me like that, took control, and rubbed herself all over my cock. She looked like a damn goddess with her flawless warrior body, her long, dark, voluminous hair, her pert breasts with prominent, perfect nipples. I was helpless under her, in awe of her power. I'd never felt so out of control in my life.

Even now, standing here, thinking of her, my body reacted like a desperate fool. I gritted my teeth. Pathetic. I was pathetic.

I was so used to demure, submissive women. And there was nothing wrong with them. But, *boginya moya*! That. That was so unexpected and . . . I didn't even have words for it. It was something beyond mortal understanding. That was otherworldly. For those few moments she was riding my shaft, I had forgotten everything—the war, the pack, my family that was now gone, this barren nothing that would be our future pack land—everything.

I'd almost surrendered completely. Part of me still regretted not yielding fully to her, allowing her to have her way with me, to take as much pleasure from me as she desired. Sate herself by using me.

But then, that unwelcome and irritating thing I called my conscience had slapped me in the face. It started as a whisper in the back of my mind. She was the sister of the alpha—the sister of the alpha! And I, the leader of the pack he was hosting so selflessly, was coming as close as possible to fucking his princess of a sister. How much I, myself, would have tortured any man who was given the hospitality of my pack only to then turn around and fuck one of my sisters. And how I'd promised her father I wouldn't touch her, that he trusted me to keep her unharmed during this journey.

The more I tried to push it away, the louder it became, until it was deafening. Until my stomach turned with shame.

Even though I'd never had such an incredible sexual experience before, even though I was only a handful of her thrusts from possibly the best orgasm of my life, my chest tightened and bile rose to my throat.

It took every ounce of willpower I had, but I managed to stop her. To end it before it went any further. Before we'd gotten to the point of no return. Because once the line of consummating this arrangement was crossed, I knew I wouldn't have the willpower to cross back.

At the first moment I could leave without being a complete dick, I bolted out of that cabin, transformed into my wolf, and ran at least a kilometer away. Only then did I feel safe enough to finally alleviate the heavy ache in my balls. Like a mad man, I shifted back into my human form, hunched behind a tree, and gripped the hot, throbbing monster in my hand. It only took a few strokes, and I was growling in ecstasy with tears spilling down my face, spraying come all over the bark of that tree. It was below freezing, and I was buck naked, cold biting into my exposed ass, with my bare feet sinking into the snow, my come turning into icicles as I experienced the most ethereal, earth-shattering orgasm of my life.

I actually cried! Fucking tears. Over what? Over a woman who wasn't mine, who I wasn't allowed to have? Over the fact that I'd had the best orgasm of my life and all I'd touched was my own damn hand?

And if I got *that* just from masturbating, what would the real thing with her have been like?

I was a fool to believe that would be the end of it. I still had to spend a few more nights sleeping in the same small room with her, inhaling her mesmerizing scent while I was asleep and vulnerable, dreaming of her. Even sleeping in our wolf forms to stay warm, with a silent agreement not to sleep touching, even if it was normal to do so on these types of missions, I couldn't control my nagging desire for her. Now that I'd had a taste, there was nothing else that would ever satisfy me again.

When we finally returned to the packhouse, I stood under an ice-cold shower and breathed a sigh of relief. I'd made it back without another incident.

It was for the best. I needed to think of my pack first.

But something still nagged at me. Every time I looked in her eyes, I felt the mate bond. Could I be imagining it? It didn't make sense. There should be more certainty, more proof. Wouldn't she have said something? Was I really the only one feeling it?

And what about the mark? Who had given that to her? I was desperate to ask her. Did she have a secret mate? Had she cheated on him? Or perhaps they had one of those open relationships. But why not tell me? It seemed like pertinent information.

However, as she'd stayed in her wolf form during the remainder of the time, there was no opportunity to ask. So I continued to wonder, and both want to speak to her but also to stay away as to not feed the flames.

But that mate thing still nagged at me.

A few days after we returned, I found myself in the office with Tyce. He pointed toward some packages sitting next to his desk. "Hey, bro, so we got all these sports bras for your pack."

"What?" I blinked a few times, not understanding why, out of every supply our pack could possibly need, he'd gotten *bras* for us.

"Oh, Terri didn't tell you?" He looked up at me from the paper he had in his hand. "She asked me to get your pack some sports bras. Said your female warriors needed more support. So Gigi measured all of them and put in the order, since I'd obviously have no idea what I'm doing." He smiled and shook his head.

"Terri asked for these to be ordered?" I asked, making sure I heard right.

"Yeah, she's a good kid," Tyce replied. "Always thinking of other people. I constantly tell her she needs to take care of herself too. Not sure where she got it from. Couldn't be from our parents." He chuckled.

We unboxed the packages together and double-checked the order. Then we chitchatted a bit. Tyce, as usual, snuck in words about his mate, about how well she was doing with her own warrior training. He lit up every time he spoke of her. He was truly in love, and I couldn't help but envy him. I hadn't felt that way previously when he'd spoken of her, but all of a sudden—it was as if small pieces of my frozen heart were cracking bit by bit—I wanted that. I wanted that in a way I never had before in my life.

When there was a pause in the conversation, I cleared my throat and hesitated for a moment. Was this something I really wanted to ask? But I pushed forward. "So, your mate."

"My mate? Gigi?"

"Yes, Gigi. How do you know she is your mate?"

"It's like they say." Tyce lit up with a smile. "You just know."

"But there are also . . . physical signs, yes? I have heard this. But I do not know myself."

"Oh, yeah!" He slapped his hand on my shoulder. "Bro, you're gonna love it when you find your mate. When you touch her skin, it's like sparks. And you can feel her emotions through the bond. When you do something to make her happy, you feel it. And when she's"—he lowered his voice—"horny"—he winked and elbowed me a bit—"you feel it too."

I nodded, taking in the information. I'd heard similar from others. But it was good to confirm anyway. I didn't have any of the other symptoms of the mate bond. While it was practically electrifying to touch her, I wasn't sure I felt physical sparks. And while she did seem to wear her heart on her sleeve, making it simple to interpret what she was likely feeling, I couldn't say I'd actually *felt* her emotions.

Either way, I did have to thank her. I wasn't sure I understood the choice, but she must've had a good reason to believe we needed the bras she'd gifted to my pack.

I found her later that day in the gym, not long after we'd distributed all the bras. All of the women were surprisingly elated. And they worked that much harder during our drills. I'd had no idea that something so simple could solve so much.

Most days since we'd returned, I ignored Terri's presence, keeping my focus on training my pack. It wasn't that I didn't want to talk to her or even be on friendly terms at the very least. It was that I knew it was for the best to act as if nothing had ever happened between us.

But to not thank her would be brutally rude.

I approached her as she was adding weights to her bench rack. I quickly did the math in my head of what she'd already loaded. Shocked, I blurted, "You bench more than this?"

She swiftly turned from where she was about to grab another weight and slowly backed up. "Umm, well, I don't know. I was going to try it today. I'm not sure if I can actually bench that much."

"But you put more weight? So you must know you can do this much?"

"Oh, yeah, I guess."

"Holy shit."

She stared at me like a deer in headlights and didn't respond.

"I had no idea women can bench this much weight. This is how much a male warrior lifts."

"Oh. Maybe I put too many weights by accident. Let me remove some."

"Why you do that?"

"Do what?"

"Act like you do not bench that much, when clearly you do."

She fiddled with her hands behind her back and looked down at the ground. "It's complicated," she finally replied after a pause. "Someone once made me feel bad about it. And now I just feel weird telling people how much I lift."

"Whoever made you feel bad is idiot. Probably jealous. This is most amazing thing I have seen. It gives me hope for my own pack. That my female warriors can do it too."

"They definitely can!" Terri practically shouted. "It's, of course, more work than it is for a man. But I've seen how hard they've all been training. I believe in every single one of them."

I nodded, accepting her praise of my pack. "That is why I came here. To thank you for what you did. For ordering sports bras. They made big difference."

"Oh, it's no problem." Her cheeks reddened. "I could just tell they really needed them, so I did what any ally pack member would do. I let my brother know so he could help if we had the resources."

"No, not any ally pack member would do that. Most packs think of their own interests above all. They would not even think of helping another pack without wanting something in return. But you . . . you did not even try to take credit. I only know because your brother told me. So thank you." I paused for a moment, admiring the glow of her tan skin, the thick lashes that surrounded her luminous amber eyes, and the way her cherubic cheeks dimpled when she smiled. Without thinking, I added, "You are beautiful, both inside and outside."

Her cheeks flushed even more. And I couldn't help but think, in any other circumstance, how much I would have begged her to be my mate. I had clearly misjudged her. She was not the princess I'd thought she was. You didn't fight like she fought or lift like she apparently lifted without serious grit and mental toughness.

"Good workout," I finally said and returned to my pack, an ache in every step away from her.

Who was the lucky bastard that had gotten his teeth into her?

Chapter 22

Nikolai

"Morning," Tyce greeted Sasha and me as we entered the warrior gym to get our workout in before our pack arrived for training. I glanced around, taking in all the empty equipment. The gym that was usually fully packed by now only had a handful of Tyce's warriors in it.

"Where is everyone?" I asked. "Outdoor training today?"

"Nah," Tyce replied. "They have the next week off. The first sunrise of the year is in six days, so we kicked off our sunrise festival today and gave everyone the time off. Feel free to use the gym as much as you want." I nodded, and he continued speaking with a glint in his eyes. "Be careful out there. You'll be seeing a lot of plastered wolves on the prowl. Lotsa drunk, horny she-wolves too." He gave me a friendly punch in the arm. "Used to be my favorite time of year. But I'm a changed man. They're all yours now." He lit up with a bright smile and then turned to load up a barbell on the ground.

Sasha smirked and shook his head as we headed toward the dumbbells. "Start with bent-over rows?" he asked.

I nodded, and we grabbed our chosen weights. We took our places at benches next to each other. After we got a few reps in, I turned to him and said, "I can't figure out how that American pack knew where to find me."

"Maybe they've been tracking you," Sasha replied. "It wouldn't be unheard of."

"But why that pack? And how would they know? You think the Chernoye Nebo Pack knows we're here?" A shiver traveled up my spine. I had hoped they'd never figure out where we'd gone. Even though I'd forbidden my pack from using social media, I still wondered if someone slipped or perhaps disobeyed my orders.

"Kolya, what you have is very powerful. He wanted it enough to not only destroy our pack but to continue fighting even after we'd killed off the majority of their warriors. You know he won't give up until he gets it, even if it means tracking you down on another continent."

I switched to a heavier dumbbell and grunted through my next set. Cursed was the day my father put me in possession of possibly the most powerful object in the world. An object no one should have known about. An object that led to the demise of my entire family and most of my pack.

"Where'd you hide it anyway?" Sasha asked.

I looked up and glared at him. Stupid man. Asking for that kind of responsibility. "It's better you don't know."

"You don't have to bear this burden alone."

"That's where you're wrong. It is my, and only my, responsibility," I said firmly, making it clear it was the end of the discussion. While I trusted Sasha, he tended to get on my nerves. For a long time, I chalked it up to my irritability and terrible state after the war. But after some time, I realized I didn't have the same ease and comfort with him that I'd had with my late beta, Andrey.

But there wasn't much that could be done now. Sasha had been part of my friend group and one of my best warriors before the war. There was no better option. And as far as being a beta, he'd done a phenomenal job. He'd kept up morale better than I was capable of, and had worked just as hard as me to train everyone. So any personal issues with chemistry were minor grievances as far as I was concerned. He was a good guy, and he had taken on the responsibility of his title fully, even without having the lineage or the lifetime of training his predecessor had.

We spent a couple hours working on upper body before our pack filed in. And then it was the usual agenda. Warm-ups, running, weight training, and sparring. I did have to admit that everyone was improving. Although they weren't where I wished they were, I did consider where they'd started and felt pride in my pack for the first time in a long time. It finally seemed possible that I'd be able to make warriors out of wusses.

I decided to take a page out of Tyce's book and give everyone the next day off to join the festivities of the Jade Moon Pack. A day wouldn't hurt. And we did need to boost morale.

"Someone's lightening up," Sasha teased after everyone left. "Did you finally get laid or something?"

I froze for a moment, but reminded myself that nobody knew. I believed Terri when she promised she wouldn't tell anyone. "Laid by whom? I'm a lone wolf now, Sasha."

"Maybe it's time to take Tyce's advice then and find a nice she-wolf who's breaking loose tonight." He winked.

"I have better things to do," I replied and grabbed my gym bag, swinging it over my shoulder, indicating it was time to go. Sasha shook his head at me and subsequently picked up his own gym bag.

Later that evening, I agreed to go out with Beta Liam's family and Sasha to enjoy some of the festivities.

"Tonight they're doing a cookout at the ice-skating rink," Liam explained on the way. "Which mostly just means burgers and hot dogs. But the pups love it."

When we entered the building, we were greeted by loud thumping music, multicolored lights, and a huge, rotating disco ball hanging from the ceiling. Families were in line at a window with a big sign over it that read SKATES FREE TODAY. Liam's mate ushered their children over while Liam led us toward the concession stand to grab food and the spiked version of whatever the kids were drinking.

Everyone congregating around the rink was in good spirits. I even spotted some of my own pack members enjoying themselves. Sasha and Liam rambled on next to me while I grunted here and there, acknowledging their presence. At least Sasha had found someone to converse with him. I wasn't in the mood. Everything still weighed heavy on me, and I couldn't find it in myself to just let go. But maybe the drink would help. I tasted it, and it actually wasn't bad. It was some warm, sweet apple juice that someone had poured bourbon into with a heavy hand.

A few of my pack members greeted me as we made our way through the bleachers. I managed to be friendly and warm toward them, although I felt the opposite. I kept reminding myself that morale was low. I had to at least appear positive and hopeful even during the times I felt the most negative.

We finally took our seats in a reserved section, where the alpha and beta families had gathered. I noted that almost everyone from the packhouse was there except a certain someone who wouldn't leave my mind. I hated that I noticed. And I hated even more that I was disappointed by her absence. I reminded myself it was for the best, especially as both her parents were present. The last thing I needed was more matchmaking attempts by Yulia, or more threats of chopping my balls off from Lance.

I sipped on my drink while I watched young pups and teenagers skate around the rink. I even managed to crack a small smile when the orphaned boy I'd carried during our trek here waved at me from the ice rink, appearing joyful while holding hands with the woman who had adopted him. Perhaps a small droplet of water had managed to drip from my frozen heart.

Tyce and Gigi made conversation with me, so I politely turned to give them my attention. Sasha and Liam both made sure I was never without a drink. I had to admit the apple drink was pretty damn good, and before long, I was feeling a buzz.

It must have made me more social than usual because Sasha exclaimed, "We should hang out and drink together more often. It's good for you. You're too wound up. It's not healthy."

"What's not healthy is what happened to our pack," I bit back.

"Goddess, you've changed," Sasha snapped at me. "You used to be cool. But now, you're just this miserable little fuck. I know what happened sucks, and we've all been mourning everyone we lost. But we're alive! What point was there in battling so hard for our pack's survival when you have no plan to actually live?"

I was thankful our dispute was in Russian, so the others sitting near us didn't know what we were saying. Except maybe Yulia, but she seemed to be off somewhere else at that moment.

"Sasha, give me some space."

He backed off. Thank Goddess.

What had previously been a nice buzz now filled me with anxiety and anger. I crumpled the empty cup. I couldn't understand how Sasha could be moving on so easily. What happened still haunted me. It wasn't something I was going to be able to shake off overnight. My entire family had perished in the battle. I had witnessed my eldest sister being beheaded, helpless to save her from our enemy. It was the Goddess's mercy that the murder of my parents and other two sisters had happened out of my line of sight. It was traumatic enough to live with the one visual.

I clenched my fist, the drink now sitting like acid in my gut. I wanted to leave, to let the cold air numb the growing ache in my chest. I was about to get up and head back to the packhouse to sleep off my misery when I looked up.

A flash of white skates sliced across the ice. A figure moved effortlessly, like she belonged to the rink, like she belonged to the sky itself. My breath caught.

I knew it was her immediately.

Even though she was wearing a chunky scarf and oversize beanie that obstructed my view of her face, I would have known her anywhere, with any amount of clothing covering her.

She was in the middle of the ice rink with a small group of other women her age. All of them were spinning, leaping, and showing off a number of other tricks. But my eyes were held hostage by just one.

I watched intently as her bright white figure skates glided across the streak-covered rink. With how elegant she was, one would never have guessed that the Zamboni was well past due. She did beautiful spirals, showing off her flexibility, glided on the ice while she performed backward crossovers, and completed a few axels.

Was that drool that I wiped from the side of my mouth?

The disco lights bounced off the smooth skin of her face and the tendrils of long hair that peeked out from her ensemble. The leggings she was wearing accentuated her thick, toned thighs. Her quads and hamstrings flexed against the tight, insubstantial fabric. I swallowed, far too aware of the movement of her body.

Even as I watched her skate, the unease from earlier lingered. That pack had found me too easily. If they could, so could others. I should have been thinking about that. I should have been focused on protecting what little I had left.

"That's my baby!" Lance shouted beside me, instantly taking me out of my trance. My whole body jerked and guilt filled me. I took a deep breath to calm myself, certain no one had noticed where my eyes had been planted a second earlier. I turned to the man who had disturbed me. Alcohol wafted off his skin. He'd certainly had his fair share to drink. Certainly more than me.

"She's good," I commented.

"The best," he responded. "Used to perform in high school. Our pack has a synchronized skating club." He then turned back to the ice and banged his fists against the glass separating us from the rink. Once he had the attention of just about everyone in attendance, he shouted, "You show them, Terr! Double axel! Double toe loop! Traveling camel spin!"

My face heated with second-hand embarrassment. I subconsciously slunk down in my seat, attempting to differentiate the alpha I was from how this one was behaving.

"Lance, stop!" Yulia approached from seemingly nowhere. She tugged at his arm and he swatted her away. She tried again to pull him away from the glass, this time with more force. "The pack is watching."

"So what!" he snapped at her. "I'm the alpha! I'll do whatever I damn please!"

"Lance," she responded in a warning tone. He turned, and the two of them seemed to be stuck in a staring competition.

"Fine, fine!" he finally acquiesced and allowed her to lead him away.

Once the two of them disappeared from my view, I turned back to Terri and noted that her cheeks had reddened. She was no longer doing tricks and had switched to skating around the rink along with everyone else. Her group of friends followed. Surely her second-hand embarrassment had to be far worse than mine.

As she skated past me, we made eye contact. I felt it again. The bond. The strange bond that didn't make any sense.

Part of me wanted to stay longer, but I knew I couldn't continue to sit there like a stalker creep. I managed to get up and pry my eyes from her. No matter how much I admired and felt drawn to her, I knew it was best to push the feelings away.

As I moved to the exit, I stopped and wished a good night to some pack members on the way. They did seem to be in good spirits tonight, and that cheered me up, especially after the sour mood I'd been in not much earlier. I slipped through the doorway into the dark, cloudy evening. Even with my night vision, I could barely see my path ahead. I hadn't made it far when Sasha caught up to me, clasping his hand on my shoulder.

"Look, I'm sorry for back there," he said.

"It's fine," I replied. "I shouldn't have snapped at you like that. Especially not in front of everyone."

"We need to be a team," he said.

"Yes, a team," I replied, letting out a deep breath.

"That's why I was offering to have drinks and hang out. So we can work better as a team."

"Sasha," I said, trying my best to keep my voice even, "I need space, okay? I'm not going to make a good hangout buddy right now. It's nothing personal. I just can't."

He didn't say anything in response but walked the rest of the way back to the packhouse with me. When I said good night, he understood and disappeared into the beta wing.

When I crawled into bed, I replayed the evening in my head and vowed to myself to try to be more friendly toward Sasha. We had at one time been very close friends. Maybe I could try to remember how it had been so easy before, how there was a time when he didn't constantly irritate me.

I knew I was being unfair. Sasha wasn't the enemy. He had suffered too. But that was the problem, wasn't it? He could move on. And I couldn't.

I took several deep breaths in an attempt to quiet my mind. I did my best to think of nothing. Nothing like what we had left. Nothing like the pack land I had found. Nothing, like the dark, sunless Alaska sky.

Chapter 23

Theresa

Early in the morning, I kicked all the layers of sheets and blankets off me. My body was drenched in sweat. For a second, I had to remind myself that it was, in fact, the middle of winter, and I hadn't suddenly overslept several months and found myself waking on an uncharacteristically hot day in the middle of July.

When I unlocked my phone, I was greeted by the alert I dreaded from my period tracking app every month. *Ovulation.* I groaned into my pillow and then whispered a prayer of thanks to Artemis that it was a day when most people would be out of the packhouse for the continuing sunrise festival and I was unlikely to be bothered. For once, something was going right. I just had to make it through today without incident, and I'd be golden. By the time ovulation rolled around again, I'd be back at school, secure from detection.

Fortunately, I was mostly safe within the confines of the packhouse. No one in my immediate family would notice, which was just about everyone who stayed in the alpha wing. The beta and gamma were both mated, and all of their pups were too young to have wolves yet. Those who did the housework were all women. While I had heard rumors there were women who could sense heat, I wasn't sure if that was true. It left very few for me to worry about.

To be safest, I would stick to my bedroom for the day and avoid anyone and everyone. Besides feeling warmer than usual, the heat hadn't really come on yet. I'd gone through it enough to know that I usually had about an hour after the first signs appeared before I succumbed to the worst of it. I decided to sneak downstairs to grab enough water and snacks to tide me over for the day.

I was relieved to find the kitchen empty of Tasha when I entered. The last thing I needed was her reporting my "unhealthy eating" to my mom. The sad part was, she wouldn't even suspect anything other than that I was gaining weight behind her back, circumventing all her efforts to keep me as bony as possible. I quickly found the stash kept on hand for Tyce's bulking and hoarded as much as I could in the tote bag I'd brought down with me. Lots and lots of protein, which would do the trick to keep me sated.

Just as I felt satisfied that I'd acquired enough supplies to keep myself comfortable for the remainder of the day, the familiar symptoms began to take hold of me. My legs weakened and my breath turned to pants. Before long, my belly was fluttering with arousal, and my panties were sticky and moist against my skin. I shut the door to my bedroom before my scent could be carried to other parts of the packhouse and immediately fell in a heap beside it.

My skin was so sensitive, so needy for touch. My leg muscles contracted, desperate to feel a man's body between them. For months, I had gone through this and no one specific came to mind. I just knew I needed to be touched, needed to be filled. And when I couldn't take it anymore, I'd found a willing human. It wasn't difficult, living in a co-ed dorm. It also wasn't hard, being a woman living among college-aged men. And no matter what I felt the next day, it had been worth it in those moments. It curtailed the raging fire that couldn't be put out.

But today, I wouldn't have anyone. I'd have to go at it alone and pray I didn't scorch myself.

I crawled across the floor and heaved myself into my bed. Then, once I was ready to let go and *ménage à moi*, the thoughts that had previously been occupied by a faceless man suddenly weren't so faceless anymore. I lost all ability to rationalize or suppress my fantasies. All I knew was that every naked part of him I had seen in that cabin was now broadcast in HD in my brain.

The way his face had contorted in satisfaction as I'd ridden him, the way his muscular forearms had stiffened when he'd grasped my hips, his well-toned glutes that I'd gotten a peek at when he'd added wood to the fire, and his thick, sturdy back. Was there a single part of his body that wasn't perfect?

An hour or so later, and I had probably imagined sex in every physically possible (and maybe some not) position with him. I was left with a cramped hand, gasping for air, and praying for relief. No matter how much I strummed and plucked and rose to crescendo, it wasn't enough. I switched from right to left hand, thinking about symmetry when working out—and this was a workout—then switched back again.

When I didn't know how much more I could take, practically crying from exhaustion, my body must have given in. Because I finally found some respite. I took deep breaths, shook my hands out, found the shorts I'd previously discarded and pulled them back on. Then I grabbed a protein bar and water bottle from my stash and gulped both down as if I hadn't had food or water in weeks.

Maybe that would be it. Maybe it was over. But probably not. Heat had a way of hanging around for hours. It was never just a simple wham, bam, never see you again.

But I savored the peace while I could. I stretched out my limbs, ending up in a starfish position in my bed, and allowed my lids to shut. I had barely relaxed when I found myself drifting into sleep.

When I awoke, it was with a gasp. Nothing looked familiar. Where I'd closed my eyes was not where I opened them. And staring down at me was a very shirtless Nikolai with just a towel wrapped around his torso and his blond hair dripping wet. "Why are you—" he started, tight features and a scowl on his face, his fists clenched, and his eyes shooting daggers at me.

I looked around while adrenaline shot through my system, trying to make sense of how I'd ended up where I had. My chest tightened, and a choking sensation took hold as more and more came back to me. I had fallen asleep and somehow ended up in Nikolai's room. Yes, I'd been having issues with sleepwalking, but he didn't know that. From where he was standing, this looked very, very bad.

"I sleepwalked," I still tried to explain, blurting out whatever came to mind. "It's been happening. I swear. This wasn't . . . I wasn't . . . I just fall asleep sometimes and wake up at your room. Well usually not in, but outside at your door. And—" I stopped when I noticed his nostrils flaring as he was clearly taking in a scent, and his pupils dilated to twice the size they'd been.

Oh shitake mushrooms!

"*Techka . . .*" Nikolai murmured.

"What?" But I was pretty sure I knew what that word meant. Because while I'd been temporarily distracted by the compromising position I'd found myself in, the physical symptoms of my predicament were making their presence known more and more as the seconds ticked by, especially with a very shirtless, very built, very toned Nikolai glaring at me.

Whatever I'd imagined in HD hadn't even done him justice.

He is hot.

His pecs glistened from the moisture of the shower he'd stepped out of. His arms were bigger than I remembered. His normally scruffy hair was weighed down in an undeniably sexy way. Even the way his lips took on different shapes with every change in his emotion . . . Gosh, I couldn't stop thinking about them on me, on every single part of me. How badly

I wanted my own lips on him, to trace the sharp angle of his jaw, to trail them down his broad neck . . .

"It's what happens . . . to women . . . *Techka*." He interrupted my thoughts. "You must have word in English." His voice almost seemed pained.

"Heat," I responded, now quite aware that I was not really in control of myself. Whoever Terri was, she was no longer me. I was now a rabid wolf, with only one goal on my mind.

He backed up, clenching the towel around his waist. What had at one point been a look of irritation had now been replaced by wide eyes and a slight tremble in his lower lip. I got up off the floor and approached him. With every step forward, he took one back, until his back was flush against the wall. His abdominals flexed with every breath he took. He smelled absolutely divine. The clean, soapy scent that clung to his hair and skin mixed with his natural, carnal scent that, while musky, was also slightly sweet, with notes of dark honey. I was intoxicated, with a need to inhale every last drop of his aroma that penetrated the air around me.

I stepped so close we were practically touching. His body heat warmed my skin. His heavy breathing fanned the top of my head. I planted my hands on his chest. My fingers vibrated with pleasure as I stroked them along his skin, savoring the smooth texture, relishing the slight tickle of each blond baby hair. I brushed my palms along his pecs, taking in the landscape of hard muscle.

"How is it possible?" he managed to ask. "You're marked."

"Half-marked," I replied, not able to concentrate enough to elaborate. I needed him, and I needed him now. Every instinct in my body was telling me to get closer, touch him more, make him helpless in my presence until I could have what my wolf wanted.

"What is half-marked?" He wrapped his large hands around my wrists, stopping their movement along his chest, but not removing them.

"I never marked him. My wolf . . ." I groaned at a shiver that traveled the length of my back. We were so close. His scent and warmth were surrounding me. My nose was extra sensitive to his pheromones and his arousal. I was so close. "My wolf wants to mark. I can't stop her."

Because his hands were wrapped around my wrists, I used my hips instead. I pushed my pelvis into him, luxuriating in the feeling of hardness behind his towel. His hands strengthened around my wrists as he let out a pained, baritone moan. He wanted it just as much as I did. I had no doubt. He was powerless as the soft plop of his towel falling to the floor alerted us to the fact that he was no longer shielded in any way, shape, or form.

And that was all it took for the string of his self-restraint to break. His mouth was suddenly on mine, our tongues twining. We switched places as he pushed me up against the wall and urgently pulled my T-shirt off, revealing that I wasn't wearing a bra.

"*Boginya* . . . you are so perfect," he murmured and his mouth latched onto one of my nipples. I cried out as he swirled his tongue eagerly around it, suckled as if he were starved, eventually shifting to softly nibbling at my breast.

"Don't stop," I whined, savoring both the pleasure and the slight prickles of satisfying pain as his teeth grazed my delicate skin.

He switched to the other one, savoring my other breast as much as he did the first. Soon his large hand was traveling the inside of my thigh, burying itself inside my cotton shorts. He easily slipped his large fingers beneath the fabric of my panties. "So wet," he moaned. "You are so fucking wet."

"Don't stop," I begged, tears building behind my lids.

He slid a large digit inside me, and I didn't think I'd ever felt anything so delightful before. I cried out as if he'd just saved my life.

"Keep going." I rocked my hips with desperation. He slipped a second digit inside me and brought his thumb to my clit. I cried out again.

He worked his fingers in and out of me and simultaneously swirled his thumb around my sensitive bud. It felt so good, but . . . "It's not enough," I whined.

He withdrew his hand and backed away, giving me space to move away from the wall. I paced to the center of the room and turned back around to find him watching me, daring me. I stared back into his silver eyes as I grasped the elastic of my shorts and panties, and allowed them to fall down my legs. His eyes darkened and didn't leave me. His breaths came out heavy.

I took all of him in. He was completely bared to me, his well-toned body on full display. My gaze roamed over the broad expanse of his shoulders, the way they tapered into thick, sculpted arms, honed by battle and relentless training. His chest was just as impressive, leading down to the deep grooves of his abdominals, each ridge cut like stone, flexing subtly with every breath he took.

Then my eyes drifted lower, and—*my gosh*—I had never considered myself a leg girl before. But his? His were something else entirely. Thick, powerful, like tree trunks. They looked strong enough to crush logs or pin me beneath him for hours—and I suddenly realized just how much I wouldn't mind that.

The light of his room reflected off a trickle of precome. I stepped backward until my legs touched his bed, and I fell back onto it, spreading my thighs, inviting him in. "Do whatever you want. Just please, put it inside me."

At first, he obeyed. He climbed into the bed and positioned himself between my legs. He fisted his hard length and stroked it a few times. He stared down the length of my thighs and then up at me. His jaw was clenched, and his eyes appeared pained, his brows deeply furrowed.

"I can't," he finally choked out.

"Of course you can!" I demanded. "Just put it in!"

"It would not be right . . . you're . . . you're . . . I . . . I do not think straight. *Blyad!* Why . . ."

"Please," I begged again, and a tear escaped and trailed down my cheek. "Please. I need this. Please, Nikolai."

"It's not right," he said, but I could tell his resolve was weak. He said no, but he wouldn't move.

"It's just sex," I bargained. "Just casual sex. You've had casual sex before, right?"

He didn't answer.

"Have you never had casual sex before?" I demanded.

"Of course I have!"

"So, why can't you have casual sex with me?"

He, again, didn't say anything.

"I promise, it won't mean anything. We'll just go on after today as if it never happened. It'll be like we were strangers who met at a party or something and then never saw each other again. Please, Nikolai." More tears formed and fell. I couldn't hold them back. A soul-destroying throb pulsed throughout my groin. "Please. I need this. Please, can you? Please."

His resolve faltered more. His hands were now on my knees, stroking me, sending soothing vibrations up the length of my legs.

"Please, Nikolai," I whispered through my tears. Desperate anxiety overtook my whole being. What if he refused me? I would perish.

"Kolya," he practically whispered.

"Kolya?"

"Call me Kolya. It's my familiar name."

"Kolya." I tested it out. "Kolya, please."

His eyes were so soft now as they glanced down at me. He swallowed, and his Adam's apple bobbed. He took one of my hands in his and finally spoke. "After today, we can't do this again."

"I know," I replied with an ache in my throat.

"It's not you. I can't be with anyone now."

"It's okay, you don't have to. And you're not the first person I've come to for this," I said, hoping it would make him feel better, assure him that I wouldn't cling to him or expect more. "I've done it a few times already. At school. So you don't have to worry about me getting attached. During heat. I went and found someone—"

"Stop," he said. "I don't need to know about others."

I nodded, and the sides of his mouth lifted into what was almost a smile.

Kolya wrapped his massive hands around my thighs, yanking me closer to him. And although my thighs were thick with muscle from all the working out, they appeared petite in his alpha hands. He positioned himself at my entrance and then trailed his eyes along my stomach, my breasts, and face, until his silver eyes met mine. And I knew this was just a one-time, casual thing. But for a moment, I felt something. Tenderness radiated from his body, and the way he looked at me was a way no one ever had before. I felt absolutely gorgeous for the first time in my life. His face showed nothing but pure admiration.

"You're okay?" he asked.

"Yes, keep going, please." I couldn't keep the desperation out of my voice. He was so close. Just a small movement away. Every second he didn't proceed tormented me.

He took a deep breath and brought himself to my entrance. I stared up at him in anticipation, unable to breathe.

His luminous silver eyes didn't leave mine as he, at long last, pushed himself inside me. I let out a relieved moan as Kolya breached my entrance and stretched my insides to the max. He had to withdraw and push back in a few times before I could fully accommodate his massive size. I'd been with a handful of men by that point, but no one even close to as huge as Kolya. I'm sure it should've hurt. But all I could feel in that moment was freedom from the desperation I'd been suffering moments earlier. As he thrust forward, my insides practically sang from satisfaction.

"Fuck! Is so good," he moaned and rocked himself back and forth. "You're so wet, so tight, so beautiful." All of a sudden, the man of few words was speaking, unable to control himself. "So sexy. Perfect."

"Keep going. Don't stop," I said, needing more.

He obeyed, pushing himself inside to the hilt. I let out a satisfied cry. I savored each movement, each brush of his hips along the inside of my thighs, each hot breath that fanned across my face, each groan from his own pleasure. No detail was missed. At some point, it came to me that I was in the middle of the best sex of my life.

"Harder," I whispered.

"I want it to last," he replied, continuing his steady, controlled movements. "You feel very good. If I do it harder, that's it."

"It's okay." I wanted it to last too. But my body and mind were not my body and mind in that moment. I'd been possessed by a need that outweighed all rational thought. I couldn't rest until that need was fulfilled.

The expression on his face was pained. And it occurred to me that perhaps he felt the same way I did. What a pity that the best sex I'd ever had was about to end, and then it would never happen again. But that part of me was too weak against the greater demands of my wolf.

He thrust into me with his full force, and I let out a carnal moan. Kolya gently pushed a bit of blanket into my mouth.

"I want to give you everything," he whispered, "but people are home."

I nodded, my eyes wide and pleading. A whimper escaped, begging him not to stop. Tears were prickling my eyes. I was so close.

He clearly understood the assignment, because he was back at it, this time with more zeal. I moaned into the blanket, and he seemed pleased as he accelerated, driving into me faster and harder. And then he did it again, somehow hitting a spot that let off hot sparks. My eyes rolled back into my head, and I pulled the blanket out of my mouth. "Right there," I moaned. "It feels so good right there."

He pushed the blanket back and rocked back on his hips, and he managed to hit the same spot again. My toes literally curled. Was that my G-spot he'd found? He diligently thrust into the same spot over and over again, and I could barely breathe, think, or see. I bit into the blanket, allowing it to muffle the screams that would have otherwise been audible in the beta wing. He picked up speed, and my whole body shook under him, my insides flamed. And then he hit it again. The world exploded, stars burst behind my eyes, I convulsed uncontrollably. An earthquake wreaked havoc on my body as the best orgasm of my life spread through me.

He jerked himself out from inside me and let out a loud, satisfied moan as his hot come rained down onto my stomach.

My labored breathing was halted when a trance abruptly came over me. The world around me disappeared as my eyes turned to crosshairs, zeroing in on Kolya's neck. I surrendered to the feeling and followed my instincts, getting onto my knees so I could reach. I opened my mouth and . . .

"What are you doing?" Kolya exclaimed, stopping me by my shoulders.

My neck jerked back, and I came to. "What?"

He stared at my mouth and then asked, "You were going to *mark me*? Why are your teeth like that?"

I touched my canines, and he was right. They had expanded. Something that had never happened in my human form before. Tears of shame tumbled down my cheeks. "I didn't mean to," I tried to explain. How could I explain? I really hadn't meant to do that. I would never mark someone against their will, without discussing it ahead of time. And I definitely wouldn't mark someone just because we had sex once. "I really didn't mean to," I said again, not sure how to convince him I wasn't lying.

I stared at him, wondering how he'd react. Would he yell at me? Would he tell me to never look at him again? Would he think I was crazy and trying to mark an alpha for my own gain?

"I believe you," he said in the end. I let out a sigh of relief.

"I promise, it's true. I would never mark someone without their permission." I hoped he understood what I said, since it all came out as mumbles with my enlarged canines in the way.

"Is that what happened to you?" he asked, gently touching my mark.

I nodded, and another tear slipped out. He brought his finger to my face and wiped it away.

"Here," he said and grabbed for his towel where it had been abandoned on the floor. He gently dabbed at my stomach. Once he was satisfied I was clean, he threw it into a hamper and lay down in the bed. He then surprised me by opening his arms to me.

I crawled into them, and he wrapped me up against him. As soon as my skin touched his, the anxiety dulled and warmth spread through me. Suddenly, everything was okay. I was protected and safe within his large arms. Slowly, my teeth receded back into my gums, tingling a bit, until I could tell they were back to normal.

"He was your mate?" Kolya asked.

"No," I replied.

"This has happened before? Your teeth doing that?"

"No. I never slept with him again after that. And the others were all humans. I think it's because you're a werewolf. Now that I've been marked, my wolf needs to mark back. I think that's why I keep going into heat."

We were silent for a long time. I curled into him, listening to his heartbeat. Even though we were practically strangers, something about being with him was so familiar. As if we'd known each other in another lifetime and met again in this one. My body melded into his like soft butter.

But something felt off. I could sense that, although he was calm on the surface, holding me softly against him, something was seething under his skin. When Kolya finally broke the silence, he said, "Whoever he is, he deserves death."

"Don't say that," I responded, not even sure why I was being defensive.

"Rape is punishable by death. What he did, it's no better. And if I ever learn who he is, it will be his last day on earth."

I tensed but didn't say anything. A warning. To never tell him who he was. I could sense that nothing Kolya said was an empty threat. In fact, I knew. I'd grown up with three alphas. And any of them would have done the same.

Chapter 24

Julia

29 years ago

When I was first introduced to the future alpha, Lance, I knew he'd be mine. There was no length I wouldn't go to make sure of it. But I also knew he would be a challenge. His brother, Gabe, had been child's play, just a little mouse I'd bounced around in my claws before swallowing him whole. Lance, on the other hand, was a mongoose. And he would not go down so easily.

"Pleased to meet you, Julia," he'd said, barely even acknowledging my presence before turning to his father to discuss some other pack they'd been dealing with. I was an afterthought, a passing breeze, something beneath his notice.

"And this is my little sister, Miriam." Gabe brought my attention to a mousy, lanky girl with a shiny black French braid that fell to her lower back, who appeared more overgrown ten-year-old than the fifteen-year-old Gabe had told me she was.

"Hello," Miriam said as she shook my hand. She tilted her head slightly and put on what was clearly a forced smile.

As we'd both predicted, my visit to his pack was tense, and it would be a gross understatement to say I was unwelcome. To his parents, I was vermin that had made myself at home in their otherwise pristine house. It went without saying that Alpha Bruce and Luna Catherine, both devout worshippers of Artemis, were adamantly against chosen mates. But I had to give some credit to Gabe. The bit of alpha genetics he had came out at the dinner table, where he would make sure there was always a setting for me and argue loudly with his father, the current alpha.

During the third dinner, things escalated. "Julia is going to be my mate, whether you agree or not!" Gabe threw his water glass straight at his father's head.

Alpha Bruce dodged at the last moment, it shattered against the wall behind him, and he stood. "I've had enough of your disrespect!"

"And you think I haven't had enough of yours?" Gabe spat back.

"I'm the fucking alpha! You sit your ass down, you ungrateful dingbat!"

"Let's take this outside! Wolf to wolf!" Gabe's muscles and veins strained against his skin. He clenched his hands into fists and jumped back and forth on his feet, readying himself for a fight. "Then we'll see who should really be the alpha."

"Gabe, stop!" Luna Catherine shouted. "This is not necessary."

"Stay out of it, Mom," he bit back. "This is between me and Dad."

"Shut up and sit your ass down!" Alpha Bruce bellowed. He must have used his alpha aura, because Gabe immediately went quiet and took his seat. Gabe's nostrils flared, and his eyes were wild. But he couldn't speak.

I did what I could to comfort him after dinner. "You were so brave against your father. I was very impressed."

"My dad's an asshole," Gabe replied. "I totally would have taken him. But he won't even let me fight him."

"He only takes easy way out because he knows you would easily beat him in fight," I agreed.

"You get it." Gabe smiled.

Before long, he was on top of me, pulling off my clothes, touching me everywhere I allowed him. He was in a more aggressive mood that night, pressing so hard on my breasts they probably bruised. But I pretended I loved every second of it, as if he were the best and only lover I'd ever had. He pumped into my hand until he spilled his seed all over my chest, letting out a high-pitched cry as he came.

I used the T-shirt he'd discarded to clean myself off. Then I allowed him to hold me, and told him how amazing he was and how lucky I was to have such a great lover. One thing I'd realized over time was, as long as a man had a good time, he'd believe everyone had had a good time. And so, much like all men, Gabe didn't even question how I could have possibly enjoyed myself.

After enough time had passed, I told him I needed to go for a run to cool off. He rolled over and was snoring before I'd even finished re-dressing myself. I quietly snuck out of his room and made my way downstairs, then through the back door. I found my usual place to undress and store my clothes while I went for my nightly run in my wolf form. After performing all day for Gabe, I needed this to let go and just be, to merely run on instinct.

I spent at least an hour sprinting through the Alaskan wilderness, imagining it as my new home. Honestly, it wasn't too different from back home—we also lived in the middle of nowhere. But here, there were some undeniable luxuries. The houses were beautiful, like something out of a TV show or movie. Running water and reliable electricity were standard here, unlike back home, where some pack members still used outdoor latrines; pack members that—I reminded myself—I could be mated to. Being with Gabe wouldn't be so bad. As long as I kept reassuring him, he'd be happy. And most importantly, I'd never have to return to that shithole of a pack again.

But still, I could do better.

It was as if Artemis had been listening to my prayers. Because what I saw that night changed my life forever.

I stepped behind one of the few rocks scattered across the expansive backyard of the packhouse, turning off my night vision in preparation for shifting. I wanted to avoid drawing attention to my naked body, in case someone happened to glance out of a window.

As I quickly scanned my surroundings, the faint lights at the back of the packhouse revealed a shadow moving stealthily along the perimeter. I stilled, lowering my body behind the rock, my eyes locked onto the figure.

It scaled the wall, climbing up the siding with the ease of someone who had done it before. As it ascended, its outline sharpened, revealing a wolf. By its massive size, it had to be a male. My gaze shifted upward to an open window. A welcome intruder? There was no other explanation for a window being left ajar in the middle of the Alaskan winter.

Just as I'd anticipated, the wolf slipped through the window. Not even a second passed before it closed behind him.

I smiled as I counted the windows, mentally mapping out the layout of the bedrooms. I was nearly certain whose window the wolf had entered. After I gathered my clothing and watch, I noted the time. Something told me this wasn't a one-time visit. That wolf had been far too confident and familiar with the climb he'd made.

The next morning, while everyone was out and I was left behind, I decided to hunt for the tools I needed. My search led me to the basement, where I discovered their neatly organized collection of common tools, each perfectly labeled. It didn't take long to slip out a screwdriver and a few washers.

My second-oldest brother, who'd turned to thievery in his teenage years before eventually being banished by the pack, had taught me a thing or two back when we were still in contact—one of which was how to disable a lock.

It took me only minutes to do what I'd set out to. I smiled and practically skipped down the hall to the guest room where I was staying. Then I made myself as invisible as possible for the remainder of the day.

I endured the nightly fight that was becoming a permanent fixture of dinner, then soothed and reassured Gabe that he was a big bad wolf who could easily take down his father. Once he felt better, I allowed him to remove my clothes. To speed things along, I grabbed at his erection as soon as my panties were removed and said, "You make me feel all these things I never felt before." I stroked him up and down and stared up at him like he was a god.

"I can make you feel even more things." He pushed me down into his pillows.

"Like what?" I asked, giving him my best doe eyes.

"I want you to feel what it's like to go all the way."

"I told you. Only after marriage. I am good girl."

"I brought you here. I told my family I'm taking you as a chosen mate. It's as good as done." He grabbed at my knees and pushed my legs apart.

"No!" I cried out. It took everything in me not to slap him across the face. But I knew if I did that, it would all be over. Instead, I resorted to thinking about sad things. I forced out my tears and put on the waterworks. "Gabe, how could you?" I sobbed. "I am not ready. I trusted you. Maybe this was terrible idea." I grabbed at my clothes and covered myself.

"Julia, no!" Gabe reached out to me. "No, I'm sorry, Julia. Please don't cry."

"I thought you believe in Artemis's teachings."

"I do!" he reassured me.

"Artemis tells us to wait until marriage. And I will not sin, Gabe, I will not!"

"Of course not, Julia. I would never expect that of you."

"So I can trust you?" I sniffed and fluttered my eyelashes.

"Yes, of course. I'll always take care of you," he replied. Soon he was holding me again and agreeing to just a hand job.

After he passed out, I snuck out again and made my way out of the packhouse for my nightly run. When I returned, I stayed hidden with most of my body concealed behind the backyard shed, my night vision turned off, with just the moon and dim packhouse lights allowing me to see.

As predicted, the wolf returned. He moved with the same confidence, the same ease. As soon as the window shut behind him, I shifted, dressed, and padded into the packhouse, each step calculated, avoiding the creaky floorboards I had already memorized.

Soon I'd made it to the room that coincided with the open window and brought my ear to the crack between the door and the floor.

Quiet groans being swallowed by kisses. The squeak of the bedspring. The pounding of flesh hitting flesh. It was exactly as I'd suspected.

I rose to my feet, took a deep breath, and swung the door open.

The light of the hallway spilled into the large bedroom, illuminating the tangled bodies on the bed. And there, caught midact, were two very large, very naked men. Performing unmentionable things with each other.

Although I'd been expecting it, it was quite another thing to play witness to something I'd only ever heard rumors about. The gasp that left my lips was authentic. Same with the wide, terrified eyes. For a moment, I was rendered speechless and completely forgot what I was going to say.

The soon-to-be Alpha Lance and his mysterious partner stared back at me, frozen. Faces twisted into cold, raw, unfiltered terror.

"I . . . I . . ." My voice trembled. I shook my head, my thoughts scrambling for the right words. "I opened wrong door . . . by accident. I'm sorry!"

Without waiting for a response, I slammed the door shut and bolted down the hall to my guest room. The dash, though part of the plan, was as genuine as my gasp. I collapsed onto my bed, clutching my pillow, panting as adrenaline coursed through me.

That moment would be seared into my memory forever.

While Lance had likely faced countless fears in his life, the look he'd given me was one of pure dread. His worst nightmare had come to life. I'd uncovered the one secret he'd intended to keep buried forever, especially from his brutal, strictly religious father.

Check, mongoose.

Chapter 25

Theresa

After the whole heat situation, I was at a loss. Some might call it spiraling, maybe the beginning stages of insanity. Parts of me felt deep shame. I'd basically taken advantage of the man, twice now! A man who'd made it very clear he had no interest in me. A man my mom was actively attempting to seduce on my behalf . . . and here I was, being an extension of her. Ugh!

Why hadn't I been stronger?

Why didn't I bolt from his room the moment I woke in it?

Why, after the many times I'd sleepwalked only to be stopped by a locked door, was that the one time it wasn't?

What kind of person does this twice? What kind of woman forces herself on a man who already said no?

I didn't force him. I didn't. He wanted it too.

But if he wanted it, why did he resist at first?

Because he has a conscience, unlike you.

And not knowing how he felt about what had happened was driving me deeper into crazy. Of course, he had to know heat made one senseless and incorrigible. It had to be the same for men when they smelled it, right? He would have been as defenseless as I was.

I tried to think back. Beyond his clear desire, had there been antagonism? Had he felt like I had done it on purpose to take advantage of him, especially after the whole cabin situation? Did he think I was some sicko who was hell-bent on getting him inside me?

The specifics were blurry. The day had put me into a daze, but as I thought more about it, details emerged. Yes, he had resisted initially, but he'd eventually given in. And he'd wanted it to last. He'd wanted it to last! I clung to that. He'd been going slowly so he wouldn't finish too early.

And when I'd done the unthinkable—the thing that made me want to puke all over my room when I thought about it—he hadn't accused me of what I'd thought he would. No, he'd believed me. My heart stuttered and melted at the thought. He had not a single reason to, but he'd chosen to anyway.

And the sex—my gosh—the sex! I didn't even know it could be so good.

But I'd have to forget it. It would never happen again. Maybe I could pray that someday I'd meet someone else who would make me feel half as good as Kolya had. And, I hadn't even thought that was possible, so perhaps I'd even have better one day.

When I couldn't take my overthinking and anxiety anymore, I finally got off my butt and made my way to the home of the one person I knew could make me feel better. Sophia already had her door open by the time I was halfway up her driveway.

As soon as I entered, she wrapped me in a huge bear hug and whisked me up to her bedroom, the place that had become my safe haven over the years.

"How are you, you big bad bitch?" she sang out as soon as we were behind closed doors. Sophia was the most adorable little blonde thing with the most vulgar mouth. She mostly got away with it because she was so gosh darn cute and unassuming. "What's going on? What's been happening with the asshole that should have been a wet spot on his dad's sock?"

I couldn't help but chuckle. "He keeps texting. He keeps making new phone numbers. He's like a cancer. It's like a stupid game of whack-a-mole."

"You know, we both know some people who would end that game for you."

"Sophia," I sighed.

"I know, I know!" She rolled her eyes.

"He can feel everything, you know?" I said. "He knows when I'm—" I hesitated for a moment. Even though Sophia was the last person who would ever judge, I couldn't help a lifetime of forced modesty. "When I'm in heat."

"Gross!" She made a gesture of throwing up.

"Look at these texts." I handed her my phone. "From yesterday."

She took a moment to read the text I'd pulled up for her. "He's disgusting. I can't believe he would text you that! 'You know you want my cock inside you.' I would let your brother kill him just for that!"

She handed me back my phone. I took it and showed her the list of all the messages that had been moved into my Spam & Blocked queue. "Look at all this! All him!"

"Fucking Artemis! He's such a parasite. Let me see." She took the phone to scroll the long list.

I sat back in the chair in her room and sighed to myself. At least talking about this got my mind off the prior day.

"What's this?" Sophia questioned. I stiffened, suddenly recalling something I hadn't wanted her to see. "'Why does it hurt so much! Why do you have wolfsbane in you?' What is he talking about?"

"Oh, that's nothing." I grabbed my phone back from her.

She put her hands on her hips. "It's obviously not nothing. Why did he think you had wolfsbane in you? Did you actually . . . ?"

"It's not a big deal," I replied. "I'm fine now."

"Dude! Wolfsbane? Wolfsbane!" She raised her voice. "You mean the only poison known to kill werewolves? The shit that's a death sentence if any pack member's found in possession of it?"

"Stop! It's okay!" I tried to hush her. "Keep it down."

"What aren't you telling me? Because this is really freaking me out. And I know you can handle yourself, but I'm legit worried."

I sighed, weighing what to tell her. Finally, I settled on saying, "I went on a mission with Alpha Kolya. Well, Nikolai, but his nickname is Kolya. And some crazy wolves had wolfsbane on them. But we killed both of them, so there's nothing to worry about."

"What the fuck?"

"Seriously, Soph, don't worry about it. It's better that you don't. It wasn't anywhere near our pack. It was just some random attack. Probably some wolves who went rogue after getting banished from their pack." I didn't believe a single word of what I told her, but I also didn't want this information to ever leave this room. While I trusted Sophia, I was afraid that trust was only good up until she truly feared my life was in danger.

"Terri, Terri, what am I going to do with you?" She shook her head.

"Just be my friend," I replied.

"Of course. You're my best bitch!" She smiled. "And a fucking badass. You and Alpha Nikolai took out two other werewolves? That's nuts! I didn't know you had it in you to kill."

"I didn't actually do the killing, but it's like my dad always said. Kill or be killed."

"Yep. Which is exactly why we should enlist your dad to kill the piece of shit that sends you disgusting texts when he's supposed to be blocked."

"You know I won't do that."

"Sometimes I wish you weren't such a kind person." She let out a heavy sigh. "Fine, let's talk about something else. So who did you manage to fuck yesterday during heat? Anyone hot in the pack? What lucky bastard got to have a piece of the beautiful, majestic, and badass Alphette Terri?"

I froze. My whole body tensed, and my skin burned.

"Oh my Goddess! You fucked someone yesterday. Seriously? Who?"

"You know I tell you everything, but I can't tell you this."

"Why?"

"I promised I wouldn't. If my dad or Tyce ever found out . . ."

"Tyce? The same Tyce who's put his dick in half the pack? You need to stop being afraid your brother is going to care that you're also trying to live your best life."

"He would care about this one. Just trust me."

She snickered and covered her mouth. "Damn! You fucked Damien, didn't you?" she teased, guessing the name of my brother's best friend.

I couldn't help but snicker at the thought. Damien was practically a third brother to me, so I didn't see him that way at all. But a part of me did find the idea funny. Tyce would be *pissed*. "Don't guess!" I finally responded. "I'm not going to tell you."

"Fine fine!" she replied, waving her hand. "But unless you say otherwise, I'm just going to assume that you and Damien are sneaking around behind Tyce's back."

"Assume away!" I replied, laughing again at the thought. Tyce did always act extra protective of me around his friends, especially after I started wearing a bra. While I loved my big brother, it was also fun to get a rise out of him sometimes. Although Gigi had that department covered now.

We laughed a bit more, and then Sophia's face settled. She looked me up and down and pulled me in for another hug. "Seriously, Terr, I think you should reconsider keeping this from at least Tyce. I get why you don't want to tell your dad . . ."

"About Damien?" I asked, taken aback, assuming she really thought I was sleeping with him.

She chuckled. "No, I didn't actually think you fucked him. But did you?" She pushed me away from her and stared into my eyes.

I winked. "I told you. I'm not saying anything."

"Fine! Be that way!" She shoved my shoulder. "But anyway, that wasn't what I was talking about." She let out a deep breath. "I was talking about your mark. I wish you'd consider telling Tyce about it. I just hate that he's out there living without any consequences, harassing you."

"You know as well as me what Tyce would do to him."

"He deserves it."

"Deserve it or not, I couldn't live with myself if I were the reason he lost his life. The reason his parents lost their son. I hate him, but not enough to send him to his death." I sighed. "He wasn't all bad."

"Are you kidding me? He was awful! He constantly put you down. Some of the stuff he said . . ." She clenched her hands into fists.

"I don't disagree that he has issues."

"Having issues is putting it lightly. He was abusive, Terr. Do you remember that time we all went out as a group and got drunk at the pub? And he saw you talking to some other guy for half a second and completely flipped his shit? He called you a whore in front of everyone!"

I shrugged. "He was drunk."

I could tell she was biting back what she really wanted to say. We had this conversation at least once a month, and she'd said her piece already, several times over. I understood where she was coming from and why she felt the way she did. But I wasn't ready to come clean and turn him in for his death sentence. I also wasn't ready for my parents to find out that I had dared sleep with someone before meeting my mate. Sure, Tyce had openly done it for years. But he was a male *and* the alpha heir. The rules that applied to me didn't apply to him.

I spent the remainder of the afternoon hanging out with Sophia. We went out to enjoy some of the sunrise festival before splitting up and heading back to our individual homes. As I made my way down the hall to my room, Kolya's scent alerted me to his presence before I saw him. My stomach fluttered as we made eye contact.

"Hi, Kolya!" I said, far too enthusiastically.

"*Privet*," he responded not so ardently. I did at least know that was the word for *hi* in Russian. His eyes felt intense as they burned into me.

Nervous, I cleared my throat and practically whispered, "Thank you. For yesterday. I appreciate it."

He narrowed his eyes. For a moment I thought he was angry, but then he spoke in a deep, gentle voice that was anything but outraged. "Do not ever thank me for what I did. Only person who should be thankful in that situation is me. You are gift. That I was allowed opportunity to be with you, even once in my life, is worth more than anything I could ever give back."

My mouth fell open, and my heart stuttered. I quickly closed it.

He reached out and lightly squeezed my arm, sending a jolt of pleasure through me. His touch was unreal. I practically melted from the contact, and memories flooded my mind. I quickly pushed them away. No thinking about his broad, sturdy shoulders or the deep crevices of his abs, especially not while he was standing right in front of me, touching me, breathing the same air as me. His eyes bore into mine, the silver of his irises somehow both hot and cold simultaneously as he held my gaze. "You *are* okay after yesterday?" he quietly questioned.

"Yeah! Of course!" I responded, desperate to make him see I was totally 100 percent fine, and definitely not sulking around because he wouldn't be more to me than a one-night stand. "I told you, it was casual. Totally casual."

"Casual." The corners of his mouth tilted upward, but the expression seemed somehow forced.

"Casual. Just pounce and bounce."

"Pounce and bounce."

"I've done it before. Lots of times actually. So many times!" Did he just wince? "This was no different! You're just another unlucky passenger getting pulled onto the Terri train." I thought I was easing his worries, but I couldn't help but notice the way his eyebrows pulled together and his shoulders sagged a bit. Pain shot through my chest, and I practically keeled over. It took me a second to realize it wasn't my emotions that had caused that sensation.

"Terri, any man lucky to be with you." He frowned. "I *was* lucky to be with you, even if only for few moments. But I cannot be with anyone now."

"Why not?" I asked, trying my best not to read too much into anything he was saying. "Your pack is safe in our pack." I paused and then added, "Even if not with me, I don't see why you should deny yourself."

His brows furrowed, and his eyes turned dull. He stared off, as if he were seeing something I couldn't. Melancholy seeped from him, and it took everything in me not to wrap my arms around him in sympathy. "I cannot have distractions now. Even if our pack looks safe, I do not believe the wolves we fought were coincidence." He sighed, then stared straight into my soul. "The war that killed most of my pack was not just petty dispute. I cannot tell you more, not because I do not trust you, but because it is dangerous to know more." He sucked in a deep breath and let it out. "I have something they want."

"What could they possibly want enough to follow you to another continent?"

"Something worth so much that if other packs learn about it, they would make alliances even with a pack so weak it is liability to them. Worth so much, the weak pack would risk a stronger pack knowing, even knowing the stronger pack could wipe them out of existence, just to keep it for themselves."

"Oh," I replied, not sure what else to say. I wanted to press for more, but I had a feeling I was already pushing it with how much I'd begged of him the prior day. "Can I help?"

"No, it is best you don't," he replied and turned away, ending the conversation.

I watched him disappear down the stairs. All I could think was, he didn't say he didn't *want* my help, just that it was best I didn't. I knew I was just one person, and likely couldn't offer much to his pack, but there had to be something I could do. Whatever he was trying to handle was so clearly bigger than him. And I don't know why, but I felt some sort of strange pull, like this was my calling. Like I was meant to help him. And maybe I wouldn't figure out how today, but I also knew I wouldn't be able to sit still and do nothing.

# Chapter 26

Ginger

I woke to a gentle shake of my upper arm. "Baby," the most beautiful voice whispered. "Wake up."

I turned to find Tyce standing beside the bed, my snowsuit slung over his shoulder. His soft smile dissipated my grogginess. "What's going on?" I asked. It wasn't like him to randomly wake me in the middle of the night.

"Nothing's wrong. I just have something to show you," he replied, holding the snowsuit out to me. "Put this on."

Curiosity replaced sleep as I slid out of bed. Tyce helped me into the snowsuit, steadying me when I stumbled. We crept downstairs, pulled on our boots, and stepped outside.

Crisp, frosty air pricked my cheeks. But I was instantly distracted from the cold as soon as I glanced up and gasped at the sight. "Oh my Goddess, this is amazing!" I exclaimed, taking in the night sky. I had seen the northern lights a handful of times, especially now that I was living in Alaska, but it had never been quite as vibrant and intense as it was that night. Neon ribbons of green and magenta shimmered as far as I could see.

He took my gloved hand in his and pulled me out to the middle of the backyard. A thick blanket was spread out on the snow, with Thermoses and a large, gift-wrapped box waiting for us. He gestured for me to sit, and I obeyed.

"This used to be my favorite thing to do as a kid," Tyce said, his voice tinged with nostalgia. I turned to find he had a big, wistful smile on his face. "When I got my wolf, I started doing it in that form instead. But this brings back so many good memories." He grabbed a Thermos and lifted it in a cheers gesture. I grabbed my own and clinked it against his, then took a hearty drink of what turned out to be hot chocolate.

"Did you make this?" I asked.

"I'm not completely inept."

"Really?" I teased. "I still haven't had any of that cooking you claim you're able to do. Pretty sure everything's been made by Tasha except that one night Terri got voluntold to make our dinner."

"Give me some credit! I'm capable of boiling water and stirring in Swiss Miss and marshmallows."

"Ooh! You even added the marshmallows! Overachiever!"

"Of course! Hot cocoa without marshmallows is a crime."

"Swiss Miss already comes with marshmallows most of the time."

"Well, this one didn't."

"So what happens if I don't add marshmallow when I make hot cocoa? Do I get tortured by Alpha Tyce?" I teased.

"Of course. But it's only a minor crime, so I'll still stab you, just not with a knife."

"Damn. I'm ready to commit some crimes now. Many crimes. So many crimes you'll regret not going harder on me."

"I'll go harder if you want me to, baby." He pulled me closer. I snuggled into him, sad there were so many layers between us. I craved the sparks that I normally indulged in when we were skin to skin.

"So what's with the gift?" I asked, pulling the hefty box into my lap.

"Just an early b-day prez."

"My birthday isn't for almost two months."

"Every day you're with me is a birthday." He winked.

"That was disgustingly corny."

He stuck his tongue out at me. "Well, c'mon, go ahead and open it!"

I pulled off my gloves, tore into the wrapping, and pried open the box. Inside was some sort of fur. I could easily tell by the smell. I pulled it out and turned it around in my hands, trying to figure out what I was looking at. "Are you like a cat now, presenting me with a dead animal to show what a big bad little hunter you are?"

"I did hunt a bunch of these down. But don't worry, I got rid of the guts."

"What is it?" I tried to make sense of it. At first I thought it might be a fur coat, but it didn't have sleeves, and it had a zipper down the middle of it.

"I know how insecure you are about your wolf form. Of course, I think your wolf is badass, but I know you've been scared to join in on the full moon runs. So I made you something you could wear so you feel more comfortable. I hunted down a bunch of coyotes, since their coloring is similar to yours, and brought them to the seamstress so she could turn the pelts into a little cover for your wolf. I'm happy to zip you into it any time you want to wear it. At least until you realize how amazing you already are."

"What? Seriously? Tyce!" I hit him on his upper arm.

"What?"

No one had ever done anything like this for me before. My fingers trembled as I ran them over the soft fur. My throat tightened, and I clenched my jaw, fighting back the stupid tears that were spilling over. I wiped at my face furiously, cursing myself for crying like a baby. "Stop it, stop it, stop it! No more being so sweet!"

Tyce chuckled, completely unbothered by my reaction. "You deserve for someone to be sweet to you," he said simply. Then he pulled me into his arms and nuzzled his face against my cheek. "Even if you pretend you hate every second of it when I know you don't."

I responded with a *humph.*

"Do you want to try it on? I can take a picture of you in it, so you can see what you look like."

"Okay, fine," I conceded, acting like it was a huge burden even though my insides danced with excitement. The ugly missing fur of my wolf would be covered up. I'd have a chance to actually look normal! It was everything I'd been hoping for. Granted, I'd prefer to be permanently fixed, but this was a good compromise, for now at least.

I stripped down as quickly as I could while the unrelenting cold bit at my exposed skin. That was the second reason I hated going into my wolf form.

"So sexy." Tyce whistled once I was completely bare. But I gave him the show for barely a second before I morphed into my wolf. My nails stretched into claws, fur sprouted from newly formed hair follicles, and my bones rearranged themselves into my canine form. My paws landed on the fluffy snow.

"So fucking cool." Tyce grinned with pride. "If we ever go into battle, it's game over once they get a look at you."

I tilted my head in insecurity. Sure, I looked scary, but once they got over the initial shock, I'd be taken down in seconds. Even though I was training with Sara regularly, I was also getting my ass beat regularly. It was only thanks to my new werewolf superspeed healing that my skin color wasn't black and blue. But I was determined. I would keep training, even if it killed me.

"What's wrong?" Tyce asked, furrowing his brows. He stroked my cheek, and I nuzzled into his hand.

"*I just wish I was better at fighting,*" I replied via mindlink.

"You will be. Everyone's shit at first. You should've seen how much I sucked when I started. Don't compare your beginning to someone else's middle." He bent down and grabbed the fur cover from the box it was sitting in. "Here, let me put this on you. Maybe it'll cheer you up."

He unzipped it and laid it out so I could step into the leg holes. He then wrapped it around my body and zipped it up around me. While I'd been pleased to find that my wolf was able to stay pretty warm even with all the exposed bones, it was nice having something better insulating me.

Tyce pulled his phone out of his pocket. "Now smile!"

I posed, putting one of my front legs out, then I did a spin to show off the rest of my body.

Before long, Tyce abandoned his phone, and clothes, and also morphed into his wolf. While I'd gotten used to being around his wolf, it still always surprised me just how big he was. He had to be twice the size of me.

I stretched my legs one final time, broke into a run, and headed toward the outskirts of the pack. Tyce took no time to catch up, and we were soon running side by side. With the packhouse in the center of town, getting somewhere with some privacy required running by other people's homes, so I usually didn't shift until I was well hidden. Even in the middle of the night when almost everyone was asleep, I'd be wallowing in insecurity that they'd see my half-dead wolf.

But now that I was covered, for the first time I didn't shrink back, didn't hesitate. I just ran.

We raced each other as the bands of northern lights danced above us, our paws kicking up clouds of snow as we ran toward the outskirts of the pack's land. The crisp night air bit at my exposed nose, but I barely felt it. It reminded me of the first night I'd gotten my wolf—how freeing and liberating it was to be out in the wilderness, alone with my mate, away from all responsibility and judgment, just the two of us against the world.

I let out a joyful bark, leaping over a snow mound with ease, feeling like I could take on the whole world. Above us, the neon ribbons of the northern lights twisted and pulsed, reflecting off the pristine snow, painting everything in eerie green and magenta hues. It was magic.

By the time we returned, I was in high spirits. After Tyce unzipped me, I shifted back to my human form and quickly threw everything back on. As we walked inside, Tyce leaned over and whispered, "I have one more surprise tonight."

I looked up and lifted my eyebrows in anticipation.

"I talked to Alpine Snow Pack as promised, and they agreed for you to train with them. Didn't even ask any questions."

"Wow, that's amazing!" I said with enthusiasm, but trying not to be too loud. "I can't believe they just agreed like that with no problem!"

"Yeah, they didn't even hesitate," Tyce said, rubbing his jaw with a dark expression.

"Isn't that a good thing?"

"That's the thing. Packs don't do favors without a reason. They didn't even ask for anything in return."

I frowned, trying to hold on to my excitement. Had it really been that easy?

Tyce shook his head. "It's a little sus. I don't want to rain on your parade, but it just seems odd they didn't push back. And with them being out here, sniffing around, doing who knows what, I'm just not sure."

"Maybe they're just helping a fellow pack out?" I tried.

"I have a hard time believing any pack is that friendly, Gi."

"Yeah, I guess." I relented, my shoulders sagging in response.

A chill ran down my spine, instinct warning me before my mind could catch up. I wanted to brush it off, to believe it was nothing, just a rare act of goodwill between packs. I needed to believe it. I wanted this to work. But deep down, I couldn't shake the nagging feeling that Tyce was right.

"We'll figure something out," he said, brushing my hair behind my ear. "I'll think of something."

"Thank you," I replied as his mouth brushed my cheek.

"For better or for worse, I have your back, always."

Chapter 27

Nikolai

When I stepped into the gym Saturday morning, ready to take over training from Sasha, I immediately noticed something was off. Half the group was missing.

I scanned the room, my brows knitting together. "Where are the women?"

Sasha barely looked up from adjusting the wraps on his wrists. "Your girl took them."

I stilled. "My girl?" I repeated, leveling a pointed look at him.

His lips twitched into a smirk. "Theresa."

I exhaled, rolling my shoulders to keep from reacting. I wanted to smack that look right off his face, but I held back, reminding myself that I'd promised I would be a better friend.

"Ha. Funny." My voice was flat. It wasn't funny. Not even a little. "Where are they?"

"Outside."

Without another word, I turned on my heel to figure out what was going on. I pushed open the heavy entryway door and was greeted by a chilling wind biting the exposed parts of my skin. It was certainly not warm today. I followed the tracks in the snow to what was likely a field during the warmer months but, at the moment, was just an open rectangle full of snow.

Terri was bundled up, observing as all of the women of my pack marched the perimeter of the open area with kettlebells in their gloved hands.

For a moment, I just stood there and watched. The wind howled across the open field, whipping strands of Terri's dark hair free from her hat. The tip of her nose was red from the cold, but she didn't seem to notice. Her cheeks were flushed, her breath coming out in soft, misty puffs as she shouted words of encouragement to the women. There was something mesmerizing about her in this moment, so in her element.

"What are you doing?" I yelled as I approached.

"Helping," she replied.

"Helping how?"

"I'm having them do farmer's carries. When I watched them deadlifting today, I realized the reason they're so limited is because they need better grip strength. Tomorrow, I'm going to go heavy on the shoulders with them. Women don't naturally get the same kind of shoulder strength men do, so they have to work that much harder at it. I know they're off on Monday, so the rest of the week I'm going to spend a few hours going over some fighting techniques that are good for women who may not have as much force power as their opponent." She took a deep breath. "Friday will probably be the last day I can do anything with them, so I'm going to spend time going over any questions they have, woman to woman. Then I'm going to have to get packed up to go back to school."

"You don't have to do this."

"But I want to!" she exclaimed with a big smile on her face. "Your pack members are so great! Two of them already invited me to come by for dinner with their host family, another one told me she's going to knit me a scarf, and three of the girls invited me to hang out one night."

I stared at her, not sure what to say.

"Plus, I enjoy this!" she continued. "When it's not with my dad, I actually love training and sparring and all that. And it's such a good feeling when you can see what you're doing make a difference."

"My pack isn't your responsibility." I couldn't allow her to spend her precious time doing this. She had no obligation to my pack. I was beginning to understand that she was the type to go out of her way to her own detriment, without complaint, unless someone else took it upon themselves to force her to think about herself. My skin warmed as I looked into her bright, eager eyes. It was not every day that one met such a selfless and beautiful person. My stomach twisted with unfamiliar feelings. She was just so . . . so . . . perfect. The best person I'd ever met

"Sure, but that doesn't mean I don't want to help," she replied. "There are lots of things that aren't my responsibility, but that doesn't mean I'm going to just turn my back on them. It's easy to decide you're never going to do anything good unless you're required to. But that doesn't really make you a good person, does it? That just makes you someone who only ever does the bare minimum. And I don't want to live in a world where people only do good when they have to do good."

I let out a heavy breath. She wasn't wrong. And I had nothing to refute her argument. If she wanted to help, so be it. It was only for a few days, anyway. Like she said, she'd be heading back to school. Where she apparently had troves of men willing to help her during heat. I balled my hands into fists at the thought, every muscle in my arms flexing with fury.

I reminded myself that she had every right to sleep with whomever she wanted. She was a grown woman and had the same needs we all did, even more so on certain days. As much as I wanted to imagine a scenario in which she could be mine, and I could do everything in my power to please her and make her happy, to ensure she never even thought about another man again, I knew it was futile. I couldn't give her what she wanted and needed. My only obligation now was to keep my pack safe. She could never be a priority to me like she deserved to be to someone.

"Are you okay?" Terri's touch on my arm jolted me back to reality. I hadn't even realized how far my thoughts had drifted. "You seem . . ." She studied me, her brows drawing together. "Angry? Sad? I'm trying to figure it out. Maybe . . . jealous?"

My head snapped up. "What?" I barked, taking a step back.

Her eyes widened slightly, and she winced. "Sorry. Sometimes I speak without thinking."

I exhaled through my nose, forcing myself to steady my expression. "Why do you think I feel that?"

She hesitated, glancing down at her hands. "I don't know. I just . . . sense it."

Sense it? A muscle in my jaw ticked. "What does that mean?"

"Never mind." She let out a nervous laugh. "Forget I said anything. I'm obviously just being crazy."

Crazy? No.

Because if I was honest with myself, she was right. The answer was there, burning a hole in my chest, but I couldn't bring myself to believe it. I considered pressing her further and demanding she tell me how she knew, how she saw right through me. But that would mean admitting what had been circling my mind moments earlier.

And that wasn't happening.

So instead, I let out an exasperated exhale and turned away. "I'll be inside. You know what you are doing."

I relieved Sasha so he could take his break and immediately took over where he'd left off. With the women gone, I worked the men extra hard as we practiced fighting in our human forms. I wasn't satisfied until noses were bloodied and there was more visible black and blue than skin color. Then I finally excused them for an extra-long lunch break, giving them some time to heal.

As I swung open the heavy front door to the gym, a woman's voice sounded from behind me. "Hey! Wait up!" I turned to find Terri sprinting toward me, a big smile on her face. She pulled a beanie over her thick waves as she stepped outside beside me. "Well, that went great today! I feel like we really made some progress!"

"Good," I replied, trying to hit a balance of appreciative but not encouraging.

"I wish I'd started helping sooner. I just barely started and already have to leave."

I nodded, not sure how to respond.

"Well, I guess a little bit of helping is better than no helping."

"Terri, you don't have to help at all."

"I know, I know." She rolled her eyes in an exaggerated motion. "It's not my pack! But I don't know. You'll probably think this is crazy, but in a weird way, I feel connected to them. Maybe it's because my family on my mom's side were betas of the pack going back generations. Or maybe it's something else. But something about being around your pack makes me feel at home somehow."

"I think you feel at home when you're helping," I blurted.

"There's nothing wrong with that!" she responded defensively.

"You're right. There's not. You're good person." A perfect person. An angel on earth.

"Wow, I'm surprised you don't have something negative to say about it."

"What do you mean?" I stopped in my tracks and stared at her.

"I guess, I just can't ever tell if you're bothered by my presence. Most of the time I think I'm annoying you, but then sometimes you seem okay with me . . ." She paused. "You know what, it doesn't matter. I'll be leaving in a few days anyway, so you can think whatever you want."

I let out a breath. I didn't like the idea of her believing I didn't like her. All of a sudden, it felt very important that she knew it was the complete opposite of that. "At first, I was annoyed. But that was before I knew you. I misunderstood. I did not see who you are. But more I see you with others, more I value you. Your beauty inside is so bright, and I was idiot not to see it. Blind fool. *Durak*, as we say in Russian."

She looked down at the snow and mumbled, "That's really nice."

I was going to turn around and return to my responsibilities. I'd said my piece, and I knew better than to let her get any closer to me.

But then she smiled.

And just like that, all my resolutions crumbled into dust. What was one more day of recklessness? She was leaving soon anyway.

"What your plans are for first sunrise?" I asked impulsively.

"I was just going to go to the pack celebration."

"You want to watch it with your friends and family, I am sure. But if not . . . there is place I went for last sunset. After being numb—" I practically choked as I said the words. It was only after I said them that I realized how much I was revealing to Terri, something I had absolutely not meant to do. But then she looked up at me again, with her sweet, angelic eyes, and I knew I couldn't backtrack. I finally ended my sentence: "I felt . . . something."

"Are you inviting me to go with you?" She practically gasped as she said the words.

I nearly retracted the offer. But then she looked up at me with those wide, hopeful eyes, and I knew there was no turning back.

"It would be in wolf form. And it's not close, so we must leave early."

"Yes!" she exclaimed when I'd barely finished my sentence. "Yes, I want to go with you. I know this is really important and personal, and I appreciate you inviting me to experience it with you."

Just seeing the smile she gave me made it worth inviting her.

Maybe a little bit of recklessness wouldn't hurt.

Like she said, she was leaving. This was a small, minuscule distraction. Just one day to give in to my desire to feel a little closer to the most amazing creature I'd ever met. And then she'd be gone, and it would be as if it had never happened. By the time she came back for the summer, it was very likely my pack would have already left.

Chapter 28

Ginger

When Tyce dropped me off on Sunday morning for another day of training with Sara, I was greeted by a rare smile.

"Do I have a surprise for you!" she practically squealed.

"More sparring?" I deadpanned.

"Better!" she replied in earnest. "Come, come. I've been saving him all night for you!"

"Him?" I questioned. Was she going to make me fight one of her warriors? Maybe I'd have half a chance for once.

"Oh yes. Found him about fifty kilometers outside your pack. Clearly waiting for someone to go out for a little run. But I caught him!" She smiled wide, displaying all her perfectly maintained teeth. She looked almost maniacal, with an evil glint in her eyes. And oddly peppy.

"What do you mean you caught him?" I swallowed.

She winked at me and pulled open a heavy metal door that I'd never noticed before. Probably because it was at the end of a dark hallway I'd never gone down previously. Suddenly, I was very aware of my breathing. I tried to keep it even, not to give away the bad feeling that was coming over me. Didn't they say something like, don't let predators smell the fear on you? I was sure I stunk of fear.

She flicked on a light, and led me down some stairs, into a basement. *Fuck!* Was I about to die? My wedding was only months away. Tyce and I were so close to marking each other. And I'd stupidly begged him to let me train with someone who was known to be a psychopath.

"Where are you taking me?" I asked.

"To my private chamber," she replied, as if that explained everything. As we made it to the last step, she added, "Torture chamber."

Fuck!

It was too late to turn back now. Certainly she wasn't actually planning to kill me. And yeah, I didn't exactly think that being tortured was part of the training plan, but I could technically heal now, in a matter of minutes or hours depending on the wound.

But then a body came into view as we turned a corner. There was someone else here. A young man, likely in his midtwenties, stripped of all his clothes, just everything hanging out, with duct tape over his mouth, chained to a metal chair that was attached to the wall with more heavy chains. *What the fuck?*

"Ta-da!" Sara exclaimed, simply delighted by this surprise.

I blinked, not sure what to say.

"Now it's time for the best part of your alpha training." She pulled open a drawer that, upon first glance, seemed to be a tool chest. However, inside wasn't hammers and screwdrivers, as I'd expected. No, it was a collection of knives. All sorts of knives, of different shapes and sizes.

She spent some time humming to herself, picking one knife up, then another. Testing a few out in the air. Finally she smiled as she selected one that seemed to be to her liking. "This. This is perfect for your first go round. Not too heavy but still a good weight. Recently sharpened, so it should cut through the flesh no problem. Good point, nice shape. Yes. This one is perfect for you." She handed it to me as if she were handing me the perfect pair of shoes for an outfit I was wearing.

Was she actually expecting me to stab him?

"I feel like a proud mother, bringing my pup down for her first torture." To be fair, she did look delighted, with a soft glow to her cheeks and eyes glazed with the slightest bit of moisture. "It's not every day you get to witness someone you've personally trained lose their torture virginity."

I think I'm going to be sick.

"I remember my first time. My father let me do the honors of first stab. I'd be happy to give it to you too, if you'd like." She smiled and nodded toward the victim in an encouraging way. A victim whose eyes were bulging with terror. I thought I stunk with fear, but his was overpowering, sour, rancid. And something told me Sara probably loved that smell and would wear it as perfume if she could.

"I'm okay. Maybe I should watch first to learn," I replied.

"Visual learner, got it." She pulled a different knife from the same drawer. "We'll start easy. Give him a chance to confess everything first. But I always hope they don't. It's so much more fun when they're devoted to their pack."

She turned and ripped the tape off his mouth. He let out a pained scream that echoed in the small, concrete room. I glanced around, eyes zeroing in on the numerous large brown stains on the floors and walls. I took in the smell of bleach. And more of the overpowering scent of stone-cold terror.

"Okay, Gigi, what do you want to know from this son of a bitch?" Sara nudged me toward him. "This asshole was kilometers from your pack lands. He could have been moments from raping and killing the pups in your pack. He could have been scheming to murder your mate to take his alpha title." She pulled on the collar of my shirt. "Hmm. No mark." After a beat, she continued, "And no legitimate pups. There's no one else in line."

I'd never thought of that. Just one essential organ removed from Tyce's body, and the pack would transfer to someone else. No wonder his family trained him so hard. They were entrusting him with their entire pack, which had gone back generations. It suddenly made sense why alphas were pressured to make pups ASAP . . .

"What do you want to know, Gigi?" Sara dug her nails into my bicep. "Go on, ask him. They say there are no bad questions. Same goes for torture. We try until we get somewhere."

I took a deep breath. My mind was blanking. What was I supposed to ask him? He looked so pathetic at that moment, I almost felt bad for him.

"He. Wants. To. Murder. Your. Mate," Sara emphasized.

"Why do you want to murder my mate?" I blurted out, feeling put on the spot.

He stared at us and didn't say anything. Sara chortled.

"Thinks being silent will save him and his pack." Sara stepped forward. "Dumbass." Before I could process what she was saying, she shoved her knife so deep into his stomach her hand was practically inside it. High-pitched shrieks echoed off the walls, floor, and ceiling. I clutched at my stomach as blood spluttered out of his. "First time you've been penetrated, eh?" Sara said as she pulled the knife out. "It's okay, after the first time, it only gets better and better." She chuckled. "At least for me."

At first, I just felt cold. An unnatural cold, one that seeped into my bones despite the warm basement air. Then, my head started to ache, a dull throb at my temples. The scent of iron hit me like a brick wall. My stomach clenched.

A bead of sweat rolled down my back. My knees wobbled. *No, no, no, keep it together.*

But when Sara slashed him again, a fresh spray of crimson splattered across the concrete floor, and I knew—I knew I wasn't going to make it.

I was trying so hard not to vomit, not to react, not to give away how disturbed I was. Sure, I watched gory movies sometimes. But this was real life. Sara was shoving a real-life knife into a real-life person, a person whose fear, blood, and sweat I could easily smell now that I had turned wolf. The assault of scents was still overwhelming for me after going my whole life without being able to smell so many. And now, I was being exposed to especially brutal scents, and they were fucking with my psyche.

"Ask him something else, Gigi. Let's see if he's learned what happens when he keeps his mouth shut."

I opened my mouth but nothing came out.

"Don't be shy. Ask him anything. Ask him his favorite color. It'll take longer to get answers. But that just means more fun." She encouraged me with a fucked-up Chesire cat smile.

I stepped forward, forcing myself to stay brave.

When I still didn't say anything, Sara spoke again. This time more quietly, slowly, deliberately. "Imagine, this motherfucker torturing Tyce instead, shoving his knife into Tyce's stomach." She thrust the knife back into the man's exposed stomach, cutting right into the center of his bellybutton. When she withdrew her knife just as quickly as she'd pushed it in, blood spurted from the open wound and his high-pitched screams followed.

My own stomach soured. The world around me dizzied. I gasped for air while simultaneously attempting to keep my breathing even so Sara wouldn't know how much this was affecting me. Suddenly I understood what a young Tyce experienced when his father and grandfather had exposed him to this. Why he had passed out. While the abstract idea of torture had been okay, experiencing it up close and personal was something else. But I couldn't let Sara see how weak I was. That I couldn't handle it. I wanted to be a good luna. I wanted to be a part of Tyce's world. And if this was what Tyce had to deal with, I would deal with it too. I kept my head up high even as it pulsed, signaling an oncoming migraine.

Sara continued, "Think of this bitch trying to get what he needs from Tyce. Or, worse, you walk into your bedroom one day, and Tyce is dead because he got to him. Maybe not this one, but another little bitch because we didn't get the information we need to stop him. If you don't torture for information, your whole pack is fucked. That's why we have to—" She slashed her knife across his chest, sending more screams into the room.

I tried to disassociate. The screams were the worst. The sound of pure, unadulterated pain ringing in my ears. But then I really thought about what Sara said. She wasn't wrong. Why was he so close to our pack that was in the middle of nowhere? Could he really be trying to take it over? It was so simple when you thought about it. Sara herself had obtained her pack in a matter of moments. And what would I do if Tyce were murdered? How would I live without him? He was my one and only mate. And I would certainly murder anyone that came even close to trying to take him from this life. Just the thought boiled my blood.

"Are you trying to kill my mate?" I screamed.

He didn't say anything. Sara chortled again and slashed him across the face.

"He's trying to kill your mate, Gigi. Find out why!" Sara exclaimed. "Ask him why!"

"Why are you trying to kill my mate?" I yelled at him.

He didn't say anything again, and Sara slashed at him again.

We continued like that for what felt like hours, although it was probably closer to minutes. She would egg me on, pressure me into asking questions, and I would. When he wouldn't answer, she'd stab, slash, or cut him. My whole body shook, the bile in my stomach burned my esophagus, my ears rang, my throat felt parched. I was more exhausted than I'd ever been sparring. This was a brutal exercise in faking it until I made it. And by the twentieth question, I didn't feel any closer to making it than I had with the first.

When his body was more red than skin toned, Sara paused and walked back toward the tool chest. She grabbed a cloth from on top of it and wiped her bloodied blade. Maybe we'd finally be able to take a break. But my hope was short-lived.

She held the knife out to me. "Now your turn."

Could I refuse?

Her dark eyes burned into me as she waited for me to take the knife.

What had I gotten myself into?

"Take it, Gigi. Do it for Tyce."

My hand shook as I extended it. I forced my palm to wrap around the handle. I was trembling so much, I almost dropped it, barely able to get a grip on it. I wrapped my other hand around the first just to make sure I wouldn't.

"Now, ask him something. If he answers, we can give him a break. But if not . . ." She smiled widely at him, leaving his fate unspoken.

"Are you trying to take over my pack?" I asked. *Please answer, please answer, please answer.*

But he didn't. He continued to hold his silence.

"We've got a stubborn one," Sara said. "My absolute favorite."

To be fair, it did seem like he was starting to relent. When I'd first entered the chamber, he'd seemed tougher. He was a tall, robust man. But something in his face showed the uncertainty he felt about the future. I could see why someone like Sara could enjoy this. After all, she was a petite woman, someone most people certainly underestimated, working in a field that had previously only been inhabited by men. And here she was, in her power, taking down a clearly well-trained warrior who had been entrusted to go on whatever mission he was on alone.

"Go on, Gigi. Show him what happens when he doesn't answer our questions." She nodded toward him. "Show me you can do this. Prove you have what it takes to be a warrior."

It was like she knew exactly what to say to get me to go through with it. For so long, I'd wanted nothing more than to be a warrior. The last thing I was going to do was leave with my tail between my legs in front of Sara.

I straightened up and forced my feet forward. I could do this.

Sara's watchful eyes burned into my back.

The bloodied, naked man stared at me, but didn't say a word. Was that normal? Did they never speak? Was that what they taught you in torture training? Did it normally help or hurt more? What was his end game? Did he know he wouldn't be leaving alive?

I took a deep breath. He was already so covered in cuts and wounds that were in the process of healing. What was one more?

I swallowed my whimpers.

My hand quivered unstoppably. I was a wimp. I couldn't bear to look at Sara, who I knew was judging my every move. I had no choice. I had to force myself to do it.

"Go for the stomach. No bone," Sara said in a voice that sounded far away, even though I knew she was still in the same spot, just behind me, watching.

Finally, I was so close I could smell his breath and sweat. It was the moment of truth. I stepped closer, the knife in my trembling hand. I just had to do it. Just one cut. It wouldn't even be that deep.

But my arms wouldn't move. My mind screamed at my body, *Go! Go!* But my muscles locked, frozen in place.

My stomach clenched at the thought of Tyce dead because I was too weak. My fingers curled tighter around the hilt. *Just do it.*

Before I could overthink some more, my arm jerked forward. I forced my body to lead. Pretended I was somebody else as I flung my arm forward and right into his stomach.

He cried out as the blade cut through his organs. And I let go. As I did, I realized I was probably supposed to pull the knife back out, but I didn't have it in me. All I could do was squat down into a small ball and force myself to keep in the vomit that was begging to come out. I slapped my hands against the cold wall and took labored breaths, doing my best to hold myself together.

Before long, someone was yanking me to my feet.

"Go upstairs," Sara commanded.

I was free. I didn't even have the ability to determine whether she was satisfied or disappointed with my performance. My legs felt like lead as I climbed the stairs. It was as if I were recovering from a month of leg days. As soon as I reached the top of the stairs and shut the door behind me, I collapsed on the floor. I couldn't believe what I had just witnessed. And done.

I wasn't sure how much time had passed when the scent of my mate encircled me as he pulled me toward his warm body, wrapping his large arms around me. "Gigi, are you okay? What were you doing on the floor? Weren't you supposed to be training?"

Tears flooded my eyes, so relieved to be safe with Tyce.

"Tell me, baby. What's wrong?" His voice was so soft, and kind, and empathetic. Part of me wanted to just cuddle into him and forget any of today had happened. But the other part of me felt shame over the fact that I couldn't handle this when I wanted to be a warrior and his luna so badly.

"I . . . I . . . Sara . . . We . . . We tortured."

"You tortured?"

"I stabbed someone."

"Who did you stab? Did someone try to hurt you?" A flare of his anger accosted me.

I shook my head, trying my best to pull myself together enough to form long phrases and explain exactly what had happened.

"Breathe, Gigi. It's okay. You can tell me later. Do you want to go?"

I nodded. And without another word, he picked me up without any effort. Something that, to this day, still astonished me he could do. Before long, I was tucked into the front seat of his car, and we were driving back to our pack, music filling the silence.

Chapter 29

Nikolai

Early on Tuesday morning, I jumped into a hot shower before it was time to leave. They say a full moon can make one do crazy things. And in our culture, we were especially affected by the first full moon of the year—the Wolf Moon. It was days away. And there was no reason to believe that a sunrise couldn't affect us much the same. Especially after having lived in persistent darkness for so long. I'd practically forgotten there was a time in my life when I'd walked under the sun's rays.

As planned, I met Terri at the dining table that morning, where I found her munching on some buttered toast. "Shh, don't tell my mom." Terri winked at me and giggled. I stared at her, not sure what she expected me to tell her mom. That I was taking her on a private adventure? Her mother would be elated at the news.

I continued into the kitchen, where I heated up one of the pre-prepped breakfast sandwiches Tasha always had on hand for the alphas when we'd be up early for training. I fumbled with the fancy Nespresso machine they had and was soon in possession of breakfast and coffee.

I joined her at the table. And although her hair was pulled back in a simple ponytail and she had clearly not put much effort into her appearance, I couldn't help but be awed by her natural beauty. She was astonishingly gorgeous just sitting there, being herself, doing the same thing she probably did every day. But I couldn't help but think that I wouldn't mind sitting across from her, just as I was now, every day, having the honor to be in her presence as she went about her daily life.

"Tasha does a great job on those sandwiches," she said, "but I don't know what it is about plain, basic butter on toast. It's just so good! Sometimes I add a little jam too, but I decided to go simple today. What about you? What's your breakfast go-to?"

"It's called *kasha*. I do not think you eat it here. Very common where I am from. *Prostaya yeda*—simple food. Keeps you full long time."

"I'd like to try it sometime."

"Tasha has some. She offered it to me."

"I'll ask her next time she makes me breakfast. That is, if my mom doesn't intervene." She groaned.

"Intervene?" I asked.

"Yeah, my mom is obsessed with being skinny. Not only does *she* have to be skinny, but she has to project her disordered body issues on me too. They have a phrase for it. Almond mom."

"Almond mom?"

"You know! Moms who just eat a couple almonds if they're hungry." She sighed. "It was so nice being away at school for a while without someone monitoring what I eat all the time."

"You're adult. You should make your own decisions about food."

"Tell that to my mom." She sighed.

I nodded. "Sometimes relationship with our families is difficult. Because we love them, we do not say what we wish to say. Because we do not want to upset them. So we allow them to hurt us instead. I understand."

"Oh, Goddess!" Terri exclaimed. "I'm so sorry. Here I am, complaining about my mom, and you . . ." She shut her eyes tightly, crinkling her nose. "I'm really sorry. I should be more appreciative."

I extended my arm and put my hand on hers. "It's okay, Terri. As Sasha reminds me, life goes on. You are allowed to complain about your parents." I didn't want her to feel as if she had to censor what she said to me.

"But doesn't it hurt to see other people fighting with their parents?"

"Yes." I nodded. "And I have not always been so understanding, I will be honest. But I want to be better." *Better for you. Even if only for a few days.*

"We should head out soon." She stood abruptly, picking up her dirty dishes.

I watched as she disappeared into the kitchen and then scarfed down the remainder of my sandwich. As soon as I put my own soiled dishes away, I followed her to the front door. We exited the packhouse together and trekked through the knee-deep snow to a place where we could remove what we were wearing.

As usual, she slipped behind a large rock to undress. Part of me yearned to sneak a peek, to allow my eyes to trace every inch of her naked body that haunted my mind. My cock hardened at the thought of her uncovered nipples stiffened by the cold air, her bare, round ass bitten by the frost, needing my large hands to warm it. It took every bit of willpower to stop imagining accosting her and pushing her against that very rock she was undressing behind.

I forced myself into my wolf form, and to stop thinking such unsa-vory thoughts. To think, there had been months where I didn't desire a woman at all. When the only thoughts I had were of grief and survival. And now—now I couldn't stop the intrusion of lust that had come over me.

Once she appeared in her wolf form, I sprinted forward. I tried to keep enough of a distance that she hopefully wouldn't notice the state of my male appendage. I'd worked myself up so much that even the below-freezing temperatures weren't enough to calm the raging inferno inside me.

And then she sprinted ahead of me, her tail held high, shaking her wolfy butt at me. She turned with a mischievous look on her face, and her tongue darted out of her mouth for just a second, before she sprinted forward again. She was teasing me, accentuating the throb of longing in me. I couldn't help but smile to myself as I pushed ahead of her in order to show her the path, doing the best I could to keep my mind on the task at hand. We had a long journey ahead of us. It would take several hours to reach our destination, and it was paramount we made it there well before sunrise.

The wind whipped around us, lifting fine dust from the snow and swirling it in the air, obscuring the path ahead. But I pushed onward, relying on my nose instead of my eyes. From when I'd first gotten my wolf, I'd always had a strong sense of direction. Once I traveled a path, the scent stayed with me, etched in my memory like a map. My mother had been the same.

Something hitched in my throat at the thought of her. Although I'd remained calm that morning, Terri had ascertained correctly that it was difficult to hear of others' mothers and to be reminded of mine. What I wouldn't give to hear her strong opinions today, as much as they had always annoyed me.

Terri came closer and whimpered. My attention instantly went to her. What had happened? Was she okay?

Nothing seemed amiss. I tilted my head at her in question. But she just looked at me with puppy eyes, as if she could sense what I had been feeling and her own mood sobered correspondingly. It was eerie. But I pushed it from my mind.

Once again, Terri impressed me with her sheer strength and resolve, easily keeping pace with me. She might have been small, but that had no bearing on how tough she was. As we moved through the stillness of the wilderness, I found myself wondering if, perhaps, I had met my equal. She carried herself with the confidence and resilience of a true alpha, someone who had earned her place through grit and determination. Yet, I couldn't shake the thought that she might have spent her life in the shadow of others—forced to obey her elder alphas, never given the chance to truly shine in her own right.

But I had only known her for such a short time. And it would remain short. So perhaps I'd never have my suspicions confirmed. Perhaps it was all a projection of the dream woman I wished I'd meet anyway. It always started out like a fantasy come true, didn't it? Until you truly got to know the person, and the more you learned about their shortcomings, the less you could stand them. At least in my experience.

But the hours of travel passed by as if they were seconds. Even running side by side without speaking a single word, unable to mindlink due to our different packs, I couldn't help but delight in every moment I got to spend by her side, and found myself wishing the day would never end.

When we finally reached the foot of the mountain we were about to climb, I paused, letting my gaze travel over her form from snout to tail. I sized her up, silently questioned whether she was still up for the climb. She met my stare with a glint of mischief in her eyes, and her head tilted just enough to say, *Are you really questioning my abilities?* Then, with perfect timing, she stuck her tongue out before spinning around and charging up the incline.

The snow on the slope was so faintly sunken it could hardly be called a path, but she ascended it with the ease of someone who belonged to the mountains. I bolted up right after her, pushing past with a burst of speed. As I pulled ahead, I threw my head back and let out a jovial howl.

She was soon on my heels, playfully shoving me with her hips and sending me stumbling sideways as she darted ahead. Just like that, something stirred within me—a part of me I thought had been lost forever, buried alongside the memories of my family. Here it was, resurfacing.

We raced up the mountain together, our paws carving twin paths in the snow. As we neared the summit, she surged forward one last time and her back paws kicked up a flurry of snow that hit me square in the face. I sputtered and barked despite myself as she reached the summit just ahead of me, triumphant and unapologetic.

As soon as I peaked, she danced around me in circles. I could only imagine the teasing song she'd sing if she could speak. I bowed, lowering my head to concede. As soon as I glanced up, she swiped her tongue along my cheek. A consolation kiss?

Her eyes then widened, and a quiet gasp escaped her mouth. I turned to see what she was looking at. I halted, my own mouth dropping open. It was at that moment the inky depths of the night sky softened and yielded to a pale, silvery blue that stretched over the horizon.

We stood side by side, entranced as a golden blush tinged the edges of the earth. The growing glow slowly revealed silhouettes of the world below. Gradually, the light washed the landscape in hues of peach and amber. The first rays of sunlight spilled over the horizon, gilding everything they touched with warm brilliance.

Terri stood beside me, so close that I could feel the warmth of her body. Her fur trembled as her breath came out in pants. When I turned to see her reaction, her eyes reflected the awe of what was unfolding in front of us. And I realized there was no place I'd rather have been than where I was at that moment.

If only I were given the opportunity to live a chosen day for more than twenty-four hours. Any perfect day of my life. I would have picked this one without hesitation.

I let out a loud howl, welcoming the break of dawn. Terri followed my lead, lifting her head to join me. Our breaths fogged the chilly air as the notes of our songs blended and carried in the wind, claiming this moment for ourselves while we marveled at the sun's slow return.

Before long, the entire world was bathed in natural light. What I had previously only been able to see through the small beam of my night vision, and mostly experienced through my other senses, was now alive with color and clarity. It was no longer a place I simply inhabited, but somewhere I lived as a small piece of a huge world.

Terri pranced along the perimeter of the summit, radiating pure joy. It was infectious. A force tugged at something buried deep within me. Slowly, a rare smile crept across my face, waking muscles that had lain dormant for ages. Then it hit me—a realization so startling it shocked me to my core. I was *happy*.

I couldn't remember who started it, but before long, we were play wrestling each other, rolling around in the snow, barking and growling. I nipped at her dark fur, fur that was full and glossy under the sun's rays. Absolutely stunning. She licked at my face, and I returned the affectionate gesture. Before long, our tongues were touching, licking at each other as we lay on our sides. Our paws rested against each other's faces, and our hind legs tangled. Heat radiated throughout my body, but I refused to advance things further. Especially when she couldn't verbally confirm it was what she wanted.

This was fleeting, a passing moment that could never evolve into anything more, given the inevitable end to our time together. For now, this was enough.

We stayed for the hour until sunset, lying together as colors deepened around us, shifting from gold to fiery orange, then to a rich, burning crimson. Finally, the sun slipped away, leaving behind a trail of twilight. Stars winked into existence, misty at first, then bolder as the last remnants of sunlight vanished. Terri let out a sad sigh. I couldn't help but compare what had just unfolded to my time with her. So beautiful, mystical, magical, but over in just a blink.

When we returned to the packhouse, I was relieved to find it empty. The faint sound of faraway howling and music alerted us to the fact that everyone was out enjoying the festivities the Jade Moon Pack had planned for the day and evening.

"Thank you for inviting me to come with you today. It was amazing! I couldn't have imagined a better way to spend the first sunrise," Terri said with bright, glossy, joyful eyes.

"No, thank *you*," I replied. When I didn't say more, she turned and headed toward the stairs. I couldn't help but stare, admiring the way her ass looked in the leggings she was wearing. I had to adjust myself and force myself not to follow.

Then she stopped, just before taking that first step.

I should say no.

She hesitated.

I should definitely say no.

When she turned back, lips slightly parted, those amber eyes glowing in the dim light, I knew I wouldn't.

"Hey," she said. "No one's here. Would you . . . want to come up? Hang out for a bit?"

One more time won't change anything, I told myself.

But the way my pulse pounded in my ears said otherwise.

The way she looked at me—so sweetly, so inviting—combined with those damn leggings, made it impossible to resist. It would take a level of willpower I didn't have to turn her down.

I followed her up, step by step, feeling like a man walking to his own execution.

The old stairs creaked beneath our weight. We padded down the hallway, passing door after door, until we made it to hers. She swung it open, and I stepped inside right after her and shut it behind me. As soon as the latch bolt clicked into the strike plate, I had my hands on her ass, pulling her against my chest. Our lips crashed together. Our tongues twined, and the only sound was our ravenous pants.

Before long, I was pulling off her shirt, revealing that she, once again, was not wearing a bra. I instantly had my mouth on her erect nipples. The nipples I had waited all day to taste. I hungrily sucked on one and then the other, twirled my tongue around its perimeter. "*Fuck*," I gasped.

She let out a quiet moan as I sucked her right nipple back into my mouth and brought my teeth to it, gently nibbling along the delicate skin.

Her arousal bloomed into a sweet aroma. *Blyad*! My cock was so stiff it was practically painful. She brought her petite hands to my stomach and pushed my shirt up. I assisted with pulling it over my head. As soon as it was off, I had my hands back on her, kissing down the center of her chest, between her perfect, pert breasts with the most beautiful tawny nipples. My lips trailed down the line of her torso until I reached the waistband of her leggings.

I tugged at the elastic to reveal she was also going commando. "No underwear?"

Her cheeks reddened, spreading to her ears. "It was easier. Since I wouldn't have them on long . . ." Her voice trailed off.

"No, you won't," I agreed, pulling them down her legs. As soon as she stepped out of them, I grabbed her hips to halt her, then gently forced her legs apart until I was able to fit my chin between them. *Blyad!* She smelled so fucking good. My tongue was drawn to her like a moth to a flame, desperate to taste her.

I licked her from bottom to top, tracing my tongue along every crevice until I found her clit. I sucked it into my mouth, and her hands clenched in my hair. She let out a relieved moan as I tapped my tongue against it, hastening my speed and adding more force with every flick. I ravenously lapped at her, inhaling the intoxicating scent of her arousal, taking immense pleasure in the dribble of her down my chin.

Before long, her legs were shuddering against my cheeks, her nails were digging into my scalp, and her moans were echoing off every surface of her bedroom. I ate her as if this were my last meal. Her moans turned to a euphoric scream, her thighs trembled against my ears, and I drew every bit of orgasm I could out of her. When I finally withdrew my mouth, she was left panting and limping before finally collapsing into her bed.

"Wow!" she said as she spread out in a starfish position. "You're amazing at that."

Pride radiated throughout my body. My shoulders straightened in pleasure as I basked in the vision of her rosy, glowy skin, the rise and fall of her chest as she caught her breath, and the satisfaction on her face. I couldn't help myself from climbing into bed with her, pulling her into my arms, and nuzzling against her neck to inhale her sweet, musky scent, now ripe from the day and what had just gone down.

I jolted, a surge of shock coursing through me at the sudden touch of her hand on my cock.

"You give me sass for not wearing underwear, Mr. Alpha! But I'm pretty sure you're free-balling under these sweats!"

I couldn't help but grin. "It was easier."

"Dang! You horny." She giggled and pawed at my hard, throbbing cock. Soon she was up on her knees, brushing her palm against the entire length of it through the fabric of my pants.

My muscles tensed, and a primal groan of pleasure reverberated from my chest.

Her eyes widened, and a mischievous smile appeared on her face. "Let's see what you're packing, Mr. Alpha." Her hands were soon on the elastic of my sweatpants, pulling them down until my cock popped out, practically hitting her in the nose. She stared and licked her lips. "I mean, I've seen it before, obvi. But, holy *wow*. I almost forgot how huge you are. I can't even believe you fit."

My cheeks warmed, and my chest swelled. I was desperate to fill her again, to stretch her pussy to the brink. All my salacious thoughts were running wild in my head as she tugged my pants off. She crawled back over to me. I watched with anticipation as she spread her legs and straddled my upper legs. I couldn't help but bring the pads of my fingers to her inner thighs to stroke the soft skin.

Her eyes fluttered shut, and a moan escaped her full lips. "Why does it feel so good when you do that?" she whimpered. "How do you make it feel like that?" She let out another moan. "Like electricity."

She certainly stroked my ego.

I pushed my pointer and middle finger inside her hot, swollen pussy. She was so fucking wet. Soaking.

"No." She pushed my hand away. That same mischievous smile I was beginning to love appeared on her face. "That's not what I want inside me, Kolya."

"Terri." I practically groaned again, especially at the sound of my name on her lips.

"Can you guess what I actually want you to put inside me?" She teased as she gently stroked both her hands up and down the length of my dick. Precome trickled from its head. Just seeing her petite hands on me while I was probably the hardest I'd ever been was driving me over the edge. I couldn't guarantee I'd make it even two thrusts once it was in her.

But some annoying bug nagged at me, like a buzzing mosquito when I was trying to sleep. I was so close to giving her what she was begging for, *on her fucking knees*! But I knew I wouldn't be able to forgive myself if I didn't at least try to do the right thing. I placed my hands on hers, halting her movement. I nearly cried actual tears when she stopped rubbing me. I was so desperate for her touch.

She tilted her head in question, and a deep red blush appeared on her cheeks and ears.

"Terri." I repeated her name. "I need you to understand." I paused. It was causing me physical pain to continue, to know that things might not proceed after what I was about to tell her. "It can't be more than this. It's not you. I can't be more right now."

"How many times are you going to tell me the same thing?" She practically cut me off. "Always so serious." She giggled. "I already know, and I'm cool with it. I'm going back to school soon anyway."

Why did a jagged blade punch through my chest at her relaxed answer?

And why did I feel furious at the idea of her going back to school and all those men who were apparently lined up to help her with her heat?

I took a deep breath, pushing the thoughts from my head. I was being irrational. This was just my one day to give in to my desire. And that was all it would ever be. I would enjoy it for what it was.

"So, are we good now?" she asked, giving my cock a gentle squeeze, quickly reminding me of what I had been seconds from possibly losing.

"Yes," I replied, my dick taking the reins from me.

"Good." She grinned. She undid the tie that had been holding her thick, dark hair back and allowed the gentle waves to tumble down around her. If it was possible, she now appeared even more goddess-like, with her long, voluminous hair that framed her body, toned arms that flexed with each stroke, golden-tan skin that glistened under the soft light of her bedroom, and well-defined, sturdy abs that were on full display. When she finally lifted herself and lined her entrance up with my cock, I was a goner. Any other misgivings I might have had were wiped from my consciousness.

I let out a deep, appreciative moan as she lowered herself onto me in a slow grind, rocking her hips to allow each bit of my length to methodically enter her. The inner walls of her pussy clenched around me. My hands dug into her thighs. I couldn't believe such a beautiful angel was allowing me inside her, packing every inch of me into her. She continued to slowly and carefully lift and lower herself onto me until she was filled to the hilt.

"*Blyaaad*, you feel so good!" I cried out.

She smirked and lifted her arms over her head, elevating and emphasizing her sporty, pert breasts. I couldn't take my eyes off them as they bounced with every movement. Using only her thick, well-muscled lower body, she easily slid up and down the length of my cock, impressing me with her display of athleticism.

I wrapped my large hands around her petite waist, taking pleasure in the feel of her soft skin. She sped up her movement, taking all of me in, hard and fast, slamming against my pelvis with every push. She was bringing me to the edge, and I was getting too close. I didn't want it to be over.

I swiftly rolled her onto the bed so I was on top and able to slow things down. She stared up at me with her sweet, inquisitive amber eyes. I smiled and brought my lips to her ear. "I want to last," I whispered, then trailed kisses across her cheek until my lips were on hers. I slipped my tongue into her mouth, claiming her tongue with mine. With every thrust, I swallowed her gentle moans.

Her hips fell into rhythm with mine as I drove into her. She wrapped her legs around me and dug her fingers into the flesh of my ass. In response, I quickened my pace marginally. She let out a louder moan. "Don't stop," she pleaded.

Her wish was my command. I continued my methodical pace, leisurely dragging my girth along her inner walls with every push and pull, revering each movement, every moan and whimper, her natural fragrance, the feel of her pebbled nipples against my chest, her hot, drenched cunt. I appreciated every sensation and moment. I never wanted to forget how it felt to be in the arms of an angel on earth.

"Take me from behind," she rasped.

Boginya moya! I'd never been with a woman who was so assertive in bed before. And I couldn't lie and say that her confidence to demand what she wanted wasn't driving me absolutely wild. Who knew an alpha would appreciate someone else taking control so much?

I relented to her immediately and switched positions. Her ass was soon in the air, with her swollen pussy inviting me inside. I pushed into her, relieved with the feeling of being back home as soon as I entered her. She similarly gasped with delight. *Goddess, she is majestic.*

As much as I wanted it to last for hours, to keep fucking her all night, she soon had me back at the edge. I knew I didn't have much longer and brought my fingers to her clit, taking the little bean between my thumb and middle finger. Before long, I had her crying out and writhing under me, her inner walls clamping down on me, and her hands digging into the bedsheets. I worked her until she was shaking and screaming, coming completely undone. With one last punch forward, my climax exploded through me in a thousand-volt shock. My arms and legs went frigidly numb. I pulled out just as I spilled my release down her lower back, sputtering and gasping for air. I practically collapsed on her as I tried to catch my breath and make sense of the mind-blowing event I'd just experienced.

The high lingered for a moment. Then came the silence. My body still buzzed from the aftershocks of pleasure, but my mind . . .

What the fuck am I doing?

I clenched my jaw, pushing the thought down.

Then I noticed her body had gone stiff.

"Terri?"

She wouldn't look at me. Her entire body was tense, and her face was pushed into the comforter, her shoulders hunched inward.

"Are you okay?" I asked.

She gave me a thumbs-up.

I pulled my shirt off the floor and mopped up the mess I'd left on her. When she finally rose from the position she'd been in, she kept her hand covering her mouth.

"What happened to your mouth?" I asked.

"Nothing," she responded, her reply slightly muffled.

Needing to know what she was hiding, I pulled her hand away to reveal the cursed fangs peeking over her lower lip.

"I'm sorry," she apologized, tears forming in her eyes.

"It's not your fault," I said, taking pity on her. Although that mark pissed me off every time I even glanced at it, it had been given to her against her will. Any side effects it caused weren't something she could control. "Don't be embarrassed."

She nodded, and looked at me with the most pathetic little puppy eyes that made me want to tear up myself. Running purely on instinct, desiring to do anything I could to fix the pain in her eyes, I wrapped her in my arms and brought her to lie with me in the bed. I wanted to know more. I wanted to know who gave her that mark, who caused her all these problems. Mostly so I could kill him. But moreover, I wanted to know this amazing woman.

Chapter 30

Theresa

I stirred awake, blinking against the lamplight. Had I fallen asleep? I glanced upward to find a pair of silver eyes meeting mine.

"Oh, shoot! Sorry. I didn't mean to fall asleep," I stammered, scrambling to get up. Gosh, last thing I needed was for him to think I believed this to be a relationship where we spent the night together and stuff. Besides, my family was likely getting back soon, and it was in my best interest to scram before they figured us out.

As I sat up, readying to grab my clothes and get out of his way so he could leave, his hand closed gently around my wrist. "Wait."

I glanced back at him, searching his face for a clue to his thoughts. As usual, his expression was unreadable.

"Would it be wrong to want to spend little more time with you?" he asked.

"Oh," I replied, caught off guard.

"When we can speak with each other," he added.

I blinked, then smiled faintly, the tension in my shoulders easing. "Look who wants to talk all of a sudden," I teased, playfully poking him in the chest, right between his perfectly toned pecs. He really was hot. Not only the hottest man I'd ever been with, but likely the hottest man I'd ever seen. I was having a hard time believing he was real, and that I actually *had* had sex with him. Twice! And it had been incredible. Better than anything I could have imagined. My cheeks heated as the memories flashed in my mind.

His eyes crinkled, and he pulled me down against his chest, wrapping his large arms around me, encompassing me in his warmth. Even if he weren't holding me as if keeping me prisoner, I wouldn't have been able to move anyway. It just felt *so good* when my skin touched his. I'd never felt a similar sensation before. Like my skin was alive and glimmering from within, my nerves sensitive to every movement of his limbs.

He placed his fingers under my chin, tilted it upward, and pecked me on the lips. Again, he moved his mouth to mine, deepening the kiss. I closed my eyes and sank into him. He brushed the back of his knuckles along my cheek and jaw, and finally made it to my neck, tracing a path toward my collarbone. His thumb found the most sensitive part, and he circled it. I gasped, slightly pulling away. Why was he touching my mark?

"Will you tell me what happened?" he asked.

I hesitated, shrinking back.

"Please," he added.

I suppressed my smile as an idea came to me. "If I do, you have to answer one of my questions. Any question I want. And you have to promise to answer honestly."

He exhaled through his nose, his silver eyes darkening. "Terri . . ."

A long silence stretched between us. His chest rose and fell. Unsavory feelings seeped from his pores. How did I always seem to understand what he was feeling?

Seconds ticked by with no answer. Perhaps we wouldn't talk then. I could feel his resistance, like an invisible force. He was about to refuse. I could sense it.

"You don't have to tell me anything," I said, suddenly unsure. "I just thought . . . if I'm opening up . . ."

His jaw tensed. Then, finally, his features softened. "Okay."

A tingling warmth spread through my chest. I couldn't help but smile. Maybe we could be more than this hookup situation thing we had. This amazingly hot alpha was willing to try for a deeper connection.

I sat up fully, hugging the blanket around me. It wasn't modesty—not exactly—but something about being so open with him made me feel exposed in a way I couldn't explain.

Kolya leaned back, propping himself up on one elbow, watching me intently. His gaze was penetrating, but not in a way that made me uncomfortable. Instead, it made me feel *seen*.

"All right," I said, my voice steadier than I felt. "Where do I start?"

He didn't answer, just waited, giving me space to tell my story.

I took a deep breath and began. "Even though dating before meeting your mate is forbidden by the temple, it's not like anyone actually follows the rules. People at school were always hooking up, sneaking around. And I wanted that too—so badly! It seemed fun, exciting. The idea of being with only one person my entire life felt . . . criminal. I mean, Tyce has to have been with hundreds by now." I wrinkled my nose, grossed out by the thought. "Why couldn't I have some fun before settling down too? But of course, with a family full of alphas—my dad, my grandpa, and my brother—no guy would come near me. No one wanted to risk it."

I let out a bitter, self-conscious laugh. "I thought maybe I'd meet someone in college. But the idea of doing it with a human weirded me out back then. I know we're all anatomically the same, but it just felt . . . wrong. So while my friends were all hooking up, I stayed a virgin. A twenty-year-old virgin." I cringed at the admission. "How embarrassing."

"Why that is embarrassing?" Kolya asked in a calm, reassuring voice.

"It just feels so old! Everyone else seems to lose it in high school. When did *you* lose it?" The question escaped before I could stop it, and I quickly added, "That doesn't count as my question!"

He chuckled. "Fifteen."

"See!" I exclaimed.

"It is double standard. Alpha sons have no one standing in their way. No idiot would be dumb enough."

"And alpha daughters . . . we're wrapped in Bubble Wrap," I groaned.

"I do not believe this about you," he said. "You are tough. Like stone."

His words warmed me, but only for a moment. "I guess," I murmured. My thoughts drifted to Tyce, and the lashes on his back. Whatever I'd been through, he'd had it worse.

Kolya nodded, as if he understood where my mind had gone. "Alpha sons have their own problems."

I shook my head, pushing the thoughts away, and then continued, "Everything changed this past summer break when I came home after my sophomore year of college. By then, I'd mostly gotten used to the idea that I'd stay a virgin until I met my mate. And then . . . I met *him*. My now-ex."

My mood darkened at the thought. Kolya seemed to sense it, as he gave my upper arm a squeeze.

"Honestly, I didn't even like him at first. He was a friend of a friend of a friend. My friend Kaylynn had a crush on this warrior whom she invited to a party she was throwing. He had duty and couldn't make it, but he asked her to invite one of his friends, who he said was kind of a loner, in his place. Said he was trying to get him to meet more people. And Kaylynn, of course, agreed.

"We were all just sort of hanging out. I made some silly joke, teasing him in a flirting sort of way. And instead of laughing, he flipped me off. I don't even remember what I said, but I'm sure it wasn't anything that rude."

"He sounds like *suka*," Kolya spat. "Like bitch."

I couldn't help but smile at his response. "I should've trusted my instincts," I admitted. "But my friends are really welcoming, so we kept inviting him to things. Over time, I started to see a different side of him. He listened when I talked. He was . . . helpful when our friends drank too much and things got out of hand. And I started to think maybe he was a good person, deep down. Now, looking back, I wonder if it was all an act."

I frowned as memories started to slip back. "Now that I think about it, he never knew his limits when he drank. Once, we all drove out to the middle of nowhere to avoid pack gossip, so our parents wouldn't hear about it. He downed like half a bottle. We kept telling him to slow down, and he kept insisting he was fine. Before long, he was sloshed. When we tried to take his keys, he refused and, instead, threw them into a river. A bunch of us had to shift and track them down because the current carried them away." I was embarrassed to admit how dumb I was to ever date this guy. Ashamed to even be telling this story.

"When he was sober, he was honestly okay," I added. "And he was the first guy who ever really pursued me. He asked me on dates. He didn't seem intimidated by my family. For once, it felt like it was my turn to have what everyone else seemed to have. And I think . . . I think I just liked the attention." I sighed, considering how pathetic I was.

"Terri," he said. My heart stuttered at how he said my name, in his sexy Russian accent. "You were young. It was exciting. Don't be so hard on yourself."

I leaned into him, taking comfort in his warmth. "At first, it was fun," I said. "We spent a lot of time together, sneaking around, laughing, just . . . being young. But then, his moods started. He'd get upset over the smallest things. Like once, I joked about going skinny-dipping at the lake, and he got weird about it. Asked me why I wanted to do that when I didn't even know if he'd like how I looked without clothes on."

Kolya's hand clenched into a fist. "What the hell is wrong with him?"

I looked away, ashamed. "What was wrong with me for staying? I should've shifted and run home. But I was so stupid. I think I wanted to believe that I misheard, or, I guess, I was hoping to finally lose my virginity, and I knew if I dumped him, I could be celebrating my twenty-first birthday with my v-card intact." I hung my head. "He eventually apologized. And he showed up the next day with flowers."

Kolya cupped my chin in his hand and tilted it upward. His silver eyes pierced right into my soul. "You are absolutely beautiful. Stunning. Body of goddess. I question sanity of this man. He is not man. He is boy."

I flushed, biting my lip. "But I am pretty muscular for a girl . . . and my boobs are itty-bitty. They're completely flat when I lie on my back!" I demonstrated.

Kolya's lips quirked up into a smirk as he thumbed my nipple. A shiver of electricity rippled through me. "Your boobs," he murmured, " . . . perfect. Perfect handful."

I closed my eyes and sighed. I couldn't believe how wonderful this man was being to me.

"Besides, Terri. You are more than beauty. You are whole person. Warm, wonderful . . . angel of person."

Heat rushed to my face, and my cheeks burned hot at the unexpected compliment.

"What happened after he said this?" Kolya asked softly. His voice pulled me back to the story.

I took a shaky breath. "The cycle started. Things would be good for a while, then he'd flip out over something else. Like one time, I went down to Anchorage with Beta Liam to pick up supplies for the pack. While we were there, I stopped by Barnes & Noble. My ex called, so I answered. When he asked where I was, I told him, and he said, 'What's Barnes & Noble?' Surprised, I blurted out, 'You don't know what *Barnes & Noble* is?' He exploded, accusing me of treating him like an idiot. No matter how much I tried to explain that I was just surprised—it's such a well-known store—he wouldn't hear it.

"I started to feel like I was constantly walking on eggshells. The smallest things could set him off. If I mentioned an actor in a movie was good-looking, he'd get upset. If I wanted to hang out with friends instead of him one night, he'd throw a fit. If there were any guys in the group, he'd call me a whore. He even started dictating what I could and couldn't wear. The relationship stopped being enjoyable. Instead, it felt like I was stuck in a never-ending cycle of damage control, trying to avoid triggering him.

"I know you probably think I'm stupid for not breaking up with him sooner. I guess a part of me cared about him. He'd had a tough life—his parents were chosen mates, not fated ones, and they fought constantly. When he was a kid, it sometimes got so bad that they'd forget to feed him. He didn't have many friends either. Really, his only friend was that warrior I mentioned before, and even that friendship wasn't a close one."

Desperate to justify myself, I added, "If I'm being fair, not everything was bad. Some things were good. Really good. We'd have times where we'd just hang out and talk, and he could actually be sweet. Those moments made it harder to walk away.

"Sometime in early August, I told him I was ready to have sex."

Kolya tensed beside me.

"We did it one afternoon while his parents were at work. It was horrible. One of the worst experiences of my life. He was so nervous that he couldn't get it up, and he took it out on me. He kept being mean, blaming me. I can't even remember what he said—I think I blocked it out. I just remember asking him, at one point, to please be nice to me. Eventually, he changed his attitude, and when he finally got hard, we did it. It hurt. A lot. But I muscled through."

"Terri, I am sorry." Kolya gathered me into his arms and pressed me against his chest. "You did not deserve this. You are good person. You deserved someone gentle. Your first time should be special. You should be appreciated." His voice roughened. "You should not need to beg for man to be decent to you."

A tear slid down my cheek. I'd never told that story to anyone before, and it was cathartic for someone to validate my feelings after all this time.

"It eventually got better," I continued, "but the relationship got worse. I decided to break up with him two days before going back to school. I went to his house, brought him a small gift, and gave him this whole speech about how wonderful the summer had been, but I thought we should just be friends. He got quiet, and I knew I should leave.

"But he started kissing me, begging me not to go. I didn't want to, but he begged for one last time together. So I gave in." My voice cracked as I gripped the sheets. "I just lay there, waiting for it to be over. Then, toward the end, he said, 'You're mine.' I didn't think too much of it, but after we finished . . ."

The memory slammed into me like a tidal wave. I clutched at my chest to try to steady my racing heart, and I pushed through to finish the story. "After we finished, he bit my neck. I screamed and tried to push him off. But it was too late. He'd done it." Tears spilled down my face, unstoppable, as the pain and horror hit me all over again. "He marked me." A raw, strangled sob tore from my chest.

Kolya's silence was deafening. When he finally spoke, his voice was ice-cold, deadly. "If I ever meet this *mraz'*, his life is finished. Nothing would give me more pleasure than to claw him to death, slow, piece by piece."

Panic flaring in my chest, I exclaimed, "No! You can't!"

His gaze snapped to mine. "Why not? He did not hesitate when he took from you. When he marked you without consent, chained you to him forever." His eyes blazed, filled with contempt. "What was your crime, Terri? That you tried to be good girlfriend? That you tried to love this broken man? He showed you worst, and you still saw good. You gave him kindness, he repaid with harm. Again. Again. Until he took even your freedom."

"But to kill him?" I whispered.

"I do not know single pack where marking without consent is not death sentence!" His voice thundered with such force that it felt as if an earthquake had ripped through the room. His skin burned, and his muscles trembled with a barely contained rage. His fury reverberated through me, shaking me to my core. "Mate bond, it is most sacred. Most powerful bond a wolf will ever have. The fated bond is gift of *Artemida* herself. For him to steal your right to a true mate, to claim you without consent, bind you for eternity—unforgivable. Abomination."

I whimpered, not sure how to respond.

Kolya's eyebrows knitted together, and his demeanor softened. He reached out and brushed a stray hair behind my ear. "When you told story, it sounded like you blame yourself. It's not your fault, Terri. You could not know what he would do."

"I just . . ." My voice cracked as I struggled with the words. "I just feel like I should have known better."

"How could you know? It was your first relationship."

"But he was so horrible!" I blurted, the frustration and self-reproach spilling over.

"Someone once told me . . . we love what feels familiar." His voice was tinged with both sorrow and understanding. He paused, as if choosing his next words carefully. "Alpha families . . . they are difficult. Trauma passes through generations. Our packs depend on us to be strong, always. Even when weight of responsibility almost crushes us. So fathers beat out weakness. Beat out emotions. And then . . ." He sighed. "Then we pass it to our children."

"Our mothers too," I added softly, a sudden clarity taking shape in my mind. Something about his words clicked, unraveling a truth I hadn't considered before.

I stared at my hands, the memories flooding in.

My mother's voice, nitpicking my body.

My father's disappointment when I didn't live up to his expectations.

Tyce and Trav, both trained until their skin bled, never allowed to show pain.

I'd spent my whole life under the weight of constant criticism and impossibly high expectations from my parents, never stopping to think how deeply it affected me. Of course I'd stayed. It felt familiar.

My breath hitched. "I never even realized . . ."

Maybe that same crude judgment was what had drawn me to my ex in the first place, without me even recognizing it. It was why I felt so at ease around him, why his behavior hurt but never felt out of place.

I let out a deep exhale. For the first time in months, the idea of forgiving myself felt possible. But I was too exhausted to unravel all the complex thoughts that had suddenly formed.

Instead, I glanced at Kolya and smiled faintly. "You still owe me an answer to a question."

He raised his eyebrows but didn't speak.

"What is the Russian pack after? Why did they go to war with you?"

His muscles stiffened against my body, and he pinched his lips together.

"You promised," I reminded him.

With a resigned sigh, he sat up and crossed his arms. "I promised," he echoed my words like a surrender. He met my eyes and, in a serious tone, asked, "And I can trust you'll never tell a soul?"

"Never! I pinky swear!" I put out my pinky for him. He looked at me like I had three heads. Then I realized he probably didn't know what that was. "It's a thing in America. We shake with our pinkies to prove that we promise."

"And if you break this . . . pinky promise?" His eyes lit up with amusement.

"Your pinky gets cut off!" I joked. "Just kidding. Though I'm pretty sure my dad *would* cut a finger off for breaking a pinky swear with him."

"I would do same." He caught my pinky between his thumb and forefinger, studying it. "Nice pinky. Would be shame to cut it off."

"Not worried!" I grinned. "My word is as good as gold!" I put out my pinky again, and he hooked his far larger digit with my petite one.

He lay back into the pillow, and his expression grew distant. His features tightened with unease. "My family has heirloom, passed down for generations, from so long we do not know from where it came. It's small red stone, pierced and worn on gold chain. We call it *krasnyy kamen'*. It means 'red stone.'"

"You'd think something that started a war would have a more dramatic name."

"It did not come with mystical name, like in books or movies. We just call it what it is."

"Kind of disappointing, Kolya!" I teased, nudging his arm.

He didn't laugh. Instead, his expression darkened. "There are things about this stone more disappointing than name. It is curse on my existence." His voice was laden with bitterness. "No one was supposed to know about it. But legends survive. There are written records, preserved for hundreds of years in other packs. Someone pieced the truth together and traced it to us."

"What does it do?"

He seemed reluctant to answer, hesitating for what felt like an eternity. Finally, he said, "It grants one wish. Only one. Must be very specific. Otherwise . . ." He hunched his shoulders, as if burdened by experience. "You get what you wish, but not in way you want."

A sense of lightness washed over me. Hope bloomed in my chest. I touched my mark and smiled. Just as I opened my mouth to speak, he interrupted.

"There are three things it can't do," he said firmly. "First, it cannot remove mark."

I wilted as disappointment crashed over me.

"I know." His voice was quiet and empathetic. "I thought of it too."

I rubbed at my mark reflexively, its permanence sinking in. Even this powerful, ancient stone couldn't erase it.

"It can't bring dead back," Kolya continued. "And it cannot make someone your fated mate. It does not interfere with will of Goddess."

"Does your pack use it often?"

He shook his head. "No. Too dangerous. Too risky. What if someone wishes to be new alpha? Or harm their packmate? Once a wish is spoken, it cannot be undone."

I nodded my understanding.

"We only allow most desperate to use it, like mother with ill pup."

"Have you ever used it?" I asked, my curiosity getting the better of me.

Kolya stiffened, his expression hardening, and he snapped, "You already ask your one question." The harshness stunned me into silence. But then his voice softened. "I would rather not talk about it."

His reaction could only mean that he *had* used it. Follow-up questions churned in my mind, my curiosity eating at me. But I didn't want to press—clearly, the topic had upset him. Still, the thought of never knowing, especially with only days left before I returned to school and his imminent departure from our pack, gnawed at me.

But I kept my mouth shut as he rose from the bed and began gathering his clothes. "Your family will be back soon. I should go."

I nodded, knowing he was right.

After he slipped his pants on, he returned to the edge of the bed. I glanced up at him, and he met my gaze. His silver eyes bore into mine with a quiet intensity. He leaned down, brought his hands to the sides of my face and brushed his lips against my forehead. "Thank you, Terri. Today was happiest I feel for long time."

He kissed me gently, then without a word, he left, closing the door softly behind himself as he walked away.

I sank back into the bed and let out one final sigh. It lingered in the air as I stared out into the empty room.

Chapter 31

Julia

29 years ago

The day after the incident, I made sure to wear my tightest, lowest-cut black dress to dinner. Even Gabe's father, who otherwise loathed my existence, couldn't keep his eyes from skimming the tops of my breasts.

Gabe clearly noticed, because at one point, during the meal, he leaned in and gripped my wrist under the table. "What are you wearing?" he hissed, his voice barely audible over the clink of silverware.

"What?" I fluttered my eyelashes and acted dumb. "Is something wrong?"

He scowled but said nothing else, though his tension was palpable. Across the table, Lance's piercing gaze found mine. Unlike his father or Gabe, his attention wasn't rooted in lust. His eyes narrowed, assessing me, silently questioning me. I met his stare with a shrug and resumed eating, unbothered.

After dinner, Gabe, as usual, whisked me up to his bedroom. I went through the now-expected motions, stroking his ego and his dick. I excused myself at the earliest moment I could. I had big plans, and I needed Gabe satisfied and out of my way. I showered quickly, washing away any trace of his touch, and slipped back into my black dress.

The house was quiet as I wandered through the dimly lit hallways. I passed Lance's room, the door ajar, revealing only darkness within. He wasn't there. Hmm.

I made my way downstairs and sniffed around, looking for a fresh bit of his scent. Finally, I caught his trail and followed it down the hallway to a room I'd only been in once, when I got the official tour.

The door to the small library creaked as I pushed it open. Inside, a fire crackled in the hearth, its golden glow dancing over the antique furniture. Lance sat on the couch, a glass of amber liquid in hand.

"Hello, Julia," he said without looking up, his voice calm and resigned.

I sauntered toward him and perched on the arm of the couch. "I will not tell anyone, you know."

"What do you want?" His eyes remained fixed on the fire.

"Why you think I want exchange for silence?"

"Gabe might be a dumbass, but I damn well know you didn't come here because you love him."

I smirked. "And what you know about love?"

He turned to me, and his gaze met mine. But instead of the anger I'd expected, I found something else, a flicker of pain, of vulnerability behind his eyes.

"You love him?" I said as it became clear to me.

He didn't reply.

"Is your mate?"

"Doesn't matter," Lance muttered, taking a long sip from his glass. The unmistakable scent of bourbon filled the air. The nearly empty bottle at his feet explained the haze in his eyes.

"You avoid the question," I pressed.

"It doesn't fucking matter," he snapped, though his voice lacked conviction. "Can't. Not long-term."

The words hung between us, heavy and bitter.

"Have you always preferred company of men?" I asked in a tone that was intentionally light.

His lips twitched, almost forming a smirk, and he said flatly, "I prefer both."

"So . . . you like both. But our Goddess is fickle. She sent you man as mate," I mused.

Lance drained his glass and set it down with a soft clink. "I know what you're doing."

"Then you are not so stupid as your brother," I said, letting my smile curl wider.

"And what makes you think I'll agree to your terms?"

I slid off the arm of the couch, lowering myself to my knees in front of him.

His posture stiffened, his legs spread just enough to invite me closer.

"I can make you happy," I whispered, dragging my nails up the inside of his pant legs. "I tell Gabe I am virgin. He liked this. But you . . ." I leaned in, lips hovering near his crotch. "You want someone who knows what she is doing."

Lance remained still, his eyes locked on mine, unreadable.

I reached for his belt, working it loose with deliberate slowness. He didn't stop me.

"We could have perfect arrangement," I murmured. "Mutual benefit. Your parents never need to know truth. All they see is, at first, I agreed to be Gabe's chosen mate, but fate . . . fate had other plan."

"And why would I go along with this?" His voice was low, almost a growl.

"Because," I said as I leisurely drew down his zipper, "I am only one who can give you what you want. Discretion. Freedom. Loyalty. I look away while you . . . enjoy your other preferences." My fingers brushed his underwear, coaxing his limp cock out. He still didn't stop me, and I lowered my mouth to him, testing the waters, hoping the alcohol wasn't enough to dull his senses.

He watched me, eyes narrowed. "What won't you do to get what you want?"

I met his gaze with unwavering intensity. "For you, Lance, there is nothing I will not do."

I returned to my task, took him into my mouth, and deliberately worked him. I was pleased when he began to respond and gradually grew and hardened against my tongue.

He scoffed. "You're no virgin."

I smiled and licked down the substantial length of him, gripping his base. "Ah, but I am, Lance. Virgin until marriage."

His hand shot into my hair, and he thrust himself into me, his eyes glinting with challenge. He pushed me down, and I gagged as he hit the back of my throat. A sneer crossed his face. "You think I'm just going to bind myself to you without even a test drive?"

As soon as I was able to come back up for air, I replied, "There is loophole. Back door." I grinned. "You can test me same way you test man."

With a violent tug of my hair, he pushed me off him. I stumbled back, barely managing to catch myself before I collided with the floor.

"Undress," he commanded. "Let me see what I'm buying."

I scrambled to my feet. My hands trembled only for a second, then I forced them steady. If this was what it took, so be it. Without a word, I unzipped the back of my dress and allowed the fabric to drop around me. His eyes burned into me as I unsnapped my black lace bra and bared my breasts to him. My body was shaking, but I refused to let it be from fear. Let him think he had won.

He gave an appreciative nod. I pulled the matching panties down my legs and stepped out of them.

He motioned with a single, authoritative flick of his finger. "Turn."

I turned. I let him see everything. If he thought I was prey, then I would play the part. For now.

"I can see why Gabe likes you." I glanced over my shoulder, meeting his gaze as he stood to his full, imposing height. He took a few deliberate steps toward me. "Now," he commanded, "face the fire and get on your hands and knees."

I obeyed, allowing the flames in the hearth to warm my naked body. Behind me, I could hear the rustle of fabric and the soft thud of his pants dropping. Soon he was so close, his body heat warmed the back of my legs. The crackle of the fire was punctuated by the loud sound of spitting.

Soon the flesh of his erection was against the cheeks of my ass. My heart raced in anticipation, and I almost faltered, wondering what I was getting myself into.

He thumbed the delicate entrance. I moaned, imagining that was what he wanted to hear.

In response, he slapped his hand against my mouth and held it there. "Quiet." After he removed it, the silence was broken by the quick intake of breath and another soft *ptuh* of spitting.

He lined himself up with my anus, the head of his cock throbbing against my rim. Without another word, he drove into me, pushing his girthy, substantial length inside. The first thrust ripped a cry from my throat that I swallowed down, biting it back into silence as my body was torn apart. Searing heat shot through me like fire. As he pushed himself farther and pulled back, the pain didn't stop; it lingered and spread, a burning, throbbing ache that radiated outward. Every breath felt strained and every movement unbearable. My mind struggled to grasp the reality of the physical agony and emotional shock. Tears streamed down my cheeks.

But even as I cried silently, another part of me detached, watching from the outside. Calculating. *He thinks he's breaking me. He thinks I will crawl, beg, whimper.* No.

His grasp on my hip tightened violently when he finally came. He spluttered, almost sounding pained. Loud gasps of air followed. Eventually, his grip on me loosened, and he withdrew, leaving me trembling in the aftermath. "Stay," he instructed, speaking to me as if I were a dog.

Behind me, I heard the soft rustle of fabric and the zipper of his pants sliding upward, followed by the distinct sound of his belt buckle being fastened. I hesitated before glancing over my shoulder. He sneered, tossing a stack of bills onto my back. "I'll think about it," he muttered coldly, then turned and exited without another word, the door clicking shut behind him.

Chapter 32

Ginger

By the time my final training session with Sara rolled around, I'd—*mostly*—recovered from what I'd experienced during the previous one. Tyce clearly sensed something was off during the drive, because he kept trying to interlace his fingers with mine, but I wouldn't give.

"I'm sure you did amazing for your first torture, Gi," he tried. "You'd be surprised at how many grown-ass men throw up and pass out."

Phantom sensations echoed in my mind. The screams. The knife cutting flesh. The smell of blood, thick and metallic, clinging to my nostrils.

My stomach turned.

Tyce reached for my hand, but I pulled away.

"You couldn't have done any worse than me," he added.

"You were ten!"

As soon as I said it, I regretted it. His face darkened, shadows flickering in his eyes.

"I'm sorry." I winced. "That was really insensitive of me to bring up."

"You're not wrong," he replied softly.

I exhaled, searching for the right words. "I guess . . . I just feel so behind. All those years I didn't have a wolf, I couldn't train. And now I'm trying so hard to catch up. I just wish I could be like Sara, or your sister. Or my sister. Or Jasmine. Basically all those other women who are so cool and badass."

The words hung in the air. Tyce didn't reply, just reached over and squeezed my hand. The gesture was comforting, but it didn't erase the gnawing inadequacy in my chest. I was sure he was sick of hearing me lament the same thing over and over again. But how could he understand how I felt?

When we arrived, Sara and Trav both greeted us, bringing us into their sitting room.

"I'm sure you've got some intel to share," Tyce said. "Gigi told me you caught someone."

"That little fucker was a good one." Sara grinned. Her eyes lit up with a predatory gleam. "He and I had fun for hours. He lasted all night. Not a lot of men out there with his stamina."

Trav shot her a look.

She smirked and added, "I didn't say none." The tiniest flicker of warmth softened her otherwise cold demeanor as she gave his cheek a playful squeeze. The rare display of affection was odd coming from someone as ruthless as Sara.

Huh. Maybe she wasn't completely heartless after all.

Tyce cleared his throat. "So . . ."

"Unfortunately, in the end, he didn't have much info. Trust me, I worked him hard. Not a single inch of him was left untouched. All he revealed was that he'd been given a scent to capture, a woman. Didn't even know the name of the pack she's from. Was just told she'd be in this area. Smart alpha. Gives the bare minimum info. Someone else in his pack had gone after her but got himself killed instead. Seems this fucker met the same fate."

"Do you know who he was after?" Tyce asked, leaning forward.

"He didn't have a name. No one from my pack," Sara replied. "And not a single report of an attack. What about yours?"

"Same on our end," Tyce confirmed. "Haven't heard of a single attack and definitely haven't heard of anyone taking down a stranger wolf."

"Maybe it's not someone from either of our packs then," Trav guessed.

"If not our pack they're after, then whose?" I asked. "There isn't another pack around here."

The room fell into a thoughtful silence. No one seemed to have an answer.

"Maybe a rogue," Trav offered. "That's all I've got."

"I'll keep hunting," Sara said with a dangerous glint in her eye. "That was a lot of fun. I could go for another round."

After we got up and headed toward the gym, Sara and I split off from the brothers. They headed to the equipment room to lift weights together while Sara took me to their sparring gym. At least we'd be indoors today.

"It's time we see what your wolf is made of," Sara exclaimed.

"My . . . wolf?"

"Yeah, your wolf. Most of the time you won't be fighting in your human form. So let her out!"

I fidgeted slightly. "But I haven't even beaten you in my human form yet."

Sara snickered. "Obviously! I'm not a fair opponent. The point wasn't to beat me. It was to give you a challenge for once, since your mate was never going to. A shark in a fish tank will only grow eight inches, but in the ocean, it'll grow eight feet. The shark never outgrows its environment. You need to go to the ocean, Gigi."

I bit my lip.

"So," she said, snapping her fingers, "let's go. Strip."

My stomach churned as I hesitated. The muscles in my body twitched with nervousness, and a fluttering panic settled in my chest. Still, I forced myself to peel off each layer of clothing with trembling hands. My heart pounded in my chest, each beat echoing in my ears.

With a shaky breath, I let go and allowed my body to shift. Bones cracked, skin stretched, and in moments, my wolf was revealed. She was monstrous with patches of fur missing, exposed bones, and eyes that glowed a devilish red. I kept my gaze low, bracing myself for her reaction.

"Sick!" she exclaimed, vibrating with energy. "Holy fuck. That is the *sickest* wolf I've ever seen!" Her eyes gleamed with awe.

I blinked. I hadn't expected that reaction.

"I can't believe you've been hiding *that* all this time! Damn. I've got to train you for war." She clapped her hands in excitement. "The other side will never expect you!"

Hadn't she seen my wolf when we'd gotten stranded on that island together months ago? Maybe she'd been too distracted to notice. There was a lot going on.

"Okay, time to give me a challenge!" Sara couldn't seem to hold in the joy on her face. The fluttering in my chest slowly shifted. A tiny spark of pride began to flicker. "I'm going to spar you in my human form. Show me what you've got!"

I ran and leaped, targeting her with my claws. She swiftly ducked and grabbed me by the torso, plucking me out of the air and slamming me onto the large mat underneath us. So much for giving me an advantage.

I tried again. This time, I lunged. Fast.

Or at least, I thought I was fast.

Sara sidestepped me like it was nothing. A blur of motion before I felt a brutal force against my ribs.

My body slammed into the mat, air rushing from my lungs in a painful burst. For a moment, all I saw were stars.

"Again," Sara ordered, pacing around me. "You're not using your claws enough. You're letting your opponent dictate the fight. That's how you get yourself killed."

Gritting my teeth, I scrambled to my feet, forcing my breathing to steady. I had to land at least one good hit. Just one.

I pushed forward, snapping my jaws toward her shoulder, but she twisted midair, flipping over me before slamming her elbow into my back. My knees buckled, pain shooting through my spine.

"Still too slow," she teased.

The rest of the session unfolded much the same way. While I felt pretty dejected by the end, I couldn't lie and say I wasn't supremely impressed by how good Sara was. For anyone else in human form, facing off against a wolf, trained or not, would be a massive challenge. But Sara handled the large predator with ease, anticipating and countering every move.

After I shifted back, and put my clothes back on, Sara gave me a friendly slap on the back. "Just keep training. And maybe one day you'll have half a chance." She winked.

Tyce returned with his brother and then led me out to his car. I let out a deep sigh as soon as I sat down.

"How was training?" he asked.

"I mean, I still suck."

"I don't think you need to have parents who are hard on you. You're hard enough on yourself."

"I just wish . . ."

"You just wish what?"

"I just really thought training with Sara would work better than it did."

"Have you sparred anyone who's not Sara yet?"

"Well, no."

"So how do you know you haven't improved then? In video games, you generally start with the basic opponents before you get to the boss level. You essentially *started* at the boss level. Maybe you should try out some of the basic dudes before you decide you suck."

I shrugged.

"Gigi, I really hate when you get like this." He took my hand again. "Do you want to know what I wish?"

"What?"

"I wish you could see yourself through my eyes. How fucking amazing you are. I was beaten to comply with my training. You're already a shit ton more motivated naturally than I'll ever be. I bet if you keep up with it, you'll be kicking my ass one day. Because you have heart. And I hope my heir has the same heart you do one day."

My mouth dropped open, and my heart swelled as I fought to stay composed. Forcing a playful tone, I said, "Tyce, stop! You're hurting my teeth again!" But deep down, I knew he could feel the way his words had hit me through the bond. Despite my protests, I was secretly basking in the glow of his praise.

When we made it back to the packhouse, I found Terri curled up on the couch in the living room, a book open in her lap. She looked up and greeted me with a bright smile, waving me over. "Hey, Gigi! How's it going?"

"Hey!" I replied, taking a seat next to her.

"I heard you and Tyce are leading the run tomorrow for the Wolf Moon!" she said, her tone brimming with excitement.

"Oh . . . yeah." My shoulders slumped at the reminder.

The excitement in her eyes dimmed as she noticed my reaction. "What's wrong?"

I hesitated, glancing away. "I just . . . hate how everyone's going to be staring at my wolf."

"Oh, yeah. I get it. I'm not a huge fan of being the center of attention either. But I've kind of gotten used to it over the years. Comes with the territory of being in an alpha family."

"It's more than that."

She nodded. "Yeah, I heard your wolf is . . . different."

"And your parents hate it. The pack's probably going to be wondering what someone with a fucked-up wolf is doing becoming their new luna."

Her eyes widened in shock. "No! The pack would never think that!"

But I wasn't convinced. I'd seen the way some of them looked at me when they thought I wasn't paying attention. The glances. The hushed whispers.

"You don't know that," I muttered.

"Gigi, don't judge the entire pack by my parents' behavior. There are so many good people in the Jade Moon Pack, people who'd be disgusted if they knew what really went on in the packhouse. Please, don't ever doubt for a second that they'll accept you because of how my parents treat you."

I looked at her skeptically, but she pressed on.

"And Tyce?" she added firmly. "He'd never tolerate anyone bad-mouthing your wolf. He'd hunt them down and make an example of them. Disrespecting a luna is a crime!" After a beat, she asked, "Hey, how about we hunt together tonight? I can stick with you as moral support."

A thought struck me, and I responded with a question of my own. "Would you mind running with me tomorrow night too? Up front. I could use all the support I can get, and it'd mean a lot to have you there."

Terri's eyes lit up with conviction. "Of course! I'd love to," she said, as if any other answer would have been absurd. Her enthusiasm was infectious.

In that moment, I realized just how much I liked Tyce's sister. She was like a beam of sunshine on a cloudy day. While I missed my sisters back home, I couldn't help but feel lucky to have gained this one here.

Chapter 33

Theresa

On Thursday, I showed up for my last training session with the ladies of Severnaya Zvezda Pack. They all gave me a warm greeting, making me feel right at home in their pack. After some warm-ups, I started them out on sparring, so I could at least teach them some good fighting techniques before I left. I was pleasantly surprised. These Ukrainian ladies could fight! I supposed that was how this group had made it out of the war.

After spending the entire morning and afternoon with them, they convinced me to join them for drinks that evening. The ten of us headed to the pack's pub together, where we grabbed a large table and settled in. Despite my insistence on paying, they wouldn't hear of it. I knew they were living off modest contributions from my pack, yet they pooled their money together and made sure I didn't spend a single cent.

Toward the end, Mariya, who had the biggest personality of the group, pulled me aside. "Alpha smiles again," she said in her heavy Russian accent.

"Oh! That's . . . great!" I stammered, hoping she didn't notice the sudden warmth flooding my cheeks.

"He is tough," she continued, "but he is fair. He will make good mate. And good father." She gave me an exaggerated wink and squeezed my arm like we were sharing some big secret.

"I'm sure he will—one day," I replied, forcing a smile as heaviness settled in my chest. The thought twisted something inside me, an ache I hadn't anticipated. Maybe I wasn't as okay with the casualness of our relationship as I'd tried to tell myself I was.

"He loves you." Mariya leaned in closer. "I know."

"What?" I choked, laughter bubbling up unbidden, though it felt forced, unnatural. "Oh, no. He doesn't love me. We're just . . . friends." The words felt hollow as I said them, like I was trying to convince both her and myself.

She shook her head, clicking her tongue in disapproval. "You will see," she said cryptically, like she knew something I didn't. For a moment, it seemed like she had more to say, but instead, she pulled me into a warm, tight hug. "Good luck with school. See you again soon."

"See you again soon," I responded, while wondering if I actually would.

As I watched her return to the group, a confusing swirl of emotions tangled in my chest. My heart somehow felt both full and hollow simultaneously. I said my final goodbyes to the group and then began my short trek back to the packhouse.

I'd laughed off Mariya's words, but they continued to echo in my head like a whisper.

As soon as I stepped inside, I shed the layers of winter clothing, pulling off my heavy coat and tugging off my snow boots. Once I grabbed my gym bag from where it rested on the floor, I hauled it upstairs toward the promise of a hot shower that called me. The stairs creaked under my weight as I ascended, echoing through the quiet packhouse.

The moment I reached the hallway, I stopped abruptly. His familiar and intoxicating scent hit me before I even saw him. My heart quickened. And then there he was—intense silver eyes locking on to mine, filled with a raw energy that made my breath catch. I suddenly wasn't so sure Mariya was wrong.

Before I could react, he stepped forward and tugged me into his bedroom, the door clicking shut behind us. My gym bag slipped from my hand, forgotten, as he pulled me into his arms. Our mouths found each other like magnets drawn together, an unspoken need igniting between us.

His hand trailed up the length of my torso, slowly and deliberately, until it found my breast. His touch sent a jolt of heat through me. I couldn't suppress the moan that escaped my lips as my hips pressed into his instinctively. The heat of his body met mine, and I felt an unmistakable hardness against me, igniting a fire in my core that threatened to consume us both.

But then, the sound of voices drifted through the hall just outside his door. I stiffened instantly, the haze of desire clearing as reality came crashing down.

We were being reckless, way too reckless. Neither of us could afford to get caught like this.

"I should go," I whispered, reluctantly pulling myself away. The words were a betrayal to my body. Every part of me screamed to stay. It took every ounce of willpower I had to step away. He didn't argue, but the glossy sadness in his eyes mirrored the ache in my chest.

We waited in tense silence until the voices faded down the hall. Once I was sure the coast was clear, I slipped out of his room, closing the door quietly behind me. My heart hammered in my chest as I hurried to my own room and closed myself inside.

Leaning back against the door, I let out a shaky breath. Mariya's words from earlier echoed in my mind again. She was wrong. This was just lust . . . a raw, magnetic, *feral* attraction. And that was all it would ever be.

That evening, I walked outside with Gigi as a team, our arms hooked elbow to elbow. The pack had gathered for the huge celebration—the first full moon of the year, the most important one—honoring our kind as a species.

The pack had gone all out, setting up a massive buffet inside a heated tent. The centerpiece was the fresh kill from the previous night, surrounded by an array of sides contributed by pack members. Outside, speakers pumped lively music into the crisp air, while strings of lights twinkled overhead, casting a warm, festive glow. The energy in the air was palpable.

Tyce led Gigi around to greet various members of the pack, and I seized the opportunity to slip toward the back of the crowd. I kept to the outskirts, ready to disappear into the shadows if necessary. The last thing I needed tonight was to cross paths with my ex. I'd managed to avoid him so far, and with any luck, I could hold out until tomorrow morning, when I'd finally head back to campus.

I was scanning the area when a familiar, unmistakable scent reached me just before I heard my name. "Terri," Kolya called softly from behind me.

I turned, spotting him partially hidden behind a snowbank, dressed head to toe in black. His night vision was dimmed, subduing his silver eyes in the darkness.

"Can I talk to you?" he asked.

"Of course," I replied, my voice steady despite the flutter in my chest. He reached for my gloved hand and, without another word, guided me away from the crowd, the shadows folding around us.

The smile on his face was radiant. He beamed down at me, his silver eyes shining. "I . . . I want to see you one more time before you leave," he said in a quiet voice. "You can run with me tonight?"

Guilt twisted in my chest as I shook my head. "I'm sorry . . . I can't," I replied. "I promised Gigi I'd run with her. She's really insecure about her wolf . . ." My voice trailed off, full of regret.

His smile faltered, and he briefly looked away, his shoulders slouching under the weight of disappointment. He let out a frustrated sigh, but then his expression shifted, as if remembering something important. When he looked back at me, there was a renewed intensity in his gaze. "I want to answer your other question."

"What?" I asked, blinking in confusion.

"The question I refused to answer before," he clarified. "When I promised you one question, but you asked second, and I did not answer. I want to answer now."

"Oh . . . Oh!" I stammered.

"I was harsh before," he said, his tone softening. "It was hard for me to speak then. Still hard. But you must know why I am like this. Before . . . before I lost my family, before I lost most of my pack, I was different man. Around you, I feel like this man again. Like life can be more than grief. You make me want to feel . . . happy."

"Kolya . . ." I whispered, my voice breaking under the weight of his words. My chest ached, and tears pricked at my eyes as I fought to hold them back. Slowly, I removed the glove from one hand and reached up, letting my fingers brush against the rough stubble of his cheek.

His eyes fluttered closed, and he leaned into my touch, as if my hand was offering him comfort he desperately needed. For a moment, we stayed like that, and I couldn't bring myself to let go.

After some time, he finally pulled away, and I slipped my glove back on, shielding it from the biting cold. He exhaled deeply, the sound heavy with the weight of what he was about to say.

"As you guessed, I already used my one wish," he began. "Problem with only one wish—you always fear to spend it. Always think, maybe tomorrow there is greater need. But when you are desperate . . . you know."

He paused for a moment, gathering his thoughts, then continued.

"Our pack, we fought many battles before. Always small disputes, nothing we could not handle. But when Chernoye Nebo Pack learned of stone . . . everything changed. You can imagine what man might wish with such power. Their alpha, I believe, already had his wish ready before he came.

"They used chaos of human Russo–Ukrainian war to cross border unseen. At first, we were winning. We lost warriors, yes, but they lost more. Still, they were relentless. Recruiting anyone, everyone. They would not stop.

"We called allies, but this help was not enough. They could not risk losing too many of their own. And when I lost my father . . ." His voice faltered, like the words were heavy in his throat. He stopped, breathing deep before forcing himself to go on. " . . . then I knew. We might lose everything. I had no choice but to use my wish."

I glanced up at him. His lips were trembling, his eyes bloodshot. My heart pounded like a hammer against my ribs as his anguish seeped into my bones.

"I wished for victory. But . . ." He took in a tremulous gasp of air. He was visibly shaking, clearly doing his best to hold himself together. "I was not specific enough. Yes, we won. But before victory came . . . my family was gone."

"Kolya . . ." I whispered, reaching out to rub his arm gently. The ache in his heart was tangible, his despair weaving into the heaviness building in my chest.

He blinked rapidly, as though fighting back tears, and then pressed on. "First, they took my youngest sister, Anastasia—Nastya, as we call her. She was not even eighteen. She was our doll, everyone's little sister. We spoiled her, loved her . . . and we failed to protect her." His voice cracked, and he looked down, shaking his head. "After this . . . morale fell apart. We were broken."

He paused, sniffing as he steadied himself. His hands trembled slightly. For a moment, I wondered if he could continue, if he should continue. But then, with visible effort, he did. "Next, they took Lena. She was like my mother. Strong, bossy. Always making her opinion known to everyone." His lips twitched with what might have been a fleeting attempt at a smile, but it quickly faltered. "If anyone could survive, it should be Lena. She was too stubborn to die. But . . ."

A pained sob tore from him, and I clutched my chest as his grief stabbed straight through my heart. The rawness of his sorrow was overwhelming. For a moment, I considered stopping him, telling him he didn't have to go on. But I realized this was something he needed to share—maybe even a release he'd been holding back for too long—so I let him continue.

"And then . . . they took Dariya." His voice dropped even further, thick with agony. "My oldest sister. She was only twenty-two. All life ahead of her." His hands balled into fists. His entire body shook. "She was sister I was closest with. Only one year and half between us. And I watched . . ." His words broke off, his breath hitching as his face twisted with anguish. "I watched an enemy wolf tear her head from her body." His voice came out hoarse, trembling. "I see it. Her head . . . gone. I was there. I was . . . powerless."

Kolya collapsed to his knees, and a sob broke through the stillness of the night. Without hesitation, I dropped to my knees beside him, cupping his face in my hands. His pain was unbearable, and I felt desperate to help him, though I didn't know how.

"I'm so sorry," I whispered, my voice cracking. "I . . . I wish . . ."

His hand covered one of mine, grounding me in the moment. "We all wish, Terri," he said softly, his voice weighted with the kind of pain no one should ever feel.

We stayed like that for a long while, wrapped in a pained silence. I searched for words—any words—that might bring him some small comfort. I desperately wished I could come up with something to say that could possibly help him. But I knew there wasn't a single word or phrase or string of words and phrases that would ever be adequate for what he had experienced.

Eventually, Kolya took another deep breath and continued, his voice quieter now, almost hollow. "After we lost Dariya, my mother, she beg me—take her to stone. I hid it so no one could find it, and I feared going back—worry we are tracked. But my mother . . ." He paused, his throat flexing. "She grieve too much. She lost her mate, her daughters, her will to fight. I cannot deny her.

"She was so weak then. Barely strong enough to make the journey. But I take her. I give her stone. So many better things she could wish for. But in the end . . ." His voice cracked, and he took a moment before finishing, "she wished for me to survive. For me . . . to find my mate."

His voice wavered, heavy with unspoken grief. "She not live long after. I think . . . she wanted to die. And once she made that wish, she felt like . . . finally, she can. And she did not fight back anymore."

By then, my own tears were streaming freely down my cheeks. I couldn't hold them back, not when faced with the sheer weight of his pain. I pulled him closer, resting his head on my shoulder as I held him tightly. Something broke deep inside me. I didn't want to let him go.

But I knew our time was limited. The pack was waiting, and I had promised Gigi I'd run with her. A promise I now deeply regretted. I didn't want to leave him, not like this, not when he needed someone. I wanted to do more, to help him in some way. But what could I do? I was just one small, broken person.

"You should go back," Kolya said softly.

"How?" I whispered, my throat thick with emotion. "How can I leave you like this?"

"Terri," he said gently, though his words carried an undeniable finality, "I am like this a long time. You just did not know."

"But now I do. I know now," I pleaded. "I can't leave you."

"You must," he said firmly, his gaze steady despite the lingering pain in his eyes.

"Kolya . . ."

"Terri," he interrupted, his tone hardening as he straightened, pulling himself away, standing. "You must leave me. You must live your life. This burden is not yours. It is mine. This is my fate, as alpha of my pack. I must be strong. I must lead."

I shook my head, my voice breaking. "You're carrying your pack, but who's carrying you?"

His jaw tightened, and for a moment, I thought he might falter. But then he took a step back, his expression cold and resolute. "I do not need anyone to carry me. I am alpha. From youth, we are beaten. To have no emotion, to be strong, to be unbreakable."

"But—"

He reached for me and pulled me to my feet. "*Pozhaluysta*, Terri," he said, his voice unyielding. "Go."

I stayed rooted, unable to tear myself away from him.

"Go," he repeated, more forcefully this time, giving me a light shove in the direction of the pack festivities. "Goodbye, Terri."

Before I could protest again, he turned and sprinted into the distance. His figure disappeared into the shadows, leaving me standing there, reaching out helplessly. A sob broke free from my chest. I let out everything I'd been holding back, my cries echoing into the void.

"Terri!" I heard my name in the distance.

"*Fuck*," I muttered under my breath, scrambling to wipe my tears, to clean my blotchy face, to pull myself together before anyone could see me like this. I adjusted my gaiter, desperately trying to mask the evidence of my breakdown.

By the time Gigi appeared, I had forced my face into something that vaguely resembled composure. She was carrying something furry, some kind of pelt, but her focus was locked on me, assessing me.

"Are you okay?" she asked in a hesitant voice, her grip tightening on whatever she was holding.

I forced a smile, willing every ounce of pain to stay hidden behind the fragile mask I'd hastily constructed. "Yeah, I'm great!" I chirped in a voice that was too high-pitched to be convincing. "Let's get into our—" My voice cracked a little, but I quickly cleared my throat. "Our wolf forms. The run's about to start, right?"

She hesitated with furrowed brows, but didn't push. What choice did she have besides to follow my lead as I stripped myself bare and scattered my clothes carelessly on the snow-covered ground.

"*Wait!*" Gigi stopped me, holding up the bundle in her arms. "Since we're shifting here, do you mind helping me with this?"

She tossed the fur contraption onto the ground and stripped. I blinked at the mess of fabric. After she shifted, she stepped into what I realized were leg holes.

Immune to the chill that was biting into my now-bare skin, holding back the tears that were threatening to break the dam holding them back, I fumbled with the material as I figured out how to zip her in. My hands moved on autopilot, my mind already distancing itself, already preparing to shut down.

And then, at last, I let go and transformed into my beast, succumbing to my animal brain, where everything outside basic survival no longer mattered.

Chapter 34

Nikolai

I must have removed my clothing at some point, but I didn't recall doing it. I couldn't even remember shifting into my wolf form. All I knew was that I was wolf now, sprinting across the vast, endless arctic tundra. Somewhere along the way, I had shed not just my human form but also the fragile remnants of my identity.

I no longer knew who I was, where I'd been, or whom I had loved and lost. I was no one. Just a nameless wolf, running through the icy expanse as the moon glared down at me. The cold air burned my lungs, and the snow crunched beneath my paws.

I sprinted faster, driven by an animalistic need to escape, to silence the flood of emotions clawing their way back. I wanted to be nothing but a creature of instinct, ruled by hunger, thirst, and exhaustion. No past. No pain. No regrets.

But I couldn't outrun my past or my losses. The heart I'd buried in a deep freezer was thawing, cracking, bits of ice chipping off. Water leaking into icicles that fell as they warmed, piercing the ground around me. Emotions were flooding back into me.

Her face wouldn't leave my psyche. I couldn't stop thinking about her thick, wavy hair, her warm, inquisitive amber eyes, the cherubic shape of her face, the way when she blushed it extended to her ears, how she was so catlike in her wolf form, the perfect, graceful predator.

And I'd let her go.

I knew there was no other choice.

I wasn't able to offer her what she deserved.

Asking her to be with me would only prolong the inevitable.

Our relationship had been doomed before it even started.

I ran for hours, until I made it back to where I'd finally pried that door open.

I dug my claws into the icy rock and began the upward climb. The wind howled around me, whipping against my face and blowing through my thick fur coat. My breath curled in the frigid air like tendrils of smoke and instantly crystallized, especially the higher I climbed.

Every muscle burned, but I welcomed the pain. It was grounding, tangible—unlike the ache in my chest, which I couldn't escape no matter how far I ran.

I continued upward. A spray of snow cascaded down from the cliffs above, forcing me to press myself tightly against the icy surface until it passed. My ears flicked, searching for any sound that might signal further danger. When I felt confident the coast was clear, I continued.

The wind shifted, carrying with it a scent that shouldn't have been here—soft, warm, and unmistakable. Her. Maybe it wasn't even the wind. Maybe it was my mind playing tricks on me, unearthing phantoms. But still, my paws faltered, my pace slowing against my will. And just like that, the memories I had been trying to outrun surged back, unbidden and unstoppable.

I thought about the prior full moon run, when she had attempted to playfully prank me and lighten the mood, and how I had reacted by snapping at her. How it felt when I first discovered she'd been marked. How impressive she was when I first spotted her lifting weights. How tough she was during that first venture out to my new pack land. Every moment, no matter how small and insignificant, played in my mind.

I felt blessed by the Moon Goddess that our paths had crossed and I'd had the opportunity to meet such a remarkable woman.

But it had been far too short-lived. From one full moon to the next. Just a single month of sunshine when all that lay ahead was darkness.

As I climbed higher, my paws sank into patches of snow and scraped against frozen rock. The slope steepened, but I pushed forward, my muscles contracting with each effort.

Finally, I crested. I pulled myself up to the summit. The unrestrained and merciless wind hit me harder here.

I stood still on that summit, staring out at the full moon in all her glory, bare, unconcealed by clouds. I threw my head back, and I howled like I'd never howled before.

A raw, unfiltered cry tore from my soul. At first, the sound was small, strangled, barely a whisper against the wind. But then it grew—raw, aching—a cry of grief and longing that rent the night. It wasn't just a howl. It was a confession. A surrender.

I howled for my family, for my pack, for her. For everything I had lost and everything I would never have. The sound echoed into the darkness, swallowed by the wind and snow as I laid my soul bare under the watchful gaze of the moon.

I cried until my throat was raw, my lungs burned, and my body trembled from the effort. For the first time since losing my family, since losing everything, I let myself feel.

My once-frozen heart was beating painfully in my chest.

When there was nothing else left inside me, I collapsed to the ground, into the icy snow. For a moment, I lay there, staring at the golden sphere in the endless, starry sky.

And then, I made my decision.

I would focus on my pack. I would be the alpha they needed—the leader who would guide them to new territory, train them to fight, and ensure their survival. I would rebuild, piece by piece, even if it meant sacrificing my own happiness.

Because that was what being an alpha meant.

For a fleeting moment, I let myself wonder—if things had been different, could I have chosen happiness instead? But duty weighed heavier than desire. An alpha carried the burdens of others, even when no one carried his.

I rose slowly. The wind whipped around me as I took one last glance at the moon. Then I descended the mountain, step by step, knowing that this was my path. My duty. My fate.

No matter how heavy it felt, I would carry it.

For them.

And for her.

Chapter 35

Theresa

I was a zombie when I made it to the runway that morning. I had barely slept the night before, and when I woke, my pillow was still damp with tears. I couldn't even remember how I'd made it through the full moon run and then home after. I must have just gone through the motions, my body moving while my mind drifted somewhere else entirely.

Earlier, as we prepared to leave, I'd walked past Kolya's room. I paused outside his door, my hand hovering over the handle, my heart pounding against my ribs. But the silence on the other side was deafening. The room was empty. He was gone. Just like that. The air inside my lungs turned heavy, pressing down on me, stealing my breath. I hadn't even said goodbye.

After stowing my bags in the cargo hold, I climbed aboard the pack's bush plane and sank into one of the narrow seats. I pulled off my mittens. Everything about me felt raw—my body, my hands, my heart. Hours of crying would do that, I supposed.

I rummaged through my backpack, finally locating my Dopp kit. Without really thinking, I pulled out a tube and began rubbing its contents onto my hands as I stared blankly out the window. The snow-covered landscape stretched endlessly, blending into the overcast sky.

"Terri!" Tyce's voice cut through my daze.

I jumped, startled, and turned toward him, blinking rapidly. "What? What is it?"

"Are you okay?" His brows knit together in confusion as he mimicked the motion of rubbing his hands together.

"I'm fine!" I insisted. "My hands are just dry."

Tyce glanced down, and his mouth twitched with restrained laughter. "Terri . . . why are you rubbing toothpaste all over your hands?"

"What?" I asked, confused, before looking down at myself. My hands were coated in a blue goop that wasn't absorbing into my skin.

I stared at the tube I'd been using. My cheeks heated with embarrassment.

"Oh," I muttered, trying to laugh it off. "Oops."

"Oops?" Tyce said, raising an eyebrow. "Didn't the overpowering smell of cool mint tip you off?"

"I wasn't really paying attention," I admitted.

"Here," Gigi interjected, handing me a small packet of hand wipes. "This should help."

"Thanks," I mumbled, grateful, and tore open the packet to wipe the sticky mess off my hands. I recapped the offending tube and returned it to its rightful place. This time, I made sure to grab the actual hand lotion I'd meant to use and lathered it onto my now minty-fresh hands.

I sagged back into my seat, exhaustion weighing me down. I leaned my head against the window and allowed my breath to fog up the cold glass, watching the soft haze form and fade with each exhale. The cabin buzzed with faint activity—Beta Liam's steady voice as he and his copilot worked through the preflight checklist, the occasional rustle of movement, and the giggling of Tyce and Gigi seated just behind me.

The familiar call of "Clear prop!" rang out, followed by the low rumble of the plane's engine sputtering to life. The vibrations beneath me grew steadier as the propeller whirred into motion, and soon, the hum of the plane filled the cabin. Before I knew it, we were airborne, the snowy landscape tilting and shrinking beneath us.

Despite my fatigue, I couldn't sleep. The events that unfolded the prior night had completely and utterly devastated me. I stared out at the white expanse below, but I wasn't really seeing it. I was somewhere else entirely—lost in my thoughts, existing in a foggy daze.

Was it possible to fall in love with someone after only a month? The logical part of me wanted to say no. But my aching heart knew better.

I couldn't stop thinking about him. Even though I'd intended for everything between us to stay casual, even though I'd known I'd be going back to school and he'd be moving to another part of the state, I couldn't shake how much he'd affected me, how he'd buried himself in my soul.

And what about him? Would he be okay? I couldn't shake his grief and how it had sunk into my bones. I couldn't forget the hollow look in his eyes as he recounted his story, as if he were reliving the pain of losing his family one by one, each memory cutting into him like a fresh wound.

But when I'd wanted to help, he'd pushed me away.

How could I be there for someone who didn't want me to be?

I pulled out my phone to check the time, more out of habit than necessity. That was when I realized—I didn't have his number. Did he even have a number? The permanence of our separation hit me then. He was really gone, and I had no way to contact him.

What evidence did I even have that what we'd shared was real? That it had been more than a fleeting dream?

I drifted in and out of consciousness, barely feeling like I even existed on that plane. Wondering what purpose my life had anymore.

"Terri . . . Terri . . . Terri!"

My name snapped me back. I blinked and whipped around, startled, until my eyes landed on Tyce, who was standing in the aisle next to my seat.

"Huh?" I asked, disoriented.

"Wow, you're really spaced out today."

"I guess I didn't get enough sleep last night," I mumbled, avoiding his gaze.

"Are you sure you're okay?" His voice softened, his concern obvious. The way his eyes bore into me made me feel exposed.

"Yeah! I'm totally fine!" I tried to brush him off. "That run just went really late, last-minute packing, you know."

Tyce didn't look convinced. He leaned in slightly, his expression shifting to something more serious. "You just seem . . . different. Off . . ." His words hung in the air, and for a moment, I thought he was going to press further. But instead, he pulled back, hesitating like he didn't know if he should push or let it go.

I forced out a laugh. "Tyson! I'm fine! Yeesh! Can't I be tired sometimes?"

"That's how he is now," Gigi chimed in, rolling her eyes dramatically. "Ever since he started taking his alpha duties seriously. He does the same thing to me. 'Gigi, do you have enough food? Is the room warm enough? Do you need more blankets? Do the rats need anything?' He's such a *dad* now!"

"Hey! Hey!" he protested. "That's *Daddy* to you!"

"Yes, Daddy," Gigi responded with a dramatic, teasing whine.

Tyce leaned back, his voice dropping an octave as a smirk spread across his face. "*Fuck!* That just did something to me. Say that again, baby."

"Da . . .ddy," Gigi purred, dragging the word out with a wicked grin.

"Oh my gosh! Can you guys *not* do this in front of me!" I complained, taking a stab at normalcy. Acting how I would if I wasn't crumbling. It felt like I was putting on a performance, playing the part of someone who wasn't dying on the inside.

What I really wanted to do was curl up under a huge blanket and cry until there was nothing left inside me.

After we landed, Tyce and Liam escorted us to our new housing, a two-bedroom apartment in close proximity to the woods that Tyce insisted we live in together for the duration of our remaining time in college. I'd already moved most of my stuff in from campus housing before I'd gone home for break.

When it was time for Tyce and Liam to head back to the pack, Tyce lingered by the entryway, his feet rooted as though he couldn't bring himself to leave. He held Gigi's hands tightly as he stared down at her with glossy eyes. His chin trembled, and his voice wavered, cracking under the weight of emotion as he began a heartfelt speech about how much she meant to him and how deeply he would miss her over the next few months.

Gigi listened, her own eyes welling up, but after a moment, she let out a small, exasperated laugh and wiped at a tear. Straightening her shoulders, she leveled him with a look. "For Goddess's sake, Tyce! You act like you're not going to be visiting every other week! And FaceTiming me every night! And being the first to heart every one of my Instagram stories! And texting me every other minute to send me some obscure rat meme you found!" Then, with a gleam in her eye, she added, "And out of respect for your sister and Liam, I won't even *mention* the Snaps you'll be sending—or the ones you'll be requesting."

He mumbled under his breath, just loud enough for us to catch, "Can I request one for the ride back?"

Gigi gasped in mock offense and gave him a hard shove. "Get out of here, you creep! You're making Terri uncomfortable!"

Liam chuckled, shaking his head. "Beta Liam appreciates you waiting until after Alpha Tyce is back at the packhouse before fulfilling any of those requests," he said with a grin, tugging Tyce's arm to drag him away.

"One last goodbye," Tyce insisted, shaking off Liam's grip. He turned back to Gigi, pulling her into his arms and lifting her effortlessly off the ground. He wrapped her in a bear hug before going in for an ardent kiss.

Liam and I exchanged awkward glances, both of us trying and failing not to look. Liam cleared his throat dramatically, and after a moment, Tyce reluctantly put her back on her feet.

Then, he turned to me, pulling me into a far more chaste hug. "Bye, Terr Bear. If you need me to beat anyone up, just say the word."

I forced a chuckle to acknowledge the joke.

"I know you're more than capable of handling it yourself," he added, "but as your big brother, I have to offer."

"Bye, Tyce," I said as he pulled away.

He turned back to Gigi, giving her one last hug and a lingering kiss, before finally leaving with Liam.

Once we were sure they weren't coming back, Gigi turned to me. Her expression softened, and she reached out, resting her hand gently on my arm.

"Terri," she said, her voice quiet but full of concern. "Are you sure you're okay? I get it if you didn't want to tell your brother. I keep things from my family too sometimes. But . . ." She furrowed her brows, her concern deepening. "Last night, when I found you alone . . . you just looked like something really horrible had happened. I didn't want to be too nosy, but . . ." She sighed, pausing for a moment before meeting my gaze again. "I just want you to know you can talk to me. I'm here for you."

"Thanks, I appreciate it." I plastered on a smile. "But I'm honestly fine. I was just getting in my feelings about leaving home. But I'm all good now!" Even as I said it, I knew that I wasn't convincing.

"Okay . . ." Gigi's voice trailed off. I could tell she wanted to say more, but she left it at that. "I guess it's time to unpack."

"Time to unpack," I echoed, thankful for the opportunity to retreat to my own bedroom and be alone.

However, instead of unpacking, I fell into my bed as thoughts swirled around my head. I thought about how emotional Tyce had been to leave

Gigi. I'd never seen him like that before. His love for her was so clear, raw, vulnerable. My chest ached at how alone I was, how broken I was, with a permanent mark on my neck. Who would want me as a mate? We'd never even be able to be proper mates.

My eyes trailed the stack of textbooks on my desk.

Maybe I couldn't have what Tyce and Gigi had. But who said happiness had to come from a mate? It was the twenty-first century, for Goddess's sake! There were other ways to build a meaningful, fulfilling life.

I could be anything I wanted to be. If I didn't join the family business, I could start my own. I could start up a whole new stream of income for the pack. Or I could be the first female warrior we ever had. I could rise up the ranks and become a senior warrior who bravely led the men into battle, taking down enemy wolves. Who was to stop me? Trav's own mate was an alpha!

From this day forward, I vowed, I would forget about my ex. I would forget about Kolya. Instead, I would focus on school, on training, on becoming someone who didn't need someone else to define her.

Chapter 36

Ginger

During my first week of school, I was surprised to find I didn't miss Tyce as much as I would've expected. Sure, there were moments when a random ache would settle in my chest and I'd long for his presence. Nights felt lonelier. My sleep was lighter and more restless than it had been before I left. Mornings sucked. The bed felt colder, too big. I'd reach out instinctively, expecting to find him there, only to be greeted by empty sheets. But I kept moving forward.

My full courseload kept me too busy to dwell on much outside of school. Between organic and biochemistry, human anatomy and physiology, chemistry, and ethics, I barely had a moment to breathe, let alone think beyond my assignments, exams, and endless notes. By the end of the first week, I was already drowning in homework, my planner was overflowing, and my nights were consumed by studying.

It didn't take long for me to fall into a rhythm. I gravitated toward the same handful of classmates each day, pulled together by our desperation to survive the semester. We formed a study group, spending lunch breaks quizzing each other over flashcards and sharing color-coded notes. They said werewolves tended to keep their distance from humans, and I noticed the few I spotted on campus often sat alone. But for me, blending in had always been second nature. I'd practically grown up around humans. This world wasn't new to me at all.

By the time Friday rolled around, I could hardly believe an entire week had already passed. Time blurred when every second was accounted for. That afternoon, I lingered after my human anatomy and physiology class, hoping to ask my professor a quick question.

Professor Langley was a kind, soft-spoken woman. She'd been a nurse since the midseventies and was now semiretired, teaching college courses to pass the time. What I had planned to be a brief question turned into a deep, unexpectedly fascinating conversation about her time as a nurse. Her eyes lit up as she regaled me with stories of the challenges she'd faced throughout her career and the countless lives she'd saved.

Before I knew it, I was telling her about the time I helped deliver a baby. Of course, I left out the part about it being a werewolf baby, and about the pack that had been trying to take over ours, but left in just enough details to illustrate what had happened.

"That's incredible," she said. A warm surge of pride spread through my chest, chasing away the self-doubt that had lingered at the back of my mind. I hadn't realized how much I needed to hear the admiration of someone I respected.

By the time I left the classroom, an hour had passed, but I didn't care. I felt lighter, as if I had finally reaffirmed something within myself. This was where I was meant to be. This was what I was meant to do.

I now felt fully confident in my decision to pursue nursing over premed. Professor Langley even suggested that, if I ever wanted to advance my career later, becoming a nurse practitioner could be the way to do it.

As I headed for the exit, replaying the conversation with my professor in my mind, a pretty brunette with bangs and stick-straight, shoulder-length hair stepped into my path, forcing me to stop abruptly.

I inhaled instinctively, and the unmistakable scent hit me. She was a werewolf. Her pack's scent seemed familiar, though I couldn't place it. I was still working on distinguishing all the different pack scents, something most people my age had long mastered. At least I could now tell if someone was from my old pack, Midnight Maple, or my current one, Jade Moon. Beyond that, it was a guessing game.

"Gigi?" she asked, catching me off guard. Her face didn't look familiar. Or did it? I was having trouble keeping track of all the people I'd been introduced to that week.

"I'm sorry if we already met, but I can't remember your name," I replied, racking my brain and trying to think of which one of my classes she might be in.

"I'm Grace," she said with an easy, friendly smile. "I was in your chem class for a day, but I transferred to a different section."

Had there been another werewolf in my chem class? The week had been so overwhelming, it was entirely possible I'd forgotten.

"Oh, right," I said, hoping I sounded convincing, not wanting to offend her that I didn't remember her when she so clearly had me. "Sorry, Grace. I'm terrible with names sometimes."

"It's fine," she said, brushing it off. "I'm sure you've met tons of people this week. I have too. But since we're both, *you know*"—she gestured vaguely but meaningfully—"I figured I should catch you. I'm still in chem, just at a different time. If you ever need to swap notes or anything, I can give you my number."

"Thanks!" I pulled out my phone, typing in the digits she rattled off. I quickly sent her a text. "Now you've got mine too."

She glanced down at her phone and smiled. "Perfect. Honestly, it's so strange being around *them* all the time," she said, nodding toward the humans bustling through the hallway. "It's nice to meet someone like me, you know?"

"Yeah, totally," I replied, even though I didn't fully agree, but I figured it would be weird if I responded otherwise. I wasn't about to give her my entire life story.

"Hey," Grace said, her tone brightening, "my friends and I are going to a party tonight. The party'll be mostly *them*, but me and my friends will be there too. Want to come? I can introduce you to everyone!"

"Oh, that sounds great!" I said, genuinely excited. *My first party! New friends! Werewolf friends!*

"Awesome! I'll text you the deets." She gave me another warm smile before walking away. I watched her for a moment, trying again to remember if we'd met and conversed before. But then I let it go. Clearly it couldn't have been that interesting of a conversation if we, indeed, had had one. Besides, maybe she'd just remembered my name from attendance and noted who I was because we were both werewolves.

I finally found the exit and stepped outside into the cold, crisp air, inhaling the scent of winter, pine trees, and Alaskan wilderness, something that was far more abundant down here than up where I'd been living.

The off-campus housing Tyce, or someone else in the pack, had found for Terri and me was practically next door to campus, making the walk home fairly easy. While the cold would have certainly bothered me before I'd gotten my wolf back, since turning full wolfy, I'd discovered extreme cold didn't register the same way anymore. Heat, on the other hand, was a different story. While I hadn't experienced it firsthand yet, I'd heard trips down south were sweaty, miserable getaways.

Thankfully, Hawaii's weather seemed to be fairly moderate, so my dream of a tropical island honeymoon—where Tyce and I spent the entire time fucking with the ocean as our backdrop—hadn't been crushed. We planned to leave the morning after the wedding and take advantage of my spring break to wrap ourselves in each other for an entire week. With how hectic and busy my life had turned at school, I was only looking forward to it more now.

When I got back to my temporary home, I opened the door to our open floor plan and immediately spotted Terri on the floor, hunched over a textbook at the coffee table. Her face was red and blotchy, her expression utterly devastated. My chest tightened with guilt.

Even though I wasn't spending much time at the apartment, every time I crossed paths with Terri, she looked like a shell of herself. It was clear something was deeply wrong, but we'd only just met and hadn't had the chance to get close. I didn't know how to get her to let me in and tell me what was wrong.

Still, I squared my shoulders and resolved to try.

Dropping my backpack by the door, I approached her quietly and slid onto the floor across the coffee table. I watched as she stiffened, like she was bracing herself for something. "Hey," I said softly, "how's it going?"

She quickly wiped at her face, pasted on a too-bright smile, and straightened her posture. "Oh, it's great! I'm learning so much. It's great to be back!"

Liar.

I took in the dark circles under her eyes, the way her hands gripped the textbook just a little too tightly. She was trying so hard to seem okay.

"That's . . . great," I replied, keeping my voice even. Then I added, "But how are you? Like, mentally? Coming back after over a month at home can't be easy."

Her smile faltered for just a second before she forced out a soft chuckle. "It's nice to get away from home, honestly. My parents, you know how they are . . . A break from them is like a vacation."

"Sure." I narrowed my eyes and nodded slowly, studying her. "But you must miss *someone* back home, right?"

This time, her hesitation was more obvious.

"Of course! I miss my friends. But I'll see them again during summer break."

I sighed. I wasn't getting through. Terri had built up a hard shell, and it would take more than just some gentle prying to break it open.

My phone vibrated in my back pocket, and I pulled it out to find a text from Tyce. A smile tugged at my lips before I slipped it back into my pocket, deciding to reply later. For now, I had to focus on Terri.

Maybe . . . maybe if she thought I needed her instead of the other way around? It wasn't a lie, exactly. I would feel awkward going alone. But as soon as the thought crossed my mind, guilt prickled at the edges of my conscience. Was it wrong to use that? Even if it was for her own good?

"Hey! I made a new friend today, and she invited me to a party tonight. We should go! Celebrate surviving our first week and get out of the apartment for a bit."

She hesitated, and I could see the protest forming on her lips.

"Please?" I added quickly, before she could speak. "I always feel so awkward going to parties alone. And we haven't really had a chance to bond yet. It'd mean a lot if you came with me."

While I didn't know Terri super well yet, I had gathered that she was always sniffing around for a way to help others. If I framed it like *I* needed her, I knew that who she was at her core wouldn't allow her to say no. Her expression faltered. Her internal struggle played out on her face. For a second, I felt a twinge of guilt for manipulating her, but I genuinely believed this would do her some good. She couldn't just stay here, sinking deeper into despair.

Finally, she said, "Yeah, of course." Though her tone was anything but enthusiastic.

"Yay!" I cheered, maybe a little too eagerly. "My sister and I always help each other with hair and makeup before going out. Let me help you with yours! I can even help you pick out an outfit. Something sexy, so maybe you can meet someone *crazy* hot. They always say the best way to get over something is to get under someone."

Her lips twitched into a faint laugh, more air than sound.

She clearly wasn't feeling it, but I'd been miserable before. I knew that sometimes you had to force yourself out of the funk, even if it felt impossible. And maybe this night out would be good for both of us. If nothing else, it might help her trust me enough to finally open up.

I wasn't sure I could help, but I was damn sure going to try.

Chapter 37

Theresa

I didn't protest as Gigi rummaged through the sparse contents of my closet and my still-packed suitcase. She sifted through my collection of T-shirts, sweatshirts, sweatpants, gym shorts, and an admittedly excessive number of turtlenecks. The truth was, I didn't really *do* sexy.

"Ooh la la!" Gigi held up a lacy bralette, twirling it around like a prize. Okay, so maybe I *did* do sexy in one area. I kind of liked the idea of someone being surprised to uncover my underthings after expecting something totally different based on the comfy, casual clothes I regularly wore.

I knew I was probably supposed to react to Gigi handling my intimates, but I couldn't bring myself to care. Hey, at least someone other than me was seeing them.

She laid various options out on my bed, pausing to step back and think. Then, she darted back to my closet or suitcase, dug around some more, swapped out different pieces, and repeated the process. I sighed, too lost in my own thoughts to be of much help. But she did, at least, seem to genuinely enjoy doing this.

She returned to my closet a final time and rummaged through it, pulling apart the hangers. Something seemed to finally catch her eye. She grabbed it and held it out to get a good look. "I *knew* you had to be hiding something like this, you little vixen!"

It was a tight, indecently short black turtleneck sweater dress I'd impulsively ordered during a moment of optimism. I'd never worn it, but at the time, I'd hoped I would someday.

"Put it on!" Gigi insisted, practically bouncing on her heels. "I can leave the room if you want."

"It's fine," I said with a sigh, taking the dress from her. I turned my back, careful to keep my mark hidden, and stripped off my sweatsuit.

"And she wears a thong!" Gigi whistled. "Damn, Terri. I never would've guessed!"

I rolled my eyes but couldn't help a small smile as I slipped into the dress. When I turned and did a half spin, Gigi clapped enthusiastically.

"Damn, girl, you're *hot*! You should wear tight clothes more often. Your ass looks incredible in that dress."

"It's about to fall out," I joked, attempting at normalcy.

"I see no problems," Gigi shot back with a wink.

Something about her energy tugged at my heart. I'd been so wrapped up in my own problems, I'd almost forgotten what it felt like to have someone care.

When we were done, I followed her to her room to return the favor, though she clearly didn't need much help. She already had a vision in mind and quickly settled on a bright red, long-sleeve top, with straps that crisscrossed at her chest in a sexy way, paired with a black leather miniskirt. She finished the look with tall black suede boots.

Once she put it on, I had to admit, I could see why my brother was so into her. She had curves in all the right places and carried herself with a self-assured confidence that was magnetic. She practically *reeked* of sex.

"You look great," I said with a forced smile, attempting to be as encouraging to her as she was to me. "You clearly have this whole sexy thing down."

"Why thank you," she replied, flipping her long strawberry blonde hair dramatically.

Gigi then had me sit cross-legged on the floor while she plopped down behind me, her arms full of different tools. She immediately got to work, spraying my hair, clipping it up, and meticulously curling it. I did feel a little bad because I had *a lot* of hair. The whole process took over an hour, but Gigi didn't complain once.

When she finished her work, I returned the favor and curled her hair for her as she guided me. I found myself laughing for the first time in days as I fumbled through it. Admittedly, this was something I'd never done much of, but I found myself enjoying the bonding experience.

While I worked, Gigi wistfully commented, "This is so nice." Her lips tugged into a smile. "It reminds me of my sisters. I miss them so much."

"Paige and Heidi, right?"

"Yeah . . . Heidi just had a pup too." I noted her eyes growing glossy as she continued, her voice tinged with longing. "His name is Grayson. We FaceTime all the time, but I just wish I could hold him. He'll be coming here for the wedding in March." She sighed. "It just feels so long away. I wish time would hurry up so I can finally meet him in person."

Although now mated, neither of my siblings had had a pup yet, so I wasn't exactly sure how Gigi felt. I had to admit, I'd never felt particularly motherly. It always felt more like something that was expected of me than something I genuinely wanted.

But then, unbidden, Kolya came to mind. And suddenly, I could imagine a scenario where a pup would be a welcomed guest. The idea of creating a life out of the love two people had for each other seemed . . . nice. Better than nice. Like a satisfactory piece of a love story.

"It must be really hard being so far from your family," I said after a moment, breaking the silence. "It seems like you're all really close."

"It is," Gigi agreed. "And we are." She paused, then added thoughtfully, "I know your parents are tough, but Tyce and Trav both really care about you."

"Yeah, they've been good brothers."

"Tyce told me you used to stick together growing up."

"Yeah, that's true. They used to sneak me food when my mom was being extra crazy about what I ate. Her favorite phrase was always, 'Once on the lips, forever on the hips.' Or 'You're not hungry, you're just thirsty.'" I sighed. "Recently, I've realized it has nothing to do with me. It's her own insecurities. While I guess she and my dad seem to work together okay, I always got the feeling she was afraid to lose him for some reason. Which is weird. Why would you be afraid to lose your fated mate?"

"Are you sure they're fated mates?" Gigi asked.

"Of course!" I responded emphatically. "They're both super religious . . ." My voice trailed off as I thought back to my mom's antics. "Well, my dad is super religious at least. I couldn't imagine him ever marrying someone who wasn't his fated mate. And I can't imagine my grandfather ever *accepting* it either. My dad never crossed him."

"It's just . . ."

"Just what?" I leaned in closer, curious.

"Something your uncle, Gabe, I'm pretty sure his name was, said at your grandpa's funeral. Something along the lines of, 'Julia, we both know he's not your mate.' I didn't think too much of it then, like maybe he was bitter that his brother was mated to the person he wanted. But now . . ." She appeared lost in thought.

"Well, how would he know the difference?" I mumbled to myself, recalling my mother's words from a month earlier.

"What?" Gigi asked.

"Oh, nothing. I was just remembering something," I replied, not sure I wanted to share.

"I guess it's just something to think about," Gigi said. "But it would make sense, right? Like, I never once felt like Tyce was unhappy with any aspect of me. He always makes me feel like I'm that perfect person who dropped down onto planet Earth just for him, that I could infest our bedroom with an army of rodents and he would still smile and say, 'thank you.'"

I couldn't help but giggle despite myself, recalling Tyce's fear of rodents. It was one of his more endearing traits. Although I did feel bad that our dad and grandpa always gave him so much shizz about it.

After I twirled the last bit of hair around the wand, Gigi pulled out a large cosmetic case and got to work on my face. I realized then that my mood had been lifted. As much as I'd been dreading the party, perhaps that evening wouldn't be so bad.

Chapter 38

Miriam

29 years ago

"Are you fucking *serious*?" Gabe roared, jolting the table when he stood. As if that wasn't enough, he grabbed the solid oak piece of furniture and shook it violently. Plates jumped, glasses tipped, and wine splashed across the tablecloth.

I instinctively reached out, trying to steady my own plate while simultaneously scooting back to dodge the onslaught of food missiles.

"That's enough, Gabe!" My father, Alpha Bruce, rose to his full height, his presence radiating fury. "Stop it!"

Gabe let out a strangled, guttural noise, his movements freezing abruptly, clearly because he had no other choice.

"Look," Lance interjected, his voice steady despite the chaos, "this wasn't my choice. Honestly, neither of us wanted this. Out of love and respect for you, Gabe—"

"Respect?" Gabe spat, his voice dripping with venom.

"Yes, respect," Lance pressed on, undeterred. "You think I want to be mated to the woman my brother loves and planned to marry? Do you think Julia wants this? We tried to fight it, both of us. But Artemis clearly had other plans."

"You're a liar, Lance!" Gabe's rage exploded. "You think that, because you're going to be alpha, you can take whatever you want from me? You've always been a jealous little shit—always needing to prove you're better than me, always trying to dominate me! You're just insecure because you know if it weren't for birth order, I would be the alpha! You should be grateful I haven't killed you yet."

"I'd love to see you try!" Lance snapped, slamming his hands onto the table as he leaned forward. His eyes locked with Gabe's in a deadly glare.

"Gabe! Enough!" Bruce's voice boomed, his alpha aura so thick we could all feel it. Everyone fell silent under the pressure of it.

Bruce's piercing gaze shifted to Lance. In a more subdued and controlled voice, he asked, "Are you really mated to . . ." He paused, his eyes flicking down to Julia as though she were something vile and unworthy of acknowledgment. "*Her*?"

"Yes, I am," Lance replied evenly, his expression unreadable, his voice calm despite the tension in the room.

Bruce's jaw tightened, and his disapproval radiated. For a long moment, he didn't say anything. His expression was unreadable. Finally, he exhaled heavily and said, "None of us has the power to override the Goddess's will."

His words hung in the air as a final, indisputable verdict that settled over the room.

Unable to speak, Gabe stormed out with wild and destructive movements, slamming and flipping furniture on his way. His heavy stomps reverberated down the hallway, culminating with the slam of the front door crashing shut behind him.

My gaze turned to Julia. She sat perfectly composed, her back straight, not a single hair out of place. If I didn't know better, I might've thought she was *pleased*—smug, even.

Lance didn't so much as spare her a glance as he silently stepped out of the room. His departure was swift and unapologetic, and he didn't even bother to excuse himself. Once he was gone, Bruce soon followed, and my mom and I were left gathering all of the dinnerware and throwing away anything that was now broken.

Later that night, I found myself outside Lance's bedroom door. I hesitated for a moment before knocking.

"Come in," he said.

I pushed the door open and stepped inside. He was perched on the edge of his bed, his head cradled in his hands. His hair was a chaotic mess, as though he'd been running his fingers through it since he'd left the table.

I grabbed a chair from his desk and sat down.

"Yes?" he asked, glancing up at me briefly.

"You can't really be mated to her."

"Why not?" he replied in a clipped tone.

"She's . . . she's not even your type." I fumbled for the right words. "With most mates, it makes sense. But you and Julia . . . you don't make any sense at all."

"And what is my type, Miriam?" he asked with a penetrating gaze. There was a restrained but unmistakable flash of anger in his voice.

"I don't know exactly," I admitted, stumbling over my words. "But I know it's not her. She's . . . she's so snobby, like she thinks she's better than everyone else. The way she talks to me—it's so patronizing. I don't trust her, Lance. And this whole thing with Gabe? Taking him as a chosen mate? Do you really believe she ever *loved* him?"

"Miriam," Lance fired back, "do you realize you're insulting my mate?"

I stood there while frustration bubbled up inside me until it spilled over. "If she's your mate, Lance, then why do you look so *miserable*?"

"Did you miss what happened tonight?" he snapped. "How I had to tell my own fucking brother that I was taking his mate from him? Do you know what that feels like? And then there's Dad—he couldn't even say Julia's *name*. His disapproval was written all over his face. Do you think having a mate is all sunshine and daisies? Sometimes there are consequences, *real* consequences. And sometimes your mate"—he hesitated, and his voice cracked slightly when he continued—"isn't right for you at all. But Artemis chooses to send that damned person to you. And they make you happy, and you can see a future with them—you *want* a future with them—but it's not that simple, Miriam. You don't just get to live in a dream world where everything works out. You have responsibilities, *duties* as an alpha, as a leader. You have to make hard decisions . . ." His voice trailed off.

For a moment, I wondered if he was still talking about Julia or if there was something, or someone, else. At some point, his speech had spiraled beyond Julia, and I felt lost, struggling to piece together his meaning. What was he really trying to say?

"Miriam," he said with a hard gaze, his tone shifting to one of finality. "I am mated to Julia. Julia is my fated mate. I intend to marry her and take her as my luna. The sooner you accept that, the better it will be for all of us."

"For all of us?" I repeated. Something about the way he said it made my stomach churn, like there was something deeper he wasn't saying.

"Yes," he said firmly, his expression unreadable. "Now go. And close the door behind you. Don't make me use my alpha aura on you."

A frustrated sigh escaped me as I pushed the chair back into his desk. He wasn't going to elaborate. I walked to the door and paused, hoping for . . . something. A hint, a crack in his resolve. But there was nothing. I stepped out of the room, closing the door softly behind me.

Even as I walked down the hallway, my thoughts raced. Something didn't add up. Julia. She had to be manipulating him somehow. But *how?*

What leverage could she possibly have? She was just some foreigner from a nothing pack in a former Soviet country. Sure, she came from a beta family, but what power or influence could that pack possibly have here?

Chapter 39

Ginger

By the time we made it to the party, Terri seemed to be in a much better mood. I felt pleased with the progress I'd made. She was opening up more and actually laughing, a huge contrast to earlier that afternoon.

"Let's go get some drinks!" I exclaimed and led her into the kitchen of the small house we'd come to. They had a huge bowl of jungle juice set out, so I filled our Solo cups with generous pours. We tapped our cups together and made it out to the living room where music was blasting and students were gathered. I sniffed around, but only humans seemed to be in attendance so far.

"How'd you hear about this party?" Terri asked.

"It's kind of funny," I said. "I met another one of our kind earlier today at school. She gave me her number and said there'd be more of us here tonight."

"Oh," Terri replied, but she didn't seem as enthusiastic about it as I thought she'd be. "Do you know what pack she was from?"

"I couldn't tell," I replied. "And she didn't say."

"It's usually good to ask. I try to stay away from people in packs we've had disputes with in the past."

"Oh, I didn't even think of that." I bit my lip, realizing how much I still had to learn. I didn't even know what packs Jade Moon Pack had

had disputes with. I made a mental note to ask Tyce later for a list, so I could make sure to avoid them.

"It's okay," Terri said, giving me a small smile. "I'm sure it's fine."

We wandered through the party, occasionally stopping to chat with people Terri recognized from her classes. Though she introduced me, it was clear she wasn't particularly close with any of them. The whole interaction reinforced how guarded werewolves could be.

As our cups emptied, I refilled them, and before long, we both had a good buzz going. We found a couple of empty chairs and settled in, eventually launching into a game to entertain ourselves.

"He's a ten but . . ." I began, scanning the room.

Terri grinned and pointed to a guy in a plaid shacket with his hair slicked back with way too much gel. "He's a ten but . . . he's one of those alpha male podcasters."

I burst out laughing and nodded toward another guy, this one wearing a wool coat indoors. "He's a ten but . . . he kisses his BMW good night every night."

Terri chuckled and gestured toward a tall, gangly guy with oversize glasses. "He's a ten but . . . he says 'That's all folks!' after every joke he tells."

We both doubled over in laughter.

I pointed at a shorter guy in a bright, colorful sweatshirt. "He's a ten but . . . he writes erotic *Dora the Explorer* fan fiction."

Terri nearly choked on her drink. When she looked up, she said, "He's a ten but . . . he's not potty-trained." Then she motioned toward a guy in JNCO jeans.

We kept the game going, making up increasingly ridiculous red flags for every guy who passed by. Each joke left us bent over with laughter, tears streaming down our cheeks. For a moment, everything felt light and uncomplicated.

Eventually, our cups emptied. "I'll grab us another round," I said, getting up and heading back to the kitchen. When I returned a few minutes later with two fresh cups in hand, Terri was no longer laughing. Her shoulders were slumped and her gaze distant. I handed her one of the drinks and sat down beside her. "Hey, are you okay?"

"Oh, yeah, I'm fine," she replied. She took a sip, sniffling quietly, and I caught the glint of a tear sliding down her cheek before she wiped it away.

"Terri," I said gently, leaning closer. "Are you *sure* you're okay?"

"Yeah, yeah. I just . . ." Her voice trailed off. It seemed like she might finally open up when her head suddenly snapped up and she sniffed the air.

"What is it?" I asked.

"Alpine Snow Pack is here."

"That's the pack in the Anchorage area, right?"

"Yeah . . ." she said, but didn't elaborate. She seemed to be lost in thought and no longer present in the moment.

I looked up and noticed Grace in the distance. "Hey, that's my new friend over there. Do you mind if I quickly go say hi?"

"Oh . . . yeah," Terri replied, though it didn't seem like she'd even registered my question.

I made my way over to Grace as it all clicked. The scent from the jar Tyce and Sara had been analyzing and the man Sara had tortured. Grace's scent was familiar because she was from the same pack. If Grace was part of the pack scouting near Sara's and our territory, this could be a golden opportunity. I could gather intel to help Tyce and Sara out. *Keep your friends close and your enemies closer*, right?

"Gigi!" Grace greeted me warmly. "You made it!"

"Yeah, this party is great. Thanks for letting me know about it!"

"Of course! Hey, come meet my friends!"

She led me to her group, and I immediately recognized them as were-wolves—all part of the Alpine Snow Pack. Their territory wasn't far from here, so it made sense many of them attended this school. If Grace didn't have useful information, perhaps someone else in her group would.

She introduced me to everyone, and they were surprisingly welcoming, offering me big hugs, warm smiles, and promises to hang out again in the future. I sipped my drink, the buzz in my head shifting to something closer to drunk. Everything felt warm, wobbly, and slightly surreal, and I was genuinely enjoying myself.

"Hey, I should check on my friend," I said after realizing how long I'd been away from Terri.

When I found her, she seemed zombie-like again, her earlier cheer completely gone.

"Hey, if you want to head home, we can," I offered.

"What? No!" Terri stood abruptly. "I think I just need to use the bathroom. Everything's totally fine. We should stay longer. I'll be right back."

She walked off, joining the line for the bathroom down the hall. I was about to take a seat when Grace appeared beside me.

"Hey, can I get you something else to drink?" she asked.

"Oh no, I'm good. This is probably my last one," I replied.

"How's your friend?"

"She's fine. She just went to the bathroom."

"You're not leaving, are you? We just got here."

"No, no, she wants to stay," I assured her. "I can introduce you when she gets back."

A man approached us and stood next to Grace. I struggled to remember his name. Bill? Brian? Ben? Something with a B.

"Hey, do you wanna?" he asked, tapping his right nostril meaningfully.

"Gigi, have you tried it before?" Grace placed her hand on my arm in a friendly gesture.

I shook my head.

"Oh, you have to. It's amazing. It makes you feel so good, like you don't have a care in the world. You've gotta try it!"

The idea was tempting. I'd missed out on trying coke at my bachelorette party, which I'd always hoped would be much wilder than it turned out. Of course, I was grateful for everyone that had thrown it for me. But I really wanted to have more interesting life experiences before I settled down. Plus, Terri was feeling so low. Maybe this would cheer her up. Besides, we were werewolves. We could handle things like this far better than humans. What harm could it really do?

"I'm in!" I said, excitement bubbling up. "Once my friend gets back."

Grace beamed, and we stood chatting until Terri returned. But the moment she stepped into the room, her eyes widened, scanning the crowd.

"You're Theresa, right?" Grace asked.

Wait—had I told her Terri's name? And why'd she call her *Theresa*? I'd never heard anyone use her full name before, except maybe her mom sometimes. But maybe they'd crossed paths in a class or through pack business. That would explain it.

"I am." Terri studied her, but her eyes were glossed over, and her brain was probably feeling just as foggy as mine by this point. We had drunk a lot, even by werewolf standards. "And you are?"

"Grace," she said brightly. "We were just about to head downstairs for some fun. We were waiting for you."

The group began moving toward a doorway leading to a staircase.

"Where are they taking us?" Terri asked me quietly.

"Just to hang out," I assured her, grabbing her arm as we followed.

We made our way down to a finished basement with a couch, a few chairs, and a handful of people lounging on the floor. Grace claimed the couch, patting the cushions beside her with an inviting smile and waving us over. "Come on, sit!"

The air in the basement was thick with the smell of sweat, cheap beer, and something sickly sweet—probably the jungle juice we'd been chugging earlier. The bass of the music upstairs was so strong I could even feel its vibration down here, thrumming against the ceiling and walls.

I led Terri to the couch and sat down, but a nagging unease began to creep into my gut. Even in my drunken haze, something about the room felt *off*. I glanced around, trying to identify the source of my anxiety. People were lounging, sipping drinks, chatting. Maybe it was the unnerving way their gazes lingered on us.

Terri must have felt it too. She stood abruptly. "You know what, Gigi, I thought I felt okay, but I don't. I think we should go home."

"Oh, don't worry!" Grace said in an overly cheerful tone. "We've got something coming that'll make you feel *so* much better."

"I think the only thing that's going to help right now is my bed," Terri responded, grabbing my arm.

"I should get her home," I added quickly, rising to my feet. "Sorry, maybe next time."

"Aww, but the party's just getting started!" Grace pouted. "You just got comfortable."

"Yeah, I know," I replied, forcing a chuckle. "But I think we're good for tonight."

I turned toward Terri, but Terri wasn't looking at me anymore. She was staring at the two massive men who had just stepped in front of the staircase.

My pulse stuttered.

"Gigi," Terri murmured, shifting closer to me. Her voice had lost all traces of drunken haze.

The room felt suddenly smaller. The air too heavy. The bass was still pounding, but it felt too far away now, like it belonged to a different world.

"Where do you think you're going?" one of the men asked in a low, menacing voice.

My heart raced as I tried to process the situation. On impulse, I took a step back. "We're just leaving," I stammered.

Something was wrong.

Terri's grip on my arm tightened.

But, before I could take another step, a sharp, stabbing pain pierced the back of my neck.

"*Ow!*" I yelped, my hand flying up instinctively to touch the spot.

Beside me, Terri cried out. "What the heck—"

Realization hit me. We were surrounded. The two men blocking the stairs were joined by others behind us—massive figures that could only be warriors from the Alpine Snow Pack. My training with Sara flashed through my mind, and I tried to recall the moves she'd drilled into me. I knew I needed to fight, to resist, but my limbs felt sluggish, my thoughts fuzzy.

The world started to blur.

"Gigi . . ." Terri's voice was faint and distant, and then she collapsed against me.

I fell to the floor with a thud, Terri's weight pinning me down. My vision blurred as the room tilted and spun. The air felt heavy, suffocating, and my body refused to obey me.

Four dark silhouettes loomed, their eyes gleaming with something too cold, too calculating.

And as my vision tunneled to black, one final thought burned in my mind: *Tyce, please find me.*

Chapter 40

Nikolai

"I don't understand! Where the *fuck* is she?" Tyce's booming voice echoed down the hallway as I stepped through the front door on Sunday evening, sweat still cooling on my skin after hours spent pushing my body to exhaustion. I walked farther into the packhouse, and his voice grew louder. "We need to get that plane out tonight. I need to go to Anchorage immediately."

I followed the sound of his shouting, rounding the corner to the common area to find a red-faced Tyce with bulging eyes, fists clenching and unclenching at his sides.

Across from him, Beta Liam stood firm, arms crossed, with a calm but unreadable expression.

"Tyce, it's not possible," Liam said with a measured tone, a stark contrast to the raging alpha.

Tyce's chest heaved. His nostrils flared. "I don't care if we crash the fucking plane," he snarled. "I have to get to her. Do you understand? She's out there, and we're just standing here, doing nothing!"

Liam's jaw tightened, but his voice remained steady. "The conditions outside are horrendous. If we try to fly now, we won't make it. What good would that be?"

Tyce's teeth clenched so hard I thought they might crack. His hands curled into fists.

After a brief pause, Liam added, carefully, "Besides, it's possible she just lost her cell phone."

"But Terri's not answering either! I've been calling both of them all fucking day!" Tyce's frustration was teetering on the edge of fury. "What are the chances *both* of them lost their phones?"

"I mean, yeah, it's unlikely," Liam admitted, "but not impossible."

A bolt of panic shot through me. Terri? Missing? My breath caught in my throat. Before I could think it through, I blurted, "Terri is not answering your calls?"

Both men turned toward me. Tyce's glare was immediate and cutting, and I realized my mistake too late. Why had I asked about *his sister* specifically? It was reckless, and the suspicion in Tyce's gaze made that abundantly clear. I could practically hear the wheels turning in his mind, analyzing, assessing, trying to unravel the real reason I cared so much.

But the worry clawing at me outweighed my misstep. "When was last time you heard from them?" I asked, carefully including Gigi in the question.

Tyce didn't respond right away. His eyes bore into mine with a mixture of distrust and irritation. He was clearly scrutinizing me and deciding whether to tell me anything at all.

I pressed on, unwavering, as if this was just another pack matter to me. As if my pulse wasn't hammering in my ears. As if the very idea of Terri in danger wasn't making my wolf thrash under my skin, demanding I do something. Keeping my voice measured, I said, "If something is wrong, I want to help. You have done much for my pack. I cannot stand by if your luna or your sister are in trouble. Consider me your closest ally."

Something in my words must have cut through his suspicion. The rigid lines of his posture eased, just barely. Slowly, his jaw loosened and some of the sharpness in his expression dulled. A flicker of trust. Just enough.

"Gigi texted me on Friday night," he began in a strained voice. "She said they were heading to a party. I told her to text me when they got home, but she never did. At first, I figured she got drunk and forgot. But when I didn't hear from her *at all* yesterday, I knew something was wrong. I've been calling both her and Terri nonstop for the past two days, and nothing. No replies, no answers. And now"—he shot a glare at Liam—"flying conditions are shit, so I can't even get to her. I don't want to tell my dad yet. If it turns out they just lost their phones at a party, he'll blow it out of proportion. But the longer this goes on . . ." His voice trailed off.

"Why don't we take this to your office?" Liam suggested. "Right now, you're practically inviting the entire packhouse to get involved."

Tyce hesitated, then nodded and followed Liam down the hall. I trailed behind, the knot in my stomach tightening with every step.

Inside the office, the air felt thick, suffocating. The tension pressed from all sides of the room as we silently took our seats around Tyce's desk.

Tyce sank into his chair as if the weight of the world had collapsed onto his shoulders. His head fell into his hands, and his knuckles dug into his temples like he could physically hold himself together. His usually dominant presence had been dulled.

"Tyce," I said, attempting to keep my voice steady, "I give my word, and my beta Sasha's, that we will help track them. Whatever it takes, we will find them."

His only response was a slight nod. He remained slouched, with his hands shielding his distraught face.

The three of us sat in silence, the gravity of the situation hanging heavy around us. My own thoughts spiraled, fixating on Terri. Was she okay? What could have happened to her? College had seemed safe enough, but then I remembered the wolves who had tracked us down—the ones from near her school. A chill ran down my spine as a terrible possibility took root. *What if . . .* Would they have assumed the two of us were involved, to the point I'd risk my pack to save her?

The idea seemed absurd. Those wolves couldn't have communicated anything. We'd killed them. And she was so far from me now. There was no trail, no connection that should link us. *But still . . .*

"Can you handle that, Beta?" Tyce asked suddenly, his voice cutting through the silence. He lifted his head from his hands, revealing an expression that was a mix of exhaustion and frustration.

Liam didn't hesitate. "On it," he said, already rising from his seat. He walked briskly to the door, leaving without another word.

I glanced at Tyce and furrowed my brows in confusion.

"We just got a mindlink," he explained, shaking his head. "Some stupid playground fight with some of the warriors. Nothing important."

I nodded, acknowledging his explanation.

Tyce leaned back in his chair, dragging his hands back and forth through his dark hair. The movement left pieces of it sticking up in all different directions.

"I just wish . . ." He trailed off, exhaling audibly. "I just wish I'd marked her." His voice cracked. "I wanted to. But she was so damn adamant about waiting until marriage. She didn't want to look bad in front of our parents." He let out a bitter laugh, shaking his head. "That shit's so outdated. It's not like they don't already *know* what we're up to."

His shoulders sagged as he let out a heavy sigh. The weight of his regret was palpable. "If she were marked," he rasped in a raw voice, "I'd at least know where she is. I could feel her. I'd know she was safe. But . . ." His voice faltered, splintering into something dark and helpless.

Crack! With a strangled roar, he slammed his fists against the desk. The violent sound shot through the room.

I flinched. Not at the outburst, but at the raw emotions and vulnerability it exposed. I knew exactly how he felt. Because I felt it too.

I wanted to tell him I understood because Terri's disappearance was clawing at my insides too. But I stayed silent, biting back the words. I couldn't let Tyce know how close I'd gotten to his sister. That conversation wouldn't end well.

"What if she's hurt? What if she's scared? I should be able to feel her. I should be able to—" Tyce didn't complete the sentence.

A thought struck me, so intensely it forced me upright.

I should tell him.

I *had* to tell him.

But then . . . I sank back into my chair.

Terri had trusted me with her secret, sworn me to silence. I knew how important it was to her that no one, especially not her family, ever found out. But now . . .

I tried to weigh my options. On one end, there was her potential kidnapping and the possibility that revealing her secret might help us find her faster. On the other end, was her trust, her confidence, and the promise I'd made.

If I told him, I risked betraying her in the worst way possible.

If I stayed silent, I possibly risked her safety.

It felt like an impossible decision. Both sides of the scale were equally important to me.

And it was possible that time wasn't on our side. If someone had taken her, who knows what they might do to her. Tyce was teetering on the edge of a breakdown, and I couldn't deny that I was too. I was just better at hiding it. I didn't have the luxury of openly mourning Terri's absence, not without raising questions. Tyce, on the other hand, was allowed to openly grieve his mate.

And what was Terri to me? In an ideal world, I would have made her my mate. But I'd pushed her away instead, convinced that her future would be better without me in it. I wanted her to live her life, to find someone who could be the kind of partner she deserved.

What was I to her now?

Time ticked by. The air between us was thick with hopelessness. Tyce sat hunched over his phone, endlessly texting and calling. But there was no answer.

Finally, I knew I had to end it. Sitting here in mutual misery wasn't solving anything. We were both exhausted and not getting anywhere.

I stood, crossing the room to him. His hands trembled as they gripped his phone. His knuckles were white with tension. Gently, I placed a hand on his shoulder. "Tyce," I began softly, "I know this sucks. But better we stop for tonight. In morning, we will meet again. If you do not hear from them by then, I will bring Sasha to help."

His body tensed under my hand. His fists clenched and unclenched as if trying to wrangle his emotions into submission. With a loud exhale, he let go of his phone. I could sense the battle raging inside him.

"Maybe the flight conditions will improve by morning," I offered. "If not, we will figure out something else. But tonight, there's nothing more we can do."

Tyce didn't respond. His jaw was tight, and his gaze remained fixed on his phone, as though staring hard enough might force a response. I knew he wouldn't stop trying. I could already picture the hundreds of missed calls and messages that would greet Gigi and Terri when they regained access to their phones.

Realizing there was nothing else I could do without breaking Terri's trust, I removed my hand from his shoulder and stepped back. "Good night, Tyce," I murmured, though I doubted he even registered my words. His eyes were still locked onto his phone, his fingers twitching with the urge to text again, to call again, to demand answers from silent phones.

I left the office and closed the door behind me. Returning to my room, I prepared myself for what I knew would be a long, sleepless night. Even as I dropped onto the bed, the tension in my body refused to ease.

The room was too quiet. Every creak of the floorboards made my ears twitch, every gust of wind against the windows sent a fresh jolt of unease through my gut. I flipped onto my back, staring at the ceiling, willing my mind to shut off. But every time I closed my eyes, I saw her.

She was gone. And I had no way to reach her. No way to know if she was okay. Helplessness burned through me.

I made my decision. If I greeted Tyce in the morning to find that he still hadn't heard from the women, I would tell him.

Chapter 41

Nikolai

As feared, by the next morning, Tyce still hadn't heard from Gigi or Terri. Thick and suffocating dread was settling in. It was looking less and less to be a case of a couple of lost cell phones.

While everyone else was at the morning temple service, Sasha and I met Tyce in his office, where he was seated in the same spot I'd left him.

Tyce looked exactly how I felt, like hell. His eyes were bloodshot, shadowed by dark circles. His hair was even more disheveled than it had been the prior day. Overgrown stubble dusted his jawline. He was a ghost of his former self—an alpha taken down by his biggest weakness.

He arrived in the same clothes he'd been wearing, now wrinkled from his clearly sleepless night. The muffled sound of a generic voicemail box rang through the air.

He let out a heavy breath and rubbed his temples before running a hand through his hair. "Flight conditions are still a no-go," Tyce muttered in a voice that was rough with exhaustion. "This weather sucks. Seriously, *fuck my life*!"

His fist slammed against the desk. Sasha and I both jolted and looked at each other in response. He exhaled shakily and gestured toward the chairs. "Take a seat. Do you want coffee or something? Looks like we're not going anywhere."

Sasha glanced at me before pulling out a chair and sitting down silently.

I followed, perching on the edge of the chair I'd claimed the previous day. My mind raced as I tried to find the right way to say what needed to be said. I took a deep breath, steeling myself. "I know Gigi is not marked—"

"Don't even *fucking* remind me!" Tyce snapped.

I hesitated after his outburst. He was hell-bent on setting the whole place on fire. And as much as I hated to add fuel to it, what I had to say couldn't wait.

There was no good way to do this. I had to just rip the Band-aid off.

"Terri, on other hand—"

"Terri, what?" Tyce's tone sharpened and his bloodshot eyes narrowed on me.

"Terri is marked," I said, my voice steady despite the tension in the room.

Tyce blinked. Once. Twice. As if his brain had momentarily short-circuited, refusing to process what I had just said.

And then, he snapped.

"TERRI'S WHAT?" The walls practically shook with his voice.

He shot to his feet, and his rolling chair crashed against the wall behind him.

"Who the fuck marked my sister?" His chest heaved as he advanced on me with fists clenched so tightly his knuckles had turned white. "Who the *fuck* marked her? *Did you mark her?!*"

"What? No!" I said quickly, holding my hands up in protest. "I did not mark her."

"Then who?" His voice dropped to a low, dangerous growl.

Sasha shifted beside me and gave me a cautious look, but he didn't speak.

I took a deep breath, knowing the explanation I was about to give would not help the situation at all. "Terri had a boyfriend during summer," I began.

Tyce's entire face changed. His lips pressed into a tight line. I could see the moment the realization set in. He had no idea. She'd hidden it well.

"The relationship . . . it was not good," I continued carefully. "He was not good to her. She tried to end it, before she went back to school. But . . . he did not take this well."

"So he marked her?" Tyce's eyes burned with murderous rage. He clenched his fists as if readying himself to drive them into someone's skull. His chest swelled as if he were holding together an explosion that was about to go off.

When he spoke again, his voice was low and dangerous with barely suppressed violence. "Who *the fuck* marked my sister?"

I sighed, my own frustration bubbling beneath the surface. "I don't know. She would not tell me."

Tyce's eyes burned into mine. "Why the *fuck* did she tell *you* when she never even told *me*?"

"Tyce," I said, forcing my voice to stay calm, "I promise you, I feel nothing but respect for your sister. Complete res—"

"Respect?" he cut me off. "*Respect?* Have you been fucking my sister under my roof? While my pack has been providing yours with *charity*?"

"It was not like that—"

"Then what the fuck was it like?" He stepped closer, looming over me with rage radiating off him.

I stood to meet his eyes, refusing to let him intimidate me. "Tyce, please," I said, my voice steady, though edged with frustration. "I care for your sister, *very much*. That is why I tell you this. I worry for her same as you."

If only I could make him see how much I adored Terri. How much she meant to me. How much I admired, no, *revered* her. That I wasn't just some creep that took advantage of someone in close proximity. How hard I'd fought my growing desire for her. But how could I make him see that?

If only he could feel how desperate I was to know she was okay, same as him.

His jaw tightened. "I should—"

"*Tyce*!" I shouted, cutting him off this time. "I *know* you are upset. But now is not time for this. We must focus on saving them."

The tension hung heavy between us. Finally, Tyce seemed to register the situation. He let out a breath and sank back into his chair, gripping his phone as if willing it to give him answers. His breaths were labored, and when he finally set the device down, his shoulders sagged, defeated.

After a moment, he spoke. His voice was quieter now, but no less desperate. "Who marked her, Nikolai?"

"I tell you truth. I do not know," I insisted. "Like I said, she never told me. She did not trust me not to kill him. And she was right. Because believe me, I *want* to kill him. Whoever did that . . . he deserves to die."

Tyce's hands clenched into fists again. "I really want to fucking kill him," he growled. "How *dare* someone mark my sister? *My* sister! An alpha's sister! This motherfucker has *balls*! Balls I'd like to chop off and feed him."

I sighed heavily, leaning back in my chair. "I understand. But right now, we need him. Whoever he is, he may be our best chance to find Terri . . . and Gigi. We need him alive. We need him to cooperate."

"How do we find out who he is?"

"You are alpha," I suggested. "You could ask your pack. Someone must know who she dated. And if they don't, you will find him anyway."

For a moment, Tyce seemed ready to act on the suggestion. His body tensed, and his eyes narrowed as though he was considering who he might interrogate first. But then, his shoulders slumped in defeat, and he shook his head. "I can't do that," he muttered. "I can't do Terri dirty

like that. She obviously didn't want anyone to know. If people found out
. . . it would ruin her reputation."

The room fell into silence again, each of us lost in our thoughts.

Sasha broke it by clearing his throat. "If I may," he began, "you cannot
question whole pack. But Terri must have told someone. Someone she
trusts."

Tyce stilled. His head snapped up, his eyes alight with sudden clarity.
"Sophia!"

Chapter 42

Tyson

I finally understood what it meant to straddle the edge of sanity and madness.

I hadn't slept in days. The world around me felt surreal, like I was walking through a dream—or a nightmare. Every time I bumped into a wall or grazed a piece of furniture, I'd catch myself wondering why I hadn't just passed through it. I was a ghost, a shadow of myself.

Losing Gigi was like losing my purpose. Without her, what was the point of any of this? I scrolled through our old messages, rereading the last text she sent me.

Gigi: Love you, send you some snaps later

As if the words might change. As if they could tell me where she was now.

But the screen remained the same. No new messages. Just a string of my frantic ones.

They said the definition of insanity is doing the same thing over and over again and expecting a different result. Well, here I was, proving it. I must have called and texted both Gigi and Terri a thousand times. At this point, my fingers were moving on autopilot. The result was always the same: No response. Straight to voicemail. Silence.

They were gone. Both of them. Just . . . vanished.

I was losing my fucking mind.

I clenched the steering wheel as Nikolai and Sasha climbed into my G Wagen. The leather creaked under the pressure of my grip. I needed control over something, anything, even if it was just this damn car. We were heading to Terri's best friend Sophia's house, which was a fair distance from the packhouse. Thankfully, I knew the route well enough that it didn't require much focus because, let's be honest, I had no business being behind the wheel. I might as well have been drunk or high for how out of it I was.

The drive blurred past, mile after mile, without me registering a damn thing. My foot was heavy on the gas, but I hardly cared. The only thing that snapped me back to reality were the sudden, brutal gusts of wind that slammed into the car, rattling it off-kilter.

When we finally pulled up to Sophia's modest-size family home, the windstorm greeted us with full force. The same high winds that had canceled our flight down south now howled through the open landscape, lifting loose snow and whipping it into chaotic white spirals.

We fought against the brutal gusts as we climbed the driveway and stairs to the front door. My body ached, not just from the cold but from the weight of everything. The sleepless nights, the helplessness clawing at my chest, the waiting. I had no patience left. I barely had enough focus to string together a list of questions.

I rang the doorbell and crossed my arms and ground my molars together to keep from snapping.

The door creaked open, and an older woman with graying curls peeked out, her eyes widening in surprise. "Alpha Tyce, is . . . everything all right?" she asked. It wasn't every day the alpha showed up unannounced at someone's doorstep.

"We need to speak with Sophia," I said in a clipped voice.

She hesitated, her brow furrowing. "Oh, I'm sorry, Alpha. Sophia isn't home right now. You just missed her. She always goes for an extra-long run on Monday mornings after temple."

I bit back a growl. My jaw tightened. Of course, she wasn't home. I was taking all Ls these days.

"It's very important," I said, trying to keep my tone polite. But what could her mother do? If Sophia was in her wolf form, she wouldn't have her phone.

The woman frowned, clearly picking up on my irritation. "Is it something I could help with? Or perhaps my mate?"

"No," I replied curtly. "Only Sophia can help."

She sighed. "I see. Well, I'm sorry. There's not much I can do. She's likely well out of mindlink range by now. But she usually gets back around lunchtime. If you want, I can let her know you were looking for her the moment she returns."

I let out a heavy breath. "You're sure there's no way to reach her?" I asked, my voice strained as I barely held back my frustration.

Her mother frowned. "Alpha, I—"

My vision swam with red. My wolf snarled inside me. I forced myself to stay still. This wasn't her fault. But *fuck*.

"Just . . . let her know we came by," I ground out.

We exchanged brief goodbyes, and I turned back to the car with Nikolai and Sasha trailing behind me. Once inside, I tried a mindlink to Sophia, just in case, but it was futile. Just as her mother said, she was out of range.

Slamming my hands on the steering wheel, I groaned in frustration.

"She will be back soon," Nikolai said.

I glanced at him, and my blood boiled. Nikolai, who had fucked my sister. Nikolai, who sat there like nothing was wrong, as if he hadn't crossed a line he never should have.

Terri had always been a kind soul, so sweet and genuine with everyone she met. But men mistook her friendliness for flirting. Even when she was just minding her own business, simply existing, they would leer at her. They had since she was a preteen.

I'd spent years protecting her from assholes like that, slapping smug grins off their faces and making sure they kept their distance. She deserved better than their pathetic, predatory attention. And now . . . *Nikolai*?

My fists tightened on the wheel, and for a moment, I envisioned throwing him out of the car and beating the shit out of him right there in Sophia's family's driveway. But I couldn't. Not yet at least.

As much as I hated to admit it, I needed him right now. For whatever reason, Terri had confided in him. He apparently knew more about her situation than I did. And, to his credit, he'd come up with the best plan we had so far. So, for now, I swallowed my anger.

I sent out mindlinks to the senior warriors on duty, instructing them to keep an eye out for Sophia's return and to alert me the moment she crossed the border. Then I let out a long, frustrated groan and dropped my forehead to the steering wheel.

The weight of it all pressed down on me—the sleepless nights, the damn flight conditions that refused to clear, the constant worry. I just wanted to hold Gigi again, to feel her safe in my arms, to know she was *okay*.

We returned to the packhouse, made our way toward my office, but I barely registered my feet moving.

"I promised Boris I spar with him in wolf form today," Sasha said, distracting me from my melancholy. "You know he's been working on that roll. You need me now?"

"It's okay. You can go," Nikolai grunted.

Sasha didn't hesitate, disappearing down the hall, leaving me alone with Nikolai.

"Do you want something to drink? Eat?" Nikolai asked and, after a beat, added, "I can go to the kitchen."

I let out a bitter laugh. "I'd love a fucking bottle of vodka right about now. But we need to focus."

"Tea then," he said and walked away.

Tea. At a time like this.

I returned to my office and sank into my chair, feeling like deadweight. Beta Liam had agreed to take over my alpha duties for the day and promised to make up some believable excuses for my dad to keep him from sniffing around. It wasn't like my father wasn't already used to me being a disappointment. He'd probably just assume I was descending back into my old ways.

The truth was, my dad *could* help, and I had considered telling him everything. But now that I knew about Terri's marking, I *couldn't*. He'd lose his fucking mind. Plus, I knew he was the absolute last person Terri would ever want to find out. I'm pretty sure she'd rather die. We'd go rescue her, and she'd bring herself right back to whoever had taken her.

Nikolai returned and set a cup of tea in front of me before taking his own seat, sipping his drink like we weren't in a crisis.

I ignored the tea. Instead, I pulled out my phone and called Gigi *again*.

Straight to voicemail. *Again.*

I let out a breath. "Now what?" I muttered, frustration seething through my veins.

Nikolai leaned back in his chair, setting his cup down. "We wait."

I stared at my phone. My fingers itched to redial Gigi's number. I tapped the Call button.

Voicemail.

Again.

I gritted my teeth, my wolf howling inside me.

Wait? Fuck waiting.

Chapter 43

Ginger

As I woke, I fought against a dull, aching exhaustion pressing down on me. My eyelids felt impossibly heavy. My mouth was dry, my head pounding. Every muscle in my body throbbed, sore as if I'd run a marathon the day before.

This has to be the worst hangover of my life.

Slowly, the fog in my mind began to clear. I inhaled the scent of crisp air and wet earth. Was I outdoors? I groaned, trying to roll over. A sharp *clink* echoed through the silence.

My eyes snapped open.

Coldness nipped at my skin—no, at my *fur*. My stomach dropped as my sluggish brain scrambled to make sense of it.

The room—*is it even a room?*—was cloaked in darkness, the only illumination coming from the faint glow of my red night vision. The outlines of my surroundings took shape. Cold, empty space, stone walls, and metal bars blocking the only exit. The scent of damp earth and frost hung heavy in the air.

I tried to move, but the harsh clink of metal stopped me short. I looked down. My breath hitched.

My paws—*paws*—were shackled in thick metal cuffs, which were attached to chains that were bound to the wall behind me.

I was trapped.

Panic surged through me. I yanked at the restraints, but they held firm, cold and unyielding against my skin. My mind scrambled to piece together how I'd gotten here.

The party. Terri. *Grace.*

Alpine Snow Pack.

Fuck.

A crushing sense of panic crashed over me. I'd thought I was so clever, trying to outsmart them, playing the role of an unsuspecting partygoer and gathering intel. But while I'd been playing checkers, they'd been playing chess.

I squeezed my eyes shut, fighting the surge of nausea that rolled through me.

Tyce.

Did he know I was missing yet? Was he searching for me? Did he blame himself? The thought of him finding out, the thought of his face when he realized I was gone, *hurt* more than the chains biting into my legs.

I'm supposed to be a luna. A leader. A warrior.

And yet, here I was. Shackled. Helpless. A pawn.

I hung my head, shame overtaking me. I had failed.

A quiet rustling came from beside me, followed by a voice slipping into my mind.

"Gigi, are you awake?"

Terri's mindlink was faint, as if she were fighting the same sluggishness I was. I turned my head and caught the familiar golden glow of her night vision maybe a foot or two from me.

"Where are we?" I asked, my voice raw even through the mindlink.

My stomach twisted and hunger gnawed at me. I hadn't eaten since . . . I didn't even know how long it had been.

"I don't know for sure," Terri replied in a tone laced with quiet dread. *"But if I had to guess, this is Alpine Snow Pack territory. They must have brought us here after we passed out."*

I swallowed. My eyes flicked to the bars confining us. *"Are we . . . outside?"*

"Yeah," Terri confirmed. *"This is a cave. It's an old torture tactic. They're using the cold to force us to stay in our wolf forms."*

A chill crept up my spine. *"Why?"*

She hesitated before answering. *"They're playing the long game."*

My stomach tensed.

"Instead of torturing us with weapons, they're making us slip into our animal brain, hoping we'll lose our grip on rational thought. When that happens . . ." She trailed off in a voice strained with hopelessness.

"They think it'll make it easier to manipulate us," I finished for her, my pulse pounding in my ears.

"Yeah," she said softly. And then, after a pause, she added, *"But that doesn't mean they won't still use weapons."*

A heavy silence settled between us.

My heart pounded as the reality of our situation sank in.

We were prisoners. Trapped.

"Just whatever you do, don't—"

Terri's words were too late as a loud roar tore from my throat. A sharp, searing pain shot through my legs. I was left whimpering from my attempt to shift back to human, only for the unyielding metal to bite into my bones.

I glanced at Terri to see her cringing expression. *"That's why they put the shackles on us. Sorry I didn't tell you sooner."*

Not only were we trapped, but we were stuck in one spot. Were we supposed to just *go to the bathroom* where we slept? This was not only terrifying but also deeply humiliating.

And it was all my fault. *How could I have been so stupid?*

"Terri, I fucked up," I choked out through the mindlink. Guilt clawed at my chest. *"I should have known better."*

Terri let out a regretful sigh. "I *should have known better*," she echoed. *"I've been trained for this. I knew to stay away from Alpine Snow Pack. They attacked Kolya and me. I was just so drunk, so in my head, I wasn't paying attention. I should've been on alert.* You *couldn't have known."*

I froze. *"Wait . . . they attacked you?"*

"Yeah . . . I didn't say anything because . . . because Kolya was hiding something, and he didn't want anyone to know. I didn't want to break his trust."

My mind raced. *"Wait . . . you're the person they attacked?"*

"What?"

My breath hitched as I pieced it together. *"Sara caught someone snooping around and tortured information out of him. He said they'd* almost *caught someone. Trav thought it might have been a rogue!"*

Terri let out another long, exhausted sigh. *"I should've told Tyce . . . I thought I was doing the right thing, but now I've only made everything worse."*

I shook my head. *"It's not just you. I should've been less trusting. I actually thought this* rando, *Grace, wanted to be my friend. And now look where I got us."*

Terri didn't answer right away, and I knew we were both thinking the same thing. No matter how we tried to justify it, we had made mistakes. And now we were paying the price.

The sound of distant footsteps sent a spike of dread through me. Was someone coming?

I tensed. A hushed voice murmured something I couldn't quite make out. Another voice snorted.

"Think this one'll last longer than the last one?"

"Doubt it. You saw what happened to the last guy."

My stomach turned. I exchanged a look with Terri, who was just as tense as I was.

What happened to the last prisoner?

But the voices faded, and we were soon back to silence.

After some time, Terri's voice entered my mind again. "*We can't kick ourselves. That's for later. For now, we need to focus on surviving.*"

I flexed my muscles, preparing. But . . . "*For how long?*"

Terri shook her head sadly. "*It's hard to say. It can take months to really break someone down. And who knows how long it'll be before anyone in our pack figures out where we are. Or if they'll be able to find us.*"

"*What do we do?*"

"*We need to keep as much of our humanity as we can. We need to mindlink each other, talk, think about complex subjects. Anything that forces us to think like people and not just wolves. It's so easy to retreat into our simpler brain in this form, and we have to proactively fight against it.*"

I straightened, determination replacing my despair. "*Coronal, sagittal, axial, median. Superior, inferior, medial, lateral, anterior, posterior, proximal, distal.*"

Terri's ears perked, and she tilted her head slightly. "*What?*"

"*Sorry, I was thinking about the new vocab I learned in one of my classes. I figured that would do the trick.*"

She huffed out an amused sigh. "*Well, I guess you may as well teach me. It's not like we're going anywhere.*" She lay down and turned toward me, giving me her full attention.

"*All right, we can start with the planes of the body . . .*" And just like that, I launched into an impromptu anatomy lesson, one I was sure Terri had never signed up for.

Chapter 44

Nikolai

The silence stretched between us, broken only by the rhythmic tapping of Tyce's fingers against the wooden desk and the occasional muffled sound of a voicemail message cutting in and out.

Every few minutes, he tried again. Calling. Mindlinking. His expression flickered between frustration and outright fury every time the connection failed.

Each passing minute felt like an hour.

Tyce was relentless. Again and again, he dialed, pressing on the chosen contact of the moment, only to be met with the same voicemail recording. Calling and mindlinking like a maniac.

I couldn't deny I would have done the same. I just didn't have the same means to attempt contact. So, I determined my job, albeit impossible, was to attempt to keep him calm.

Honestly, I wasn't doing any better. My mind screamed for action, but all I could do was sit there, forcing myself to remain still. I kept blocking out the worst-case scenarios. If I let myself think about Terri in the hands of whoever had taken her, I wasn't sure I'd be able to keep my composure.

So I made myself move. I got up, refilled my tea. Tyce's remained untouched. I rummaged through the kitchen for snacks, but they sat abandoned on his desk. Neither of us could stomach food. The thought alone made bile rise to my throat.

Another call. Straight to voicemail. Another attempt at mindlinking. The same flicker of his eyes to the ceiling, searching for a connection that wouldn't happen.

I lost count of how many times he called. How many times I watched his expression crumble, only to harden again as he tried once more. Again and again.

Then, as the clock ticked past two, something inside him snapped.

His fist slammed against the desk with a forceful thud.

"This is *bullshit*." His voice was raw with exhaustion. "She should be back by now."

And that was when I felt it too. That sick, gnawing certainty in my gut that something was wrong.

"Let's go," I said, standing.

He immediately knew where, rising to his feet to follow.

When we opened the garage, we were greeted by practically whiteout conditions. What had started as a severely windy day had turned into a full-blown blizzard.

Before I could even fully shut my door, he threw the car into reverse, tearing out of the garage and driveway in a blur of screeching tires.

The car lurched forward as he floored the gas, paying no attention to speed limits or the erratic swerving of his own movements. He white-knuckled the steering wheel so hard, I thought he might tear it clean off the dashboard.

The roads were nearly invisible beneath the barrage of snowflakes. Tire tracks were erased as quickly as they were made. The wind pushed against the car like a physical force, the vehicle shuddering. The headlights did little against the swirling snow. Beams caught on endless flurries, making it feel like we were moving through an abyss.

Each sharp turn he made was barely controlled. The tires skidded on the slick road before regaining just enough grip to keep us from spinning out.

When one unfortunate car dared slow him down, he slammed his hand on the horn and held it, the blaring sound slicing through the air like gunfire.

"*Move.*" The word was low, guttural, laced with barely restrained rage.

When the car finally veered aside, he didn't so much as flinch before pressing harder on the gas, tearing down the road like a maniac.

Tyce didn't even bother to park properly. The car skidded to a stop at an awkward angle in the driveway, tires kicking up a spray of loose snow. He was already out before the engine fully cut off. He slammed the door shut behind him and bolted up the front steps.

Before we could even knock, the door flew open.

Sophia's mother appeared, pale faced, with wide eyes frantically darting between us. She gripped the doorframe as if it were the only thing keeping her upright. "Alpha!"

Tyce didn't hesitate. He was already stepping forward, his presence overwhelming the threshold. "Where's Sophia?"

"She never came home," she choked out while her hands trembled. "She's never been gone this long. Never! And with the weather like this . . ." Her voice cracked, and she shook her head. "She would have come home."

Tyce's jaw tightened. "You haven't heard from her at all?"

Sophia's father emerged, his face lined with worry and his mouth pressed into a grim, thin line. "We tried mindlinking her. We tried calling. Nothing. Her cell phone is here, in her bedroom where she left it. And she's too far out of range for mindlinking."

"Alpha, where is my daughter?" Sophia's mom's voice wavered, just this side of hysteria. "Why were you looking for her?"

"Leslie." The man reached out and gently brushed his mate's arm. He was clearly trying to comfort her. But it was useless.

She shook him off. "Please, Alpha. Where is my daughter?"

For a moment, Tyce looked lost. Unsure how to respond.

Her gaze flickered desperately between Tyce and me, searching for answers neither of us had.

I stepped in. "Sorry, ma'am. We do not know. We are hoping you would."

Tears streamed down her face, and she let out a sob. "Something's wrong, isn't it?"

"We don't know," I said, even though it was becoming more and more clear that something was.

"Please," she pleaded, the word cracking. "Why were you looking for her?"

Tyce finally snapped back. He took a step forward and, in a gentle but firm tone, replied, "I'm sorry. It's confidential. But I'm putting out a search immediately."

At his words, Leslie collapsed to her knees. Her mate reached for her, tried to pull her up, but she pushed him away, sobbing harder. "Please get my daughter home safe, Alpha. Please!"

Tyce's hands trembled at his sides. His shoulders rose and fell unevenly, like he was fighting to keep himself together. For a moment again, he looked young and lost, like a small boy. But he quickly shook his head and straightened his shoulders.

"I'll do my best. I promise." Tyce's voice was raw, quieter than before. His fingers flexed at his sides before he turned away, blinking hard. Finally, he turned back and said, "Give me something with her scent on it. Alpha Nikolai will help too."

Sophia's father rushed back into the house, returning seconds later with a winter hat. He handed it to Tyce, who passed it straight to me.

I took a deep breath, inhaling Sophia's scent, locking it in my memory before handing the hat back.

I was sure Tyce felt the same as I did. Someone had reached Sophia before we could. And now, standing in the aftermath of our delay, it was impossible to ignore the sickening certainty that we had waited too long.

We turned back toward the car and battled the snow that was quickly piling up.

Tyce's head tilted upward, and his eyes glazed over as he connected to his warriors through mindlink, his breaths coming out in wisps of white vapor. Heavy flakes came down around us, but he stood rigid, unmoving. He was doing exactly what he'd promised Sophia's mother he would. Commanding his soldiers to venture out into the terrible conditions and track Sophia down.

Moments later, he exhaled audibly, and his shoulders sagged under the weight of both defeat and guilt. Without a word, he slid back into the car and started the engine.

The windshield wipers worked furiously, but the snow came too fast, too thick, half blinding us as we pushed forward. The heater blasted warm air, but it couldn't cut through the chill that had settled deep inside both of us.

He drove us to the edge of his pack, parking on the last bit of road that was rapidly being buried. We stepped out. "This is the area where she passed the borders this morning, according to my warriors. It's our best shot at finding her." His voice barely carried over the storm.

Without another word, he shifted into his wolf, a much larger and fluffier version of Terri's. I immediately noticed the resemblance, and an intense ache of longing knifed through my chest. Outside of the anxiety I'd been wrapped in, I missed her. My chest burned without her close presence. I'd had breakups in the past, but nothing like this. It was as if a piece of my soul had been torn from me.

I shook the thought off and followed Tyce's bear of a wolf into the wild void. The wind's howls drowned out the sound of my own breathing. My paws sank into the snow deeper than expected, the icy flakes clung to my fur. Tyce's massive wolf was a shadow against the whiteout. His powerful frame pushed through the storm with unrelenting force.

We pressed forward, noses to the ground, scanning for even the faintest trace of her scent. At first, we caught something. It wasn't much, but it was enough. Enough to spur us on, to make us fight through the drifts that threatened to swallow our limbs with each step.

The blizzard fought us. The wind slammed into us, knocking us sideways, forcing us to lower our heads just to keep moving. Every inhale was thick with frost.

Tyce growled ahead of me. We were losing against nature.

I inhaled deeply again, trying to pick the scent back up. It had been here. But the storm was swallowing everything whole—the scent, our tracks, even the very ground beneath us.

We continued to push, battling the storm. Even as it became clear the wind had likely carried off whatever bits of snow held her scent, fresh snow had buried her paw prints, and subzero temperatures had frozen any moisture particles, reducing the spread of odor.

I forced myself forward, inhaling deeply, searching, praying for *something*, anything! But the storm had devoured everything. The scent was gone, erased as if she had never been here at all. I growled low in frustration, and my ears flattened against my head.

Tyce's snarl cut through the wind like a blade. He clawed at the frozen ground, his breath coming out in heaving pants, his massive shoulders rising and falling with the weight of his despair. I knew that feeling. That sickening, penetrating feeling in your gut when you knew you were too late.

His head snapped toward me, his glowing golden eyes burned through the swirling whiteout. A question without words. *Did you catch any-thing?*

I shook my head.

Tyce let out a furious snarl. His claws dug into the packed snow beneath him as if he could tear through the layers of permafrost and find Sophia buried underneath. But there was nothing.

He lowered his head and tucked his tail slightly. I felt my own tail instinctively dip as well. The weight of our defeat pressed down on both of us. The walk back to the car felt longer. Heavier.

We found the car covered in the same blizzard we'd battled.

Tyce shifted first. His hands shook as he pulled open the trunk and extracted the clothes he'd left behind. I followed suit. Once dressed, we worked together to clean the car off, before climbing back in.

For a long moment, he just sat there, gripping the steering wheel, staring at nothing.

Finally, his grip tightened, and in a voice hoarse with frustration and something dangerously close to helplessness, he muttered, "She's gone."

Then, without another word, he revved the engine back to life.

Chapter 45

Nikolai

The warriors continued to battle the terrible conditions well after Tyce and I had given up, working late into the night. But, in the end, they had no better luck than we had. Any scent of a werewolf that may have existed at some point was wiped away by the storm. Sophia was gone.

"You look like shit," Tyce remarked the moment I stepped into his office the next morning.

I dropped into the chair across from him with a heavy sigh. "I haven't slept for two nights."

Tyce lifted his head, finally making eye contact. His sharp gaze flickered over me. After a long pause, he leaned back and folded his arms across his chest. "You really do care about her, don't you?"

I nodded.

Silence settled between us as we both sank into our chairs. Tyce lifted his coffee mug, taking a slow sip. I drank mine too—more out of habit than necessity. The caffeine had long stopped working, but at least it gave my hands something to do.

Tyce finally broke the silence. "Liam said flight conditions are still shit. But they could finally clear up by tomorrow morning, if we're lucky."

"And what?" I raised a brow at him. "We go to Anchorage with no plan?"

"Obviously we need to track down the motherfucker that marked my sister and bring him with us." His voice was laced with rage. "But . . ."

I finished the thought for him. "But you do not want to question your pack."

Tyce exhaled through his nose in frustration. "No. If we don't come up with another idea, I'll do it. But I know she wouldn't want that."

I nodded my understanding.

"Then we must search bedroom," I said, pushing back from my chair. "Maybe we find something—gift, letter, diary—where she confesses everything."

Tyce let out a long, helpless sigh, raking a hand through his already messy hair. "I know Terri. We have cleaners in and out of our rooms all the time. Our parents even go through our shit occasionally. She wouldn't leave behind anything obvious, especially not while she's away at college."

I met his gaze. "We must try."

He didn't argue. He stood and led the way upstairs.

We began to methodically go through her room. Tyce took one half, and I took the other.

Tyce started with the bed, lifting the mattress and box spring with ease, revealing nothing but the wooden support slats beneath. He pulled out the drawers from under the bed, rummaging through the neatly stored belongings. Notebooks, greeting cards, old letters, extra bedding, childhood toys.

Meanwhile, I scoured her desk, pulling books from the shelf, flipping through them in search of something hidden, perhaps a letter tucked neatly within the pages. I checked the inside covers for inscriptions. Nothing.

I moved on to the drawers, sorting through loose papers, notebooks, and old homework. Most were just notes, study guides, and other school assignments. I held my breath as I checked the margins for doodles, hoping maybe she'd scribbled her beau's last name next to hers, like my sisters used to when they had a crush. But there was nothing. Not even a drawing of a heart.

I turned to her dresser, pulling open drawers, sifting through piles of soft, worn-in T-shirts, sweatshirts, yoga pants. My mouth curled into a weak smile as I took in the clothes that smelled faintly of her. Then I reached the last drawer and paused.

Lingerie.

I swallowed hard. A line I shouldn't cross, but if she was hiding something, it would be in the one place no one would dig through.

My large fingers brushed the delicate lace, trailing along the sheer fabric with a reverent touch. Based on the mostly empty drawer, she'd taken most of her underwear with her to school. But what she had left behind . . . *Boginya.*

I turned slightly, glancing over my shoulder to make sure Tyce wasn't watching before closing my hand around one of the fragile pieces. The thought of her wearing it sent a sharp pang of longing and regret through me, a bitter ache that settled in my chest. What I wouldn't do to see her in it.

I held back a sob that was desperate to come out as the short period of time we'd known each other replayed in my mind. I thought about the way the soft curve of her hips molded against my hands, the way her thick, brawny thighs looked wrapped around me. And I thought of her angelic heart, the way she'd come up with different, unique ways to help my pack. I'd had the perfect woman in my grasp, and I'd let her go.

I clenched my jaw, forcing myself to exhale slowly, to shove the drawer shut before I lost it. There was no time for this.

I turned back to the search, forcing myself to continue. The laundry hamper was empty. Tyce had already moved on to the closet, pulling down boxes from the top shelf and rifling through them without hesitation.

When my side of the room seemed exhausted of possibilities, I started lifting furniture, checking underneath.

The desk turned up nothing but dust bunnies and lost pens. I moved on to the dresser, gripping the heavy wooden frame and letting out a loud grunt as I hoisted it away from the wall.

Tyce glanced over at the noise but, seeing nothing of interest, went back to his own search.

That was when I saw it.

A dark lump, covered in gray fuzz and months' worth of dust.

I pulled it from the filth, shaking off the debris. What emerged was a simple black thong, crumpled beneath the dresser.

A strange, uneasy feeling curled in my gut.

I lifted it to my nose without thinking, and immediately, her scent consumed me.

Terri.

Soft. Feminine. Warm. A delicate, intoxicating fragrance that clung to the fabric, undisturbed, unwashed, untouched for who knew how long. The moment it hit me, something in my chest tightened, something raw and primal.

I should have dropped it.

But I didn't.

Instead, I inhaled deeper, greedy for more, letting the scent wrap around me like a drug. A ghost of her lingered here. And as wrong and as depraved as it was to be inhaling the soiled cotton like a starved animal, I couldn't bring myself to stop.

But there was something else. Something that didn't belong.

My nostrils flared as I took in a second scent, my muscles tensing instinctively. Male. A man from the Jade Moon Pack. Unfamiliar. Unacceptable. I went still as white-hot rage pulsed through me.

It had to be him.

"Tyce," I called, my voice low, controlled. Too controlled.

He turned, brows furrowed at my tone. I held out the evidence.

His gaze flicked to the fabric in my grip, then snapped back to my face in horrified realization. "Is that . . . my sister's *thong*?"

"It has his scent on it."

His face twisted in disgust. "Bro! Are you sick? I'm not smelling my sister's fucking *panties*!"

"Tyce, I don't know who he is," I gritted out, barely reining in my temper. "You must smell them."

"Fucking Artemis!" His hands shot to his head, fingers digging into his scalp as if trying to physically rid himself of the thought.

"I know is not . . ." I inhaled. "Ideal." Understatement of the year. "But maybe you recognize him."

"How do you even know it's him?"

I met his eyes in a hard, unyielding stare. "Who else would leave scent on her underwear?"

Tyce let out a frustrated, agonized groan. His whole body stiffened with resistance. "I can't fucking believe I'm doing this."

With a swift, angry motion, he snatched the panties from my hand. Then he just . . . stared at them. Like they were radioactive. For a long second, he stood there, gripping them between his fingers, face contorted in sheer dread.

"Just do it," I said.

His glare snapped to mine, heated with betrayal. Then, with a quick inhale—he did it.

The reaction was instant.

He threw the fabric to the ground as if it had burned him and doubled over in a coughing fit. "I CAN'T BELIEVE I JUST FUCKING DID THAT!" His voice was raw, violated. "I think I'm gonna be sick!"

I barely held back an eye roll. "Well?"

Tyce braced himself against the dresser, taking deep breaths, face twisted in a mixture of fury and shame. But then, as he straightened, something shifted.

His expression hardened. Rage eclipsed every other emotion. His hands clenched into fists, and his body was rigid with barely restrained violence.

"I know who he is."

Chapter 46

Nikolai

"Joe Shmoe," Tyce spat from the driver's seat. We were back in his car for the fourth—or maybe fifth—time in two days.

"His name is Joe Shmoe?" I asked, raising a brow.

"Joe. Joe nobody. Joe should-be-fucking-ashes."

Once again, Tyce was white-knuckling the steering wheel with his foot hitting the gas far too hard. At least the weather conditions had improved, and the roads were freshly plowed. But the tension inside the car may as well have been a storm in and of itself.

The barely contained rage rolled off Tyce in thick, heavy waves. Even as someone who wasn't part of his pack, I could feel his alpha aura penetrating the air, clouding the small enclosure. He was in it to kill it at this point.

I understood. The moment I'd smelled the scent of this man—if you could even call him a man—I'd wanted to lose control too. My fingers twitched, aching to wrap them around Joe's throat.

"We need him alive," I said, just as much to myself as to Tyce.

"That motherfucker doesn't deserve it," Tyce snapped, his anger palpable.

"I do not disagree. But we need him now. Alive."

Tyce's jaw tightened as he shook his head. "The second we don't, I'm slicing his throat open and watching his blood run cold."

The image sent a visceral thrill through me. The thought of ending this faceless monster, of making him suffer the way he had made Terri suffer, stirred something dark inside me.

"No." The word tore from my throat before I could stop it.

Tyce's head snapped toward me, eyes burning. "What, are you developing some sort of empathy for this asshole now?" His voice was thick with incredulity, dripping with disdain.

"No. Trust me, I have no empathy," I replied. "He deserves torture. He deserves death. He deserves to have freedom ripped away, same way he stole Terri's. But—"

"But what?"

"It must be Terri's choice."

Tyce blinked, his fury flickering.

"She was the one marked against her will," I continued. "She must decide his sentence. Not us. If we take her choice, then we are same as him—stealing what is hers."

A muscle ticked in his jaw, and he grumbled under his breath. He didn't say I was right, but it was clear he agreed.

Joe's family's home was small and unassuming. I took in its structure and surrounding snow-covered yard, curious about the man Terri had been with before we'd met. What was it about him that had drawn her in?

Tyce and I climbed the front stairs, reining in our fury. I could hear Tyce's steady, heavy breaths beside me, each one measured, controlled, but barely. We both would have preferred to storm in with guns blazing, ready to tear Terri's ex apart limb by limb. But we needed him alive. *For now.*

Tyce took the lead, pressing the doorbell. The chime echoed inside. We listened, picking up the muffled shuffle of footsteps. Then the door swung open, revealing a middle-aged man with a graying black beard and a beer gut.

The moment his eyes landed on Tyce, he stiffened. "Alpha," he stammered, stepping back instinctively. His gaze flickered between us. His confusion was clearly laced with unease.

Tyce didn't wait for an invitation. He stepped inside immediately. His presence filled the cramped entryway. "Where's Joe?"

I stepped in right behind him, and I was immediately greeted by the thick, cloying stench of cigars. It wasn't fresh. This was the kind of smoke that had settled deep, soaked into the walls, the curtains, the bones of the house. For a brief moment, nostalgia flickered through me. My pack had its fair share of heavy smokers, and I'd walked into plenty of homes steeped in the same acrid haze.

The man swallowed hard. "H-He's in his room. Is there— Is something wrong?"

"This is between me and Joe," Tyce responded. "No more questions. Bring him. *Now!*"

Joe's father hesitated, shifting his weight between his feet. I could see the war in his eyes—loyalty to his son battling against the instinct to obey his alpha. In the end, obedience won. He turned without another word and disappeared down the hallway.

A ticking clock filled the silence of the room.

Again, I took in my surroundings. I wanted to understand. I wanted to know who Terri was before I'd met her. And this was a part of her past. She had been inside these walls before. This may have even been a safe, familiar space for her at some point.

From my angle, I was able to peek into what I assumed was their fancy living room for guests, with floral couches from a bygone era and glass displays with various trinkets. The kitchen was small and in need of updating, with a well-worn table and chairs. At the center of the table were two ashtrays, one with leftover cigars and the other with cigarette butts, each one stationed in front of its own chair.

Somewhere in the back of the house, hushed voices.

Then, footsteps.

A young man with dark, short-trimmed hair rounded the corner. He was slight, and his clothes hung too loose on his body. The moment his dark eyes landed on us, he went rigid.

For a split second, he just stood there, catching his breath as the color drained from his face. Then his gaze darted to his father, to the door, then back to us.

Tyce stepped forward.

Joe stumbled back, nearly tripping over himself.

Tyce tilted his head, watching Joe like his prey. "You look confused," he murmured. "Like you don't know why we're here."

Joe's throat bobbed. "I-I d-don't—"

"Don't lie."

Joe flinched. I caught the quick rise of his chest, the way his fingers twitched at his sides. He was already unraveling.

Tyce took another step. "*Come,*" he ordered.

Joe swallowed hard. His hesitation was brief, just a flicker, but I saw it. His eyes skittered from room to room, door to window, trying to work out if there was a way to escape. But there wasn't. No one can outmaneuver an alpha aura. Trembling, he obeyed.

The second he was within reach, Tyce grabbed the back of his shirt and yanked him forward.

I hadn't known what to expect, but I hadn't expected *this*. He stood around the same height as Terri, 175 centimeters, if I had to guess, and he looked breakable against her alpha brother.

"Wait, please," Joe's father croaked. "Alpha, please. He's my son."

Tyce paused, turned, and looked the poor man up and down. "Your *son* took something that wasn't his. From *my* family." His voice was cold and final.

"He's just a kid," he said in a raw, desperate voice. "Whatever he took, I'll make sure he returns it."

"What he took can't be returned."

Tyce didn't wait for a response. He shoved Joe through the door, out into the cold.

Joe's father lingered behind the window, watching as his son was whisked away, powerless to intervene.

"*Don't move*," Tyce commanded as he threw him in the back seat and slammed the door behind him.

The car filled with the scent of cold sweat and terror. Joe shivered in the back, but whether from the cold or the fear rolling off him, I couldn't say.

Tyce slid behind the wheel and started the engine.

Joe's voice came out in a splutter. "W-where are you taking me?"

Tyce let out a dark, humorless laugh and shifted the car into reverse.

Chapter 47

Tyson

When we reached the penitentiary, I yanked open the back door of my car. Joe flinched but didn't resist when I grabbed his arm and hauled him out. He moved stiffly, but he didn't fight. He'd be stupid to.

Nikolai followed as I dragged Joe into the concrete building. We passed rows of cells, the few prisoners inside watching silently. A guard stepped aside, his face impassive, as I pulled open the heavy metal door leading to the basement and forced Joe through.

The temperature dropped as we descended the narrow staircase. The dim, flickering lights cast jagged, erratic shadows along the damp walls. The steps creaked beneath our weight. The harsh stench of fear mixed with the odor of bleach and stale air.

Once we made it to the bottom, I shoved Joe into an old wooden chair that was darkened by stains from those who had sat there before him, most of whom had never walked back out.

"Stay," I commanded with my alpha aura.

Joe whimpered, and his body locked in place as he instinctively bared his neck in submission.

"Good," I said, circling him like a predator. "Saves me the time and effort of chaining you up."

Joe's eyes were red and moist with the tears he was holding back. "Alpha, I'm sorry," he squawked. "It was an accident. I didn't mean to . . . I just—"

"You just what?" I snapped.

He flinched, curling in on himself.

Fucking coward.

"You just what?" I demanded, my voice rising as I pushed my alpha command into the words, leaving him no choice but to answer.

Joe trembled. "I just . . . I didn't want Terri to leave me," he finally choked out in a mixture of guilt and self-pity. "She tried to dump me because she wanted to screw other guys at school. I couldn't—" His breath hitched, and his hands clenched into fists. "What she was doing was fucked-up, unethical, wrong, selfish, the list goes on. She had committed to me. I was her boyfriend."

"So you marked her against her will?" Nikolai spat, his voice dripping with contempt. "Because she did not do what you want, you decide you must control her?"

"It wasn't like that!" Joe insisted.

"Yes, *exactly* this it was!" Nikolai roared, his fury finally boiling over. His fist barreled forward, stopping centimeters short of Joe's nose.

Joe yelped, flinching so hard he nearly toppled out of the chair. His arms shot up, shielding his face as he curled in on himself. "I'm sorry!" he cried out in a voice raw with desperation. "Alpha, I'm sorry! I swear— I didn't mean . . . I didn't . . . please, Alpha."

I stared down at him, disgusted. His trembling, whimpering, *pleading* only solidified how weak he was. "You're pathetic."

He stared down at the ground without responding.

My eyes flicked to the knives laid out neatly on the nearby table. My fingers tingled with the urge to grab one, to press the cold metal to his skin, to carve my own kind of mark into his throat.

But Nikolai was right. We needed him. We'd brought him here so I could get my mate and sister back to safety.

I inhaled and exhaled several times, trying my best to reel in the rage that was bubbling under my skin. Nikolai gave me some hearty pats on the back, and I gave him a nod, appreciating the unspoken understanding between us.

I was beginning to recognize that this had gone beyond simple loyalty to my pack for our hospitality. He clearly cared about my sister and wanted to find her as much as I did.

When I finally felt like I could continue questioning Joe without snapping his neck in half, I glanced back at him, taking a step forward. "Where is Terri?"

Joe hesitated, staring down at his hands, curling and uncurling his fingers as if searching for an answer within them. Seconds passed before he finally spoke.

"I don't know," he admitted. "She's . . . far. I can feel the distance, but I usually can't tell exactly where she is unless I'm close enough."

"But you know how she feels?" Nikolai cut in.

Joe nodded hesitantly. "Yeah . . . but it's stronger when she's close. When she's farther away, I only pick up on emotions if they're really strong."

"Like if she is in pain?" Nikolai asked.

Joe nodded.

I stepped closer. "Is she in pain *now*?"

Joe's brow furrowed in concentration. Then, after a moment, he shook his head. "No."

I narrowed my eyes, studying him, searching for any sign of deception. "Are you *sure*?" I asked with my alpha aura, to make sure he was being honest.

Joe flinched as the command hit him. The moment the sting wore off, he replied, "Yes, I'm sure. I . . . I didn't feel her at all for a while. But I can tell she's out there now. And if she *is* in pain . . . it's not extreme. That's for sure."

Beside me, Nikolai let out a slow, relieved breath.

Joe's gaze lifted to mine. "Why? What's going on? Is Terri okay?"

Nikolai and I exchanged a look.

"We don't know," Nikolai answered. "We think she was kidnapped."

Joe's face drained of all color. "*What?! No!*"

Ignoring him, I turned to Nikolai and muttered, "I think we can leave him for now. He's complying." Then, turning back to Joe, I leaned in and added, my voice low and dangerous, "Which means we *won't* have to use the knives. *For now.*"

Joe visibly gulped.

"I agree." Nikolai nodded.

"Come," I commanded, waving my hand. Joe flinched from the command and instantly stood. I, again, grabbed the back of his collar and pulled him upstairs. Once on the main floor, I had one of the guards open an empty cell, and we dumped him in there to stay until we figured out flight plans.

Nikolai and I silently returned to my car. Once inside, I turned on the music, and we drove back to the packhouse without speaking.

Upon our return, we sank into the seats that had practically become our second home in my office. I mindlinked Liam, telling him to stop by when he had a moment.

He entered within minutes.

"Good news, Alpha. I checked the weather reports and flight conditions. The skies will be all clear tomorrow morning. We'll be able to head down to Anchorage. I'm making sure the runway is cleaned off and the plane is fueled as we speak."

"Beautiful," I replied, nodding in approval.

"We are back to business," Nikolai said as soon as Liam left.

For the first time in days, I allowed myself to relax—just a little. We had a plan. We were moving forward.

But something still nagged at me.

"I don't get it." I furrowed my brows. "Why take Terri and Gigi? Were they just easy targets? But why? What does someone want from my pack?"

Across from me, Nikolai shifted in his chair. His gaze flickered to the side before settling back on me.

Unease crept up my spine.

Then he cleared his throat. "Tyce," he began.

I met his gaze.

His lips pressed into a firm line before he looked away, as if debating something. Finally, he looked back at me. "There is something I must tell you."

I straightened. "What?"

He hesitated, his expression darkening. "I kept a secret," he admitted. "I did not think anyone here would find us, but . . . my pack, it has something powerful. Too powerful. It is why we went to war. And why we lost almost everyone."

Goose bumps prickled along my skin.

I leaned forward. "*What is it?*" My voice came out harder than I intended.

Nikolai exhaled, scrubbing a hand over his face. "Before I tell you, I need your word," he said carefully, "this stays only between us."

I narrowed my eyes. My first instinct was to refuse. This was *my* pack. My mate, my sister, *my* responsibility. If we were in danger, my father should know. Liam should know.

But then I caught myself.

I wanted to be an alpha in my own right, not stuck forever in my father's shadow.

After a moment, I gave him a firm nod. "It stays between us."

Nikolai studied me, then drew in a long breath. "It is stone," he said slowly. "A wish stone. Grants whoever holds it one wish. Only one. Anything they want. It has been in my family many generations. You can imagine why someone would want it. The power it gives."

The words hung between us.

I stared at him, my mind racing. A stone that could grant *anything*?

"Now that you know, I give you my word," Nikolai said, keeping his voice steady, "I will let you use it if you give me your alliance and your confidence. You and your mate, of course. And those in your pack you trust not to abuse such power."

I leaned back in my chair, letting his words sink in. A *wish stone*. The kind of power people would kill for—*had* killed for. It was almost impossible to believe. And yet, Nikolai had lost nearly everything because of it.

I exhaled slowly, grinding my teeth, deep in thought.

Gigi and Terri had been dragged into *his* war. If he had told me earlier, we could have been prepared. We would have known what that man Sara caught was really after. Maybe I could have arranged protection for Gigi and Terri while they were at school.

Maybe a lot of things.

As if reading my thoughts, Nikolai cleared his throat. "Tyce, I swear, I did not think anyone in this country even knew stone exists. Never I thought they would come for it."

I shook my head, biting back the sheer rage clawing at my insides.

"You've been living in my pack for months," I said slowly, deliberately. "My pack. Under my roof. Under my protection. And you've been sitting on something so fucking desired it put my mate and my sister in danger? And you didn't think I needed to know?"

Nikolai exhaled. "Tyce, I—"

"You didn't think anyone would come for it," I snapped, cutting him off. "And yet here we fucking are. My mate is missing. My sister is missing. And you're just now deciding to come clean?"

Nikolai met my glare head-on. "You are right," he admitted. "I should have told you. But I—"

"Damn fucking right, you should have told me," I growled, my voice low and dangerous. "I swear, if Gigi or Terri—" My voice broke off. I couldn't even say it.

His jaw clenched. "That is why I'm here," he said firmly. "To help bring them back."

My pulse hammered in my ears. I didn't give a fuck about his reasoning. My family had been dragged into this, and I had been blindsided.

How could he not tell me?

I clenched my fists so hard my nails dug into my palms. My father should know about this. Liam should know. I should have known from the second Nikolai set foot in my territory . . .

I forced myself to inhale and exhale. I needed his help now. And losing my temper wasn't going to get me any.

I studied him for a long moment, trying to make sense of why he'd kept this from me. And the more I thought about it, the more it began to make sense. Didn't it? How did he know I wouldn't have nefarious intentions once I learned about the existence of this stone? And it put him in a bad spot, with his dependence on our pack for survival. But still . . . It was wrong, even if I could understand.

But, we all made mistakes, right?

And Nikolai *had* been here. Loyal. Relentless in helping me get Gigi and Terri back.

His hiding the stone from me was clearly not due to bad intentions.

And then there was the stone itself. *A wish.*

I thought about Gigi. About her wolf.

I loved her wolf. *She* didn't see how amazing it was, but I did. But I also knew how much it tormented her. How she refused to shift around others. How the only reason she'd led the pack run was because I had that special coat made for her.

If I could give her *one thing*—it would be the chance to love herself the way I already did.

I dragged a hand down my face, then met Nikolai's gaze.

"I appreciate your honesty," I said, keeping my voice even. "I won't pretend I'm fine with the fact that you waited this long to tell me. But, right now, all I care about is getting my mate and my sister back. We'll talk about the rest *later*."

Nikolai nodded, shoulders easing slightly. "Understood."

I didn't miss the look of relief in his eyes.

Chapter 48

Tyson

The skies finally cleared, the winds died down, and the storm passed. It was time.

Beta Liam had some of the warriors running through the final pre-flight checks, double-checking the fuel levels, inspecting the wings, and ensuring the plane was ready for takeoff.

"Pitot tube looks clear!" one of the warriors called out, tapping a gloved finger against the slender probe on the wing.

Liam nodded and moved to the engine cowling, unfastening the latches to check the oil level and ensure there were no leaks or loose components. The bitter morning air carried the scent of aviation fuel and the faint metallic tang of frost-covered metal.

"Brakes are good, flaps are responding," another warrior reported as he finished testing the control surfaces.

Liam finally stepped back, his keen eyes scanning over every inch of the aircraft one last time. He reached up, gave the fuel caps a firm twist to make sure they were secure, then turned toward me.

"All checked out, Alpha," he called. "We're good to go!"

I gave him a nod, then turned as Nikolai stepped onto the runway with one of his men by his side.

"I left Sasha in charge while I am gone," Nikolai said. "This is Ivan, my best tracker."

I shook Ivan's hand, and he returned the firm handshake.

"Joe's already aboard. I have my two most trusted warriors watching him, Eddie and Tanner."

"Where I should put our bags?" Nikolai asked.

I led them to the cargo hold, helping them stow the few items they'd brought. While they boarded, I stayed behind to do one final walk-through with Liam, ensuring everything was in order.

Then, just as we were about to step onto the plane—

"Tyce!"

Fuck.

I clenched my jaw at the familiar voice and turned to find my father striding toward the runway with the same rigid authority he always had and a pinched expression on his face.

Liam shot me a knowing look, gave my shoulder a quick pat, and disappeared into the plane, leaving me to handle the storm heading my way.

I sighed, bracing myself, and went to meet my father halfway.

"Where the *fuck* do you think you're taking the plane?" he demanded as his piercing glare locked onto mine. "We're not scheduled to pick up supplies for another three days."

"Duty calls," I replied vaguely.

"Duty?" His scoff was full of disbelief, like I'd just spit in his face. "What duty? Your duty is here. This isn't some fucking day job you can clock in and out of whenever you feel like it, Tyce. You're the alpha. You don't get to run off to shack up with your mate whenever you damn well please."

A growl threatened to rise in my throat, but I swallowed it down. He didn't know. He had no idea about Gigi or Terri. To him, I was just ditching the pack to get laid.

I exhaled slowly, centering myself. "Dad, I know I haven't been the best alpha since you passed the title to me."

His arms crossed over his chest, and he looked me over. "That's an understatement."

I shifted the weight in my feet and ignored the heat rising in me. "I know I spent a while fucking around, not taking my duties seriously. I was immature. Dumb. And I get why you never stepped back. You didn't trust me."

His expression didn't shift. No reaction. Just a long, assessing stare.

I took a step closer and thrust my chest forward. "But I've changed. Since I got back from Vermont, I've been stepping up. I've been running my rounds every day, training with the warriors, checking the borders, keeping up with intel. I've been handling shit without you having to step in."

Still, nothing.

I squared my shoulders. "Have you even noticed?" I pushed. "The warriors don't go to you anymore. They come to me."

His silence stretched between us, but there was a flicker of something behind his eyes.

I inhaled deeply and felt the words build in my chest. "I get it now—what it actually means to be an alpha. It's not about being the strongest or barking the loudest. It's about responsibility. It's about making sure this pack knows they can count on me when it fucking matters. They need me to step up and keep them safe. And I am."

He released a slow breath.

I pressed on. "I'm not the same guy I was before. And honestly? A lot of that is because of Gigi. She's made me see things differently. Made me realize how important it is to be someone people can depend on. Someone who actually *deserves* to lead."

"So, where exactly are you taking the plane, Tyce? Why are you using our resources—our plane, our fuel, our beta, our warriors?" My dad's voice was even, but there was an edge to it. "I think I have a right to know what's happening with this pack. I've been running it long enough, and I'm still here."

His words hit exactly where he meant them to.

I'm still here.

He still felt as if he was needed. That one alpha wasn't enough.

"You're not going to be here forever," I said, trying my best to keep my voice even. "And when that day comes, I need to be ready. I need to be able to lead without you hovering over my fucking shoulder, second-guessing me."

His nostrils flared. "You think you're ready for that?"

"I know I am."

"You don't get to just say that, Tyce," he snapped. "You have to prove it."

"That's exactly what I'm doing!" I shot back. "And if you actually want me to be a real alpha—if you want me to succeed—then you need to back off and let me figure it out. Let me *do or die*."

His lips pressed into a thin line. For a second, I braced myself, expecting another lecture, another dismissal.

But, to my complete fucking shock, he smiled.

Not a mocking smirk, not a bitter sneer. A real, genuine smile.

Before I could process it, he grabbed me by the back of the neck and pulled me into a bone-crushing hug.

"Okay, Tyce," he murmured in his low, rough voice. He clapped my back twice before pulling away.

Just . . . acceptance?

Then, without another word, he turned and walked away, leaving me standing there, completely thrown.

For a moment, I didn't move.

If I didn't know better . . . he almost seemed . . . proud?

But I didn't have time to dwell on it. I had a mate and a sister to find. Without hesitation, I turned and climbed into the plane. Its engine rumbled and vibrated beneath me.

As I took my seat, my mind flickered back to the Seven of Wands tarot card I'd pulled months earlier. I thought about how the witch who'd done my reading had easily clocked me as a leader who didn't lead.

I inhaled slowly, letting my head fall back against the seat.

For so long, I had told myself I was rebelling, fighting back against my dad and my grandfather, punishing them for the shit they'd put me through. But sitting here now, staring out at the snowy expanse, I finally saw the truth.

I hadn't been rebelling. I'd been running.

I had been so afraid of failure, so afraid of disappointing my father and letting my pack down, that I hadn't even tried. Because how could you fail if you never put yourself in the game?

But I didn't want to be that guy anymore.

I didn't want my dad to see me as an immature, annoying kid he had to micromanage. I wanted what had just happened between us. For him to finally trust me. To believe I could stand beside him as an equal, as the alpha I was meant to be.

And more than anything, I wanted to make my mate proud.

I wanted Gigi to look at me and know she was mated to the right man. Someone she could depend on. Someone she could trust. Someone she was proud to stand beside as the pack's luna.

I didn't want to be an overgrown man-child anymore.

I wanted to be a man.

Chapter 49

Theresa

The chains were cold. Unrelenting. Unforgiving.

The metal dug into my fur, pressing against my skin so tightly I could feel the bruises forming beneath it. The cuffs clearly weren't just meant to restrain me but also to remind me of my place: helpless, caged, powerless.

They bit into my bones, reminding me that no matter how strong I thought I was, no matter how much I fought, I wasn't getting out of this.

I'd told Gigi we needed to keep our minds astute. To keep mindlinking. To keep fighting against our animal instincts. But it wasn't easy.

I curled up tighter and rested my chin on my paws. My body ached from being in the same position for too long. Moving took energy. And I had none left.

How long had it been?

Days? Weeks?

No. It hadn't been weeks. It just felt like it.

I was starving. I'd been starved before. This was the kind of hunger that made my stomach curl inward, that made my vision dim at the edges every time I lifted my head too fast. But even worse than that was the weight pressing down on my chest that had nothing to do with hunger or exhaustion.

I'd already felt the loss before all of this. Before the chains, before the cave, before the cold.

I'd lost Kolya.

To be fair, I'd never had him. And to truly lose something, it had to have been yours at some point. Our relationship was over before it had even begun.

I squeezed my eyes shut, but his face stayed imprinted in my mind, like a tattoo. The way he'd looked at me the last time I saw him. The way I'd tried to grab for him, to keep him with me, and the way he turned and . . . just left me.

I'd been so dumb. I'd reassured him that I was okay with casual. I was fine with just getting off with him a few times.

But I wasn't, was I?

I'd gotten in way over my head.

Once again, I had been too trusting. Trusted that a man wouldn't hurt me.

But they always did, didn't they? Even if they didn't mean to. They just did. I let out a quiet whine, no longer able to keep my feelings in.

Gigi shifted beside me. The soft rustling of her fur was barely audible over the howling wind outside. At least she was still here. She was the only thing keeping me from going off the deep end.

The sound of boots scraping against snow and ice pulled me from my thoughts. The guards were coming. I lifted my head, blinking slowly as they approached. Two men bulked up in their winter gear. One of them carried a tray, and my stomach clenched before my brain caught up.

They placed the tray in front of us. With two metal bowls. Filled with *dog food*.

The smell of the nauseating mix of stale meat and chemicals hit me hard. My stomach lurched, both from hunger and from disgust.

Dog food.

Because that was what we were to them.

Gigi was the first to react. She lifted her head, stared at the bowls, then huffed and looked away. I swallowed hard and did the same.

The guards chuckled. One of them crouched down, tapping the edge of the bowl with his fingers. "C'mon, girl. You must be hungry."

I bared my teeth. He just laughed.

Gigi let out a low, warning growl.

The guard smirked and stood. "Suit yourself." He nodded at his companion. The two of them gawked at us, pointing and laughing at the cruel joke they were playing on us. My ears burned with shame. I hated how powerless I was. How I couldn't do anything.

"*Goddess, I wish I could tear through their faces with my claws!*" Gigi mindlinked me. "*As soon as I get free, I'm taking them both down!*"

"*Do your best to ignore them,*" I encouraged, although I couldn't disagree with Gigi's sentiment. "*They're just trying to break us down.*"

"*But do they have to be so shitty? And dog food? Seriously?*"

"*I know,*" I replied with a sad exhale.

"Get a load'a that one!" One of the guards pointed to Gigi. "What happened to that wolf?"

"I don't know, but that's one chopped wolf."

They laughed, and my chest ached on Gigi's behalf. How dare they? We were already suffering. Why did they have to humiliate us on top of that?

"*Don't listen to them, Gigi,*" I mindlinked my friend. "*There's nothing wrong with your wolf.*"

I didn't miss the look of defeat in her eyes.

"*Gigi, don't pay attention to them. Just mindlink me and drown out their stupid laughter. They're clearly just dumb pawns who are trying to make themselves feel more important than they are by torturing us.*"

"*They're not wrong though,*" Gigi replied. "*My wolf is messed up. It's my own fault. I killed my wolf by accident when I was a kid. And I finally brought it back to life . . . and I guess this is what a zombie wolf looks like.*"

"But, Gigi, that's amazing! That you were able to bring your wolf back to life! It's a miracle. Your wolf has battle scars. Why would you be embarrassed of a wolf that has literally been to the other realm and back?"

She seemed to brighten a bit but then lowered again as the guards' laughter increased in volume. They'd probably said some other mean, horrible thing.

"Just keep mindlinking me," I encouraged, not wanting Gigi to listen to anything else they had to say.

She looked up at me and seemed to hesitate as her eyes met mine. She tilted her head and finally asked, *"Are you okay, Terri? . . . Obviously we're not okay. But you've just . . . You've seemed really down, even before we got here."*

I lowered my head, wondering how much to reveal to Gigi. At this point, nothing seemed to matter anymore. It wasn't clear if we'd even leave alive. I decided to just go for it. If anything, at least it would distract from the jerks humiliating us.

"I'm just . . . I'm just devastated." My throat practically closed in on itself at the onslaught of emotion. *"I was so dumb, Gigi. So, so dumb. I had a fling with Alpha Nikolai. I told myself it was casual. But . . . at some point, I fell for him."* My chest seized, like I had just admitted it to myself for the first time. *"And now . . . now, I miss him so much it physically hurts. I feel like I'm bleeding inside, like I'm dying, and no one can see."* I had to confess, getting it off my chest lightened the burden just the teeniest bit. I let out a breath.

"Wow, Terri, I had no idea."

"I know. It was supposed to be a secret. We tried to hide it, obviously. Can you imagine what my dad would do if he found out? But now I'm left carrying this pain, and I can't even tell anyone what happened."

"You can tell me." Gigi nudged me with her snout. *"I swear, Terri. You can trust me. We're going to be sisters soon, and I want us to be just as close*

as I am with my blood sisters. I would never tell anyone—not even Tyce—if you didn't want me to."

I lifted my head and stared at Gigi in appreciation. *"I'm here for you too. Anything you need."*

"I know. You are one of the kindest people I've ever met. And I'm so happy I get to have you as a sister now."

The warmth between us, the *hope*, was enough to make me believe, even if just for a moment, that we would make it out.

"We're going to survive this. We just have to stick together," I said with conviction.

"Hell fucking yes!"

The faintest flicker of light sparked in her eyes.

But the moment was short-lived.

Shadows danced over us as the guards crept closer.

"Looks like the bitches ain't eating," one sneered.

"You know what that means." The other let out a sinister chuckle.

The first one pulled out a pouch and dropped a couple items into his hand, passing one to his companion.

Needles.

Instinct took over, and I yanked against my restraints, fighting even though I knew it was useless. Gigi thrashed beside me, but she was just as powerless.

The guards closed in.

Clearly to avoid our mouths, which still posed some risk, they chose our backsides instead. The cool metal easily pierced through the soft layers of skin and muscle on my butt. I yelped at the intrusion, the sharp metallic sting that stabbed through me.

The effects were almost immediate. My muscles went slack, and my head lolled to the side. My vision blurred, and I barely heard Gigi snarl before she, too, was injected. I tried to fight it. Tried to lift my head, my paws, anything.

But the world was already slipping away.

The last thing I felt was Gigi's body pressed against mine, her warmth the only thing keeping me from drowning.

And then . . . darkness.

Chapter 50

Nikolai

I gripped the armrests so tightly my knuckles had gone white. The leather creaked beneath my fingers. My whole body was rigid with restraint, as if forcing myself to be still would keep me from snapping. Every nerve in me screamed to move, to do something. But all I could do was sit and wait.

The second Liam got the okay to land, I had to force myself not to storm into the cockpit and demand we go faster. I could already see the ground rushing toward us through the narrow window, but it wasn't fast enough.

I needed to get to Terri.

A suffocating pressure coiled within my ribs. It felt like I had been holding my breath for days now. I knew I did a good enough job keeping my cool in front of Tyce, trying to hold myself together as a leader. But, inside, I was crumbling. The closer we got to her, the more my fears threatened me.

The thought of losing her—truly losing her—was unbearable.

I had already lost my home, my family, and most of my pack. I had genuinely believed I had nothing left to lose at this point.

But then Terri came blazing into my life like a wildfire, burning through every wall I'd built around myself.

I'd told myself it was just a few good moments. That it was better this way. But I'd been lying to myself. I was an idiot—*durak*—to ever think I could spend one day giving in to my desires and then just be able to walk away like nothing ever happened.

I had to be the biggest fool in the world to believe I could ever forget her.

She had imprinted on me in every way possible without physically marking me. She had thawed my frozen rock of a heart, and it was beating again. The *thump, thump, thump* in my chest kept me keenly aware of her absence.

I needed her.

I loved her.

The realization slammed into me, knocking the air from my lungs. *I loved her.*

It didn't matter that I was an alpha. It didn't matter that my pack was in ruins.

I needed her.

And if I had to choose between being a leader or being with her, then fuck the title. Fuck the responsibilities. I would choose her.

I swallowed hard, forcing my breathing to stay steady. If I lost her now, after everything, after finally allowing myself to feel again, I didn't know if I could survive it. I was as good as dead without her.

The plane jolted violently as we touched down on the small, icy runway outside Anchorage, the tires skidding slightly before catching traction. The sharp jolt rattled through my bones, but I barely felt it. My pulse pounded too loudly in my ears, drowning out everything else.

Outside the window, the world was a blur of white and gray, the tarmac slick with frost, the surrounding landscape swallowed by a thick layer of snow. The engines rumbled as we slowed to a crawl.

We were here.

The moment the plane finally rolled to a stop, I unbuckled, and I was already rising from my seat before the cabin door even opened. The others followed suit, moving with tense urgency.

Joe was the last to stand, his shoulders hunched, his face pale and drawn. He didn't meet anyone's eyes as Tyce's warriors closed in on either side of him. Tyce followed behind, his gaze locked onto Joe like a wolf ready to tear into its prey.

Once we disembarked, the group of us huddled together.

"Well?" Tyce glared at Joe.

"I—" Joe swallowed. "I lost her."

"What the fuck do you mean you lost her?" Tyce's voice boomed. His alpha aura cracked against Joe, who stumbled backward, but Tyce was already on him, grabbing him by the collar of his coat and yanking him forward.

"Start talking!" Tyce bellowed.

"I-I don't know what happened!" Joe stammered. "I could feel her before, but now, she's just . . . gone."

Tyce's eyes burned. He tightened his fist around the material of the coat, practically pulling Joe up by it. "Is she dead?"

Joe's face twisted with panic. "I-I don't know! I don't think so! I don't know what it feels like when someone . . . when someone dies through the bond!" His voice cracked. "I've never—"

Tyce shook him. "You better not be fucking lying to me!" His eyes were wild, feral. "Because if you are—"

"Tyce." My voice cut through the chaos.

His head snapped toward me. His breath came out labored as he straddled the thin line between rationality and insanity.

"You would feel it." I held his gaze. "Think. You are alpha. Terri and Gigi are both in your pack. You feel when bond is cut, if . . ." My voice cracked as I recalled the feeling—how it felt as my pack members perished one by one in the war. It still haunted me to this day. That snap of the fragile connection that holds them on earth. "If they die."

Tyce's grip loosened.

Joe let out a strangled breath but didn't move, too afraid to even attempt an escape.

Tyce's jaw was clenched so tight I thought his teeth might break. His nostrils flared, his chest heaved. Then, slowly, he let go.

He turned and ran a hand through his hair. His body was still rigid with tension.

"She is not dead," I said again, my own voice raw. "But something happened. And we must find out why Joe cannot feel her anymore."

Tyce exhaled audibly. "Fine. Let's go."

Stalled, with no way forward until Joe could feel Terri again, we checked into a hotel.

Joe was chained up in his room, guarded by Eddie and Tanner. Tyce booked the rest of us a couple rooms. I'd be sharing with Ivan while Tyce bunked with his beta. None of us were in the mood for sleep, no matter how exhausted we were.

The hotel room was suffocatingly quiet, save for the distant hum of the heating system. The cheap carpet smelled faintly of industrial cleaner, and the low light from the bedside lamp cast shadows across the walls, making everything feel smaller, tighter. I sat on the edge of the bed, rubbing a hand down my face. My body ached. The weight of everything settled over me, dragging me deeper into my own thoughts. Terri was out there somewhere. Cold. Afraid. Maybe hurt. And I was sitting here, useless.

That evening, Tyce convinced me to sit in the nearly empty hotel lounge with him to eat and drink, though neither of us had much of an appetite.

The waitress had barely disappeared after taking our order when Tyce leaned forward with his beer bottle hovering near his lips. "I didn't forget about the stone."

"I did not think you had."

He studied me for a long moment, then sat back, stroking his chin before taking a sip of his beer.

"Does my mom know?" he asked finally.

I hesitated, considering. "I don't know. She left before I was born. But I doubt it. The stone was always secret, very closely guarded. Even my late beta, he never told his family."

Tyce nodded with lips pressed into a firm line. He appeared deep in thought as his fingers tapped idly against the table.

"Tyce, I swear," I continued, my voice severe with conviction, "I never thought anyone would find stone here. If I even suspect—" I stopped, my mind flashing to that day in the wilderness. To the wolves who had attacked.

Tyce's eyes flicked back to mine. "What?"

Damn it.

I took a deep, pained breath and forced myself to meet his gaze. "Something happened. And I did not tell you. Too much was already going on." Guilt pressed down on me, tightening in my chest. "I owe you, your pack, more than I can ever repay. I will make it right."

Tyce's expression darkened. "What. Happened."

I hesitated. There was no good way to say it, no way to soften the blow. I grimaced and forced myself to speak. "Terri came with me, to prepare land where my pack will move in spring. On way, two wolves found us. American wolves. They attacked."

Tyce's entire body went rigid.

"But—" My mind replayed that day, the way Terri had moved with such raw strength, with courage. How she had fought beside me, like an equal. Like she had been built for war.

"But?" Tyce disrupted my thoughts.

"But we fought back. Your sister . . ." My voice dropped and something like reverence crept into my tone. "She is incredible. I never seen woman fight like that. She helped me kill them both."

Tyce pinched his lips together.

Lowering my head, I exhaled slowly. "I should have told you."

Tyce slammed his beer bottle onto the table. He ran a hand through his hair, visibly seething. "I knew the Alpine Snow Pack had been sniffing around, but we had no disputes with them. Nothing. So I didn't take it seriously enough. If I'd known—"

I nodded, my throat tightening. "If you'd known, maybe Gigi and Terri would be safe." It hit me like a punch to the gut.

Tyce blew out a breath and looked away. His shoulders were rigid, his frustration and guilt so tangible it weighed heavy between us.

I leaned forward slightly, trying to break through his anger. "I can't change the past," I said, keeping my voice steady but firm. "I was wrong. I did not think. I made mistake."

The words felt heavier than I expected. Because this wasn't just about this particular incident. This was about all of them. The past year, the choices I'd made, the regrets that haunted me in the dead of night.

"I made many mistakes, Tyce," I admitted. "We all do our best as alphas. We make calls, we try to protect our packs. But sometimes we miss. Sometimes we make wrong choice. And when this happens, we must own it. That is why I am here. Of course, I want Terri and Gigi safe. But I also want to fix this."

Something in my words must have hit home because Tyce's shoulders finally relaxed. The hard edge of his rage dulled. He slumped back in his chair.

The waitress appeared, setting down our food. Neither of us moved to touch it.

Tyce took a sip of his beer before he finally spoke. "You living in my pack . . . we have to have trust. We have to communicate. This can't happen again."

I met his eyes and nodded. "It will not."

He picked up his fork, pushing his food around without taking a bite. I stared down at my own plate. My appetite was long gone.

Then Tyce glanced up, a faint smirk tugging at his lips. "Well, it's nice not being the one who fucked up for once."

I almost laughed. Was that his version of an olive branch? Maybe. It wasn't full forgiveness, but I didn't expect that. It would take time to earn back his trust. And honestly, I didn't blame him for being pissed. If someone had caused my mate to disappear . . .

"We will get them back," I vowed, my tone leaving no room for doubt.

A beat passed. Then I added, "And if we do not succeed . . . you have my permission to end me."

Tyce's head snapped up, eyes widening.

"Just . . . please help my pack," I continued. "None of this is their fault. They are good people. Loyal people. They will be loyal to your pack."

"Damn, bro," Tyce muttered, looking at me like I fell from the moon.

"I mean it." I met his gaze, unwavering. "If we do not get your mate and your sister back, I give you my life to take." I swallowed hard. "That is how important this is to me."

And besides, I thought, there was no more life for me without Terri.

Chapter 51

Nikolai

A loud bang on my hotel room door tore me from sleep.

My body snapped awake instantly, my instincts kicking in before my brain could catch up. The dark room around me blurred as I reached for the knife I always kept under my pillow. Across the room, Ivan had already lurched upright with tense muscles and eyes scanning for threats.

Bang. Bang. Bang.

"*Blyad*," I muttered under my breath, blinking away the haze of sleep as my grip on the knife tightened. The pounding at the door was relentless, urgent. Whoever it was, they weren't waiting.

I immediately slid out of bed and stalked toward the door. Bracing myself for what waited on the other side, I gripped the handle tight. Through the heavy metal, I could hear ragged, uneven breathing.

I yanked it open.

Tyce stood in front of me, disheveled, his face a storm of raw panic and barely contained fury. His hands were clenched at his sides, like he was physically holding himself together. "Joe's got something."

I was already moving and grabbing my boots before he finished his sentence. Ivan immediately followed.

When I entered his room, Joe was sitting on the edge of the bed, hunched over, with his fingers digging into his skull. Eddie and Tanner were stationed by the door with tight expressions and wary eyes.

"He just started acting like that a few minutes ago," Eddie said. "Said he could feel Terri again."

Tyce moved toward the bed and grabbed Joe's shoulder with a violent grip. "Where is she? Can you tell where she is?"

Joe's bloodshot eyes flicked up. They were unfocused and glassy. His breath came out in shallow gasps. "I can feel her," he rasped. "But it . . . it's bad."

A knot tightened in my stomach. "What do you mean, 'it's bad'?" I demanded, stepping closer.

Joe let out a strained breath, and convulsed with the force of whatever he was experiencing. "I don't— I can't tell. It's just too much."

Tyce and I exchanged a look of dread.

"Is she hurt?" I asked.

Joe shook his head quickly. "No, not physically. It's . . . She's . . ." His face twisted, his body locked up. "It's bad. Really bad."

Tyce swore under his breath and paced the room with agitated strides. "We need to move," he exclaimed. "Get in the car, drive, something—"

Joe groaned and doubled over, clutching his stomach like he'd been struck. He let out a choked sound and squeezed his eyes shut.

"What the fuck is happening?" Tyce shouted.

"I— She—" He stopped. Shook his head violently. "I don't know—I don't— *Fuck*, it's too much!"

"What's too much?" I demanded.

His breaths were coming too fast. He pressed his palms into his forehead like he was trying to keep something inside.

"She's trapped," he whispered in a voice raw with horror. "She's trapped." He let out a strangled sound, somewhere between a sob and a growl.

"What does that mean, Joe?" Tyce barked.

Joe's mouth opened. Closed. He shook his head rapidly, frantic. "Can't—can't—"

Then, he went completely rigid. His face twisted in terror. He wasn't breathing. He fell back onto the bed, and trembled violently. His fingers dug into the sheets as he let out a ragged groan. His suffering was visceral. Whatever Terri felt was tearing through him.

"Where is she?" Tyce demanded, pushing his alpha aura behind the command.

Joe whimpered but didn't respond.

Whatever was happening to Terri outpowered even an alpha aura. My whole body ached with anguish at the sight. Bile rose to my throat. I felt so powerless, watching Joe struggle like that, well aware that it was in reaction to whatever was happening to Terri.

"*Artemida*, please let her be okay," I said in Russian.

Tyce's nostrils flared. I could sense his control slipping.

"Where is she?" he demanded again, raw with deepening desperation.

Joe didn't respond. The silence stretched, the tension growing thicker as the seconds ticked by.

Tyce's fingers twitched at his sides while his control slipped inch by inch.

Then—SNAP.

Tyce spun and slammed his fist into the nearest wall. The impact rattled the entire room, sending a framed picture crashing to the floor.

"Fucking useless!" he roared, his aura surging so violently the air felt electric.

"Tyce!" I snapped, stepping toward him. "Breaking hotel room will not help."

He turned on me, wild-eyed with fury. His chest heaved. His wolf was clawing for control.

Everyone braced themselves. Liam, Tanner, and Eddie stiffened. Their eyes locked on Tyce, watching him like an unstable threat. Ivan took a step forward, readying to intervene if necessary. Every breath I took was like inhaling pure tension.

Tyce exhaled, and his hands flexed like he was fighting the urge to rip something apart. Then, with visible effort, he turned away with rigid shoulders and began to pace.

We let out a collective breath, though no one relaxed fully.

Tyce continued to pace the room. His fists clenched and unclenched at his sides. He kept running his hands through his hair, over and over. Time dragged.

I stared at the floor, grinding my teeth.

Stay in control.

My pulse pounded in my throat, but I forced my face to remain still. I couldn't spiral. Not like Tyce. Even if I was just as fucking terrified.

Where are you, Terri?

I ground my teeth more. If something happened to her . . . if she didn't make it out of this—

NO.

I balled my hands into fists. *Get a grip, Volkov.* I couldn't panic. I forced myself to keep my breath steady. But my wolf was restless. Prowling inside me.

We waited for Joe to be coherent enough to say something useful. But he was barely responsive. Every question we asked only got vague, agonized answers, if we got anything at all. He barely even seemed to register the fact that we were in the room with him.

She was hysterical. That was all he could tell us.

Tyce suddenly stopped midstep. "What if—" He turned to me with feral eyes. "What if they're torturing Gigi in front of her?"

Joe flinched but didn't deny it.

The question sent dread through me. Now that he'd said it out loud, I couldn't stop the thoughts from flooding me. Of Terri being forced to watch as her sister-in-law had a knife, or worse, driven into her. It was what someone would do for answers, right? But what answers could Terri have?

I shook my head, forcing the visions to stop.

Tyce's breathing picked up again, bordering on panic. "That would explain it." His voice cracked. "If they're trying to break her, they'd use Gigi against her—"

"Stop." I stepped in front of him before he could spiral further.

"Don't fucking tell me to stop!" Tyce shouted. "That's my mate we're talking about!"

"You do not know something is happening to her!" I shot back. "You only assume."

Tyce's entire body vibrated with tension. His shoulders rose and fell with deep, labored breaths.

"Joe would feel if she was in real pain," I said, forcing my voice to remain steady. "You heard him. Terri is not hurt physically. She is just . . . breaking apart inside."

Joe groaned again. His body seized, reacting to whatever Terri was feeling.

Tyce ran both hands through his hair, tugging at the strands in frustration. He looked like he wanted to keep arguing. Like he needed this fight.

I placed a hand on his shoulder. He tensed but didn't shove me off.

"You must not let your mind go there," I said. "Your imagination, it is your worst enemy now."

Tyce turned on me, his gaze wild with barely restrained fury. "How the fuck are you so calm right now?"

"I'm not!" I snapped. "But panic will not bring us closer to finding them."

Tyce let out a frustrated growl, his fists clenching and unclenching at his sides again. I understood how he felt—the helplessness, the burning rage without a target to hit—but we needed to keep it together.

Joe let out another ragged gasp. His face twisted in agony. His body shuddered violently. His fingers clawed at the sheets under him.

Tyce turned back toward him. "Joe, focus! Try to give us something, anything."

Joe curled in on himself, panting. "I'm . . . I'm trying," he rasped. "She's stressed. Panicking. She feels . . . trapped."

"What fucking good are you?" Tyce snarled, grabbing the front of Joe's shirt and hauling him halfway off the bed.

Joe's head lolled back.

I grabbed Tyce's wrist. "Let go."

Tyce's head snapped toward me. "Are you fucking kidding me, bro? He's the only connection we have to them! If he can't do his job, then what the fuck are we waiting for?"

"Tyce," I cut in, my voice more demanding this time. "Enough."

"Don't tell me to calm down, Volkov!"

"I am not telling you calm down." I stepped in closer, locking his gaze. "I tell you, focus. You want to save them, or you want to lose your shit?"

Tyce's breathing was still heavy, his muscles still locked tight, but I saw a flicker of clarity.

"Joe feels her," I reminded him. "Is already better than yesterday."

Finally, he let out a slow, reluctant breath. "So what do we do?"

"We wait," I said, the words grinding my throat. "Now, something is happening. But not forever. When . . ." I took a deep breath. "When Terri is not so hysterical, then we can go to her."

"Fucking Artemis," Tyce muttered. He stumbled back, dropping into a chair and burying his face in his hands. "What are they doing to her?"

I clenched my jaw and went back to staring at the floor. I wished I knew. I wished I had an answer. But I wouldn't let my mind go where

Tyce's had again. I couldn't. The truth was, I wasn't sure how much longer I could keep it together either.

The thought of her out there, terrified and trapped, cut into me like a blade, twisting deeper with every moment. And if I let my mind go there, if I pictured her broken, afraid, calling for help that wasn't coming, I wasn't sure I'd keep my sanity.

Chapter 52

Theresa

A dull, throbbing ache pulsed through my body as I drifted in and out of consciousness. My head felt too heavy, my limbs numb and useless. My eyes fluttered open, but my vision was blurry, distorted from the lingering effects of the tranquilizer.

"She's awake," a voice murmured beyond the gate that kept us confined in this cave. Not that the barrier was necessary. The heavy chains ensured we weren't going anywhere.

I turned my head with effort. My muscles were stiff and achy. Gigi's eyes were already open, staring ahead.

"*How long were we out?*" I mindlinked her.

"*I don't know. I don't even know what day it is anymore.*"

"*They're doing this on purpose. They want us to lose track of time. They want us disoriented.*"

Gigi let out a loud breath. "*Well, they can go fuck themselves.*"

I was weak, becoming weaker by the day, starved, and breaking down bit by bit. They knew what they were doing. I just had to hope Gigi and I were both strong enough to overcome their tactics. Who knew where we were being kept or if anyone would be able to find us. We could legitimately be stuck here for a long, long time. I was about to respond to Gigi when—

A wail ripped through the cave, breaking the silence.

My body jerked, and my head snapped up.

The sound of boots stomping against the ground traveled closer and closer along with the screaming. Then, the turning of a key and the scrape of metal against the hard ground.

When the gate opened, the first thing I noticed was the matted, curly blonde hair on the woman. She was kicking and thrashing, restrained by a heavy metal chain around her wrists. I recognized her scent immediately, as well as the fact that whatever she was wearing was not hers. It was clearly several sizes too big and must have been issued to her as a temporary solution to cover her up. Had she been caught in her wolf form?

My stomach heaved violently. *No. No, no, no.*

"SOPHIA!"

Panic consumed me. *This isn't happening. This isn't real.*

Adrenaline flooded my body. I yanked against the chains with everything I had, every fiber of muscle. I had to get to her. I had to protect her. The cold, hard metal tore into my limbs. The scent of my own blood laced the air. I yanked and thrashed like a wild animal.

"Sophia!" I mindlinked her, desperate to reach her.

She lifted her head to reveal a face streaked with dirt. Our eyes met. "Terri!" she sobbed in a cracked and raw voice.

One of the guards struck her across the face. Her head whipped to the side, and a strangled cry tore from her throat.

I roared, seeing red.

Beside me, Gigi shook with rage. *"What the fuck!"*

The guards dumped Sophia on the frozen dirt floor. The moment she tried to crawl toward me, a boot slammed into her ribs, sending her sprawling onto her back.

A growl tore from my throat as I fought against the restraints. I was going to kill them. Every single one of them.

Then, a shadow moved.

A man stepped forward. His towering frame was unmistakable. Broad shoulders, large build, even larger with his winter coat, and cold, calculating emerald eyes.

Alpha Wes.

I had met him before, back when I first arrived at school, before his pack turned against us.

He stepped over my best friend as if she were nothing more than a pile of trash to him, stopped just out of my reach, and smirked. "Hello, sweetheart."

I had never been more disgusted by a smile in my life.

"You have some information we need," he continued. "And the sooner you give it to us, the sooner we stop torturing your friend."

I met his gaze head-on, narrowing my eyes. If I could, I would have spit in his face.

He then turned toward Sophia and crouched beside her. His fingers grazed her bruised face. She flinched violently.

I bared my teeth and growled.

"Now . . . Sophia, is it?" His tone was sickeningly casual, as if we were all gathered here for a friendly chat. "I'm going to ask you a couple of questions. Theresa will mindlink you the answers. And all you have to do is tell me what she says."

His fingers trailed down her arm, pausing at her wrist.

"But if you refuse . . ." His grip tightened.

Sophia whimpered.

"Let's just hope it doesn't come to that."

He straightened, crossing his arms, surveying the scene. Then he clapped his hands together. "Now, Theresa, why don't you let your friend know where the stone is?"

My stomach clenched so hard I thought I might be sick.

Sophia lifted her head, her wide, stricken eyes locking onto mine. But there was something . . . missing. Her usual fire. Her fight. How much had they already tortured her?

I let out a low whine. Sophia had nothing to do with this. She should never have been dragged into this. This was my fault.

"Sophia, I'm so sorry," I mindlinked her.

"Terri, what is he talking about? What stone?"

"I don't know where it is," I replied desperately, knowing it wouldn't be enough.

Sophia stared at me, but she didn't speak.

Wes grabbed a fistful of her blonde curls and yanked her head back. She let out a cry.

"Well?" he pressed.

"She said she doesn't know."

Wes let out a low, malicious chuckle. "You think I believe that?" He shoved her forward. She crashed onto her knees, catching herself as best she could with chains wrapped around her wrists.

"Now," he continued, "get her to mindlink you and tell you."

"I swear, Sophia! I really don't know!" My desperation bled through the link.

"She really doesn't know," she repeated, her voice breaking.

Wes tilted his head. "Hmm." He looked down at her as if he were deciding whether or not to break her. Then, he exhaled and shook his head. "I think your friend Theresa doesn't believe me. She thinks I'm bluffing."

Sophia shook violently.

"I think," Wes continued, rolling his shoulders, "we need to demonstrate just how much I'm not joking."

A fresh wave of terror surged through me. I yanked against my chains again, putting every last bit of strength I had into trying to tear them from the wall. Blood dripped down my legs. I knew it was pointless. But I couldn't just sit there. Not while he—

Wes grabbed Sophia's arm and twisted. A sickening pop echoed through the cave.

Sophia's screams shattered me.

Her pain was visceral, piercing, unbearable. My best friend, the girl who had always been my rock, the one who was always there for me, was being dragged into this thing she had nothing to do with, being tortured.

And I could do nothing.

Her body was convulsing, curling in on itself as she gasped through the white-hot agony.

Wes watched her suffer with nothing more than mild curiosity, like he was observing an insect struggling under his boot.

"You see," he said, "I don't think you understand just how serious I am. I want that stone, and you will tell me where it is. One way or another."

I bared my teeth, a deep, guttural growl ripping from my throat, but it only made him smirk.

"You're not looking so brave anymore, sweetheart," he taunted. "Starting to feel a little helpless? A little . . . powerless?"

I thrashed against my restraints, my desperation overriding reason, my claws digging into the cold ground beneath me as I fought uselessly against the chains. The scent of my own blood mixed with the frozen air.

"I swear, Sophia! I don't know! Please believe me!" I mindlinked, praying that somehow, some way, she understood.

She was panting, her face twisted in pain, but she nodded ever so slightly. She believed me. I could see it in her eyes.

But Wes . . . Wes didn't.

"You're wasting my time." He sighed, rubbing his jaw as if all this was just an inconvenience. His eyes flicked toward the guards. "Let's see if we can speed this up, shall we?"

One of the men stepped forward, and before I could even process what was happening, he brought his boot down, hard, right on Sophia's dislocated shoulder.

A raw, animalistic shriek burst from her lips. Her entire body arched violently against the pain.

"*SOPHIA!*" I howled through the link, my mental voice shattering with despair.

She let out a gasping sob, her body writhing on the ground. Gigi was snarling beside me, vibrating, her claws scraping furiously against the stone floor.

"She still doesn't want to talk?" Wes said, shaking his head in mock disappointment. "Tough little thing, isn't she?"

I whimpered. I was hopeless. I couldn't speak out loud. My only vessel of communication was Sophia, and I had nothing I could give her. Kolya had trusted me with the knowledge of the stone, but he'd never told me where it was. And even if he had, I couldn't tell them. Seeing Sophia like this made me want to, just to get them to stop. I couldn't bear to watch my friend be hurt in front of me anymore. But I had nothing to offer. The stone's location was a secret that I was not privy to. They were wrong to assume I was.

"Sophia, please tell them I really don't know. That hurting you won't change that fact. I'm so sorry, Sophia. This has nothing to do with you." I whimpered again. My chest was so tight I was having trouble breathing. I was trapped, hopeless, and now my best friend was suffering.

Sophia repeated exactly what I told her. But he simply shook his head and said, "Wrong answer."

Then, before either of us could react, he grabbed Sophia's wrist and wrenched her upright by her dislocated shoulder. A guttural, bloodcurdling scream erupted from her. Her entire body shuddered with agony. But he continued on as if her anguish was nothing more than a slight annoyance.

"Let's try this another way," he said, shifting his grip. His fingers curled around Sophia's thumb. "You know this one, sweetheart, don't you?" he asked, his voice dripping with mockery. "This little piggy went to market."

SNAP. Sophia's body jerked violently as a ragged, choking scream tore from her throat. The sickening sound of bone breaking echoed through the cave.

"This little piggy stayed home," Wes resumed casually, snapping her index finger. He continued, breaking each finger one by one.

I howled in desperation, pulling against my chains. But it was useless.

When Wes finished breaking her pinky, he let go of her wrist, letting her broken hand fall limply against the dirt floor. She cradled it to her chest, staring at it, waiting for it to heal. She curled around her ruined hand, shaking. Trembling. Her breath came out in short, shallow gasps, as if every inhale was excruciating.

"Sophia, I'm so sorry," I mindlinked. *"This is all my fault. I'm so sorry."*

"Well?" Wes looked at me intently. "Are you going to tell us where it is now?"

"Tell him to torture me instead," I mindlinked Sophia, my desperation choking me. *"Please. Tell him to let you go and torture me instead!"*

Sophia didn't lift her head.

Didn't say a word.

"Sophia, PLEASE!" I begged and screamed through the link, but she remained silent. *"This has nothing to do with you. They should be torturing me for the answers they want!"*

She wouldn't say it. Wouldn't ask.

"Please, Sophia," I tried again.

"She doesn't know!" Sophia finally said with conviction. "She doesn't know where your damn stone is!"

Wes sighed dramatically and shook his head. "That's a real shame, sweetheart." Then, without warning, he crouched right in front of me, invading my space. His cold, lifeless eyes locked onto mine. His breath was warm against my muzzle, but it made my blood run ice-cold. "Because your friend is going to keep suffering until you remember."

I lunged, snapping my jaws an inch from his face. He didn't flinch. Just smirked. *Mocking* me.

Beside me, Gigi let out a feral growl, yanking violently at her chains. The sound of metal clanking against metal rang through the cave, but it was useless. We were trapped. Forced to watch this brutal exercise in cruelty.

They hit her. Kicked her. Broke her bones. Over and over, they battered her like she was nothing.

When that didn't work, they brought out the knives. Cut into her flesh. Took pieces of her.

I had witnessed torture before. My father had made sure of it, forcing me to watch from a young age, trying to desensitize me to violence. I had been exposed to it over and over again, pushed past the point of repulsion, forced to stomach it. But this? This was different.

Because this was Sophia.

My best friend. The person who had always been there for me, who had held me together when I was falling apart, who didn't deserve a second of this.

And I could do nothing.

I retched at one point, but there was nothing left inside me. Just bile. I hadn't eaten for days.

I didn't know how long it lasted. Minutes? Hours? At some point, time stopped making sense.

My mind slipped somewhere dark. Somewhere I didn't think I could ever come back from. Maybe the endless days in my wolf form wouldn't have broken me. Maybe I could have survived the starvation, the cold, the chains.

But this?

This would destroy me. How could I live after this? How could I ever be the same? How could I look in a mirror and not see the blood of my best friend reflected back at me?

They made her beg. Beg me to give them something. Anything. But the truth was always the same.

"*I don't know!*" I howled through the link, again and again, my voice fractured, raw, desperate. "*I DON'T KNOW!*"

But my words meant nothing. The torture continued.

Sophia's cries grew weaker. Her body stopped fighting back. I could see it—the light fading from her eyes, the slow, agonizing unraveling of her life.

One of the men hovering nearby shifted uncomfortably. "Alpha, I think she might be telling the truth. Maybe she doesn't know."

Alpha Wes sighed, almost bored, and snapped his switchblade shut.

My chest heaved. Would he finally stop? Would he finally believe me? Would Sophia finally be left to heal?

He turned back to me, locking his cold, pitiless eyes on mine. "Is that true, sweetheart?" he asked. Mocking. Amused. "You really don't know where the stone is?"

I tried to force it into him. Tried to shove my words into his mind, desperate to make him understand. *I don't know. I DON'T KNOW. Please, just stop!*

But there was no way to mindlink him.

Alpha Wes tutted, shaking his head. "It's a damn shame, sweetheart. I guess that means your friend is useless to me."

My breath stalled. *No. No, no, no—*

"I'll give you one last chance," he drawled, crouching beside Sophia again. He lifted her chin, forcing her battered face toward him. She didn't even flinch anymore. She just let him touch her.

"Sophia, sweetheart," he murmured, almost gently. Like he wasn't the same man who had spent hours torturing her. "Go ahead and ask your friend to tell you where the stone is."

Sophia barely moved. Barely breathed.

"She doesn't know," she rasped.

"Ask her out loud."

She sighed. A broken, resigned sound. She didn't even look at me when she said it. Her voice was soulless and empty. "Terri, where is the stone?"

I sobbed through the link. *Sophia, I'm so sorry. Sophia, I love you. I never wanted this to happen to you. You are my best friend, and I can't—"* My whole body trembled. *"I can't believe what he did to you. Sophia. I love you. I truly don't know where the stone is."*

She let out a small, broken sniffle before her chin dropped. "I know," she mumbled.

"What was that?" Alpha Wes's voice was louder now, laced with cruel amusement.

Sophia swallowed hard, and her shoulders quivered. In a quiet but firm voice, she forced the words out. "She doesn't know."

Sophia turned her head to me. Her expression was so soft, so accepting. Like she had already given up. Like she knew.

"T-Terri," she whispered. "I love you."

Alpha Wes flicked his wrist, signaling to his men.

The guards surrounded her, grabbing her limbs and holding her in place, as if her broken body still posed a threat.

I thrashed against my restraints, my own limbs already bruised and cut raw by the metal. But I couldn't stop. I needed to get to my friend. I needed to help her. And I would fight until the very end.

But it was futile.

Wes stepped behind her, placed his hands on either side of her head. And twisted.

The sharp, sickening crack of her neck breaking echoed through the cave, cutting through the air like a gunshot.

But Wes wasn't done. No, that wasn't enough to finish a werewolf. He flicked a hand to signal to one of his guards. The man stepped forward, pulling something from the bag they'd dragged in with Sophia.

An axe.

My heart stopped. I dry heaved. I was so frantic I began hyperventilating, gasping for air, choking on my own saliva.

They sprawled her out on the ground like a discarded animal. *I couldn't stop him.* And with one clean, merciless swing, the axe came down.

Sophia was gone.

Silence.

An oppressive, deafening silence.

My vision blurred. The world tilted.

The chains bit into me as I threw my head back and howled. A sound so raw, so broken, it didn't feel like it belonged to me. It was agony, grief, rage, every emotion I had ever felt, condensed into a single, soul-shattering scream.

Gigi cried alongside me, her own howls mixing with mine, our chains rattling as we both fought against them.

The guards only stood there, blank faced, watching us like we were nothing more than entertainment.

But I couldn't see anymore. The world was a haze of red. My best friend. My Sophia. Gone.

I kept howling as the guards hauled her body away to be burned.

She was gone.

Chapter 53

Ginger

I didn't know what to do. I didn't know what to say. I felt truly, utterly helpless.

After the howls stopped, long after they'd taken Sophia away, Terri fell into a heap and hadn't moved since. She just lay there. Her body was eerily still while her eyes stared out into nothing. Comatose.

I could still hear the snap. Still picture the way Sophia's body had hit the ground. Still hear the sound the axe made as it severed her cervical vertebrae. Still see the guards dragging her away. That moment would be forever burned in my mind. While I thought I'd gone through a lot in my life, nothing had even come close to what I'd just witnessed.

My stomach twisted with a sickening realization. When Sara had tortured that man—the one she had captured and interrogated—I had hesitated. I had tried to convince myself there had to be another way. That torture wasn't necessary. But now?

If I had known, if I had witnessed something like this first, *I would have done it*. I would have carved the answers out of his flesh without a second thought. I would have made him talk. And maybe, just maybe, we wouldn't be here right now.

I turned my head slightly and glanced at Terri. "*I—*" I started, but stopped. What could I say? *I'm sorry?* What good was that? There was no "fixing" this, no comforting words, nothing I could do to undo what had just happened.

Still, I had to try. "*Terri, I—*"

"*I think I'd rather be dead.*"

I stiffened. "*What?*"

"*It just hurts so much.*" Her voice trembled through the link. "*I lost my best friend. I watched him torture and kill her. And . . . and Nikolai . . . I can't stop wishing he was my mate. But he's gone too. He pushed me away. And it doesn't matter anyway.*"

A lump formed in my throat. "*What do you mean it doesn't matter?*"

She hesitated. She lowered her head and stared at the ground for so long that I wasn't sure she was going to answer at all. Then, finally, she replied, "*Gigi, I'm marked.*"

I blinked. "*What?*" I tried to get a look at her neck, even though I knew I wouldn't be able to tell when she was in this form.

She gazed out into the distance as she responded. "*I was marked . . . by someone. So I can't be anyone's mate now.*"

Shock ripped through me. "*Wait, what? You were marked? By who? Not by Nikolai?*"

"*Not by Nikolai. By someone else. My secret ex-boyfriend. And he was horrible. He did it against my will. I'd rather die than be with him.*"

I felt sick. "*Terri . . .*" I didn't even know where to begin. What the hell could I say to that?

She exhaled, closing her eyes. "*I can't go back to my pack, Gigi. I can't face them. Not after this. Not after . . .*" Her whole body shook. Then, slowly, she lifted her head and looked at me. Her amber eyes were once so warm and so bright. And now, they were empty, hollow. Dead.

"*Sophia was my best friend,*" she continued. "*Now she's dead because of me.*"

"*She's dead because of Alpine Snow Pack,*" I said fiercely. "*This isn't your fault.*"

She didn't answer.

"*Terri, it's not your fault.*" I tried again. Maybe if I kept saying it, she'd believe me.

She was silent, staring off into nothing. Maybe she needed space for now. I shifted, trying to get into a comfortable position, as difficult as it was. Finally, she spoke.

"*Can't you see, Gigi? It's all my fault. I should've never gotten involved with Kolya. I should have stayed away. They somehow figured out I was connected to him. I have no idea how, but they did. They knew I might know where the stone is. They figured out that Sophia is my closest friend and that if there was ever a chance I would talk, it would be through her. And I stupidly never told Tyce about when Kolya and I were attacked. Because I was trying to keep his secret. But look what happened. I wasn't even thinking at that party. It could have all been so easily prevented, and I'm . . .*" She shuddered. A sad whine escaped and echoed in the enclosure. "*I'm so stupid. I should have known better. I was trained . . .*" Her mindlink trailed off.

"*Terri, it's not your fault!*" I said with sincerity, wanting desperately for her to believe me. "*I know you think your choices led to this, but you were just making decisions based on what you knew at the time. There's no way you could've known we would end up here. And, anyway, we're the victims in this scenario. You, me, and . . .*" I hesitated, finding it hard to say her name, but I pushed through it. "*Sophia.*" I paused. My throat swelled with despair. "*They're the ones hurting us. They're making the choice to do this to us. All for what? For some stone? What's the big deal about this stone anyway?*"

Terri didn't reply. She was back in her stuporous state.

I tried to fight the frustration building in my chest. This wasn't right. The Terri I had met, the one who had always radiated happiness and warmth, was gone. In her place was a hollow shell, a ghost of the person she once was. I barely recognized her.

Sophia's death had broken her.

I turned away, swallowing the lump in my throat. The truth was, I felt just as lost. I had spent so long believing I wasn't strong enough, that I would never be a warrior, that I wasn't good enough for Tyce, too ugly in my wolf form to even show myself to the pack.

And now, all of it was proving to be true.

Because if I had been better, if I had trained harder with Sara, if I had understood earlier how evil people could be . . .

Maybe we wouldn't be here at all. Maybe I could've even gotten us out by now. I was certain Sara would know how to get out of this situation. But I was useless.

I was ashamed to take on the title of luna. I was no luna. I was just a worthless, practically human, fucked-up wolf, no-good nothing.

My jaw ached, my throat burned, my chest was tight. I was so starved, so dehydrated, and so anguished, my head was spinning.

Goddess, why hadn't I done more? I should have been smarter. Stronger.

And now Terri was blaming herself. But she shouldn't. It was my fault.

I was the one who had led us down to that basement. I'd been so fucking stupid. So trusting. Even after knowing about the wolves that had been stalking our packs. Even after Tyce had told me he didn't trust the Alpine Snow Pack. Even after the torture with Sara.

What was wrong with me?

I wanted to cry. To sob. But in this form, I couldn't.

Still, my tear ducts tingled, like they were filling with something. My eyes burned. And the longer I thought about everything, the more I stewed in my grief, my guilt, my rage, the hotter that burning became.

A sudden, penetrating heat flared behind my eyes and cut through the despair like a firecracker. I sucked in a breath as a strange sensation pulsed through me, *anger, grief, regret* all coiling into something hot. Something alive.

The air in front of me warmed.

Terri lifted her head slightly, her eyes widening as she stared at me. "*What the . . .*"

I blinked, trying to figure out what she was reacting to, then caught the faint glow reflecting off the icy ground.

Flames.

I was creating flames. They flickered from my eyes. Heat radiated outward, melting the frost-laced ground in front of me.

Terri's mindlink came again, stronger this time. "*Gigi. Your eyes. What the heck was that?*"

My pulse hammered.

"*I don't know,*" I admitted, stunned.

"*Do it again.*"

I hesitated, my heart pounding. She lifted herself slightly. Suddenly, she wasn't drowning in grief. She looked . . . hopeful.

I squeezed my eyes shut. What had triggered it? What had caused the fire?

Sophia. Her screams. The way her body crashed to the ground. The way the guards had just looked on, unaffected, amused.

The heat surged again, filling every inch of my body, curling behind my eyes like an inferno ready to burst. Dread and anguish bubbled in my chest and stomach, boiling me from the inside out.

Flames poured from my eyes, hotter, stronger, melting the frozen ground in front of us into mud.

"*Holy cannoli!*" Terri's voice rang through the link in a mix of shock and wonderment.

I panted, struggling to process what had just happened. Had I really just . . . done that? I turned to Terri, searching her expression, needing confirmation that this was real.

She blinked rapidly. Her ears perked up. Then her energy shifted. "*Wait.*"

I turned toward her "*What?*"

Her eyes locked onto mine, wide with wonder. "*Are your red eyes magical? Is that why they're red?*"

"*I . . . I don't know.*" Could that really be why?

"*Is that the first time that's ever happened?*"

I nodded, still dazed, my thoughts racing. What did this mean? Was my wolf really magical?

Terri appeared just as lost in thought, her gaze distant, unfocused. Then, something must have clicked in her mind. She turned to me so suddenly and so energetically, I flinched.

"*Gigi!*" She met my eyes, and I could feel her energy shift again. "*I remember learning something once,*" she said, her mindlink coming faster now, manic. "*If you heat metal and then cool it down rapidly, it weakens. Makes it easier to break.*"

The gears turned in my head as I caught on to what she was telling me.

"*Gigi, you can burn my chains. The cold air will cool them down quickly . . .*" She tugged at her restraints.

"*But . . .*" I hesitated, recalling the books I'd entered into the database over the summer. "*But aren't werewolves highly flammable?*"

"*Only slightly more than humans I think,*" Terri replied. " *. . . Maybe a bit more than slightly.*"

I swallowed. One wrong move, and I could set her on fire.

This was too much pressure. I had just learned I could even do this. What if I couldn't control it? At the same time, this was our ticket out of this hellhole.

"*Let me practice first,*" I said. "*I need to make sure I can aim.*"

"*Try for that rock!*" Terri pointed with her snout at a small stone, partially buried in the ground with the top sticking out.

I locked my gaze on it, concentrating. I thought back to everything that had happened. Let the devastation consume me, let it pool behind my eyes, stinging, burning.

And then, just like before, when I felt like my body couldn't handle any more—

The flames came again.

They landed exactly where I was looking, bouncing off the exposed rock, heating it until it glowed.

This could work! We're getting out of here!

A surge of adrenaline shot through me, wiping away some of the exhaustion weighing me down. I inhaled deeply, straightening myself despite the tightness in my chest. "*Tell me what to do.*"

Terri twisted her body slightly, stretching out the chain attached to her back leg closest to me, giving me the best possible angle and the most room to work with.

"*Focus on this,*" she instructed, pulling the restraint taut. "*Heat it as much as you can, but the moment it glows red, stop. I'll pull it apart before it cools completely.*"

I nodded, trying to steady my breathing. My body trembled from hunger, from exhaustion, from the sheer strain of what I was about to do—but I shoved it all aside.

I focused.

I let myself sink into every ounce of pain I had ever felt. I thought about the day I lost my wolf. The day I saw its exposed skeleton, its grotesque form. My own freakish reflection staring back at me with eerie red irises.

My body heated from the inside out. A violent surge of energy coiled in my core.

Then, flames.

They burst from my eyes, slamming into the chain, turning the metal a molten red. I gasped and snapped my eyes shut.

Terri wrenched at the chains with everything she had, muscles straining, claws digging into the cold earth for leverage. But it wasn't enough.

"*Again,*" she urged.

I sucked in a breath, digging deeper, dragging up every dark thought I could reach. Every rejection. Every whispered insult. Every moment I had felt like I wasn't enough.

Flames surged again, scorching the metal until it glowed.

We continued, doing the same thing over and over again. Going at it until finally, Terri roared as she pulled with all her strength. The metal groaned, then, with a sharp crack, it gave way.

Clunk.

The broken chain crashed to the floor.

I gasped. We both shook with barely contained energy. Terri's eyes flooded with excitement that matched my own.

It worked.

We didn't have time to celebrate, not yet. I immediately turned to the next restraint.

One by one, I burned. She pulled. The chains snapped.

But with every round, it got harder. My vision blurred at the edges. My stomach twisted with hunger so intense it was painful. My entire body felt like it was running on fumes, my reserves of energy flickering like a dying candle.

Yet I pushed through.

We were so close.

When we reached the final chain, I could barely hold myself upright. I was dizzy, weak, my breaths unsteady. Flames sputtered from my eyes in shorter bursts now, the strength behind them waning. My body was failing.

But I forced one more surge of heat. One last burst of power.

The chain flared red-hot.

Terri snarled, throwing her entire weight into her final pull.

CRACK.

The last chain snapped.

With a gasp, Terri stumbled forward, her legs shaking beneath her as the heavy metal links crashed onto the frozen floor.

She was free!

Chapter 54

Theresa

The sound of approaching voices sent a jolt of urgency through me.

"*Gigi, stay quiet. Act normal,*" I mindlinked, my body going rigid as my ears flicked toward the entrance. "*I'm going to pretend I'm still chained.*"

I hurried back to my original location and quickly arranged the chains and myself to appear as if I were still bound.

The heavy gate creaked open, scraping against the ground.

Two guards stepped inside, the scent of their sweat and stale breath clinging to the cold air around them. They weren't cautious. Weren't paying attention. They weren't expecting anything.

The taller one, a stocky man with a thick brown beard, carried a metal tray with more dog food and water.

The other, a wiry-looking man with red stubble, muttered something under his breath as he picked up the untouched bowls in front of us.

The stocky guard replaced them with the new bowls. "Eat up, bitch-es."

I didn't move, didn't even react. I waited.

They turned their backs.

In one swift motion, I lunged.

The redhead had barely taken a step before my claws slammed into his back, sinking deep into the thick down of his coat. He choked out a stunned gasp, but it was already too late. My jaws snapped shut around his neck, slicing through skin, muscle, and bone. The sickening sound of his vertebrae splitting under my sharp teeth cracked through the air.

His head separated cleanly from his shoulders before he could make a sound.

Blood sprayed in hot, pulsing bursts, painting the dirt floor and my fur. The scent of iron flooded my nostrils.

One down.

But I hardly had time to register the kill before the second guard spun toward me, his face twisted in shock. Then instinct took over.

He shifted.

The sound of bones snapping, flesh tearing, clothes shredding to pieces as thick gray fur erupted from his skin echoed through the cave. Feathers spilled into the air, floating around us as if we were in a snow globe.

And then he lunged.

He crashed into me like a boulder. We hit the dirt floor hard, tumbling over each other in a violent clash of claws and teeth. He snapped at my throat, grazing the sensitive skin just beneath my jaw. I jerked away, twisting, and instead of my throat, his jaws closed around my shoulder.

I snarled as the pain of his teeth puncturing my flesh stabbed through my body. But I had no time to focus on the pain. With a vicious growl, I twisted beneath him and kicked. Hard.

My back paws struck his stomach, knocking the wind out of him and sending him sprawling backward.

I was on my feet in an instant, claws skidding against the blood-slicked floor as I dodged his next attack. He came at me fast, barreling forward, but I dropped low at the last second and slammed into his ribs, knocking him sideways.

The impact sent us both tumbling into the cave wall, dust and ice crumbling from above. He recovered fast, shaking himself off, his glowing eyes locked onto me.

Then he charged at me again.

We collided. His claws raked across my ribs, tearing through fur and skin. I growled, as the harsh, piercing twinge of the wound pounded through me, but I pushed past it, running on pure adrenaline.

Why hadn't I picked off the bigger one first?

He was strong. But I was faster.

I darted to the side, feinting left before striking right. My teeth sank deep into his flank. He howled, twisting to shake me off, but I held firm, tearing through muscle and sinew before he finally managed to throw me off.

I hit the ground hard, rolling to a stop, but I didn't stay down.

Before he could recover, before he could shift tactics, I launched myself at him again.

This time, I aimed for his throat.

But he anticipated it. At the last second, he jerked back and I missed. He lunged for me again. We struggled, his claws slashing at my sides, my back, my legs, shredding fur, drawing more blood. He twisted, throwing his weight into me, and I hit the ground with him on top of me, his jaws snapping inches from my face.

I kicked and clawed, fighting to get the upper hand. Fighting to survive.

Then, I saw my opening.

His weight shifted just slightly, just enough.

With everything I had, I slammed my head upward, cracking my skull against his jaw. He reeled back with a yelp, momentarily stunned.

That was all I needed.

I was finally able to use the claws of my front paw to tear into his torso, pushing past muscle, past ribs, until I found what I was looking for. I had never done this with a wolf before, but I had practiced enough times on prey that I figured it out easily enough.

My paw found his slick, pulsing heart. My claws clenched around the dense-yet-soft organ, and I tugged, tearing it from veins and arteries until it was freed from his warm body.

He gasped. His body seized.

The bloody muscle spasmed one last time, just a twitch, before it finally went still. The full weight of his body dropped on me. I let out a loud grunt from the impact as the slippery organ rolled out of my grasp.

For a moment, there was nothing. Then he convulsed once. And stilled.

A gush of hot blood spilled over me as I shoved his lifeless body off me. His weight hit the ground with a dull thud.

It was over.

On shaky legs, I pushed myself upright. My vision swam. Every inch of me burned. I was torn, bruised, and bleeding.

But I was alive.

I stood there, panting, blood dripping from my fur, my body shaking with exhaustion.

Then I turned to Gigi.

She stared at me, wide-eyed but ready.

We had to move.

I searched the guards' bodies quickly, sniffing until I found a key in the pocket of the first man I'd killed. The size of it told me it had to be the gate key. There was no possible way it would fit into the cuffs around our limbs. I put it aside and continue my search.

But I came up empty-pawed. The only other keys I was able to locate were very clearly house and car keys. Which did us no good.

They hadn't brought the keys to unlock our chains.

I let out a frustrated sigh. It probably would have been useless anyway. It wasn't like I had opposable thumbs in this form. I couldn't even see an obvious way I'd be able to unlock the gate. And the cuffs were still wrapped around my legs, with chain links hanging from them, preventing me from shifting into my human form.

I locked eyes with Gigi.

We were going to have to burn her chains apart too. I mindlinked her my thoughts.

She gave me a nod, though I could see the exhaustion in her stance. She was swaying slightly, her breaths shallow and uneven.

"*I can do it,*" she mindlinked.

"*Let me help,*" I responded, stepping closer.

I used my teeth to grab one of the chains binding her, pulling it away from her body, holding it taut. "*Now. Do it now.*"

She gritted her teeth and closed her eyes. Her body trembled. For a moment, nothing happened. Then—

Flames.

They flared to life, flicking along the metal links. Heat radiated against my muzzle, dangerously close to my own fur, but I held still, refusing to let go. The chain glowed red-hot. And when the flames stopped, I pulled as hard as I could.

When they didn't break, she went again, flaming her own chain. She did it again and again until, finally, the metal snapped apart.

We moved as quickly as possible, repeating the process for each of her limbs until the chains lay in broken heaps on the floor.

She swayed.

I caught her before she could collapse, my body bracing hers. "*You okay?*"

She let out a ragged breath, shaking her head. "*Dizzy. Really dizzy.*"

She had burned through everything she had left. My gaze flicked to the bowl. The dog food.

It was disgusting. But . . . it was food.

"*Gigi, you have to eat.*"

Her body tensed. "*No way.*"

"*You don't have a choice.*" My voice was firm. "*You're about to pass out. And if you pass out, we're not getting out of here.*"

She swallowed, looking between me and the food.

Then, finally, she let out a defeated sigh. And she ate. I stood guard while she forced it down, my ears twitching toward the entrance every few seconds, listening for movement. She gagged after the first few bites, shuddering as she chewed. The smell alone was bad enough, but the texture, I could only imagine, had to be worse.

Honestly, I was so hungry, I was almost at the point of joining her.

Once the bowl was empty, she finished with a dramatic cough, then lapped at the water, practically inhaling all of it in one go.

"*I swear to the Goddess, if you ever tell anyone I did that . . .*" she started, voice hoarse.

I lifted a paw solemnly. "*I'd never!*"

Her eyes narrowed. "*Oh Goddess,* definitely *don't tell Tyce. He'd bring it up* every single time *we did doggy.*"

I recoiled. "*I DID NOT NEED THAT IMAGE IN MY HEAD.*"

She grinned wickedly, licking her lips. "*Good. Now we're both suffering.*"

I scrunched my nose at her, shaking my head. But the moment of levity was short-lived. The air in the cave was thick with the coppery tang of blood mingling with the damp, musty scent of wet stone and decay. The bodies of the guards lay where they had fallen, their lifeless forms already stiffening from the beginning stages of decomposition.

It wouldn't take long before someone came looking for them. We were on borrowed time.

An idea hit me.

"*Gigi, we need to burn the bodies.*" My mindlink was urgent. "*If we get rid of them, maybe no one will realize they were killed. At least not right away.*"

Her brow furrowed as she considered it. "*But . . . the alpha will know they're dead.*"

I nodded. "*Yeah. But if we destroy the evidence, he won't necessarily know it was us. At least not immediately. That buys us time.*"

Her expression hardened with understanding, and without hesitation, she squared her shoulders and stepped toward the first corpse, the one with a gaping hole in his torso.

I watched as her eyes glowed and flames burst forth. This time, the fire took on a blue hue, clearly stronger now that she'd finally eaten. At first, the body refused to ignite. Without accelerants like gasoline or kerosene, it took time. But eventually, the fire caught, its hungry tendrils licking the limbs, curling over the corpse like a vengeful spirit. At least once a werewolf caught fire, it would burn all the way to the bones, leaving nothing behind.

As soon as the flames devoured the first guard, she turned her focus on the second, the beheaded one. Again, it took multiple attempts, but finally, the fire spread, consuming the remains.

My ears flicked toward the entrance. Time was running out.

"*We need to move,*" I said, my frustration creeping into my mindlink. "*I just can't figure out how to maneuver the key into the lock without opposable thumbs, and my body's too big to fit through the bars.*"

Gigi turned toward the exit, her ears twitching, expression hardening as she came to the same realization.

I let out a loud exhale. "*I think our best bet is to do what we did with the chains. Heat the metal, weaken it, and pull it apart until it breaks and we can make a big enough gap to fit through.*"

She met my gaze, her eyes sparking with purpose.

"*Okay,*" she said. She shook herself off, standing tall.

Determination surged between us.

Here went nothing.

Chapter 55

Nikolai

I'd seen that look before. I recognized it instantly.

Tyce's entire body went rigid. His breath caught in his throat. Something unseen, tragic, passed through him. His fists clenched into balls, and his face twisted, eyes squeezing shut as he braced against it. Then, just as quickly as it came, it was gone.

He blinked a few times, then collapsed into the hotel chair like his legs had given out.

"Tyce?" I approached him cautiously.

For a moment, he looked lost. Like a child searching for something just out of reach, grasping for answers that wouldn't come. Vulnerability flickered across his face.

Then, his expression hardened.

"Sophia's dead," he said in a flat voice. With a heavy sigh, he dragged a hand down his face.

I stared at him. "Dead?"

"Dead," he repeated. His jaw clenched so tight a muscle twitched beneath his cheek. "*Fuck*."

"Fuck," I echoed, the weight of it settling over us like a dark cloud.

Tyce let out a loud exhale. "Terri's hysteria . . . that must be why. It has to be. And look." He nodded toward Joe, who was now rolling around in the bed, moaning. "You know who would be freaking the fuck out right now? Someone who just watched their best friend get killed."

I nodded grimly. The moment hit far too close to home.

Suddenly, I saw myself in Joe. I saw the hollow wreckage I had become after losing my pack, my friends, my family. It was a pain I wouldn't wish on anyone. And now, Terri was experiencing it. I wasn't there. Bile rose in my throat. My stomach churned. I needed to get to her. I needed to make sure she was okay.

I sank onto the bed, mirroring Tyce's posture. Neither of us spoke. The silence stretched between us, broken only by Joe's quiet moans.

Tyce folded over. His elbows dug into his knees, and his hands gripped his head. His breathing was shallow and uneven, like he was struggling to hold himself together by sheer force of will.

"I've known her since I was a kid," he finally said in a raw voice. "She was like a second sister to me."

His fingers curled into a fist, and he pressed it against his mouth, biting down onto it. His shoulders rose and fell with short, gasping breaths.

I reached over and squeezed his shoulder, offering silent acknowledgment of his grief.

His breath hitched. A sharp, choked pant tore from his throat.

"Is okay to cry," I told him. If anyone understood this kind of pain, it was me.

His jaw clenched, and his body went rigid with resistance. "I'm not a little bitch," he muttered.

I turned slightly, catching a glimpse of his face. His eyes were blood-shot now, rimmed red, the first tears slipping down his cheeks. He swiped at them so fast, so aggressively, like he was trying to erase the evidence before it could betray him.

"Just got something in my eye," he said hoarsely.

I arched a brow. "I think I am supposed to give you hug now."

"Don't hug me." He shot me a glare and punched my shoulder, though it lacked any real force. "Tell me to buck up or something. Stop being a pussy."

"Tyce, is okay."

"Give me a whipping, then. Now."

"Who do I look like, your father?"

"You're an alpha. Close enough." His voice cracked on the last word, but he covered it up with a forced laugh.

I shook my head.

The tension broke, just slightly, but we both turned when we noticed Joe had stopped writhing. He was no longer moaning, no longer rolling in agony. Instead, he lay on his back, staring at the ceiling.

"Hey, Joe?" I called out.

His head turned slowly toward us.

"Is Terri okay?"

He swallowed, blinking as if he'd only just realized we were in the room. He took a long breath before answering. "No . . . she's not. She's in a lot of pain."

Tyce leaned forward, rubbing his face hard before exhaling. "But can you tell where she is now?"

Joe hesitated and looked around. Then, slowly, he sat up. He rolled his shoulders back, straightening. "Yeah. I think so."

We loaded into the SUV Tyce had rented. It was one of those massive, blacked-out vehicles that could plow through just about anything. Beta Liam drove while Tyce sat in the passenger seat. Joe stayed in the second row with me, and Ivan, Eddie, and Tanner squeezed into the back row.

"Definitely west," Joe muttered, giving directions.

Liam did his best to find roads that followed Joe's intuition while Tyce kept glancing toward the back to make sure Joe was doing his job.

After his latest instruction, Tyce turned back toward the front as he made sense of the map on the GPS, to figure out where we were heading.

"Right up there," Joe said.

Tyce looked up as Liam was about to make the turn.

"Fucking Artemis!" he barked. "Stop the car!"

Liam slammed on the brakes. The SUV skidded onto the shoulder, jolting all of us forward against our seatbelts.

Tyce pressed his fingers against his temples before twisting in his seat to face us. "We can't go any farther. I know where this road leads. This is the main road to Alpine Snow Pack. We roll in now, we're dead. We're outnumbered."

He wasn't wrong. Walking blindly into enemy territory was suicide.

"We need a plan." He raked a hand through his hair.

Everyone started talking at once, spitting out half-formed ideas, most of them useless. We were all well aware of how difficult it was to get past the guards most packs had lining the border, keeping watch.

I thought back to Ukraine, to the ways we used to infiltrate enemy territories back home. I smirked. Talking over everyone, I said, "Back in Ukraine, we had man roll in animal shit before sneaking into enemy land. Hides the scent."

Eddie made a disgusted noise in the back. "You're joking."

Everyone else burst into laughter.

Tyce, though, just stared at me. His expression was unreadable, until suddenly, he let out a humorless laugh. "You know what? That might actually work." He turned to Joe with a wicked grin. "And we have the perfect guy for the job."

Joe went rigid. "What . . . Goddess, no," he mumbled.

Tyce ignored him, already deep in thought. "Joe's the only one who can find Terri anyway."

Joe groaned but didn't argue.

"Okay, so that covers Joe. But I need a way in." Tyce frowned, drumming his fingers against the dashboard. Then, suddenly, he leaned back, smirking. "Keira."

Liam's head snapped toward him. "Wait! The Keira?"

Tyce's smirk grew. "The one with an ass like a dump truck?"

Ivan snorted.

"Who the hell is Keira?" I asked.

Tyce waved a hand. "An old hookup. Part of Alpine Snow, used to hit her up when I came through for supply runs. Always left her satisfied, so she should be more than happy to give me a ride into the pack."

Liam pushed on Tyce's shoulder. "And what if she isn't happy to see you? You ghosted her, didn't you?"

Tyce scoffed. "I didn't ghost her. I just . . . never texted her again."

"That's literally ghosting."

Tyce rolled his eyes. "She'll still say yes. Trust me."

Liam still didn't look convinced. "And if she doesn't?"

Tyce flashed a cocky grin. "She will."

I stared at him. "This is your big plan?"

"Got a better one?"

I sighed. "So, we send Joe covered in shit, and you go with booty call?"

"Basically."

I pinched the bridge of my nose. "This is stupidest plan I ever agree to."

Tyce clapped me on the knee. "And yet, it's going to work."

Liam let out a long breath. "If we die because of your ex, I'm haunting your ass."

Tyce pulled out his phone and scrolled through his contacts, grinning when he must have found the right number. His thumbs flew across the screen.

"For the record, I'm only *insinuating* this is going to be a hookup," Tyce said loudly, then cleared his throat. "Just in case Gigi ever questions what went down."

"Yo, why's her number still in your phone?" Eddie called out from the back.

"Hey, hey, hey!" Tyce shouted in response. "We're getting in thanks to my exes living in my text-es."

Chapter 56

Tyson

Joe trudged ahead of us, his posture stiff with resentment, while Nikolai and I strolled behind him. We skirted the forest, sticking to paths as trekking through knee-deep snow wasn't quite as easy in our human forms as in our wolf ones. His entire body radiated bitterness, and honestly, I couldn't blame him. If I were in his position, I'd feel the same. But that didn't mean he didn't deserve what he had coming.

"Will this even work?" Joe grumbled.

Nikolai shrugged. "In Ukraine, this work maybe . . . half time only."

Joe's steps faltered. His face blanched. "What?"

"Well, it's a 100 percent chance that you're rolling in it. So I'd say your odds aren't looking great," I taunted. "And let's be real, at this point, the only thing keeping you alive is your usefulness to us."

Joe muttered a curse under his breath but kept walking, probably debating whether survival was even worth it at this point.

Luckily, moose were abundant in Anchorage, so it wasn't long before we stumbled upon exactly what we were looking for, a still-steaming pile of shit.

Nikolai grimaced, scrunching his nose. "Is . . . very fresh."

"Nice!" I grinned.

Joe gagged audibly and staggered back with his hands raised in a desperate bid for mercy. "No—no, no, no . . . Wait—"

I unleashed my alpha aura. "Get in there."

The effect was instant. His face contorted in a mix of horror and defiance as he fought against the crushing weight of my command. His shoulders trembled, his legs braced, and his heels dug deep into the snow like he could somehow resist the inevitable. "F-Fuck . . . you . . ." His voice was strangled, every syllable squeezed through gritted teeth. His fingers twitched like they wanted to ball into fists, but even that was ripped from his control.

Then, his knees buckled. For a second, he fought it. His entire frame quivered under the weight of my aura. But the moment his balance wavered, he lost. His legs crumpled, slamming him onto all fours. A pained, guttural sound escaped his throat. His whole body shook violently, fighting my command with everything he had. But he was fighting gravity itself. It was pointless.

His arms gave out next, sending him face-first into the pile.

Joe let out something between a gag and a strangled whimper as his entire front was smeared in thick, steaming moose shit.

Nikolai and I lost it. Laughter tore out of us, unrestrained.

Joe panted, trying to push himself up, as the pile of shit pulled him toward itself like a magnet.

"Oh, come on!" I called out, barely able to breathe through my amusement. "You're not even trying! Roll like you mean it!"

Joe let out a noise of pure suffering. But with my aura forcing him, he had no choice. He flopped onto his side like a dying fish and could do nothing but obey, dragging himself through it in slow, miserable motions.

"You missed a spot," Nikolai added.

Joe's head snapped toward him, eyes burning with murder. "Both of you can eat shit," he growled, right before his face smashed back into the pile.

This might have been the best mission I'd ever been on.

"I think your hair could use some shampooing," I mused. Then, with another pulse of my alpha command, I added, "Really cake it in there."

Joe's entire body tensed before he groaned in agony, grabbing fistfuls of the filth and smearing it through his hair like he was in a fucking Herbal Essences commercial.

Nikolai snorted. "Do not forget to wash face after."

"You heard him," I added.

Joe's eyes bulged, his brows furrowing in pure rage, but his hands moved against his will, rubbing moose excrement into his own face.

"You know what Gigi told me?" I said conversationally, turning to Nikolai. "She saw on TikTok that some men don't wash their asses." I tutted at Joe. "We can't have that. Rub your ass in that shit, bro. Get it between the cheeks."

Joe looked like he was about to slaughter us, but he was powerless as he rolled his ass in the dung, grinding into it like he had the world's itchiest bottom.

At this point, Nikolai and I were crying with laughter, struggling to breathe as we doubled over, barely able to steal glances at each other without completely losing it again.

Joe, humiliated and covered head to toe in moose shit, panted. His body shook with barely restrained rage.

And then, just as he started climbing to his feet, just as he thought the worst was over . . .

A sick, twisted satisfaction settled in my chest. After suffering for days, desperate to get to my mate, I needed this. I needed to take my frustrations out on someone. Someone who didn't deserve my mercy. Someone who had ruined my sister's life.

Maybe a better man would have stopped there. Would have let him suffer just enough before pulling back. But I wasn't a better man.

I hit him with one last command.

"One more for good luck."

Joe's eyes bulged in sheer, unfiltered horror, his lips parting in protest. But his body betrayed him before he could even get the words out. With an agonized, soul-crushing groan, he flopped back down and rolled through the shit one last time.

Nikolai actually had to lean against a tree for support, wheezing.

Joe, now utterly defeated, lay still for a second, staring up at the sky like he was contemplating every decision that had ever led him to this moment. Then, hoarse and barely above a whisper, he muttered, "I will never forgive either of you."

Nikolai immediately sobered, his laughter cutting off as he leveled Joe with a sharp glare. "That make three of us, little bitch. Or as we say in Ukraine, *suchonok*."

Then I finally released my alpha hold on him. His body shuddered as the weight of my aura lifted, and he slowly crawled out of the filth, breathing hard.

He turned and glared daggers at both of us.

For a second, I wondered if he was stupid enough to try something, if his humiliation had reached the point where he lost his survival instincts and thought taking a swing at us was a good idea.

But, to his credit, he wasn't a complete moron.

"Now," I said as I flooded him with as much alpha aura as I could dole out, knowing I'd need it to hold for a longer period of time. "Go find Terri. Get inside the pack's territory. Don't get caught."

Joe grimaced, and his body bowed under the force of my command, instinctively baring his neck in submission. His face contorted in agony. He immediately spun on his heels, his instincts pulling him forward as he followed the road toward Terri.

I watched until he disappeared into the distance, then clapped my hands together.

"Well"—I smirked, turning to Nikolai—"seems like *Plan Moose Kaka* was a success."

Nikolai snorted.

I grinned and pulled out my phone, my smirk widening when I saw the new notification waiting for me.

Keira

> **Look who always comes crawling back for more ;)**

I quickly typed my response.

Tyce

> Meet at our usual spot in 20

I shoved my phone back into my pocket and stretched my arms.

"All right," I said, turning to Nikolai. "Time for *Plan Booty*. Let's move."

He shook his head, muttering something in Russian that I was pretty sure translated to "You're a menace."

I grinned wider. "Damn right."

Liam knew exactly where to drop me. This wasn't our first rodeo.

"All right," I said, scanning the faces around me one last time. "Everyone clear on the plan?"

A few nods. Some muttered confirmations. I could feel the weight of their attention locked onto me, waiting for my final word.

"I'll sneak into Alpine Snow and find Joe," I continued. "Once I have him, he'll lead me to Terri. Since I have no idea where she is, we'll have to figure it out as we go." I glanced at Liam. "You're our communication line since we can both link in human form. The rest of you stay on standby in case this turns into a full-blown dumpster fire."

Liam exhaled audibly. "This is already a dumpster fire."

He wasn't wrong.

No one spoke after that. The tension was thick, heavy with unspoken thoughts.

I yanked open the SUV door and stepped out. A sharp, biting wind cut straight through my jacket, stinging my face as my boots crunched in the snow. I shoved my hands into my pockets, keeping my shoulders loose, my head down.

Barely a minute later, the familiar growl of an old white Honda CR-V echoed in the distance. Its tires crunched over the icy pavement as it crept toward me. The car pulled onto the shoulder, idling for a moment before the driver's side door swung open with force.

"Tyson. Fucking. Tikaani."

Keira.

She strode toward me like she owned the damn road, her hips swaying, a cocky smirk playing on her glossy lips. "Didn't think I'd ever see you again."

"Miss me?" I teased, flashing my best grin.

She chuckled. "Not as much as you missed me."

There was a time I might have. But now? Now, all I could think about was getting to Gigi. Keira was gorgeous with thick, dangerous curves accentuated by a snug winter coat and a skin-tight pencil skirt that didn't leave much to the imagination. But she didn't do it for me anymore.

Still, I slid an arm around her waist, guiding her back toward the car. And, because I'm me, I made sure to flash the guys in the SUV down the road a big ol' thumbs-up behind her back.

I could practically feel their jealous stares burning into me as they got an eyeful of Keira's legendary ass swaying in front of them.

What? You thought I was just gonna walk away without flexing what I used to hit?

"So, what brings you into town, *Alpha*?" she asked, drawing my title out flirtatiously.

I opened the driver's side door for her. "Come on. I'll tell you on the way."

She slid into the seat, and I walked around to the passenger side, my smirk fading as my mind shifted back to the real reason I was here.

Getting past the Alpine Snow Pack gates was almost too easy with her fob. No questions asked. Just like old times.

Once we were close to her place, I shifted slightly in my seat. Time to drop the bomb.

"So," I said casually, "I actually called you because there's something I wanted to tell you in person . . ."

"Sounds serious." She giggled. "Is this you trying to get me to agree to making a home video again?"

"I met my fated mate. I'm engaged. Getting married in a couple months."

The car swerved violently.

"ARE YOU FUCKING KIDDING ME?!" Keira shrieked, slamming on the brakes. My head snapped forward and nearly hit the dashboard.

"Damn, woman!" I shouted, bracing myself.

She turned on me, eyes blazing. "So you mean to tell me I drove all the way out there, picked your sorry ass up, brought you here"—she gestured wildly, narrowly avoiding taking my eye out—"just for you to tell me you met your mate?!"

I rubbed the back of my neck. "Yeah, in hindsight, a text probably would've worked too."

Keira screamed then slapped the ever-loving shit out of me. My head snapped to the side, my cheek burning from the impact.

"Get. The fuck. Out of my car!" she seethed.

I didn't argue. Opened the door. Slid out. Barely shut it before she peeled off, tires screeching.

The second she was out of sight, I grinned and fist-pumped the air.

Success!

I scurried away from the road, crunching through the snow as the taillights disappeared in the distance. The cold bit at my ears, but I barely noticed. My heart was pounding with the familiar rush of pulling off some reckless, questionably ethical, undeniably effective shit.

I ducked behind a tree, pressed myself into the shadows, and reached out with a mindlink.

"Joe. Talk to me. Where's Terri?"

Chapter 57

Theresa

Gigi gritted her teeth, her eyes burning a molten red as she focused on the metal bars in front of us. The icy air hissed and crackled as her flames licked the frozen steel, the grates slowly turning a dull orange under the intense heat.

I pressed my shoulder against the gate, muscles straining and claws digging into the frozen ground.

The metal groaned.

I felt it shift—just barely—but enough to make my heart leap. I braced my paws, shoving with everything I had. The bars shuddered, bending just a fraction more. But it wasn't enough.

Gigi gasped. Her eyes flickered with exhaustion setting in. The flames sputtered and weakened.

After another agonizing attempt, I stumbled back and shook out my limbs, trying to ignore the bone-deep fatigue creeping in.

Gigi sagged against the metal, panting hard. *I need a break.*

I let out a deep breath and nodded. She was right. The fire had done some damage, but not nearly enough. And if we burned through our strength now, we wouldn't stand a chance if—no, *when*—Alpha Wes arrived.

I lay down, my ears twitching, listening for something beyond the eerie silence that surrounded us. My body buzzed with adrenaline, ready to spring at the first sign of movement. *"He'll definitely be coming soon,"* I muttered.

Gigi's tail flicked. She didn't respond, but I saw the same thought reflected in her weary eyes.

Then, something . . . odd . . . wafted through the air. Swampy, fermented, sour grass. Pungent and barnyard-like.

I lifted my nose and inhaled. *Moose poop?*

Gigi sniffed as well. Then gagged. *"What the hell?"*

The scent was overwhelming. Thick, rancid. And it was getting closer.

A shadow shifted beyond the gate. Before long, a figure emerged.

I went rigid. My muscles locked as a different kind of nausea took hold.

I would have recognized that scent anywhere, even masked by the foul odor. I would have recognized *him* anywhere.

My ex-boyfriend stood on the other side of the gate.

Covered. Head to toe. In moose poop.

My brain short-circuited.

I couldn't believe it at first. I had to be hallucinating. This had to be a dream. I hadn't eaten in days. At some point, I did consider eating the dog food, but Gigi had already eaten it all.

I pawed at myself, clawing at my leg. The prick broke the skin and sent a hot sting racing through my nerves and blood dripping down my leg.

Nope. Definitely awake.

Okay, then I was becoming *delirious.*

"Terri?" Joe's voice cracked with disbelief.

I just stared at him. His eyes were wild, his hands shaking.

What. The. Heck.

He blinked rapidly as if he couldn't believe what he was seeing. Then his face shifted, eyes softening, mouth parting. "Oh my Goddess, Terri!" His voice rose in alarm. "What happened? Why are you covered in blood?

Are you okay? Oh Goddess, I'm so glad I found you. I'm so glad you're alive."

I didn't move.

I didn't speak.

I just . . . *watched* him.

How was he here? *Why* was he here?

"*Do you know him?*" Gigi's mindlink broke through my spiraling thoughts, her head tilting in confusion.

My gaze flicked between her and Joe, my heartbeat thundering in my chest.

This wasn't happening.

This *couldn't* be happening.

"*Joe?*" I finally mindlinked, my voice slow, measured. "*What are you doing here?*"

He swayed slightly. His skin was clammy. His fingers twitched at his sides. His face twisted in something that resembled longing, desperation. "I missed you so much! I'm so glad you're okay." His voice grew more frantic. "Please, Terri. As I've said in my texts, I *can't force you*, but I'm trying to go above and beyond to show you that you're special to me, that things will be *permanently* different if you just give me another chance. I *can't control* if you will, but at least I tried *everything* I could. You're avoiding me, and that's disappointing because you're not even letting me *prove* that I've changed. I understand why I upset you, but it *will* be different. I swear—"

I flinched.

This wasn't happening.

"—I'm honestly *attracted* to you, Terri. I think you're *beautiful*. I know I messed up, but I've *changed*. I got rid of all my flaws, kept my good traits—"

"*Stop!*" I finally cut him off, my mindlink laced with pure exasperation, my stomach *churning*.

What was happening? *Why is he here?*

Gigi turned to me, her eyes wide. "*What the fuck is going on?*"

Then, amongst all the chaos, the confusion, the *randomness*, a very lucid thought came to me. *The key!* I had the key to the gate! I could hand it to Joe, and he could let us free!

I turned to go grab it, already envisioning our freedom. But as I dipped my head to scoop it from the ground where I'd left it . . .

A blur of movement.

Joe turned, and his eyes locked onto a massive figure emerging from the shadows. The blood drained from his face.

The hit came too fast for him to even react.

Alpha Wes's fist met his stomach with brutal force, and Joe crumpled instantly. His body hit the frozen ground with a heavy thud. His skull and the icy stone collided with a loud *crack*.

My blood ran cold.

The towering man stepped forward, his green eyes glinting with malice and amusement.

Alpha Wes.

He took his time. His gaze lazily dragged over Gigi and me like we were nothing more than an inconvenience.

"Well, well, well." His voice dripped with boredom. "Looks like some wild animals got loose."

I bared my teeth. Every hair on my body stood on end. I *knew* I had no real chance against him, not in this weak, half-starved state. But I wasn't about to let him see my fear. I wasn't about to go down without a fight.

He sighed dramatically. "What does a man have to do to get a nap around here?" He stretched his neck and rolled his shoulders like this whole situation was a personal offense. "Now I have to deal with *this* nonsense."

That was when I noticed it.

Beneath his heavy coat, he wasn't even dressed for a fight. He was wearing silk pajama pants.

Of *course* he was.

I will not die at the hands of a man in silk fricking pants.

Summoning every last shred of strength I had left, I squared my stance, lifted my head, and locked onto him with my fiercest alpha glare.

Gigi followed my lead, but where I had to *pretend* to be terrifying, she actually *was* terrifying.

Her wolf appeared as if she'd been summoned from the underworld, complete with exposed bones and glowing, haunting red eyes. She looked like she'd crawled straight out of a nightmare. A vengeful demon, ready to claim the souls of her enemies.

Alpha Wes chuckled. *Chuckled.*

"You think you scare me?" He shook his head, utterly unimpressed. "You have no idea who you're dealing with." He raised a hand, lazily flexing his fingers. "All I have to do is snap, and an army will be here before you can blink. And you can't mindlink anyone outside this cave from in here, even if there *were* anyone to mindlink."

He tapped a finger against the stone. "That's why we use this place," he said with a grin. "The walls are thick with magnetite and quartz. Impenetrable." He chuckled again. "Your screams don't go anywhere."

I exhaled slowly. My body buzzed with tension. My heart hammered against my ribs.

Gigi's snarl deepened. Her body was rigid, poised. But then something flickered in her eyes. A shift. A spark of something volatile, something dangerous. The air around us thickened. I instantly understood where Gigi's mind had gone, and a lightness fell over me.

Alpha Wes smirked, unaware of the force about to be unleashed upon him. He was so confident, so self-assured in his dominance, that he never even considered us a threat.

Gigi's gaze flicked lower.

Directly to his crotch.

I saw it moments before it happened. The way her red eyes darkened to something molten, something alive. Heat rippled outward, distorting the air like a mirage.

Wes chuckled, shaking his head, completely oblivious.

WHOOSH.

His pants ignited in an instant.

At first, he didn't even realize it. The flames spread too fast, too hungrily. The silk fabric of his ridiculous pajama pants took to the flames immediately, golden-blue fire feeding ravenously on them.

Alpha Wes's laugh faltered. His nose twitched. He glanced down. Confusion flickered across his face. Then horror.

A bloodcurdling scream tore from his throat.

He stumbled backward, his body jerking violently as fire raced down his legs and spread upward toward his torso. His hands slapped wildly at his thighs, but the flames only spread faster, creeping up his abdomen, engulfing his arms.

The scent of burning hair hit me first, followed by the sizzle of flesh.

His face twisted into a grotesque mask of agony.

"HELP!" he shrieked, thrashing, rolling, trying anything to smother the flames.

But it was futile. Once flames latched onto a werewolf body, you were as good as dead. His flesh blistered, the sickening pop of bursting skin filling the air. His legs were like overcooked meat. His charred hands grasping at nothing.

The smell of scorched, burning skin, organs, and fat thickened in the air, sinking into my fur, filling my lungs.

Alpha Wes tried to run, but he stumbled backward. His knees buckled. He crashed to the ground, his hands clawing at the dirt, leaving deep, blackened furrows where his fingers used to be. He attempted to crawl.

His raw and primal howls rang out, and the cave walls carried his agony, amplifying it.

His wild and panicked eyes darted to Gigi and me. The flames climbed higher, curling around his throat. Then his screams weakened. His body convulsed. He slumped forward.

His voice died in his throat as the fire crawled up his jaw. His head tilted back. His mouth opened again.

The scream never came.

His body spasmed violently one last time. His hands twitched, scraping at his own throat, like he could still feel it burning.

Then, suddenly, his jaw fell open. A cloud of bitter black smoke poured from his mouth. His last breath was nothing but soot. Finally, he collapsed.

The fire shot up, consuming the last of him, turning him to ash.

My chest rose and fell with heavy, uneven breaths, struggling against the taste of smoke and death. Beside me, Gigi trembled slightly, staggering.

Then, a sound.

Footsteps.

Gigi's ears perked up. I whipped around, stiffening.

A shadow cut through the dim light of the cave.

Someone must have heard their alpha's shouts for help.

"Holy *shit*."

I let out a relieved breath as Tyce burst into our line of sight, skidding to a stop as he took in the scene before him.

His eyes were wide as they flicked from the embers to Gigi, his mouth slightly agape, like he couldn't quite process what had just happened.

"You . . ." He pointed at Gigi, blinking rapidly. "You just . . ." He motioned wildly at the smoldering remains of what used to be Alpha Wes. "That was *insane!*"

Gigi huffed, exhausted but smug. "*I know,*" she mindlinked both of us at the same time.

Tyce barked out a short laugh, running a hand through his hair as he shook his head in disbelief. "Gigi," he said, still grinning, "that was *metal as hell.*"

I cut in, "*Can we save the celebration for* after *we're free?*"

Tyce sobered. "Right. Good point."

I spun around without hesitation and lunged for the key where I'd left it earlier. Clamping it between my teeth, I bolted back toward Tyce. My claws scratched at the frozen ground as I rushed, unsure how much time we had.

Reaching the bars, I thrust my snout through the gap, letting the key drop neatly into his waiting palm.

Our eyes met, mine filled with unspoken demand.

"*Here,*" I mindlinked. "*Make yourself useful.*"

Chapter 58

Theresa

Tyce stood near the gate, key in hand, scowling down at Joe, who still reeked. His lip curled in disgust. "Absolutely not," he said flatly. "No."

He shook his head, taking a step back as if just being near Joe might infect him. His nose scrunched. "We are *not* bringing him. He can walk himself out."

I sighed, glancing at Joe's limp form. Blood pooled beneath his head. "*Joe looks concussed,*" I mindlinked. "*He's not walking anywhere.*"

Tyce let out a heavy, long-suffering sigh.

I stared at Joe, trying to summon even a *single* emotion that might make me feel bad for him. But all I felt was exhaustion. He was just . . . *pathetic.*

Sure, leaving him would be easy. And yet, it didn't feel right.

"When I made him roll in that shit," Tyce grumbled, glaring at Joe like this was all his fault, "I *did not* think I'd have to *carry* him out of here." He flung out an arm in frustration. "This is a *new coat!*"

I barely held back an eye roll. "*Tyce,*" I said patiently. "*Are you even planning to walk out in your* human *form anyway?*"

His mouth opened, then shut.

"*We can't just* stroll *out of here like we're not enemy number one to these people. I think your coat's a loss either way.*"

"It's a *Canada Goose*!" he whined.

Gigi let out a weak snort. "*Well, now it's a Canada* Moose *Shit.*"

"Fine," he said, rolling his shoulders back like he was mentally preparing for war.

I turned my focus back to the chains that were still clamped around Gigi's and my legs. Technically, we could escape with the heavy metal cuffs and pieces of chain, as there wasn't any need for us to immediately shift into our human forms. But it would be difficult. We wouldn't be able to outrun anyone. I was already becoming dizzy whenever I made any fast movements.

I lowered my head, sniffing the ground, searching.

We were somewhere out in the woods of the pack, possibly on the outskirts somewhere. They must have discovered this cave early on when they'd claimed this land and thought how lucky and how perfect it would be for keeping prisoners. It was clearly well isolated from their main living area.

"*How did you even find us?*" I asked Tyce.

"Lucky, I guess," he said. "I was staking out near the packhouse when I saw Alpha Wes leave in his car. I followed him as far as I could. Eventually, the car got too fast, but I stayed on the road he'd been on anyway, and it took me right to where he'd parked. I followed his scent, and there he was, just fucking around, shooting the shit with a couple warriors who were probably supposed to be guarding this place. The second he disappeared, I took them out."

He let out a little laugh, as if he were sharing some inside joke with himself. "This must be bitch duty, because neither of them was on their game. I didn't even have to shift!"

To think, this entire time, the only thing standing between Gigi and me and freedom, other than the gate, was a couple of incompetent duds.

The three of us made our way out, Tyce carrying the brown-covered Joe, and there they were. Still knocked out.

"I took a rock to their heads after, to make sure they'd be out for a while," Tyce commented.

I sniffed their pants until . . . My nose twitched. Metal.

I shoved my snout into his pocket, maneuvering it until I felt the cold sensation of frozen metal. I bit down, pulling them free.

Tyce moved in instantly, throwing Joe off his back without a care for how he landed, and snatched them from my mouth. He worked fast, barely pausing between locks. The second the final shackle dropped from my leg, relief flooded me.

Gigi groaned as her final chain hit the ground, stretching out her stiff limbs.

"All right," Tyce said, peeling off his many layers of clothes, including his expensive four-figure coat. "We move *fast*. We can't risk being seen."

We nodded, readying ourselves as he shifted into his massive bear of a wolf.

Tyce turned to Joe and let out another long-suffering sigh. Then, reluctantly, he crouched down and slung Joe onto his back in a wolfman's carry, his nose wrinkling as the smell of moose dung engulfed him.

"*Someone kill me*," Tyce growled through the link.

"*Stop being so dramatic*," I responded and then bolted. They immediately followed.

Tyce eventually took his place next to me in front, and Gigi kept pace just steps behind us.

For a second, just a second, I thought we were in the clear.

But then we heard howls, movement.

Warriors burst from the tree line, one after another, surrounding us in a matter of seconds. Glowing eyes. Bared teeth. There were *too many*.

A low, guttural growl rumbled from Tyce's chest as he threw Joe off his back again, sending him tumbling into the snow.

Then, slowly, he lowered himself into a battle stance.

I mirrored him, my own muscles flexing, my claws digging into the frozen ground. There was no other choice. If we didn't fight, we wouldn't make it out.

A warrior lunged. I moved first.

Teeth clashed. Claws slashed through fur. I met him head-on, barreling into him with the full weight of my body. We rolled. Kicked snow up around us in a whirlwind of white. He thrashed, twisting violently, but I sank my teeth into his foreleg, biting down hard, twisting.

SNAP.

A howl of agony tore from his throat.

I shoved him off me, dodging just as another wolf came flying toward me, claws swiping so close they grazed my cheek. Too close. I snarled, turning sharply, aiming for his throat.

Tyce used the force of his massive frame to bulldoze through the warriors. He slammed his weight into an enemy, sending him tumbling. The wolf barely had time to recover before Tyce was on him again, his teeth sinking deep into his side, ripping flesh like it was paper.

Another came at him. And another . . .

I threw myself into the fight, attempting to dodge attacks while lunging at a warrior who was closing in on Gigi. My claws dug deep into his exposed flank, bloodying my paws. He howled, but I didn't stop. I couldn't. I twisted my jaw, preparing to tear . . .

But there were so many of them. I did my best to just do and not think about how outnumbered and overpowered we were. A haze was settling over me. A sickly ache gathered in my head.

It could really be over.

And Gigi . . . I stole a glance at her.

I could see it. The way her flames flickered. She'd already given everything she had. Her body trembled with the effort, her head lowered, her breathing labored. Where there should have been fire, there were puffs of flame. Like an old lighter running out of fluid.

Tyce was overwhelmed, as the majority of the warriors had chosen to take him as an opponent. I could *feel* the worry as he kept glancing toward Gigi.

"*Please help her!*" he linked me, sounding desperate.

I growled, trying to force every last drop of energy into my muscles. I was fading. I hadn't eaten in days. I had already fought, I had already pushed myself to my breaking point. The edges of my vision blurred, a static buzz filled my ears, my head pounded with a deep, growing migraine.

The world spun. I had no strength left. I knew it. They knew it. This was how it ended.

I stole a glance at Gigi.

Somehow, somehow, she managed to dodge, to claw back, to keep moving. Somehow she managed to stay in the game.

And Tyce . . . Tyce was surrounded. His growls were strained, desperate. Blood dripped from his muzzle, painting the white snow red. He fought like all heck, but there were too many. His body was buckling. His attacks were slowing, weakening. His gaze kept flicking back to Gigi.

I barely had time to react to each attack before another wolf launched at me. I threw myself forward, dodging, twisting. My claws sliced into exposed flesh. My enemy yelped, but I couldn't stop. Another attack was already incoming.

There were too many of them.

Tyce howled.

A warrior ripped into his side. The sound that tore from his throat sent ice through my veins. His blood streaked the sky, then splattered onto the snow. It painted the ground beneath him a dark and horrifying crimson. His body lurched. His legs buckled.

He toppled over as if lifeless.

My breath caught. Was he . . . ?

Gigi's body stilled.

Then, suddenly, a rumbling, earth-shattering roar ripped from her throat, followed by a surge of golden-blue light.

The air sizzled. The temperature spiked.

The warriors around her staggered back. Their bodies seized with sudden confusion. Then panic. And screams. Piercing, agonized screams filled the forest.

One of the wolves ignited. His fur burst into flames. Fire crackled across his body, consuming him like he was nothing but dry kindling. He convulsed, writhing, twisting, dropping, flailing in the snow, trying desperately to put himself out.

He didn't get the chance.

Before the flames swallowed him whole, Gigi was already looking at the next one.

WHOOSH.

Flames engulfed another warrior.

Their bodies collapsed into the snow, screaming in agony, their fur burning away in seconds. The fire fed on them hungrily, climbing higher, stronger, faster.

Soon warriors were running away, fleeing her destructive path. Realizing they were fighting a losing battle, they disappeared into the forest with their tails between their legs.

And just like that, adrenaline spilled back into me. We wouldn't lose.

We fought like no one's business until the last brave soul was similarly scorched, his fur igniting instantly, his body wrapped in a deadly, fiery cloak.

And finally, silence. Nothing but the smoldering embers, the scent of charred fur and burned flesh.

Tyce stared at Gigi, his chest heaving, his head lowered slightly, eyes wide, and expression a mixture of awe and horror.

For a second, we just stared at each other, as if we'd forgotten why we'd ended up here.

Tyce broke the silence with yet another long-suffering groan, found the knocked-out, filthy Joe among the wreckage of the battle, and threw him onto his back once again.

Then we ran.

We didn't stop running until we cleared the border.

The moment we crossed that invisible line, my legs nearly gave out. My body screamed with exhaustion, every muscle shaking, my lungs gasping for air.

But we didn't stop. Who knew how long before they came looking for us.

Finally, we burst onto a desolate road. A massive SUV sat parked in the shadows, strategically tucked behind a thicket of trees. As soon as we arrived, the doors swung open, and several figures spilled out.

Kolya.

My gaze locked onto his. My breath hitched.

He was really here.

And yet neither of us spoke. We just . . . stared. Frozen in place, both too stunned to move, but I could feel the silent exchange passing between us, thick with unspoken words. His eyes searched mine, as if he was making sure I was real.

Then, without a word, he turned, popped the trunk, and rummaged through a bag. A moment later, he pulled out clothes and handed the first set to Gigi before making his way toward me.

I sank into a seated position, staring up at him, trying to process the fact that he was standing right in front of me.

"Here," he murmured, crouching beside me. "Put this on."

His voice was deep, gentle, rough around the edges.

And something else was woven into it.

Tenderness. Worry.

Then I felt it. His emotions flooded me. Sadness. Relief. Raw, aching concern. I whimpered before I could stop myself.

Not sure what else to do, I took the clothes from him, turned away, and slipped into the forest to change.

As I shifted back into my human form, I clutched the fabric to my chest, inhaling deeply. The scent was all him. Gosh, I could just live in this scent. It was like being drunk on a warm summer day when bad things hadn't happened.

I could drown in this. For a brief moment, I let myself exist in that feeling.

But it wasn't long before a crushing weight slammed into my chest.

The survival. The escape. The fighting. Now that I was safe, the truth hit me like a Mack truck.

Sophia.

She was gone. Really and truly gone.

I squeezed my eyes shut and forced my shaking hands to pull on the sweatpants, to tie the waistband to keep them from slipping. I threw on the hoodie, yanking the hood up over my head. The fabric was warm, too big, covering me completely, shielding me in more ways than one.

By the time I made it back, everyone was gathered around the SUV with its doors flung open.

Joe, still limp and absolutely filthy, was unceremoniously dumped into the trunk of the SUV.

Tyce slammed it shut, then quickly rubbed his hands through the snow. "All right, everybody in. Let's get the fuck out of here before they send more warriors after us."

Everyone scrambled inside, packing the car up to its maximum capacity.

Then the smell hit us.

"Oh, Goddess." Eddie gagged from the back row. "What the hell . . ."

Ivan cursed in Russian.

Tanner covered his nose with his sleeve, heaving like he was about to hurl. "You put him in the trunk?! He smells like a dead moose's ass!"

Tyce let out an exasperated sigh. "Would you prefer he was up front with us?"

Silence.

A collective shudder passed through the car.

"Eddie, crack the window," Tanner groaned.

"IT'S FREEZING OUTSIDE."

"Do you want to suffocate on *eau de moose crap*? OPEN THE WIN-DOW."

The window rolled down immediately.

The cold air rushed in, mercifully cutting through the stench, but it still lingered.

Gigi groaned, pressing her forehead against the window. "I survived being tortured and locked up for days just to perish in a moose toilet."

Everyone continued to commentate on the smell as I zoned out, the grief creeping back in. Like a shadow. Like a weight settling deep in my chest, threatening to crush me from the inside out.

Sophia was really gone. It hadn't been a dream.

A warm hand closed around mine. I looked up, startled, to find Kolya staring down at me, a crease between his eyes, his brows deeply furrowed.

I was still speechless, still too shaken to say anything, but I accepted the small comfort.

Chapter 59

Theresa

The SUV rumbled beneath us as we sped away from Alpine Snow Pack. The tension in the car was still thick, even though we'd escaped. None of us were naive enough to believe we were in the clear yet.

I stared out the window, my thoughts a tangled mess of exhaustion, grief, and the strange, magnetic pull I could feel radiating from beside me.

Kolya.

He hadn't let go of my hand since he first reached for it. His grip was firm, grounding, but not demanding. Like he was silently telling me: *I'm here. I've got you. You're safe now.*

Cutting through the conversations and murmurs, Tyce announced, "All right, we're stopping at the hotel, and we'll regroup there while Liam figures out when we can head home."

Once we parked, everyone scrambled out of the car while Tyce went inside to arrange our stay. Liam was busy on his phone, presumably checking the weather and figuring out the flight schedule for the next day. The others began unloading the bags from the trunk.

"So what do we do with moose shit over here?" Tanner questioned while staring into the trunk.

"I'm pretty sure Tyce is gonna book one of those rooms in the back, and then we can just bring him in through the patio door," Eddie replied.

"Goddess, I hope this scent didn't seep into my luggage."

"The real question is, Who's going to be in charge of bathing him?"

Tanner groaned. "Can't we just hose him down out back or something?"

Eddie chortled.

Tyce returned and began assigning rooms to everyone, obviously putting Gigi in his. Then, when he got to Kolya, he did something I'd never expected. He pulled him in for a huge hug and said, "Hey, bro, thanks for helping get the girls back."

Kolya made a small, acknowledging sound, patting Tyce's back once.

Tyce pulled away, handing him a key card with a sly grin. "And hey…" He winked, clapped a hand on Kolya's shoulder, and said, "Good luck."

And just like that, he was gone.

I blinked, my mouth slightly agape. "Did my brother … Did he … *did he just give you his blessing to sleep with me?*"

Kolya exhaled a soft chuckle. "His blessing, it was only so we are left alone. He would not want to picture … what maybe comes after."

Something about him had changed. I couldn't quite put my finger on it, but it was there. He wasn't as tense. The usual furrow in his brow had softened. His shoulders, which normally carried the weight of the world, were lighter.

Had it really only been a couple weeks or so since I last saw him? Because suddenly, it felt like a lifetime had passed.

He grabbed a heavy bag from the ground and gestured for me to follow him. Before long, we'd found our room.

While we'd been intimate before, something about this felt different. I was off-kilter. *Hesitant.* The pull between us was there, undeniable, but my heart was weighed down by something heavier.

And then it hit me—*I* had changed too.

There was a pressure in my chest now, something suffocating, pressing down on me. An ache that had nothing to do with the physical pain I'd endured the past few days.

Kolya tapped the key card against the door and held it open for me. "I am sure you want to use bathroom first."

My body *desperately* needed a shower. I'd been living in that filthy cave for days, blood from the fight was still dried and caked onto my skin. My stomach rumbled loudly, betraying another desperate need.

"And you are hungry," he said.

I nodded, then asked, "Do you need to pee? Before I take a shower?"

"No," he said simply, then hesitated. "Wait." He rummaged through his bag, pulling out yet another hoodie and a pair of sweatpants. He stepped closer, offering them to me. "Something clean to put on after."

Holding them against my chest, I said, "Thank you."

I turned to go, but before I could step away, his fingers caught my wrist. A warm vibration rippled through me at his touch, spreading up my arm and settling deep in my bones.

His scent filled my lungs. Warm, musky, slightly sweet, and something purely *him*. It was intoxicating.

When I tilted my head up, my eyes locked on to his silver ones.

"Terri, I . . ." His voice was low, rough. "I was so worried about you."

The words hung between us, heavy with meaning. There was something else he wasn't saying. Something just on the edge of breaking free.

I swallowed hard. "I guess that's why you came down to Anchorage with Tyce?"

He nodded, but something flickered in his gaze. Hesitation.

Then it hit me. *Joe.*

The pieces clicked together in an instant. "That's why Joe was here," I whispered. "Because he knew how to find me. Which means . . . Tyce . . ."

I closed my eyes.

The weight in my chest grew unbearable.

Heavy. It was so heavy. It was like my chest was caving in. My friend was dead. I had been chained for who knows how long. I'd come so close to death more than once. And now, my family knew.

"Terri . . ." Kolya started.

"I need to shower."

There was too much to process.

He seemed to accept my wishes and let his hand fall to his side when he let go of my wrist. I slipped into the bathroom. The second I turned the shower on, I stripped down and stepped under the scalding water. It burned, but I welcomed it.

I needed to scrub everything off. The filth. The blood. The lingering sensation of chains wrapped around my wrists and ankles.

I pressed my forehead against the cool tile, my chest rising and falling as I tried to breathe through all the unease. My hands curled into fists.

And then, I broke.

Tears spilled down my face, blending with the rushing water. Silent sobs racked my body. I grieved for Sophia. For the way she died. For how *undignified* it was. She hadn't even had a proper funeral.

She had deserved so much *more*.

And it was all my fault.

I wasn't sure how long I stayed in there. Long enough for my skin to prune and my limbs to go numb. Eventually, I turned off the water, wrapped myself in a thick towel, and wiped the steam from the mirror.

Like I thought. Something was definitely different about me. There was something *hollow* in my gaze. A shadow of something that hadn't been there before. My eyes suddenly seemed so much more like my father's.

I dried off and pulled on the clothes Nikolai had given me, pausing only for a moment to inhale them deeply. His scent clung to the fabric, comforting in a way I didn't fully understand.

When I finally stepped out of the bathroom, I was stunned to find a cart with a hot meal waiting for me. Nikolai stood beside it, pulling out a chair. "Sit."

I didn't argue. I dropped into the seat, barely registering the way he silently served me first before taking his own plate.

I hungrily devoured everything until my stomach bloated and ached. I couldn't even remember the last time I'd eaten that much food.

Then I noticed the *one* king-size bed.

For someone who wouldn't be imagining what might happen during our private time, Tyce sure booked the perfect room for that exact thing to happen.

I hesitated.

While I'd longed for Kolya every single day since he'd pushed me away, now that he was here, I felt a bit dizzy. After all, he had rejected me, hadn't he? And there was just so much that had happened since the evening of the full moon run.

He must have sensed my hesitation. "I can sleep on floor," he offered. "I want you to be comfortable."

"No, I can't let you sleep on the floor," I responded, horrified. What kind of awful person would I be to do that? It wasn't like we hadn't shared a bed before. Why was I acting so strange? We had been so close and intimate not so long ago, not able to keep our hands off each other.

He pushed me away before. He hurt me.

Part of me wanted to make him work for it. Wanted to ask, Why now? Why not then?

But as I looked at him, at the raw honesty in his eyes, I realized . . . I already had my answer.

He stepped forward, taking my hands in his. His fingers were rough, warm. "Terri, I know this week was hell. And last time we see each other, I was not . . . kind." His thumb brushed against the back of my hand. "So, if you prefer to sleep alone, I will find somewhere else."

"No, it's okay," I said. "Honestly."

He nodded as I moved away and climbed into the bed. As soon as my head hit the pillow, my eyes drooped shut, unable to stay open any longer. The last thing I saw before I faded was Kolya clearing the small table.

I wasn't sure what time it was, but at some point during the night, I woke to find Kolya lying next to me on his back, his night vision softly illuminating the ceiling above us in an eerie glow.

Something about the sight of him, so steady and strong, even while resting, cracked something deep inside me. A sob tore from my throat before I could stop it, my breath hitching as tears welled up and spilled over.

Kolya turned his head, his silver eyes immediately locking on to mine. "*Teren'ka.*" His voice was low, concerned, and without hesitation, he reached for me, pulling me into his arms. The way he said my name sounded familiar, and I remembered that my mom had called me the same thing when I had been very young, during a time when she had been a bit more loving, more affectionate.

I melted into him, pressing my face into his chest, indulging in the warmth and quiet strength of him, the steady thrum of his heartbeat against my cheek. For the first time since everything happened, I felt safe.

"What happened?" he murmured, his fingers combing gently through my hair.

"Now or this week?" I sniffled, trying to stem the tears that wouldn't stop falling.

"Both," he said firmly. "There is nothing I do not want to know."

I sucked in a shaky breath. "They kidnapped Gigi and me. Locked us in a cave. And then . . ." My throat clenched, the weight of it all threatening to suffocate me. "Then the alpha wanted to know where the stone was."

Kolya's entire body stiffened.

"I didn't know," I continued, my voice barely above a whisper. "But they tortured my friend for hours anyway. Over and over again, they made her ask me. And I kept telling them, I don't know. I don't know. But he wouldn't believe me . . ." My voice trailed off. I couldn't speak anymore, my throat closed up, my heart pounded, the onslaught of grief pierced me through my chest. The memories twisted like a knife in my gut, suffocating, unbearable.

"And he killed her," Kolya finished for me.

I gasped softly. "How did you know?"

"Tyce felt it," he said.

Of course. It all clicked into place.

I swallowed hard, blinking back more tears. "And he knows about Joe?"

Kolya hesitated for just a second. "Terri . . . I had to tell him. Was only way we could find you. I am so sorry. I know you trusted me with secret, but I had no choice. You are more important."

I let out a long, slow exhale, placing my forehead against his chest. How could I be mad? Would I not have done the same thing? Still . . . Tyce knew.

"Who else knows?" I asked.

"Nobody . . ." But he didn't say it with conviction. I could sense some uncomfortable feeling radiating from him that I couldn't place. It just made me feel sickly and unpleasant. After a moment, he finally said, "Sasha."

"I can live with Sasha knowing," I replied. "I'm assuming he's not a gossip. But if my parents found out . . ." My pulse quickened and body tensed at the thought.

"He is not a gossip," Kolya assured me.

"I would assume not if he's your beta. Being a beta requires the most trust and discreetness. Like, Beta Liam would never! You could tell him anything, and it would always stay between the two of you."

"Beta Liam is good man," Nikolai agreed.

I let out a relieved sigh, but the thick and suffocating grief curled back around me.

"Does it ever stop hurting this much?" I whispered.

He was quiet, rubbing slow circles along my back.

"I don't know," he finally admitted. "I hear people say it gets easier. Time makes it . . . bearable. But I do not know. For me, is not long enough."

My heart clenched. "Kolya . . ."

"I'm sorry," he said suddenly, voice rough, vulnerable. "I am sorry about full moon run. I handled it wrong, Teren'ka . . . I was numb for so long. But then you . . ." He paused as the steadiness of his voice cracked. "You made me feel again. I was not ready."

His words settled deep in my chest, wrapping around something fragile inside me.

I thought back to that night, to the way he'd pushed me away, how broken I'd felt. How I didn't understand.

But I understood now.

"I get it," I murmured. "I didn't then. But I do now."

His grip on me tightened. "I wish you didn't."

The way he said it, the way his eyes looked so intense and troubled. It did something to me, shooting a shiver right down my spine. My stomach fluttered with something . . . something feverish.

I shouldn't be thinking about this. Not now.

But the way he looked at me, the way he held me . . . it made the pain a little less unbearable.

And then, as if drawn by some invisible force, we moved at the same time, our lips finding each other in the dark.

At first, the kiss was slow, hesitant. But then, it deepened. My fingers threaded into his hair, and his hands found my waist, pulling me flush against him.

His lips teased mine, his tongue sweeping in, coaxing me to open for him. A whimper escaped me as his teeth tugged at my lower lip, his hands sliding lower, grasping my hips, pressing me closer.

Heat surged between us.

He kissed his way along my jaw, down my throat. His lips trailing warmth across my skin. Before I could stop myself, my fingers tugged at the hoodie he'd lent me, pulling it over my head and tossing it aside.

A low growl of approval rumbled in his chest as his hands skimmed up my sides. He gently thumbed at my nipples, sending a shudder through me. I let out a soft moan, arching my back, raking my hands through my hair.

He dipped his head and his mouth closed around one of the stiff peaks, rolling it between his tongue and teeth while his other hand palmed my breast. The sensation sent a jolt of pleasure straight through me.

He kissed his way down, slowly and torturously, until he reached the waistband of my sweatpants. The fabric felt too thick, too suffocating, too concealing. I let out a soft moan as he hooked his fingers into the fabric and dragged the pants down my legs.

When he returned, hovering just over me, my hands found his torso, and I slid them over the ridges of his well-sculpted abs, down to his hard stomach, until I found the waistband of his boxer briefs. I hesitated for a moment, but only for a moment. Soon I was removing them, exposing him to me, how massive and hard he was.

I couldn't help but wrap my palms around him and stroke his length in slow, methodical movements. A guttural sound reverberated from Kolya's chest. That sound only made me more greedy, more wanton. And before I knew it, my legs were falling open in invitation.

I wanted him.

I wanted him so much it was painful.

I wanted proof that he had returned, and that pushing me away had been a huge mistake.

"*Koshechka*," he whispered in a voice thick with need.

My pulse skipped. "What?" I asked, breathless.

"You're like cat, *koshechka*, in your wolf form. Strong, deadly, beautiful cat." His silver eyes roamed my face and softened. "*Moya koshechka*."

Something in my chest tightened.

"I am so lucky," he murmured, his voice barely audible.

Then, finally, he pushed into me.

A gasp tore from my lips at the slow, delicious stretch, at the way he filled me so perfectly. He moved slowly at first, savoring it, savoring me. But soon, his rhythm became deeper, faster, more desperate.

I had longed for him, ached for him. And now, with his body pressed against mine, I realized how much I had needed this, not just physically, but emotionally. Kolya, the man who had pushed me away, who had tried to deny this, was finally letting me in.

My entire body was flooded with satisfying warmth. I shuddered with pleasure, taking in every sensation, overwhelmed by a new feeling.

How right this moment felt.

How perfectly our bodies aligned, my hips instinctively mirroring his movements, as if he could read my every desire before I even realized it myself. With each shift, each precise adjustment, he found the perfect angle, drawing out pleasure that sent shivers down my spine. And through it all, he made me feel so safe and cared for.

I didn't know why I'd felt so shy and hesitant at first.

Something about being with him was just *so right*.

His fingers were soon gliding between my thighs, grazing the sensitive skin, finding their way higher until they were stroking the exact spot that sent electricity jolting through me, driving me absolutely wild with ecstasy. I quivered underneath him, letting out a euphoric moan.

The heat, the tension, the unbearable pleasure climbed higher and higher, until I shattered around him, crying out his name as my body trembled with release. Moments later, he followed, his entire body tensing as he let out a deep, carnal groan, pulling out at the last moment and spilling himself onto my stomach.

Before I could even catch my breath, a sudden haze settled over me, a magnetic force pulling me toward him. My mouth tingled as my canines extended, the familiar compulsion gripping me. But I braced myself, fists clenching, focusing every ounce of willpower on resisting. I had learned to expect it now, to fight through the overwhelming instinct to sink my teeth into him.

When the worst of it had passed, I let out a slow, shaky breath, sinking into the pillow. Kolya had already disappeared into the bathroom and returned, a warm washcloth in hand. He gently cleaned me off, his movements meticulous, unhurried. It wasn't just this moment—it was everything he'd done since we'd stepped into this hotel room. Anticipating every need, making sure I was taken care of.

"*Koshechka*," he murmured, the word rolling off his tongue with something close to amusement. He seemed to test it out, savoring my new nickname. "There's something I need to tell you."

"Mm?" I tilted my chin up to look at him.

He hesitated, his silver eyes clouding over as he searched for the right words. "When I look in your eyes, I get this feeling . . ." He shook his head as if frustrated with himself. "I cannot explain it, but I feel like you are my mate."

I stared at him, my breath caught in my throat.

"But," he continued, his voice laced with uncertainty, "I don't feel other things I am supposed to—the bond, the sparks, the emotions. Just . . . this knowing."

And suddenly it made sense. My fists clenched and unclenched as I tried to steady myself. "Kolya," I whispered, "I feel those things. I always feel like I know exactly what you're feeling. And when you touch me . . ." He reached out, brushing his fingers along my arm. I inhaled as warmth spread through me, a soft hum vibrating beneath my skin. "I think these are the sparks."

His gaze darkened with something unreadable. "But when you look in my eyes . . . you do not feel it?"

I shook my head. "No, I don't." Then something clicked. "It's like we both have . . ."

"A half of the whole," he finished for me.

"Do you think we're . . . ?" I said, just as he said, "I think we're . . ."

"Mates," we both said at the exact same time.

The weight of it settled between us.

"But we cannot confirm," Kolya said firmly, as if warning me.

I considered his words, turning them over in my mind before replying. "Maybe not. But I think the evidence is pretty strong." I hesitated, then added, "But really, does anyone ever know anything with certainty? You hear stories about fated mates who are still toxic together, because the bond doesn't change who you are. A relationship is still work. The mate bond just . . . gives it a better chance at surviving. That's what I think."

Kolya nodded slowly, his expression thoughtful. After a beat, he spoke, his voice steady, resolute. "*Koshechka*, mate or not, I am willing to take risk for you."

A slow, teasing smile curved my lips. "So . . . does that mean we're together now?"

His answer was immediate, unwavering. "You are mine, mate."

"Mate," I whispered, as if saying it out loud would make it real.

Then, without another word, he pulled me in, sealing his claim with a deep, possessive kiss.

Chapter 60

Julia

21 years ago

The house was quiet, save for the faint crackling of the fireplace and the rhythmic ticking of the grandfather clock in the hall. It was a rare moment of peace. Tyson and Travis were finally asleep, their endless energy and constant screaming temporarily halted.

I ran a hand over my swollen belly, feeling the delicate flutter of movement beneath my palm. A soft, wistful smile touched my lips before fading just as quickly. After giving Lance both an alpha heir and a spare, this child, this last one, was for me.

Alfochka.

That's what I'd taken to calling her. My little female alpha.

Even now, I could feel it in my bones. She would have the heart of an alpha, the drive, the fire, in a way her brothers never would.

As much as I loved my sons, loved them to the point that I would lay down my life for theirs without hesitation, both Lance and I knew neither of them would ever truly take to alpha training. They were too gentle, too softhearted. Sweet, sensitive boys. Had I not conceived and carried them myself, I might have wondered if they were even ours at all.

I knew it would be a difficult road ahead to bring Tyson from the tenderhearted child he was today to the ruthless leader he would become.

But this one . . . this one I knew would be different. Even though she'd never be forced into the role, she would take to it anyway.

My little *alfochka*.

Steps sounded in the hallway outside the bedroom. The scent hit me before the door even opened. Faint, at first. That scent was as familiar to me now as he was. As the door shut behind him, it flooded the oversize bedroom.

He looked exhausted.

I might have believed he was tired from the weight of his responsibilities, from the long days and endless decisions, if I didn't already know better.

He had been with him again.

Lance stepped into the dimly lit room, his presence filling the space. The firelight flickered against the hard lines of his face, casting deep shadows along his jaw and the hollows beneath his eyes. He had barely been home these last few weeks, retreating further into long nights that always ended with him reeking of someone else.

Of *him*.

He didn't speak immediately. He rarely did after these nights.

I inhaled, taking in the unmistakable scent woven into his clothes, his skin. It clung to him like a ghost, a reminder of the position I would never hold. His mate. The one he rejected. The one he still couldn't let go of.

"How are the boys?" he finally asked, his voice smooth, unreadable. As if he hadn't spent the evening wrapped around someone else. As if he could simply return and resume his place without question.

"They're fine." The words came out even, practiced. I had learned how to keep my voice measured, how to school my expression into something neutral, how to pretend.

But tonight, something inside me cracked.

Maybe it was the pregnancy, the hormones making me raw in ways I usually wasn't. Maybe it was the weight of *too many years* playing a role that had begun to feel like an ill-fitting outfit—one that had once felt like armor but had since turned uncomfortable and itchy.

I pressed a hand to my belly, grounding myself. "Did you even try to wash his scent off before coming home?"

His jaw tightened. A flicker of something—guilt? annoyance?—flashed across his face before it was gone. "Julia."

He said my name in such an American way, with three syllables, with the harsh letter *j*. In the beginning, I had loved it. It meant I had become a part of this pack, this land, this country. But now . . . now, the way he said it felt foreign. Wrong. I missed *Yulia*. The way the *i* was nearly silent, soft. But that was long gone. I was now the very American *Luna Julia*.

"It's an honest question." My fingers curled against the soft fabric of my robe. "You expect me to endure this, at least have the decency not to shove it in my face."

The agreement had been clear from the beginning. He would have his freedom, and I would have security. A fair trade, or so I had once believed.

But the mate bond had made things more complicated than I'd ever anticipated.

I could *feel* him. Feel what he felt, even when I didn't want to. And worse, I could feel what he felt for *him*.

And what I felt now, after all these years, was resentment.

Lance exhaled slowly, dragging a hand down his face. "It's never been a secret, Julia. You knew what this would be. In fact, *you're* the one who asked for this."

I let out a breath of humorless laughter. "Knowing something and living it are two different things."

Thick and heavy silence settled between us.

He wasn't sorry. Not really. He had made his choice, chosen duty, chosen me. But *not completely*. Never completely.

I'd thought that would be enough. That power, position, and control over my own destiny would outweigh the aching loneliness that had settled into my bones.

But I was starting to wonder if I had been wrong.

He walked past me without a word, without a touch, without a glance. I shouldn't have expected anything else. And yet, my body betrayed me. My fingers twitched with an unconscious, stupid need for contact. Just a brush of his fingers. Just something instead of this cold, impassive *arrangement*.

In the beginning, it had been different. After we'd married and marked each other, he had taken a strong interest in me, constantly lustful, constantly tearing my clothes off. There were days he would dip out from his rounds just to kiss me between my legs, to lap and nibble at my kitten. He was always a little rough, but I found I didn't mind it. In fact, I became quite fond of his way of making love.

He remarked at how extraordinary it was *to feel* the effects of his efforts. It made him that much more determined to give me earth-shattering, leg-numbing, roof-blowing orgasms. And he was always so enthusiastic about the fact that I had been his virgin, that no other man had ever penetrated me. Well, that was what he believed anyway. And I was happy to give him that satisfaction.

But over time, he drifted. It may have been the new responsibility of children. Tyson was conceived not even a year into marriage. And Travis came along another two years later. Through the breastfeeding, sleepless nights, continuous crying and screaming, my changing body, the constant neediness of the children, he began to change.

Sometimes I'd still see flickers of the Lance from the early days, but a lot had happened in eight years. There had been battles, some in which he'd lost friends. Lance's father had aged and become even more of a nuisance than in his younger years. More of his father's indiscretions had become gossip around the pack. His mother had not taken it well.

Poor Catherine. I'd pitied her for quite some time. The way she just *allowed* and *accepted* her mate's bulldozing.

Until one morning, when I'd lain in our enormous, empty bed, staring at the ceiling. A marital bed was meant to be shared. But how long had it been since it had felt full? My fingers drifted absentmindedly to his pillow. Cold. He hadn't come home. And suddenly, it had struck me with a terrible, sickening clarity—Catherine and I were one and the same. Shackled in golden handcuffs.

I lifted my gaze to his, searching for something, anything that might make this easier. A flicker of regret. A hesitation. A lie, even, if he could make it convincing.

But Lance was already pulling off his clothes, already making his way into the bathroom, already moving past the conversation as if it had never happened. As if *I* had never happened.

And maybe that was the cruelest part of it all.

Because in the end, he would always have the upper hand. And I would always be the one left wondering if this was truly what I had wanted.

Chapter 61

Ginger

I woke to warmth and sparks softly vibrating along my skin.

The steady rhythm of a heartbeat thumped beneath my ear. A strong arm wrapped securely around my waist, pulling me in, anchoring me. The scent surrounding me was familiar, comforting. I nuzzled closer, inhaling deeply, as if I could physically absorb the safety I felt in his embrace.

I was finally home. Maybe not literally, but in every way that mattered.

No chains. No damp cave walls. No torturous nights filled with fear and uncertainty. Just him. His warmth. His scent. The quiet reassurance that I was exactly where I belonged.

Tyce stirred beneath me, his grip tightening instinctively before his lips brushed against the crown of my head. "Morning, pyro."

A slow, lazy smile spread across my face. "Morning."

His fingers traced slow, absentminded circles on my back, a soothing motion that made my eyes want to slip shut again.

"I missed waking up to you," he murmured.

Warmth bloomed in my chest. "Me too."

We lay there in silence, basking in the moment. After everything, after the cave, the torture, the fight, I needed this. To be held. To be safe. To be reminded that I had survived.

"You almost became alpha of Alpine Snow Pack." Tyce's lips moved against my hair with his soft words.

That snapped me out of my blissful haze. I lifted my head, blinking up at him. "What?"

"If Alpha Wes didn't have a next of kin, the alpha title would have automatically passed to you, kind of like when Sara killed Alpha Vic and his father not too long ago. But Wes has a brother. So you didn't quite pull a Sara yet."

I stared at him wide-eyed.

"Just the other day you were crying that you'd never be as good as Sara." His lips twitched. "And you just barbecued an alpha's dick with your eyes."

"I mean . . . Sara is still the better fighter."

Tyce huffed a laugh, tightening his arms around me. "Who cares when you can just burn suckers alive?"

I didn't argue. I settled deeper into his embrace, feeling the tension drain from my muscles.

"Well, hopefully, it intimidated them enough that they'll back off," Tyce added after a moment. "Their pack is a fraction of the size of ours. They'd have to be crazy to keep at it."

A thought nagged at me, pulling me from my brief moment of peace. "But . . . why? Why did they do all this? The alpha kept demanding to know about some stone. What's so special about it?"

Tyce exhaled, shifting onto his elbow so he could look me in the eyes. His expression darkened slightly, suddenly serious. "About the stone . . ."

I frowned at his tone. "What about it?"

He hesitated. "It's a big deal."

I stared at him, waiting for him to elaborate.

He ran a hand through his hair. "I had a talk with Alpha Nikolai. About the fact that he had this stone this whole time but didn't tell us. When you got kidnapped"—his jaw tensed slightly—"I made it very clear how pissed I was about that."

My stomach twisted. "Wait! He has it?"

"Yeah . . ." he replied, and his tone shifted. "So that's where I was going with this. After he came clean about this stone, he offered to let us use it, as a peace offering."

I pushed myself up slightly. "Use it? For what?"

Tyce's expression softened, his hand finding mine, squeezing it. "Gigi, I love your wolf so much. Everything about her. I love how scary and intimidating she is. It's like you were ready-made for battle. And now . . ." He had an awed expression in his eyes. "Now that I know she can literally burn enemies alive—holy shit. You are incredible, Gigi."

His arms suddenly tightened around me as he pressed a series of enthusiastic kisses against my forehead. "I swear, I have to be the luckiest guy in the world to have you as my mate."

"That's great, Tyce," I said, my patience thinning, "but what does the stone do?"

He finally let go, grinning sheepishly before getting back to the point. "It can grant any wish you want . . ." He trailed off slightly before continuing, voice gentler this time. "Just one wish. And I know how much you hate your wolf. I know how much you wish your wolf looked like every other wolf. And if it would make you happy to wish for your wolf to be patched up, then I want you to be able to do that."

The breath left my lungs.

The thing I had wanted since I'd gotten my wolf back and learned what she looked like.

I could fix her.

With one wish, I could make my wolf normal. No more exposed bones, no more terrifying red eyes, no more whispers of *monster* behind my back. I could just be . . . *normal.*

My heart pounded as I stared at Tyce, my body buzzing with elation.

I could be normal. I could . . .

But what if I lost my wolf's fire? Could I really trade that away?

I hesitated.

Because . . . I hadn't felt like a monster yesterday. My wolf had felt powerful. Useful. She'd saved us. Would I still be able to do that if I wished for my wolf to change? I swallowed hard, my emotions tangling together in a mess of conflict.

Tyce watched me carefully, his expression unreadable.

"Wait," I said slowly, thoughts racing. "You said it only grants *one* wish?"

"Yeah, I guess that's the limitation on the thing. Only one per person."

Then more thoughts ran through my mind. Yes, if you had asked me a week ago if I wanted this wish, I probably wouldn't have hesitated. But now . . . Now I realized how small my problem with my wolf seemed. In the grand scheme of things, was it so terrible that my wolf looked ugly? I mean, for all intents and purposes, she still functioned like every other wolf. Better than every other wolf, actually. As far as I knew, no other wolf could make fire with their eyes. And I'd gone through various old records of special wolves over the summer. Not a single one had a power like mine.

If I wasted my one wish on this, what if something more important . . .

"Wait, you can wish for *anything*?" I asked.

"I guess there are a few stipulations," Tyce replied. "You can't wish for someone to be your mate, you can't remove a mark, and you can't bring someone back from the dead."

With that last rule, I faltered, sinking into Tyce, a dark cloud emerging overhead. I could still hear the desperate screams, still see the way Alpha Wes cut into her delicately beautiful face, still feel Terri's anguish as she fought against the heavy metal chains, trying to get to her friend. *That* was a wish worth making.

"I'm sorry, Gigi," Tyce said tenderly, as if he read my mind. "I'd wish for the same thing."

"It's not fair," I whispered, my voice cracking.

"It's not."

A heavy silence settled between us.

After a long period of contemplation, I exhaled. "It's not worth wasting my wish on my wolf. There are better things to wish for. Like, what if one day we have a pup that gets really sick? Or even one of our siblings' pups. And I wasted my wish on my stupid wolf. I'd feel like such an idiot."

Tyce cupped my cheek gently. His thumb traced over my skin. "You're not an idiot for feeling insecure, Gigi."

I let out a soft, humorless laugh. "Maybe. But . . . I don't think I'm insecure about my wolf anymore. Not after yesterday. Not after realizing what she can do." A small, almost surprised smile tugged at my lips. "I think . . . I think I'm finally starting to accept her."

Tyce pulled me into a tight embrace, pressing his lips to the side of my head. "That," he murmured, "is exactly what I was hoping you'd finally say."

Chapter 62

Nikolai

Grief wrapped around Terri like an unshakable shadow. I'd catch her staring into the distance, her eyes hollow, stripped of their usual fire. Sometimes, her hands would drift to her chest, rubbing absentmindedly over her heart, as if trying to soothe an ache too deep to reach. Even the way she moved had changed—her posture heavier, her presence quieter. It was a stark contrast to the lively, cheery woman I had first met.

After rescuing her and Gigi, Tyce and I made the unanimous decision to return with them to the Jade Moon Pack. Leaving them at school, so close to Alpine Snow Pack's territory, was out of the question. It was simply too dangerous. Even with their alpha reduced to ashes, there was no telling what other enemies might still be lurking in the shadows. And then there was his successor. We had no guarantee he wouldn't pick up where his brother left off, continuing to aid the Russians in their search for the stone, enticed by the promise of a wish in return.

But now that Terri was safe, I had to make sure it stayed that way.

Something didn't sit right.

How had they connected her to me? Perhaps the connection had been Tyce's pack to mine. Terri and Gigi were both ideal bargaining chips in that case, and I was indebted to Jade Moon Pack.

But then *how had they known about Sophia?*

There was only one person who had been there the day Tyce declared Sophia could identify who had marked Terri. My friend. Someone I would have given my life for. The person I had entrusted my pack to.

Traitor.

I found Sasha in the warrior gym, barking orders at our pack members as if nothing had changed. As if he hadn't betrayed us. The ease with which he carried on, the authority in his voice, it grated at me.

"Sasha," I called, forcing my tone to remain even, giving no hint of the fury smoldering beneath my skin.

He turned, his gaze locking onto mine. For a fraction of a second, something flickered in his expression. Curiosity? Maybe even suspicion. But it vanished just as quickly. "Alpha."

"I need you to come with me."

Something in my voice must have struck him, because he hesitated, just briefly, before nodding. "Of course."

I dismissed the pack members and led him away, guiding him toward a secluded corner of the gym where no one would overhear us. I didn't waste time. "The stone."

His reaction was immediate. His eyes widened with interest, a glint of something greedy and eager flashing behind them. And in that moment, I knew.

There was no longer any doubt in my mind.

"There are signs that Chernoye Nebo Pack has figured out where the stone is," I continued, keeping my face unreadable. "We need to move it to a more secure location. Will you come with me?"

Sasha barely contained his enthusiasm. "Of course!"

I gave a single nod and turned sharply on my heel.

The moment we stepped outside, we stripped out of our clothes and shifted, the cold biting at my bare skin before thick fur took its place. Without another word, I bolted forward, my paws striking hard against the frozen ground. Sasha kept pace beside me, eager, oblivious. Unaware of what fate lay ahead of him.

The journey stretched on longer than I would have liked. I had to maintain my mask, had to answer Sasha's incessant mindlinks as if we were still buddies, as if I had no inkling of the betrayal he had buried beneath that easy, talkative facade.

"That Alina is a little whore," he scoffed through the link. *"She's slept with at least five warriors from the other pack. I caught her flirting when she should've been working."*

I made a neutral sound in response, a low grunt of acknowledgment.

Fortunately, my silence wasn't out of character. Before the war, I might have indulged his gossip, might have even chided him that he was just bitter she hadn't slept with him.

But now?

Now, I saw how meaningless it all was.

Why should I care what Alina did in her free time? If anything, I envied her. Envied that she still had the luxury of normalcy, of moving on. Because for me, normal was no longer an option. For me, normal was a fairy tale.

We continued our run, passing through the expanse of raw, untamed wilderness. The sky stretched endlessly over the frozen tundra. Wind swept across the barren land with an unforgiving chill, carrying fine, dry snow that would sometimes get caught in my eyes. The vast silence was only broken by Sasha's constant chatter in my head.

After far too long of a journey, we finally arrived at the mountain. The same mountain where I had taken Terri to watch the sunrise. It had been a moment of peace, of stolen serenity in the midst of chaos. And now, it would be the place where I ended a war before it could begin again.

Navigating the jagged terrain, I skirted the mountainside until I found the precise spot. The stone had been here all along, concealed inside a box lined with charcoal to mask its scent.

Without hesitation, I extended my claws and began carving through the thick layers of ice that had formed over time, each stroke sending shards splintering into the wind. When I had dug deep enough, I stood back and shifted into my human form.

The cold struck me like a physical blow. It was razor-sharp, merciless. The wind whipped against my bare skin. My breath left me in short, misty puffs as I pushed my shaking hands into the crevice.

I found the box, and with a firm, deliberate pull, I pried it free. The stone's power thrummed beneath my fingertips.

The subzero air wrapped around me, freezing my toes, numbing my fingers, searing my exposed skin. I could feel the sting of frostbite creeping in, my ears burning from the cold. But this wouldn't take long.

Sasha stood a meter or so away, his gaze locked onto the box in my hands, eyes alight with something between curiosity and restrained excitement. "*We're moving it?*"

I met his gaze.

Then I let my alpha aura bleed into the air between us. "Shift."

The single command slammed into him. His body jerked, muscles locking as he instinctively fought it. His wolf resisted, but my will was absolute. His form rippled, trembled, then yielded. His fur retreated, bones snapping and reforming until his human body stood before me, bare, exposed, vulnerable.

He staggered slightly, letting out uneven breaths as his eyes flashed with confusion.

I took a step closer and spoke in a voice that was as hard as ice. "Do not speak. Do not move."

His lips parted as if to question me, but the weight of my command crushed the words before they could form. Silence settled between us.

The only sound was the wind howling through the mountains.

His lips parted again, as if on instinct, but nothing came out. His brows furrowed, and frustration flickered through his expression as he realized he physically could not disobey. His whole body trembled, and his teeth clattered.

I stepped closer, the stone still resting in my palm. "How did Alpine Snow Pack get ahold of Sophia?"

His jaw tightened. His silence stretched. My patience thinned.

I pushed out my aura, pressing down on him like a vise. "Answer me."

Sasha gasped as his control snapped. "I took her," he admitted, the words spilling out against his will. "I gave her to them. She was bait."

The world stilled.

My breath came slow, measured, but the fury beneath my skin boiled hotter with every second. I had suspected. But hearing it, hearing him say it, made it real. Final.

"You betrayed me," I said in an eerily calm voice. "You betrayed our pack."

Sasha said nothing. He couldn't. I hadn't given him permission to speak.

"Why?" I asked, forcing as much of my aura into the short question as I could.

He staggered under the force of its weight, his eyes momentarily shuttering, his fists clenching. But in the end, his body gave in, and he bared his throat in submission.

"Severnaya Zvezda is in shambles," he muttered. "Our warriors are a joke. There's no point in continuing this sad excuse of a pack." His voice turned bitter. "Besides, you don't trust me. You won't let me use the stone. Wouldn't even tell me where it was. You're no longer the person who was my friend. You're just a miserable fuck, petting a hedgehog against the grain because of some warped sense of duty."

I stared at him, letting his words settle. It was true, I hadn't been the best friend to him. But had he ever truly been a friend to me?

To Sasha, friendship meant drinking, laughing, and exchanging jokes over too many bottles. In that sense, I had failed him. But that wasn't real friendship. That was just having a drinking buddy.

A true friend understood that you couldn't always show up as the best version of yourself. They met you where you were, stood beside you even in your worst moments. And a true friend would never betray you for their own selfish gain.

Maybe some of his frustrations held merit. But if he had truly been my friend, he would have told me, he would have spoken to me, not smiled in my face while scheming behind my back.

The world would be better off with one less friend like him.

"But why?" I questioned. "What did they offer you?"

He shivered against the cold. His face was contorted, as if he were in severe pain. I didn't know if it was the cold or because he may have felt some small prickle of guilt. The answer forced itself out in the end. "They offered me a better life, a better life for my niece and my sister. A place in Alpine Snow Pack and a wish. A wish you were never going to give me. A wish you keep from everyone like a selfish son of a bitch. A wish I could have used to rebuild my family's life to be something better."

I could empathize. I could understand the desperation to improve his situation. But still, how could he stand there and call me selfish when he was so willing to betray thirty-seven people, willing to sacrifice innocent bystanders? Willing to seek out and give away an innocent woman as bait? Were their lives so meaningless to him? How did he decide his was more important than theirs?

And didn't the idiot understand that I *protected* my pack by limiting wishes. The fewer people who knew about the stone, the less vulnerable it was to outsiders. The less likely someone would wish harm to others. The less likely someone would make a wish they'd later regret.

His foresight had only extended to what he wanted. To what it would bring him. If he even wished correctly, specifically enough. Would he have even accounted for every possible consequence?

I took a step back, my gaze sweeping over him. He was hunched over with arms wrapped tightly around himself. This man, who at one time had been mistaken for my brother, now stood before me as a stranger.

The brutal wind drowned out the pounding of my pulse. As the frigid air thrashed against my exposed skin, inside . . . something flickered . . .

Memories surged through my mind, distant echoes of a past life. Skipping school to drive to the lake when the weather was nice. Taking polar bear plunges with our high school friends on crisp autumn mornings, before the water had frozen over. Late nights filled with poker and cheap beer, laughter ringing out between hands. At one point, we had even dated a pair of best friends, both gone now. I recalled the double dates, the sneaking around, the shared mischief.

But that was another time, another life. And those memories now belonged to ghosts.

Was that ever real? Did I ever truly know him?

I exhaled. The answer didn't matter anymore.

I steadied myself and stepped forward, resolute.

"You want your wish?" I asked, voice like ice. "You want to make your niece's and sister's lives better?" I lifted the stone, the power pulsing through my fingertips. "Then take it." I pressed the stone into his trembling hands. "Wish for what remains of the Chernoye Nebo Pack to perish within the next hour."

Sasha's hands shook violently as the stone's energy seeped into his skin. His face twisted, his lips parted, horror dawned on his face. But he still choked the words out as commanded.

The stone glowed red.

And before he could react, before he could even begin to beg for his life, I shifted into my wolf form and drove my claws into his chest, curling them around his still-beating heart.

His body jerked. A choked gasp escaped him. Then I ripped.

The sound was wet, visceral, final.

Sasha crumpled, lifeless before he hit the ground, his heart still warm in my paw.

I dropped it beside him, watching as the life bled from his empty eyes.

Then I shifted back, gathered the stone from where it had sunk into the snow, and placed it gently back in its box.

I crouched and returned it to the crevice, sealing it away once more. The Russian pack was dead. And so was the man who had betrayed us.

Chapter 63

Tyson

For Valentine's Day, I went classic.

A bouquet of red roses.

Well . . . mostly classic.

Gigi had been camped out in my office all week, using my desk as her personal study space. She and Terri had caught some human illness called COVID. At least, that was what the doctor's note from the pack hospital claimed, so they could take classes remotely for the time being. Gigi had tried explaining it to me, something about crown shapes, face masks, and quarantines, but honestly? I'd tuned out somewhere around *respiratory droplets*.

Because she hadn't been wearing a bra under a tank top so skimpy it might as well have been see-through. The deep-cut neckline barely managed to contain the perfect swell of her tits, and if anyone else had been in the room, they'd have known the exact shade of pink her nipples were.

Pretty sure I lasted all of five seconds before my *very* educational lesson about an infectious disease turned into me titty fucking her.

A smile curled at my lips as I lay in the dark, half dreaming, replaying the memory.

As she did most mornings, Gigi rolled into me, pressing her fine, fat ass right up against my morning wood, rubbing like she was already halfway to riding me. A sleepy little moan slipped past her lips as she stirred, and her hand slid lazily back to graze over me.

"Mmm," she murmured. "You feel extra hard today."

I smirked against her shoulder and nipped at the skin. "Special gift for a special day."

She hummed approvingly, stretching her arms overhead. The movement arched her back and pressed her ass even harder against me.

"But that's not all." I reached over to the nightstand, grabbing the bouquet I'd stashed there earlier. "For you."

The corners of her lips curled up as she sat up, plucking the flowers from my hand and bringing them to her lap. "You got me flowers?" She gasped dramatically. "Tyce, you're such a romantic."

"Nah," I deadpanned. "They're for my side piece. Just wanted to get your opinion first."

She rolled her eyes but smiled as she pulled the bouquet closer, inhaling the scent. Then, her fingers brushed against something that didn't quite belong.

Her brows furrowed. Her hands sifted through the petals, parting them to reveal the oddity among them.

A single "rose" nestled in the center. Same deep red color. Same sleek curves. But unmistakably . . . different.

Her eyes snapped to mine. "Tyce . . ."

I grinned. "Happy Valentine's Day, baby."

She hesitated only for a second before curling her fingers around the conspicuous "rose," tugging it free. The moment it sat in her palm, recognition dawned in her expression.

"Oh my god," she breathed, holding it up. "Tyce, this is . . ."

"Exactly what you think it is." I shifted, leaning in until my lips brushed her ear. "Now let's see how well this thing works. Spread your legs for me, baby."

Her breath hitched, but she didn't move just yet. Instead, she tilted her head, giving me that sly little smile that drove me insane.

"Baby," she said, tracing the top of the rose-shaped vibrator with her fingertip. "I got you a gift too."

I arched a brow, my grip tightening on her waist.

"And since you gave me mine first," she continued in a teasing voice, "it's only fair that I get to use your gift on you first."

Fuck.

She reached under the bed, dragging out a fully wrapped present. "I've had it for a while, saving it for the perfect occasion. And today's finally the day."

I took the package from her and ripped through the wrapping. A conspicuous box was revealed. My eyes skimmed the label before I read it out loud. "AlphaCock Strap-On Harness with Oversize Dildo."

I blinked.

She grinned and stuck her tongue out at me. "You promised."

I exhaled through my nose, tilting my head back in defeat. "I did promise."

Her eyes danced with amusement as she popped open the bedside drawer, pulling out a bottle of lube. She gave it a little shake for effect.

"Don't worry, baby," she purred. "I came prepared."

Once my gift was free of its packaging, Gigi twirled the AlphaCock Strap-On Harness with Oversize Dildo™ tauntingly, mischievously. Her lips curled into a dangerous smirk as she tilted her head at me. I'd never seen her so vengeful before. It was actually kind of hot.

"Looks like it's finally happening," she goaded me.

"I already told you, baby, I'll do anything to get inside that ass of yours. And if this is what it takes, I'm ready."

She playfully wielded it like a sword, swinging it back and forth. That definitely wasn't a normal dildo. That was the kind of thing that probably needed a concealed carry permit.

"I feel like I need to sign a waiver before we proceed."

"I don't see you making me sign a waiver to shove *your* alpha-size cock into *my* ass."

"Point taken."

She reached for the harness and started buckling herself in.

"Okay, but like . . . let's be clear on one thing. If at any point I tap out, we *immediately*—"

She cut me off by grabbing the bottle of lube from the nightstand and flipping the cap open with a wicked grin.

My mouth snapped shut.

I was in danger. Real, *imminent* danger. And fuck if I wasn't kind of into it.

She slicked her fingers with lube before meeting my gaze. "On your knees."

The order sent heat straight to my cock. My pulse hammered, my breath hitched, but I obeyed without hesitation, shifting onto my forearms and spreading my legs. The position was unfamiliar. *Vulnerable*, but, *fuck!* I liked it?

Her hands smoothed over my back, her fingers trailing along the raised scars, until she found my hips and tugged gently at them. "Good boy," she teased.

That did something to me.

A moment later, I felt the blunt head of the toy press against me. "Breathe, baby," she whispered. "Let me in."

She pressed forward, sinking in at a torturously slow pace, stretching me inch by inch. A low groan tore from my throat as the last of my resistance melted away, replaced by raw, searing pleasure.

"*Fuck*," I rasped.

Gigi stilled, rubbing her hands over my sides. "You good?"

I swallowed hard, my head dropping between my shoulders. Then I nodded. "Move."

She let out a pleased hum and began to thrust, starting slow, finding a rhythm that sent waves of pleasure rolling through me. Every push, every drag, every deep roll of her hips sent bliss coiling low in my stomach.

Fuck. This was so *much*. So *good*.

My breath turned ragged, my body trembled under her, against her, *because* of her. She was unraveling me, breaking me down with every calculated stroke, every teasing grind.

I had never let anyone take me like this. Never thought I'd *want* to.

But *Gigi*—she knew exactly what to do. How to *own* me.

She reached around, and her fingers curled around my cock with a firm, knowing grip. She stroked me in perfect rhythm with her thrusts.

I jerked, the dual sensations dragged me under and drowned me in white-hot pleasure. My vision blurred, and my balls tightened as I tumbled toward the edge.

"Come for me, baby," she whispered in a rough, needy voice. "Let go."

That was all it took.

With a savage groan, I *did*. My muscles seized, my hips bucked, hot release spilled into her hand as I shuddered beneath her.

I barely registered the moment she stilled, holding me through the aftershocks. My body felt weightless, floating in the aftermath of pure, unfiltered bliss.

I collapsed onto the bed, panting.

Gigi followed, curling against me, her body fitting perfectly onto mine.

I turned my head, still breathless, and met her gaze.

A slow, lazy grin spread across my lips. "Happy Valentine's Day *to me*."

She giggled, pressing a lingering kiss to my jaw. "Knew you'd love your gift."

Chapter 64

Theresa

"Come, *koshechka*." Kolya's voice was gentle as he tugged on my hand, pulling me down the hall. I followed him without question.

When we reached Tyce's office, Kolya pushed the door open and guided me inside. He led me to a chair already waiting for me and pulled another close, settling beside me. His fingers intertwined with mine in a grip that was firm yet soothing, grounding me in a way only he could.

The air in the room was heavy.

Tyce stood behind his desk with crossed arms and his face set in a hard line. It was rare to see him this serious. Even in the worst situations, my brother usually had some smart-ass remark, some way to cut the tension. But now? There was nothing but cold, hard vibes staring back at me.

"Terri," Kolya said in a careful but firm voice, "there is something we must discuss."

I looked between the both of them, already guessing what this was about before either one said it.

"We need to talk about Joe," Tyce finally said.

A sickening, gut-wrenching weight settled deep in my chest, pressing down so hard I thought I might choke on it.

"What he did is punishable by death," Tyce continued. "If he'd done this to anyone else, he'd already be dead. No discussions. No second chances. But . . ." His jaw tensed. "Because you're my sister, I made an exception."

I stared down at the ground, trying to temper the heavy beat of my heart.

"I convince him to keep Joe alive long enough so we talk to you first," Kolya added, his fingers tightening around mine.

"I know you, Terri." Tyce's voice softened, but the weight behind it remained. "I know how much you care. I know you like to see the best in people . . . even when the only good they could possibly do is choke on a sharp, serrated blade."

I let out a heavy breath.

"Can't you see?" Tyce raised his voice. "Joe is a massive vulnerability. He always knows where you are. He can feel what you feel. As long as he's alive, that can be used against you."

I squeezed my eyes shut momentarily.

Tyce swallowed and breathed in deep. Clearly whatever he had to say next wouldn't be easy. His mouth formed a thin line as he shut his eyes. When he opened them again, he continued, "Sophia was taken when we were searching for Joe to get to you." His voice cracked a bit with those words. "You think that's the end of it? You think something like that won't happen again?"

Kolya shifted beside me, his voice quieter but just as firm. "I will not allow Tyce to kill him if you *truly* want him to live." He turned slightly in his seat to face me. "If you refuse to end Joe, I will make sure he spend rest of his days rotting in prison cell, alive."

Then, he slid off his chair and knelt in front of me, taking both my hands in his. His voice changed, softened, became more intimate. "But, *koshechka* . . ." He exhaled slowly, tilting his head. "I hope you reconsider. Because I want this. I want to mark you one day."

My breath hitched as I stared into his penetrating silver eyes.

Kolya's gaze never wavered. "And so long as he live . . . I never can."

I wiped at tears that had appeared so suddenly they caught me off guard. My heart felt so heavy, and my limbs weak. But I forced myself to a standing position and looked back and forth between Kolya and Tyce.

I thought of Joe. Of how I had spent so long making excuses for him, trying to see the best in him. I thought of Sophia. Her screams. Her pain. Her suffering. How she met her end.

I let out a hollow breath, my chest rising and falling unevenly, my vision blurring as the weight of *everything* crashed down on me. When I finally spoke, my voice came out hoarse but resolute. "Sophia . . . she changed my perspective. What happened to her made me realize that maybe some people don't deserve our empathy. Some people will take our goodness and use it for their own gain. Maybe it's not malicious. Maybe it's simply that they hate themselves or have insecurities, and they hurt you and prey on your vulnerabilities to make themselves feel better.

"Here I was, protecting him, keeping what he did a secret from everyone who loves me. And what for? What was he doing for me? He only liked me as much as he could control me. As much as he got something from me.

"I agree for Joe to die. And if he's going to, I want to be the one to do it."

Tyce drove Kolya and me to the pack penitentiary. I'd only visited this place a handful of times. Mostly when I was younger and my father was adamant that my training would be no different from Trav's. That I would also be treated as an alpha spare.

It was one of the more progressive things my father did.

I often wavered on whether I appreciated him treating me equal to my brother, or if I would have preferred to keep my innocence, to not have had to see my father wielding a dagger, carving into a naked man's body, cutting off his sexual organs, stabbing into his backside as if it gave him some sick pleasure that I was forced to witness.

I never saw my dad the same again after.

The man who had previously been a steady, self-controlled, powerful rock in my life, the man who always made me feel protected and safe, had revealed the terrifying and disturbing side of himself. The part of himself that gave into messed-up desires to not only torture, but to turn the act into an all-out spectacle, take as much pleasure from it as possible, and not simply treat it as a necessary duty.

"I had one of the guards tape his mouth shut," Tyce said from the front. "I personally like the screams, but I thought you'd prefer him not to speak. We can always rip it off if you want."

"Thanks," I replied.

When we reached the back of the cells, Tyce pushed open the heavy door, revealing the dimly lit stairwell that led into the bowels of the pack penitentiary. The old wooden stairs groaned beneath our feet as we descended, and with every creak, my pulse pounded harder, my stomach coiled tighter.

And then, finally, we stepped inside Tyce's torture chamber.

Joe sat in the center of the room, bound to a metal chair, thick chains wrapped around his wrists and ankles. His head was slumped forward. He looked smaller than I remembered, gaunt, unshaven, pathetic.

But when we entered, his head snapped up.

For a moment, something flickered across his face. His brows lifted. His eyes shone with something. Hope?

Will I be able to live with myself if I end him?

Sophia's screams echoed in my head. My own screams.

No. Some people didn't deserve mercy.

A muffled noise came from behind the duct tape sealing his mouth. He wanted to speak.

I stared at him, my heart a dull, heavy drum in my chest. And, I realized, I was grateful to Tyce for having the forethought to have his mouth sealed. I didn't want to hear what he had to say. He had sent me countless unhinged texts over the past months. Texts I kept deleting.

His texts were sometimes accusatory, blaming me for what happened. Sometimes, his messages read like pure denial, like he had rewritten reality in his head and convinced himself that nothing bad had happened, that we were still together. He'd send random *I love you*s, *I miss you*s, as if saying the words enough times could undo everything. Other times, he'd try to bargain with me, swearing he could change, that things would be different if I just gave him another chance. And then there were the darker ones—the self-loathing, drunken texts riddled with typos, the ones where he played the victim, drowning himself in guilt but never for *what he had done to me*.

Every single one of his texts had been about *him*. His pain. His regrets. His wants.

Never once did he ask how *I* felt. Never once did he acknowledge what *I* had been through. Never once did he show real remorse, only self-pity.

Because, in the end, it was never about me.

It was always about what he wanted. About what he thought he was *owed*.

I'd had enough of his excuses, explanations, pleas, desperation.

He had said enough, and now, it was my turn. And he could do nothing but sit there helplessly and finally hear what I had to say. He was unable to turn away or cut me off.

Although I realized he may still not care, he may still not feel any remorse for his actions outside of how they affected him, I was being given the last word by two men who actually cared about me and had never asked anything of me. Their affection for me was not contingent upon what I did for them, how I looked, or whether I always said and did exactly as they expected. They valued me exactly as I was. And now they stood beside me, allowing me to end the man they both wanted to end, not for themselves, but for me!

"Joe," I said, my voice steady, filling the chamber, echoing off the cold stone walls. "You always believed we had a good relationship. That we were happy. That we belonged together. That was *your* truth." I tilted my chin up, my heart pounding in my chest, my breath tight in my throat. "But did you ever stop to wonder what *I* thought? Did you ever once consider *why* I wanted to leave?"

His hands clenched into fists, chains rattling softly.

"Yes, there were moments of happiness. A few good memories. But they don't erase the rest. And the rest? You were not kind to me. You made me feel *small*. You picked me apart piece by piece, pointed out every flaw, every imperfection, until I started believing *I* was the problem. Until I started *apologizing* for things I had no reason to be sorry for. You twisted my words, my actions, my very being until I felt like I was *wrong* just for *existing*."

I took a step forward.

"And when I told you I wanted out, you decided my choice didn't matter. You decided that my body, my future, my *life* belonged to *you*. You forced your mark on me. You *stole* from me."

A tear slipped down my cheek, hot against my cold skin. I didn't wipe it away.

"And for so long, I protected you." My voice wavered, but I didn't stop. "I kept your secret. I *justified* what you did. I made excuses for you. Because you had problems, because you needed help, because your past was difficult." I exhaled shakily. "But a lot of people have problems. A lot of people suffer. And they don't do what *you* did."

Joe's body trembled.

"In the end, your reasons don't matter. Your *intent* doesn't matter. What you *did*—that matters. And it is *unforgivable*."

My fingers curled into fists, my pulse roared in my ears.

"You took away my ability to ever meet my mate. The one person I was meant to be with. The future I was supposed to have. You took away *my choice*. And now, I am taking yours."

Tyce moved beside me, handing me a broad, heavy sword. The solid weight of it settled in my hands.

Joe's eyes widened, and for the first time, I saw it. *Fear.* Realization sank into his bones, his body jerking against the chains, a desperate, choked sound muffled behind the tape. I took a steady breath.

Tears streamed down my face, but I didn't falter. I tightened my grip.

As I raised the sword, a memory struck me. My father, with a depraved smile on his face, carving a blade through the flesh of a man. He'd *enjoyed* it.

I didn't.

This wasn't pleasure. This wasn't revenge. This was justice.

I closed my eyes.

And swung.

The heavy metal moved swiftly through the air before making contact. The resistance lasted only an instant, then gave way with a sickening snap as steel cleaved clean through flesh and bone. Blood sprayed, and his head struck the concrete with a hollow, meaty crack, rolling once before settling at an angle, exposing glassy eyes frozen wide in shock. His body slumped forward, and chains rattled as they caught the corpse.

For a moment, everything was silent.

Then I exhaled.

The sword slipped from my numb fingers and clattered to the ground, echoing sharply against cement. My legs buckled. A pair of strong arms caught me before I hit the floor. Kolya. He gathered me against his chest with a firm, unshakable grip while I shook against him. The metallic tang of blood accosted my nose, coated my tongue.

"It's over," he murmured, pressing a kiss to the top of my head. "You're free."

I let out a shuddering breath and closed my eyes against the storm of emotions threatening to consume me.

Free.

Maybe for the first time in my life, I really was.

Chapter 65

Theresa

After we'd returned to Jade Moon Pack, I'd forced myself to refocus on school, drowning in assignments, making up for every lecture and test I missed during my captivity. It was exhausting, but I welcomed the distraction. Losing myself in coursework meant I didn't have to dwell on the memories that still crept into my mind when the nights were too quiet. It meant I could focus on the future.

By Saturday evening, we flew back to campus. Tyce and Kolya came with Gigi and me, to help us resettle. Everything felt almost normal again.

Almost.

During a quiet moment, Kolya pulled me aside, his silver eyes studying me carefully. "*Koshechka*, what is this app you always open?"

My stomach dipped. Heat prickled at my cheeks. He'd noticed?

I had been absentmindedly checking it over and over, trying to be discreet, trying not to make it obvious how much it was on my mind. But apparently, Kolya saw everything.

His fingers tilted my chin up, thumb grazing my bottom lip. "You do not have to say it," he murmured. "I already know."

I swallowed hard. Goodness, this was embarrassing.

A part of me had hoped that the mark Joe left on me would somehow be irrelevant now, that maybe things would just fix themselves. But biology didn't always work the way we wanted. And the idea that something from my past could still impact my future with Kolya made me sick. Made me angry.

He let out a quiet chuckle. "I know it is period tracker," he admitted. "I saw over your shoulder."

My eyes widened.

"Why you hide from me?" he asked, his voice dipping into something gentler. "Let me help. You should not suffer heat by yourself . . . or with boy from class . . ."

I recoiled. "I would never—" I cut myself off, heart racing. "I mean, okay, so I did that before. And I kind of acted like things with them were the same as they were between us. But that was only because—"

"Terri," he interrupted. "I know you never do this. I was only teasing you."

Teasing me? Kolya?

The corners of his mouth quirked into a rare smirk. My pulse jumped.

"I asked Tyce if we stay one, maybe two more days," he said casually, like it was no big deal. "I did not tell him why, and he did not ask much. Poor guy. He is bigger baby about leaving his mate than she is. I don't blame him. I think I will be same when I must get on plane."

His voice turned softer. Deeper. "I booked hotel, *koshechka*. For just two of us. We stay there for how long we need."

My stomach flipped.

Kolya had thought ahead. He'd anticipated my needs before I even said a word. I didn't have to ask. He simply knew.

"You didn't have to do that," I said, even though I was ridiculously relieved.

His smirk deepened. "I wanted this. And . . . there is something I must tell you, when we are alone." His fingers threaded through my hair, sending a shiver of warmth through me. He leaned in, brushing his lips near my ear. "You don't know . . . what hour exactly it begins, yes?"

I shook my head.

"Then I think it is best we leave now," he murmured, voice laced with something smoldering, carnal. His grip tightened. "Just in case."

And then he winked—*winked!*—before tugging me toward the door.

After we settled into the hotel, the exhaustion from the day of traveling and moving back to Anchorage hit me. We both stripped away the day, pulling off our clothes, playfully kissing each other between layers hitting the ground. The moment I collapsed onto the plush mattress and pillows, Kolya followed suit, pulling me into the warmth of his arms.

"Is it okay if we just cuddle for now?" I asked, nuzzling into his chest. "I'm so tired."

His arms tightened around me. "Of course, *koshechka*," he said softly, then added with a smirk, "Better we save our energy."

I smiled against him as I curled into his embrace. His body heat seeped into me, grounding me, lulling me into something warm and safe. His fingers traced slow, lazy circles on my back.

But then he hesitated. I felt the slight shift in his breathing, the way his fingers slowed, as if he was gathering his thoughts.

"You said you wanted to talk about something?" I asked.

"Yes," he admitted. "Is about . . ." His touch drifted upward, fingers grazing my throat before landing on the spot that still haunted me. "Is about this."

I went still.

His thumb traced the remnants of Joe's mark, the barely faded scar that refused to let me forget, worse than a regretted tattoo.

"I hate that thing," he confessed in a tight voice. "I hate that another man ever touch you like that. Every time I see it, it makes me—" He cut himself off, jaw flexing.

"Angry," I whispered, feeling it as he'd spoken.

His grip on me tightened, just for a second, before his hand gentled again. "Not with you," he said firmly. "Never with you."

Shame curled in my stomach. I squeezed my eyes shut, as if that could block out the overwhelming weight of it all. "I'm sorry," I mumbled.

His fingers slid beneath my chin, tilting my face up so I had no choice but to meet his gaze. His silver eyes burned. "Don't apologize," he said. "Never apologize for what he did. When I say it makes me angry, it is because you did not deserve it. Because I wish I could have stopped it. But I cannot change past. All I can do now is promise. Promise no one will ever take from you again."

"I just wish . . ." My voice cracked. "I wish . . ."

His hands framed my face, his warmth chasing away the ghosts. "I know what you wish for," he murmured. "But I . . . I wish only one thing. To have you, exactly how you are now."

Kolya never treated me like I was damaged. He never looked at me with pity, never made me feel like I was something broken that needed fixing.

He just . . . *saw* me.

"That is what I wanted to speak with you about," he continued. "You are already marked. It is done. I know if life was different, you would imagine it happening another way. But if you must wear mark, I hope you let it be mine."

My breath hitched.

I blinked up at him, stunned. "But . . . are you sure? Once you mark me, there's no going back. We've only known each other for such a short period of time."

Kolya threaded his fingers through my hair as he studied me with something so raw, so *deep*, it sent my heart stumbling.

"I never more sure of anything," he said in a voice rough with conviction. "My mother's last wish was for pack to live through war . . . and for me to find mate." His grip on me tightened, his voice trembling. "Terri, I found you. You are her wish. I know this. I was blind before, too stupid to see. But now, it is so clear."

I could feel his emotions radiating through me, his warmth, his sorrow, his love.

"And . . . there is something else," he added in a quieter voice.

I tilted my head, searching his silver eyes. They looked so exposed, unguarded in a way that made my heart stutter.

He let out a slow, heavy breath. "I think why I fought it so hard, why I pushed you away, is because of guilt. Why should I get to find love, to feel happiness, to live when my sisters never will? When all the friends I lost will never have that chance? It felt selfish. *Wrong.*"

"Kolya," I whispered, my throat tight, my chest aching with the weight of his pain.

"But thing is," he continued, "I am alive. I still have pack. Pack that grows stronger every day. Pack that will one day resettle, stand again, heal, grow, expand. Being with you did more than make me feel. It made me want to be happy again. It gave me hope. Hope for future."

My heart trembled at his confession. I didn't even know what to say, so I let his words settle between us, giving them the moment of silence they deserved.

"Terri," he said softly, reaffirming what he'd told me before, "I'm sure."

I swallowed against the lump in my throat. "You're right," I admitted. "I always thought I'd be marked on my wedding night by my fated mate. It's how I always imagined it. But I guess sometimes things don't happen the way we expect." I exhaled. "Sometimes we're at the mercy of the Goddess . . . and she has other plans for us."

Kolya brushed his knuckles down my cheek.

"Terri," he said, his voice even softer now. "You can still be marked on wedding night. I wait. As long as you want. But I offer this now to show I am serious about us. If you must wear a mark, let it be one that means something. Something good."

My lips parted as a sudden, amused thought crossed my mind. "It *would* have the advantage of ending all my heats."

A smirk curved his lips. "You think I mind?" His voice dipped into something sinful. "This I do not mind. Not one bit. Every month, I come if it means I take care of you proper way."

A blush crept up my neck and to my ears.

A part of me grieved, just for a moment, that this wasn't how I'd always imagined it. But that ship had sailed when Joe had taken that choice from me.

And as I looked at Kolya, the man who held me like I was something rare, something worth treasuring, I felt the weight of my past expectations begin to shift. The future I had once imagined was gone. But maybe . . . maybe it had never been the one I truly needed. Maybe what I needed was this. Was him.

There was no longer any reason to wait.

And, honestly? The only real reason I would have waited was because of my parents. Because I would have been too ashamed for them to know I had sullied myself by sleeping with someone before marriage. That I had shamefully allowed myself to be marked before I'd wed.

But I was already marked. And they were bound to see it one day.

At least *this* way, I had someone by my side. Someone who made me feel strong, who made me feel like I could finally stand up for myself. Someone who I would take as a chosen mate if he wasn't my fated one.

Someone I was more afraid of losing than I was afraid that he wasn't meant for me.

Just like Kolya, I was *sure*.

"Yes," I whispered with a pounding heart. "*I want your mark. I want you.*"

When I woke the next morning, there were no warning signs.

The heat had already crept in while I slept. A gasp tore from my lips as I braced against the wave of arousal crashing over me, leaving me panting, trembling, aching.

My thighs were sticky. A wet patch had formed under me during the night. My nipples were so stiff and sensitive that even the slightest brush of the sheets against them sent an electric jolt through me. If I hadn't already been naked from the night before, I would have ripped everything off. My skin was overheated, flushed, impossibly hot.

Kolya's arm was draped heavily across my waist. The resulting sparks where our skin touched practically electrocuted me.

I was so empty. Desperate. I clenched around nothing, burning for something—*someone*—to fill the void.

I needed him.

Throwing the blankets aside, I wriggled out from under his arm, clambered onto my knees, and swung my left leg over him so I was straddling him.

I paused, taking a moment to drink him in.

The chiseled angles of his jawline. The smooth curve of his lips, slightly parted in sleep. The powerful rise and fall of his chest, his relaxed broad shoulders, his toned arms resting at his sides—the same arms that made me feel safe every time I curled into them.

I had to be the luckiest woman in the world to be able to wake up to this man. To be offered the opportunity to wake up to *this* every morning for the rest of my life.

My eyes dipped lower.

He was impossibly stiff and stood ramrod straight in front of me. I had never seen a more beautiful sight. He was huge, *straining*.

Like a moth to a flame, my hands slid down the thick length of him. Hard as steel, soft as silk, throbbing against my palm.

Kolya's eyes snapped open, immediately locking on to where my fingers were wrapped around him. I saw the exact second he realized what I was doing. His pupils dilated, his breath hitched, and the intensity in his gaze made my stomach flip.

His growl of approval rumbled through the room.

I wanted to hear more.

Feeling bold, I shimmied backward, never breaking eye contact as I lowered myself, aligning my mouth with the head of his manhood.

Then, I took him in.

Kolya let out a deep, guttural groan as my lips wrapped around him and my tongue swirled around the sensitive tip, tasting the salty tease of his precome. His hand shot into my hair, and his fingers tightened as I slowly slid him deeper, savoring the weight of him on my tongue.

I sucked him in, inch by inch, widening my jaw, taking him deeper, deeper, until he was pressed against the back of my throat. His breath stuttered as I started moving, setting a slow, torturous rhythm.

The sound he made—a strangled, nearly desperate grunt—only spurred me on. I hollowed my cheeks, sucked harder, let my tongue tease along the underside of his shaft.

Kolya shuddered violently. His muscles tensed.

Then, suddenly, he ripped himself away, pulling free from my mouth with a gasp.

I blinked up at him, dazed. "Did I—?"

He looked wrecked. His face was tight with restraint. His throat bobbed as he swallowed hard. "I almost finished," he admitted hoarsely.

I grinned, licking my lips. "That was kind of the goal."

"No, you are in heat." He brought his finger between my thighs and delicately stroked against my bundle of nerves. I cried out and was suddenly reminded of how desperately I'd needed to be filled just moments earlier.

He touched me again, and I flinched from the overwhelming crack of white-hot pleasure that poured from his finger. "You're so wet," he rasped.

No, I did not just need him moments earlier, but *now*.

I was on fire, the feeling of emptiness all-consuming.

"I felt it," he said, furrowing his brows. "Even when your mouth was on me, and my brain stopped working, I felt your need."

I inched closer, crawling up his body, sitting up straight, lining him up with my opening.

He was right. I would've had to wait out his refractory period, being tortured with desperate, incurable need. Not that there weren't other things he could do to help ease it. But *this* . . .

"Take what you need, *koshechka*," he murmured, voice thick with lust. "Use me."

This was what I needed.

Sweet, sweet relief vibrated through me as I took him in, slowly lowering myself down his sheer, impressive length, allowing him to stretch my insides further and further with each movement downward, taking all of him in until I was filled to the hilt.

I stayed like that for a moment, still, savoring the throbbing pulse that beat against my innards, the soft flickers that danced through me like electricity, the incredibly full feeling he gave me.

Kolya's hands gripped my hips, and his fingers dug into my flesh like he was barely holding himself back.

Then, instinct took over.

I lifted myself before slamming back down, and my cry of pleasure echoed through the room.

With each up-and-down motion, I cried out from the overwhelming gratification that washed over me. It was as if I had been starved, and for my first meal, I was taken to a three- Michelin-star restaurant.

He felt so *good*.

"Oh, Terri!" He cried out my name, and nothing had ever sounded so beautiful to my ears.

He brought his knees up behind me and was soon pumping underneath me as I bobbed up and down from the top. Our movements synced as we each took from the other exactly what we needed, building up that overwhelming sensation of a balloon overfilling with air.

Kolya's snarls filled my ears. His hands roamed my body, possessive, greedy, before one slid between my legs. His index finger and thumb found my little nub again, rolling it gently between them.

I screamed.

Lightning shot through me, hot enough to burn me alive.

Kolya growled something incoherent, his hips snapping up, meeting my every downward thrust as our movements turned erratic, desperate.

We were seconds away. Our pace impatient, needy, as we both hit the point of no return. And then the balloon burst, as I was ravaged from the inside out, an explosion obliterating me. I let out a brutal scream as I rode out my orgasm, my whole body quivering, my heart racing, until I finally steadied.

And just as I caught my breath, Kolya pulled out with a loud, ragged moan, spraying my stomach like a firehose.

I collapsed onto the bed, boneless, gasping, ruined.

Kolya hovered over me, his chest heaving, his gaze burning into mine. I watched in fascination as his canines elongated, razor-sharp and gleaming under the dim light. So, he had figured it out.

But . . . why did he look just as shocked as I was?

His eyes widened and his muscles tensed, as if the shift had caught him off guard.

But his expression soon softened as I offered him my neck, stretching it to its full length. His face was a mix of restraint and something deeper, something primal. His thumb brushed over the enduring scar of Joe's mark.

I cupped his face, my chest rising and falling beneath him. "Do it." It came out mumbled due to my own expanding canines.

His eyes burned into mine, searching for any hesitation. He wouldn't find any.

Kolya moved closer, and then his teeth sank into the juncture of my neck. The pain was cutting, but it was fleeting, replaced almost instantly with a rush of warmth, of completion, of something inside me snapping into place. A bond. A connection so deep I could feel the weight of his emotions pressing into my own.

I barely had time to catch my breath before instinct overtook me. I flipped him onto his back, straddling him, and pressed my lips to the spot where his shoulder met his neck. My wolf pushed forward, guiding me, and without a second thought, I bit down, marking him as irrevocably as he had marked me.

The moment it was done, a wave of energy rushed between us, cementing the bond. Kolya's eyes met mine, wide with wonder, and then he pulled me down into a kiss so deep it stole whatever air I had left.

"You are mine now," he whispered against my lips. "And I'm yours."

I smiled, feeling warmth bloom deep in my chest.

And just like that, I became his luna. His mate. His future.

THE END

To be continued: Wolfbait, Book 5 of the Wolfbane series.

Epilogue

Ginger

One month later, during spring break, I stood in front of a full-length mirror, taking in the sight of my reflection.

I had imagined this moment before. Countless times, in fact. But nothing could have prepared me for the reality of it. The gown, a masterpiece of delicate lace and flowing silk, hugged my curves perfectly, cascading down in layers of intricate embroidery that shimmered under the light. My long, strawberry blonde hair had been curled and woven into an elegant updo, loose tendrils framing my face. And on my neck, just beneath my collarbone, I'd sprayed a bit of my signature scent where Tyce would be marking me later.

A thrill ran through me at the thought.

The ceremony itself was nothing short of grand and exactly what was expected of an alpha wedding. White rose petals lined the long aisle, and twinkling fairy lights draped the temple's high beams, creating a canopy of golden stars. Thousands of pack members had gathered to witness the moment their alpha took a mate. My family was seated up front—my parents, my sisters, Heidi and Paige, their husbands, and my adorable nephew, all watching me with teary-eyed smiles. Jasmine's family had also traveled in for the festivities—her parents, her mate Blake, and her twins, Ryker and Aria, looking ridiculously adorable in their tiny formal outfits.

Then there was him.

Tyce stood at the altar, his broad shoulders clad in a sleek black tux, his amber eyes locked onto me like I was the only person in the world. And, for a moment, I forgot how to breathe.

I had never seen him look at anything the way he looked at me.

And as I reached him, as he took my hands in his, everything else faded into nothing.

The ceremony itself was long. Formal. Unbearably traditional. If it had been up to us, we would've done something different, something more *us*. But this wedding was a showcase for his pack more than anything. It was a symbol of the future led by their alpha and luna.

Still, Tyce was Tyce.

"Goddess, you're so fucking hot," Tyce mindlinked me at one point during the ceremony. *"And those tits? In that dress? Can we just skip the reception so I can grease them up and take my sweet-ass time playing with them instead?"*

I barely kept a straight face, resisting the overwhelming urge to swat at him. He was lucky I couldn't link back yet in my human form. But once he finally marked me? Oh, he'd better be ready for what I had to say.

Then, just when I thought I had gotten through the ceremony without issue, Tyce went completely off-script.

"Gigi," he said, taking my hand more firmly in his. His voice softened, his expression shifted into something raw, something so intimate that my throat tightened. "I know it's not custom in werewolf weddings to write our own vows. But I've watched enough human TV to know it's a thing. And I knew it was a thing I had to do tonight, on the night that I finally marry and mark the best thing that's ever happened to me."

A chorus of *aww*s rippled through the audience.

I blinked, my eyes already starting to burn.

"I want to declare in front of my pack, in front of our family and friends, how much I love you, how much you mean to me." He took a breath, his gaze never leaving mine. "Some of you may not know this, but when we first met, we were enemies. Gigi made some . . . *very* severe allegations about me." His lips quirked, teasing, though his voice was still thick with emotion. "And I said some unkind things back. The thing is, we didn't know we were mates at first. Because Gigi had lost her wolf when she was twelve."

A murmur went through the crowd. Many already knew our story, but I was sure there were some that may have been unaware.

"We spent a summer together, never understanding why we couldn't stay away, even when all we did was drive each other insane," he continued. "Why there was this pull, this constant, unshakable need to be near each other. And sure, you could argue it was because we are fated mates. But I don't think that's the full truth." His voice dipped lower.

"I think it's because, from the moment I really saw her—past the arguments, past the burns—I realized something. Gigi isn't just my mate. She's the strongest, most gorgeous, sharp-witted, stubborn, intelligent, and determined woman I've ever met. I fell in love with her the *human* way. Before Gigi got her wolf back and we could confirm the bond, I'd already fallen head over heels, and I knew I would do whatever it took to make her mine."

Tears spilled freely down my cheeks.

Oh fuck.

The photographer was going to get ugly-crying pictures of me. This was a disaster. My makeup was ruined.

But then, Tyce squeezed my hand, eyes still locked onto mine.

"You are the best decision I ever made, and I will continue making it every day," he vowed. "I will always protect you, always support you, whether it's in becoming a nurse or a warrior or something else, and I will do everything in my power to make sure you're happy. You are my mate, my luna, my best friend. And I can't wait to spend the rest of my life by your side."

I let out a full-on sob.

The priest cleared his throat and finally said the words I'd been waiting for. "You may now kiss your mate."

And fuck, did I kiss him.

I *may* have leaned into it a little too much, and it *may* have gotten *a little* lewd for a religious ceremony. And *oh fuck*, my dad saw that.

But who cares? Because when Tyce grinned at me afterward, when he laced his fingers through mine and led me back down the aisle, the only thing I could think was:

I'm now Mrs. Tikaani.

The reception was as extravagant as the wedding itself—fine dining, live music, an entire ballroom decorated with gold and white. Laughter and conversation buzzed around us. The air was thick with celebration. I danced, I laughed, I drank far too much champagne. Everything was perfect.

At one point, I found myself sitting between Terri and Jasmine, sipping on a flute of champagne as I basked in the warmth of their presence.

"You know," I mused aloud, swirling the bubbles in my glass, "this is why fated mates are so much better than chosen ones."

As soon as the words left my mouth, I felt the weight of my mistake settle in.

Terri's gaze snapped to me. Jasmine raised a brow.

"Oh, shit," I blurted. "I didn't mean . . . wait! That's not what I meant! Chosen mates can be just as good! Better even! In some cases! Depending on the—"

Terri held up a hand, stopping my desperate attempt at recovery. Instead of irritation, her lips quirked into something thoughtful. "I actually think . . ." she started, glancing toward Kolya with a silly, besotted smile on her face, "Kolya might be my fated mate."

Jasmine's jaw dropped. I nearly choked on my drink.

"Excuse me?" I sputtered. "Come again?"

Terri twisted the stem of her glass between her fingers. "We had agreed to mark each other before it happened. And he was going to force his teeth out, the way that chosen mates have to. But, in the end, after we got rid of . . ." Her voice trailed off, and then she continued without saying his name, "Well, after what happened, his canines expanded on their own. He didn't have to force them out. It just . . . happened."

A slow, dawning realization hit me. "That only happens with fated mates . . ."

Jasmine's eyebrows raised. "Holy shit."

Terri nodded, her cheeks flushing. "So, I don't know. I feel like it's a sign."

Silence stretched between us for a moment before Jasmine let out a breathless laugh. "You know . . . the same thing happened with Blake."

"What?" I turned to her in shock.

She shrugged. "After I rejected my fated mate, Luke, I thought I was choosing Blake. But then . . . after we finally, you know . . . *slept together* for the first time"—her face burned scarlet—"both our canines came out on their own."

I stared at them both. "So you're telling me that we all ended up with our fated mates? That even when we thought we were choosing, we weren't?"

Jasmine smirked. "Seems like fate didn't give us much of a choice after all."

Terri chuckled, shaking her head. "Guess not."

I took a hearty sip of my champagne. "Okay, well, cheers to fate being a sneaky little bitch."

We clinked glasses.

Then I turned back to Jasmine, curiosity flaring. "Speaking of Luke . . . what's going on with him and Lucy? Any updates?"

"They're working things out." She shrugged. "They agreed for her to move back into the packhouse." A slow, mischievous grin crept across her lips. "Oh, and I totally forgot the most important part. She's pregnant again."

I nearly spat out my drink. "NO!"

Jasmine threw her head back in laughter. "YES!"

As the night wound down, I found myself huddled with my sisters, my baby nephew cradled in my arms, his tiny breaths warm against my skin. Goddess, I was going to miss him. I tried to soak up as much auntie time as possible before my family returned to the East Coast.

"You're so good with him," Heidi murmured, watching me carefully.

I smiled, gently running my fingers over his chubby little hand. "I love him so much. I want to make sure he always knows that."

"He will."

I glanced up at Heidi. She had this strange, faraway look in her eyes.

I frowned. "Is everything okay?"

She hesitated, blowing out a breath. Then, softly replied, "I just . . . I just wish Kelli could have come."

My heart squeezed.

"The only reason she didn't is because of what a coward I've been about coming out and telling Mom and Dad the truth."

"You're not a coward!" Paige exclaimed. "You're in a pack that's stuck in the early twentieth century. And you can't out yourself without outing your mate and both of your beards."

"I know, but . . ." Heidi took a shaky breath. "I've been thinking about it, and I think Mom and Dad should know. It could stay in the family, just us. But instead of only my sisters knowing, my parents could too." She swallowed, then turned to me. "Gigi . . . you inspired me."

I stiffened. "Me?"

"With everything that happened with your wolf. With how brave and determined you've been through everything. With how you survived that horrible kidnapping. I feel like I'm finally ready to be brave too. Plus, I just can't imagine remaining in this fake marriage for the rest of my life because I'm so busy living in fear."

She exhaled, voice firming. "When we go home, I'm going to finally sit Mom and Dad down and tell them. And if it doesn't go well . . ." Her chin dipped slightly before she straightened her shoulders. "Well, if it doesn't go well, I'll still have both of you."

"Of course you will!" Paige declared without hesitation.

"Always." I squeezed her hand, my chest swelling with love, with pride.

And then, without a word, we pulled each other into a hug, swaying softly to the music.

When the night finally ended, Tyce led me back to our bedroom, which would now officially be *our* bedroom, unlike previously when we'd pretended I had my own.

Before I could step inside, he stopped me. "Close your eyes."

I narrowed them instead. "I swear to Artemis, if your *surprise* ends up being your dick wrapped in a bow again, I will bite it off."

Tyce snorted. "Oh, please. You didn't bite it off all the other times."

"This time I'm serious!"

He grinned, nudging me forward. I huffed but closed my eyes, allowing him to guide me inside.

"No peeking, Spicy Gi," he said as he shut the door behind us.

"Even though I already know it's your dick with a bow. *Surprise!*"

He tutted. "You wound me." I heard the distinct rustling of fabric, the unmistakable sound of his clothes hitting the floor, then the dip of the mattress as he climbed onto it.

Fucking Artemis. It was totally his dick with a bow again.

Not that his cock wasn't a gift every single time he used it on me, but come on. The man needed to *switch things up* once in a while.

"I'm getting impatient," I warned.

"Okay, open." His voice dripped with amusement.

So I did.

And . . . holy fuck.

Yes, Tyce was stretched out on the bed, naked, smirking, his very impressive erection sporting yet another damn bow.

But that wasn't what caught my attention.

Our bedroom was completely transformed. There were candles everywhere, flickering softly on the mantel, the bedside tables, the desk. Flowers, more than I had ever seen in such a small space, cascaded in vibrant reds and pinks. Rose petals created a path to the bed. And by the nightstand, a chilled bottle of champagne waited for us.

"Holy. Fuck." My eyes went wide with wonder. "When did you do all this?"

Tyce stretched lazily, like a smug cat. "Had some help, obviously."

I turned to him, completely in awe.

"I felt bad," he admitted, "with the pack being so isolated and us not being able to go away for the big event. So, I figured . . . at least I could do this to make our first night as mates, and as alpha and luna, special."

Damn it, Tyce.

I pressed a hand to my chest. "Stop being so sweet! You're gonna give me cavities. I'll have no teeth soon."

"I heard that's better for BJs anyway," he joked. "So, come on, are you going to unwrap your wedding gift or what?" He gestured at his cock.

I rolled my eyes.

"I'm just kidding," he said, getting up from the bed. "I'm going to unwrap my gift first."

I barely had time to react before he was pulling me closer, his arms wrapping around my waist, his body heat seeping into me, his scent surrounding me, enveloping me in that perfect, heady aroma of raw masculinity.

Goddess, was there anything about this man that wasn't perfect?

"You look so beautiful tonight, Gigi." His voice dipped low, thick with something dark and possessive. "I have to be the luckiest man alive."

His lips hovered near my ear, breath teasing the sensitive skin there. "This dress," he murmured, hands tracing down my back, "fits you so fucking amazing. That ass? It took everything in me not to slap it every time you walked by."

"Tyce!" I whined, heat rushing to my face.

He grinned. "But now, finally, I can touch all of you."

He pulled me in for a kiss, soft at first, a teasing whisper of lips against mine. But slowly, the tenderness unraveled, giving way to something deeper, hungrier. His fingers brushed through my hair, trailing past my earlobe, gliding over my neck, tracing the curve of my spine.

His fingers found the zipper and dragged it down, slowly and deliberately. The fabric loosened, whispering over my skin to pool at my feet, leaving me completely bare except for my thigh-high stockings and heels.

Tyce froze.

His amber eyes blazed as they raked down my body.

"Holy fuck. You were going commando all night, and I had no fucking clue?"

I smirked.

"Damn." His voice was hoarse, like he'd just been punched in the gut. "And here I thought I couldn't get any harder."

I giggled and skipped over to the bed, flopping onto my back, spreading my legs. "Come on, husband." My voice turned teasing. "Get over here and use that hard cock to fuck me."

Tyce didn't hesitate. "Well, when you put it that way, wife."

I quickly undid the stupid bow. "I know you like to spend a lot of time on foreplay, but tonight, can you just give me a quick and dirty fuck. I want you to mark me already."

"Fucking Artemis. Did I die and go to heaven?" He stared at me, his amber eyes glistening with delight and lust.

I chuckled. "We don't believe in heaven, silly."

"Well, if you're in heaven, then I'll believe in it all damn day, angel."

"Stop being corny."

He stuck his tongue out at me, his signature smirk tugging at the corner of his lips, but it didn't last long. Before I could tease him back, he was on me with his mouth slanting over mine, his kiss deep, claiming, possessive. His tongue traced the seam of my lips, coaxing them apart, and I moaned into his mouth, pressing closer, losing myself in the taste of him—champagne and something undeniably Tyce.

My fingers glided along the sculpted curves of his muscles, tracing every hard ridge and smooth plane. I lingered, dragging my fingertips over his broad shoulders, down the deep grooves of his chest, feeling the way his muscles tensed slightly under my caress. I could touch him forever, morning, night, every hour in between, and it still wouldn't be enough. My palms skimmed the taut ridges of his abdomen, marveling at the solid strength of him, the softness of his skin.

Goddess, how was this man my mate? This *god* of a man. How was he *mine*?

Awe swelled in my chest, a mix of wonder and desire as I continued exploring, savoring the knowledge that every inch of him was meant for me.

Between us, his cock throbbed, heavy and hot. My breath hitched as I reached down, wrapping my fingers around him, guiding him exactly where I needed him.

Tyce sucked in a sharp breath, his grip on my hips tightening. "Fuck, baby," he rasped in a voice rough with need.

Then, in one powerful thrust, his hips snapped forward.

A gasp tore from my throat as my body arched beneath him, stretching, adjusting, taking every inch of him.

Tyce groaned, dropping his forehead against mine, his breath ragged, uneven. "Goddess, you feel so fucking good." His voice was strained, like he was barely holding himself together.

He stilled for a moment, letting me adjust. His fingers skimmed over my sides and traced the curve of my waist before gripping my hips, like he was grounding himself in the sensation of being buried inside me. I clenched around him instinctively, and his whole body tensed, a deep, guttural growl rumbling through his chest.

Then he moved.

At first, his thrusts were controlled and unhurried, each roll of his hips pushing him impossibly deeper, teasing me, driving me insane with deep, languid strokes. Every time he pulled back, just enough to leave me aching for more, he'd slam back inside, forcing a soft cry from my lips.

His lips ghosted over my jaw, down my neck, his teeth scraping just enough to send a shiver racing through me.

I dug my nails into his back, clinging to him as heat coiled low in my stomach, burning, building. "Tyce," I gasped.

He pulled back just enough to meet my gaze. His amber eyes were dark with hunger. "Tell me what you need, baby."

"Quick and dirty." My voice came out breathy and desperate.

His smirk returned, slow and wicked. And then, he gave me exactly what I needed.

His pace turned frantic, desperate, hard and fast, exactly the way I loved it. The sound of skin slapping against skin filled the room, my moans mixing with his deep, husky groans. He pounded into me, driving me closer and closer to that sharp, shattering edge. Each thrust sent sparks racing through my veins, each grind of his hips against mine pulling me higher, closer to oblivion.

Tyce's fingers slipped between us, finding my clit, circling, teasing, pushing me to the brink.

The pleasure built, coiled, tightened in my belly until I couldn't take it anymore.

"Tyce!"

"Come for me, baby," he gritted out, thrusts turning erratic. "Let me feel you."

I shuddered under him as he brought me to what had to be heaven. There was no other explanation for the blinding white light behind my eyelids, the angels singing, the high heavens thundering in all their glory.

Tyce followed seconds later, letting out a low, guttural moan. With my new IUD in place, he came inside me, filling me with his hot warmth.

We collapsed together, panting, spent, bodies tangled, skin slick with sweat, trying to recover from our post-wedding sex bliss.

"Are you ready, baby?" he whispered just as his canines began to elongate.

I tilted my head back, baring my neck. "Always."

And then I felt the sharp sting of his teeth sinking in. The pain was fleeting, swallowed whole by a rush of something deeper, more powerful than anything I had ever felt. My wolf howled in my head, the bond snapping into place like the missing piece of a puzzle.

And as I sank my own teeth into him, completing the bond, sealing our fate together, I knew that I would never, ever belong to anyone but him.

The moment the bond sealed, a wave of raw, unfiltered energy rushed between us, cementing us together in a way that went beyond words, beyond time.

Tyce's eyes met mine and then he pulled me into a kiss so deep it stole whatever air I had left.

"You're mine now," he murmured against my lips.

I smiled, my heart thrumming in perfect sync with his. "At least for tonight."

He glanced at me with an eyebrow cocked.

"Just kidding. Forever."

Author's Note

Thanks for reading *Wolfbitten*!

If you enjoyed this book, please consider leaving me a review! Honest, authentic reviews and feedback, written by real readers, are invaluable to authors, especially indie ones such as myself. If you have a few moments to spare, I'd really appreciate it, even if it's only a quick sentence to say you enjoyed the book!

ABOUT CELIA HART

Celia Hart is a boring accountant by day and a secret paranormal romance writer by night. Like Terri, she is half-Ukrainian. Unlike Terri, she cusses like it's her second language. She lives just outside of Boston, MA with her two miniature schnauzers. When she's not writing, her other hobbies include traveling, cooking, hiking, and eating far too many Nerds Gummy Clusters.

www.ingramcontent.com/pod-product-compliance
Lightning Source LLC
Chambersburg PA
CBHW061034310726
48969CB00004B/946